PARTNERS

"My question is whether it's true that you've been dating Dan Conti," said Kevin.

"Why, yes, we've had dinner a few times." Rachel was stunned by Kevin's manner even more than by his words. His jaw was clenched as his eyes continued to rake her face.

"Was that him on the phone just now?"

"Kevin, this is not a courtroom, and you have no right to cross-examine me."

Kevin moved to within inches of Rachel's face. "That's where you're wrong. Do you have any idea what the hell you're doing? Don't you realize that Conti's using you to get at privileged information he couldn't pry out of Austin or me?"

Rachel stood her ground. "What I do on my time is my businss. As a matter of fact, Dan and I made a rule never to discuss his case or mine."

"Wonderful!" said Kevin. "The fox has agreed not to eat the chicken. He's making a fool of you, Rachel. I shouldn't have to remind you of your responsibility to avoid jeopardizing the sanctity of the attorney/client privilege. And whether it's your personal time or not, the firm has the right to insist that you avoid even the appearance of, shall we say, a 'compromising position.' "

Kevin's rudely transparent double entendre fueled Rachel's rising anger. "I'm well aware of my professional responsibility. I also think you're masking your own personal feelings behind a lecture on ethics. What I've done, Kevin, has hurt only you."

Kevin stared at her for several seconds, then stalked out of her office. . . .

PARTNERS

■

JOHN MARTEL

BANTAM BOOKS
NEW YORK · TORONTO · LONDON · SYDNEY · AUCKLAND

Partners is a work of fiction and is entirely the product of the author's imagination. Names, characters, places, and events in this novel are fictitious or are used fictitiously. Any similarity to persons living or dead is pure and unintended coincidence.

PARTNERS

A Bantam Book

Bantam hardcover edition / July 1988
2 printings through December 1988
Bantam paperback edition / September 1989

Library of Congress Cataloging-in-Publication Data

Martel, John S.
    Partners.

    I. Title.
PS3563.A72315P3   1988   813'.54   87-47796
ISBN 0-553-27807-X

Published simultaneously in the United States and Canada

Bantam Books are published by Bantam Books, a division of Bantam Doubleday Dell Publishing Group, Inc. Its trademark, consisting of the words ''Bantam Books'' and the portrayal of a rooster, is Registered in U.S. Patent and Trademark Office and in other countries. Marca Registrada. Bantam Books, 666 Fifth Avenue, New York, New York 10103.

PRINTED IN THE UNITED STATES OF AMERICA

KR   0 9 8 7 6 5 4 3

PROLOGUE

∎

The old man's mood grew increasingly brittle as he began to wrestle his Chevy Impala up the twisting grade toward the summit. The one-hour trip down U.S. 280 from San Francisco to the outskirts of San Jose had gone well enough, but his driving was rusty, and Charley Hallinan remembered now with apprehension the twelve-mile asphalt corkscrew that wound ahead of him over the hill toward Santa Cruz. The curves already seemed sharper now than they had ten years ago, the lanes more narrow. Worse, he began to fear that he might not make it to St. John's before the pain came back.

A Japanese compact shot past him in the narrow passing lane with no more than ten inches to spare, rocketing his heartbeat and producing an unwelcome giddiness. *Damn fool*, he muttered after the driver, and hunched even closer against the steering wheel, squinting over shiny knuckles like a sea captain on the lookout for icebergs.

He turned on the radio, then irritably snapped it off, noticing how poor the reception was once you got into the mountains. He listened instead to the sounds of the Detroit clunker he had borrowed for the trip, straining and groaning around the turns as if its archaic body were strung together with tape and baling wire. *Just like me*, he thought, glancing up at himself in the rearview mirror.

Charley quickly returned his attention to the road—partly for safety, but mainly out of disgust—for looking back at him from the mirror was a worn-out face he barely recognized, with yellowing, lifeless eyes and concave cheeks covered with skin as coarse as fishnet. In the center of the face sprawled a French horn of a nose wrapped in a network of merging capillaries. Loose skin hung from his cheeks, his chin. And the backs of the pale, blue-veined hands that gripped the wheel were mottled with "Hooker's bumps," so named in honor of the chemical company that had once contaminated Niagara's Love Canal. To a

1

doctor or a trained toxicologist, these ugly hand lesions usually signified even worse news within, and Charles V. Hallinan was no exception. One of his kidneys had atrophied to the size of a walnut and his overtaxed liver now steadily spilled a stream of poison throughout his body. Cancer cells had raced like Hell's Angels up his spine, using his pancreas for a starting gate, and had recently blocked the vision in one eye.

Just a few weeks before, on his seventieth birthday, the Veterans Administration doctor had told him it would be his last. That really cooked it. Happy birthday. But it hadn't kept him out of Candlestick Park that night, not with the Giants coming off a hot road trip and his friends Harry and Lou holding grandstand tickets for his birthday outing. Besides, it beat sitting around the rooming house, waiting for the clock to stop. Charley didn't even mention the bad news until the seventh inning stretch. He had been pretty low key about it, but Harry started crying anyway—maybe because he was the oldest of the three or perhaps because he was Irish or maybe just because he loved Charley the most. Charley could never quite figure Harry. Anyway, Lou had bought beers all around and tried to lighten things up, but Harry kept crying right through to the end of the game even though Atlee Hammaker threw a 5–0 shutout of the Chicago Cubs, the second of three the little guy would pitch that spring of 1983. What stuck in Charley's mind the most about that night, however, was that everyone—himself included—seemed to feel guilty about him dying.

Later, Lou persuaded him that a weekend at St. John's Catholic Retreat might be good for him. Not physically, of course. Lou and Charley both knew that miracles happened only in faraway countries: blood oozing out of marble statues or prepubescent girls possessed of eschatological visions and hot flashes from another century. Never mind miracles; Charley would settle now for a little foxhole Christianity, some peace of mind. Besides, the Giants were back on the road and he faced another empty weekend. Charley registered for a weekend seminar at St. John's.

It was boldly titled "Adventures in Dying," and it seemed worth a try, although he had never been one for yakking with strangers. Helen had done all that for both of them during their twenty-six years together. As the weekend approached, however, he began to feel a door opening to him and found himself strangely excited about the two days ahead. He quickened to a new sense of freedom (better late than never, he thought wryly) and even wondered—for the first time in years—if he might meet a woman there. Someone he could talk to, someone in his own fix.

He'd like that.

Late-morning traffic, traveling in the opposite direction—from Santa Cruz to inland San Jose—was still backed up highway 17 as far as the old man could see; bumpers welded together into a single steel caterpillar. He caught glimpses of the commuters' stone faces, staring ahead through squiggly hot air currents as if watching a bad movie at a drive-in theater, creeping toward the numerous semiconductor plants that dotted the sprawling, smoggy Silicon Valley.

As he continued his climb toward the summit of the Santa Cruz Mountains, with St. John's not far beyond, he spotted a yellow sign that warned: DANGER—WINDING ROAD—NEXT 8 MILES, and a new three-foot-high cement safety barrier that now separated the narrow northbound and southbound lanes. Charley noticed that these white concrete dividers were already streaked with black skid marks, some of them running right up and over the top. There are quicker ways to go, he thought, his face cracking with a wry smile despite the pain now spreading into his chest.

A soothing rush of suddenly chilled air and a sign reading SUMMIT ROAD—ALTITUDE 1808 FEET told Charley he was now only a few miles from the Branciforte Road turnoff to his destination. Ancient redwoods reached up on both sides—some of them fifteen feet in diameter and nearly twenty stories tall—each one surrounded by smaller oak and madrona trees, with lush manzanita, Scotch broom, and sage in between. As he began his descent, the alien scent of pine needles and clean air splashed his pain-blunted senses, and he noticed that oncoming traffic had decreased to a trickle, with nothing behind him but an old pickup truck that had been following him for the past few miles. Charley stole glances both east and west, where deep gorges of lush billiard-table green plunged down on either side of highway 17. An even broader smile started to stretch across his face at the sight, but was cut short by a shattering roar—the grinding sound of a powerful engine that seemed to materialize out of nowhere.

His good eye shot to the rearview mirror, and the image reflected there froze his heart: With incredible acceleration, the old pickup behind him had sucked up the distance between them so that its grille and hood now crowded everything else out of his range of vision—nothing there but a rust-splotched yellow hood and a grinning, jawlike grille.

Jesus, he doesn't see me! thought Charley, frantically floor-boarding his own accelerator, caught between the charging pickup from his rear and the deadly Laurel Curve coming up just 200 yards ahead. To make matters worse, the front of a giant tractor-trailer loomed into view, lumbering around the treacherous curve toward both vehicles.

Then, just as suddenly as it had appeared, the pickup backed off, leaving nothing of its deafening presence but a ringing in the old man's ears. Charley quickly applied his brakes, regaining control of the ancient Impala just as the big tractor-trailer shot past him. He willed his stiff hands to relax, but they seemed welded to the steering wheel. Looking back, he saw that the yellow pickup truck had fallen back to where it had been before its lunatic charge. *Crazy bastard's afraid I'll get his license number,* he thought, relieved that it was now just two miles to the St. John's turnoff, and that safety barriers again protected the right-hand shoulder of the roadway.

The hands that guided the rusted-out yellow pickup were younger hands, covered in snug pigskin gloves that did little to conceal their power. The driver firmly held the steering wheel at the nine o'clock and three o'clock positions, rhythmically feeling each curve of the road. His eyes glistened like wet coal drilled deep in hooded sockets as he glanced at a set of detailed road diagrams attached to a clipboard at his side, then his gaze flicked back to the lumbering Impala.

The Target.

Each diagram covered a one-mile segment of southbound highway 17, starting from a "base point" located near the warning sign where the roadway first began its ascent, and ending ten miles past the St. John's turnoff at the Scotts Valley Airport, where the plane would be waiting for him. Turnouts were noted in yellow. All safety barriers along the right shoulder were meticulously outlined in blue. Standing out in jagged-toothed red symbols were two short interruptions in the continuity of this protective barrier. The first of these breaks was a point precisely eight and one-half miles past his base point, and was labeled "Option One." The second break, "Option Two," lay just ahead and was noted on his chart at a point just six-tenths of a mile before the turnoff to St. John's Retreat.

The map was there only because it was the driver's nature to be compulsively cautious. Since being informed of the Target's itinerary, he had driven this stretch of road more than twenty times. He knew that it had to be perfect this time, for Option Two was the only remaining operational possibility—owing to the untimely appearance of the tractor-trailer at Option One.

Just a few more seconds now and it would be time to begin the next run. He double-checked his charts. He was tense but not nervous. Each curve in the road was experienced now as a sensual tug in his taut buttocks, for he was connected to the twisting asphalt like a drop of rain snaking down a windowpane. A fresh tremor of excitement rippled through his stomach and into his loins—a sensation much like the cerebral awareness of imminent ejaculation—for he realized that Option Two would not be aborted this time even if he were interrupted by the entire California National Guard. He knew this physical sensation well and called it his "zero-option high." He enjoyed it almost as much as he did the money.

His foot tingled as he began to summon the power of the big Continental engine concealed under the pockmarked yellow hood. He would have preferred his TransAm with its steel-braced front-end bumpers, but the pickup had the advantage of added weight and complete anonimity. No one at the Scotts Valley Airport would notice another pickup, particularly one with the drab colors he had carefully selected and applied. This covertness was particularly important, for the voice on the telephone had emphasized two points: First, the hit had to be dismissed by the police as an accidental death. If not, no payday. Second, they not only wanted the Target dead, they wanted him vaporized. They didn't explain why, and the driver didn't care. That was their business, not his.

Eight seconds, seven, six, less than two hundred yards ahead now lay the second break in the protective safety barrier. With luck, the Target would go all the way down—two hundred feet—to the valley floor below, but even if he didn't, the gas tank would probably blow at the first ledge forty feet off the shoulder.

The driver's thin lips curled into an uneven, joyless smile as his carbon-speck eyes scanned ahead and behind and his foot slammed the accelerator against the floorboard.

*   *   *

A burning pain in the socket of Charley Hallinan's bad eye was spreading into his lungs and groin as he saw the pickup begin to close the distance between them. *Jesus, not again!* he thought, and moved his car nearer to the shoulder on the right to allow plenty of room for passing.

But it kept coming closer, advancing until yellow and rust filled his rearview mirror again—and, oh . . . God, that awful grinding sound. Charley turned ashen, for he saw that the pickup was converging directly into him, not around him. *The damn fool was going to ram him!* To make matters worse, he noticed another break in the right-side safety barrier just ahead.

The awareness of his danger now exploded in Charley's brain, shooting an electrical current of fear through his body and short-circuiting his judgment. Instinctively, however, he veered the Chevy away from the approaching opening in the rail as the pickup charged toward him again.

The first blow struck the Impala from behind with earthquake force, snapping the old man's head back and nearly jarring his frozen hands from the steering wheel. The shock to his left rear bumper and fender would have sent him hurtling into space but for the freak presence of a giant pine tree that blocked the first part of the opening in the protective barrier. The Impala miraculously slammed against the tree and caromed back onto the narrow shoulder, skidding crazily as Charley struggled with the wheel.

Jesus, he's trying to kill me! thought Charley. He tasted blood where he had bitten through his tongue and was dimly aware of a burst of cold air knifing into his sweat-soaked flannel shirt. Already the truck's right bumper was upon him again, pounding into the left rear side of his car. Then again—crashing, pounding, propelling him closer and closer to the edge. Charley's eyes darted wildly, blinking with each staccato blow until the steering wheel finally spun out of his watery grip. The pounding in his temples now drowned out the maniacal roar of the yellow truck's steel cylinders. *Oh God,* he thought, *Oh Jesus . . . not now . . . not yet . . .*

This time the front right wheel of the big Impala shot cleanly over the shoulder of the road, and the rest of the vehicle obediently followed with the rolling motion of a horse collapsing over a broken leg.

The old man continued to pump the brake pedal with all his strength, though vaguely aware that his car was now airborne, the rocky floor of Scotts Valley hundreds of feet below him. A huge horizontal tree limb snatched the hood off the car as if it were the wing of a moth, exposing the impotent engine. Paralyzed by shock and terror, Charley dimly saw other branches lashing at him as he flew past. Then, a blinding explosion, followed by infinite silence.

The mushroom of smoke and flame was visible for miles, even to the curious "Adventures in Dying" registrants as they assembled, hopeful and uneasy, for their weekend at St. John's Retreat.

PART ONE

∎

THE CITY

∎

SPRING, 1982

What weapons has the lion
but himself?

—JOHN KEATS

ONE

■

All that most San Franciscans know about the President's Club is what they have read in the papers, yet many upwardly mobile outsiders would gladly give a day or two off their lives for just one look inside the West Coast's most opulent and exclusive men's club. Other hopefuls might even surrender weeks of their existence for a single lunch or dinner invitation there. And to attain life membership! Relinquishing a full year of their tenure on earth would seem a bargain to many of San Francisco's aspiring gentry.

Austin Barrington wasn't the type to surrender five minutes of his life for anything, and to him, the President's Club was a great place to get a bacon, lettuce, and tomato sandwich.

There was more to it than that, of course. He also relished the austere European formality of the main dining room, an amazingly faithful replication of La Conciergerie in Paris. And then there was its convenient location high atop the financial district's Arcadia Building, just across the street from Barrington's law firm and one of the few earthbound platforms in town where he could actually look down on his own penthouse office. The club's proximity allowed him to get to lunch quickly without having to suffer the street racket and the noontime crush of people. He also liked that about his own building's downstairs garage, where his Rolls could be serviced and washed every Friday without sacrificing a minute of his own precious time stuck in some seedy gas station surrounded by Arabs with flashing gold teeth and oily rags dangling from stained back pockets. Sometimes—especially during winter—he would even have his sandwich delivered by the club, so that between his connected garage at home and his parking stall at the Imperial Building, he could make it through an entire day without a moment of contact with anyone he did not choose to see.

Invitations to membership in the President's Club were every bit as rarefied as the air outside the forty-eighth-floor dining room, and the refined surroundings inside nearly as cold. Even those with the most prestigious sponsorship had a fifteen-to-twenty-year wait to attain membership, and although Stafford, Parrish, and MacAllister had never lacked for men to-the-manor-born, only Austin Barrington and Whit Stafford himself at S.P.&M. had been invited to apply for membership early enough in their careers to enjoy lunch there as a member rather than as a guest.

Barrington, a six-foot-four-inch, strikingly attractive Brahmin, had a profile that could have been engraved on a silver dollar. He looked much younger than his sixty-three years and created an amiable first impression, though just under a shock of silver-gray hair still thick enough to crown a prominent forehead lay dark, nuclear eyes that had pried the truth from many an adverse party during his thirty-five years as a trial lawyer. Whether he was interrogating a hostile witness or playing dominoes at the President's Club, Barrington's eyes were those of a man planning a jailbreak: intense, calculating, controlled—betraying his fierce temperament to any close observer.

Only his wife, Catherine, understood the dark nature of the demons that drove her husband, though fellow senior partner Adrian Fisher came close to the truth one day in a moment of candor when he'd told her, "Austin is a paradox. He strives to live down his noble pedigree the way others might struggle to conceal their humble beginnings. I could accuse your husband of being a scoundrel and a thief and escape with a sound thrashing. But call him a rich man's son and he'd surely kill me on the spot."

Barrington's longtime friend and law partner had come close but was still just scratching the surface. Only Catherine knew the secret that had sent her husband to the top of his profession: that Barrington's leadership of Stafford, Parrish, and MacAllister was the means by which he demonstrated each day to an indifferent world that he was a better man than the powerful and domineering father he passionately despised even now, years after his death.

While living, Barrington's father had been one of the ten wealthiest men in the United States and a valued client to S.P.&M. No one, of course, doubted for a minute that Austin had earned his place at the head of the firm. The national prominence William Weston Barrington II had attained as a successful New York banker-turned-developer may have provided his son a shot at success, but it was Austin's own ability and fierce determination that had carried him to the top of his own chosen field. Everywhere he went—from crew captain and cum laude at Dartmouth, to a commission as lieutenant in the U.S. Marines during World War II, then to editor-in-chief of the *Law Review* at Harvard—Austin Barrington served notice that he was not on this earth to coast on Daddy's money. Upon graduation with honors, the ambitious young lawyer turned his back on Wall Street and adopted San Francisco as his home, mainly because of the 2,568 miles that would now separate him from his father's New York City headquarters.

His choice of law firms was obvious, for Austin and Stafford, Parrish, and MacAllister were a match made in heaven, sharing an obsession with success and the competence to achieve it. His long hours as a young lawyer, combined with a succession of trial victories, had so impressed the firm that he was invited to join the partnership after only five and one-half years as an associate, rather than the usual seven. Austin's ultimate ascendancy to the position of presiding partner of the firm became even more inevitable when Adrian Fisher, himself the heir apparent to the firm's last surviving founder, became Austin's mentor.

Fisher, who awaited Barrington now at their customary table in the President's Club, had joined the firm in 1940. With Parrish and MacAllister both gone to their ultimate rewards, it was time for new leadership, and when Whit Stafford suffered his second coronary in 1945 and retired, Fisher—hard-working, hard-drinking, and thirty-five years old—was tapped. Barrington was standing right behind him.

In his day, Adrian Fisher had dominated the trial courts of the city. As a younger and more vital lawyer, Adrian Fisher had also provided solid management and dynamic trial skills to the firm for fifteen years before suffering his own health problems. Warned by his doctor and several angina attacks that his heart could no longer endure the rigors of the courtroom, and that his next drink could be his last, he retired from both the trial bar and the barroom to become the firm's full-time administrator. The unhappy medical mandate improved not only his health and his marriage, but S.P.&M. as well, for during his medical leave, Fisher was compelled to rely more heavily upon two younger partners who had become his administrative aides—Austin Barrington and Gardner White.

Gardner White, dumpy in stature, a steady and dedicated tax

specialist whose face was as pale as his name, played the perfect Mutt to Fisher's Jeff. He was a highly respected lawyer and, though lacking somewhat in imagination, had been third in his class at Columbia and chairman of the prestigious A.B.A. Taxation Committee. Moreover, he understood how money worked, unlike Austin Barrington and Adrian Fisher, who had never been without it and so never had to learn its intricacies.

By the early 1960s, however, it was clear that it would be Barrington—leonine, presentable, and successful—who would ultimately succeed Fisher and, without opposition from either Fisher or White, he quietly became the de facto leader of the firm. And now, twenty years later, Austin Barrington governed S.P.&M. with almost unfettered authority. As a token limitation on his power, he accorded respect to Fisher, now fast approaching eighty, and courtesy to the ponderous White, by running all significant administrative decisions by them, the "management committee," before taking any action. To this end, Fisher, White, and Barrington had lunched together for nearly two decades at the exclusive President's Club, always at the same table, every Tuesday and Thursday. They were known around the club—and eventually throughout the professional community—as "the Table of Three." Never were there more than—or less than—three. If one of the three of them was unavoidably out of town or otherwise unable to attend, there was simply no luncheon meeting that day.

The Table of Three's power and authority soon carried well beyond the walls of S.P.&M. Barrington and the Table were frequently mentioned in Herb Caen's column and it was common knowledge that few Republican aspirants for high state or federal office would make it far without the Table of Three's blessing—including the California governor-turned-president of the United States.

But even the most powerful firms must reckon with economic realities, and as the recession deepened in mid-1981, the Montgomery Street legal establishment had to tighten its collective belt. Many of the S.P.&M. clients began to establish austerity programs. Some simply failed to pay their bills, while others failed altogether, slipping silently into bankruptcy. Then came the unexpected decision of the firm's biggest client—an oil company that represented twenty percent of S.P.&M.'s revenues—to move its business to Anderson and Wolf, a smaller firm with lower hourly rates.

How could it be that S.P.&M., once so rich in power and influence, had suddenly found itself poorer than a firm of Catholic divorce lawyers? Bad luck, mainly, for only the most cynical economists had predicted that the federal government's deficit under the new Republican president would continue to grow, and that the new administration's laissez-faire attitude toward big business would soon all but eliminate the need for S.P.&M.'s large antitrust defense group. Indeed, most early indications were to the contrary, and the partners had optimistically supported Gardner White's 1980–1981 proposed expansion program, which added floors thirty-eight and thirty-nine of the Imperial Building—nearly doubling the firm's space—to accommodate the new associates who were being recruited to handle the projected flow of new and lucrative business. But most of this elegant space now sat empty—a gray and barren legal ghost town—and the Table of Three began to meet daily in April 1982 in an unsuccessful effort to cope with the disastrous confluence of events that had turned their projections upside down. "It's time we took *steps,*" Fisher would insist at each meeting, staring blankly into his Perrier, then pleadingly into Barrington's inscrutable eyes. Barrington would then patiently review their current efforts to stem the flow of red ink, until the older partner's eyes glazed with apathy and fatigue. *'Steps?'* Austin wanted to say. *What kind of 'steps'? What do you expect me to do about twenty percent interest rates, a recessionary economy, and a building full of lawyers without enough work to do?*

Then, yesterday, Austin cringed to remember, when things seemed to be as bad as they could get, they got worse. Their bank's loan committee flatly rejected S.P.&M.'s request for an extension on their huge line of credit, cutting the firm's lifeline and pronouncing Barrington's beloved mistress terminally ill. The city's leading law firm for nearly seventy years was disintegrating with *him*—him of all people—at the helm.

He would be the one blamed, of course. Does anyone remember the name of the lookout on duty when a ship crashes on a coral reef? No. It's the *captain* who must shoulder all blame. Little wonder, thought Barrington bitterly, that they often chose to go down with their ships.

As Austin approached the club's dining room, he could almost hear his father's ridiculing laughter, feel the condescending slap of the hand on the back of his head. *Come on, Bub,* his father would say—thank God, thought Austin, that the despised nickname had gone to the grave with its author—*when the going gets tough . . .* and on and on, for clichés had been his father's verbal toys as long as Austin could remember. Also nicknames, especially after 1945, when William Weston Barrington II let it be known that his subordinates could address him as "W.W. II."

Yes, thought Austin, good old W.W. II would know just what to do now. *Too damn bad I'm a bit busy right now,* he would say, *or I'd zip right down there and straighten out that little mess you've gotten yourself into. You're a damn decent lawyer, Bub, but you never had the touch it takes to run things. The shoemaker should stick to his last, that's what I always. . . .* Austin cast the memory aside as he arrived at the bank of elevators. "I'll show him, dammit," he muttered to himself, and turned the key next to the "48" slot on the elevator. "I'll show them *all.*"

As the elevator doors snapped open on the forty-eighth floor and Barrington strode into the lobby, Josef, the club's regal maître d', quickly assembled his most deferential bow, but Barrington's usual concession—an upward contraction of the corner of his mouth—was missing today as the senior partner plunged straight toward the dining room without a quark of recognition. The angular maître d' reddened, glanced around, then raised an invulnerable eyebrow and returned with practiced aloofness to his stand-up desk.

As Austin approached the table, he found his two partners in animated conversation. "Our own client, for Christ's sake," Gardner White was saying. White extended a pudgy hand to Barrington, who nodded to Fisher and took his usual seat. Austin noted that White was even more agitated than usual, pounding the table with clenched fists. "We've represented that bank for over three decades!"

"You did everything you could, Gard," said Fisher, his thin lips clamped tight around a cigarette. "We're not the only firm in trouble. Diamond and Pender couldn't meet payroll this week. The Jamison firm is negotiating the terms of their breakup. We're not alone."

"Small consolation, gentlemen," said Barrington, signaling Stefan that he could now approach their table with the ritual one round of drinks. Then, with the same economic motion of his index finger, he secured his partners' silence and attention. Barrington's ease in the rigid atmosphere of the President's Club was complete, as if he were chatting with friends in his own kitchen following a round of golf.

"Fact one:" he began after Stefan had retreated a respectful distance, "We shall be unable to meet payroll in six weeks according to Gardner's analysis. Fact two: Our largest client— comprising ten percent of our billable hours—filed yesterday for federal bankruptcy relief under Chapter Eleven. Fact three: If anyone outside the Table hears of our financial condition, many of our remaining clients will jump to other firms and some of our best younger partners and associates will jump with them. Montgomery Street loyalty. Like Diamond and Pender, there will be nothing left in six months but a few of us senior citizens and a handful of clients nobody else wants."

"Do you really think it's that bad?" asked Fisher, his attention momentarily engaged. "After all, seventy years is a long time, and we've faced up to problems before. Aren't we overreacting a bit here?"

"Hardly," replied Barrington coldly, but without revealing his irritation. One could see in Barrington's face, particularly in his eyes and the hard set of his jaw, that he was not an affectionate man; yet his manner toward his aging mentor never failed to reflect respect, manifested now in the uncommon patience with which he continued to address the older man. "Mark my words, Adrian, if our boy wonder, Kevin Stone, jumped out his forty-second-floor window tomorrow, half the firm would follow him."

"Well, umm, all right. I suppose you're right about that," said Fisher, slowly nodding his head, then turning toward White. "How about the business side of the office, Gard; any young Turks over there who could lead a mass defection?"

"No one with Kevin Stone's client base and charisma," said White, swirling his glass before downing its contents in a gulp, "but at the risk of oversimplifying, aren't there just two alternatives? Either we increase our revenues or we cut our costs. Since there's nothing we can do right now to increase revenues, we've simply got to slash our expenses. I suggest we start laying off associates and reducing our secretarial staff immediately. We don't have enough research and drafting work to keep them busy now anyway."

"I don't like it, Gardner," said Adrian Fisher with a vigorous shake of his elongated, noble head. "That's *the* quickest way to let Montgomery Street know we're in trouble. No. We've got to get some more borrowing credit somehow and pray for a miracle to walk in the door.''

Austin Barrington sipped his Glenlivet, feeling even more
alone than usual. Fisher was right, of course, but from a safe
distance as usual. He could pray for miracles; Barrington had to
make them happen. When at last Austin spoke, his two partners
had to lean forward just to hear him. ''Gentlemen. Upon the
assumption that miracles rarely walk in off the street, I have
taken some initiative in this matter. The cold hard fact is that we
can neither obtain additional credit nor betray our desperation by
massive staff cuts. We must, therefore, secure a quick and
substantial influx of revenue.''

''Easily said, Austin, but not so easily done,'' said White,
almost complacently, breaking another dinner roll in two and
liberally applying butter to both sides.

''Gardner's right, Austin,'' said Fisher. ''Even I know we
need a couple of million dollars just to keep the lights burning
for the next two months. That kind of retainer is rare these days
even in New York, let alone here in San Francisco.''

Barrington's eyes now betrayed his impatience. How long
would he be able to suffer these two with their simplistic answers
to complex questions, always quaking and complaining before
fate without a shred of original thinking to offer? He grasped the
arms of his chair and hunched his shoulders as if to rise. Thus
suspended, intimating that one more interruption would eject him
into space, his voice dropped even lower, yet became even more
commanding. ''Adrian. Gardner. If not entirely appreciated,
your skepticism is at least understandable. I regret that I haven't
time to deal with your many concerns, but I must leave you
now for a chat with Kevin Stone, then it's on to a meeting
that I believe may produce the 'miracle' we need. If all goes
well, you will have a memo outlining my plan first thing
tomorrow morning. Until then, I'd prefer not to get into it,
for I must tell you frankly that neither of you is going to
like it. I don't like it myself, but let's face it—we've hit a
mine, and our ship is sinking. And with due respect, gentlemen,
if my plan provides a safe harbor, *nothing* will stop me from
steering the firm into it.'' He paused and barely lifted the
corners of his mouth. ''Nothing,'' he repeated. ''Enjoy your
lunch.''

Fisher and White stared after Barrington in silence as he

threaded his way like a fullback among the tables. They watched his retreating broad back all the way across the cavernous dining hall until all but his mane of gray-streaked hair was swallowed up in the tangle of waiters, members, and guests.

TWO

∎

Kevin Stone hurried from the elevator toward Austin Barrington's corner office on the forty-second floor. The firm's premier trial lawyer, now in his early forties, was not used to being summoned on short notice, even by S.P.&M.'s acknowledged leader. Nor did he relish being asked to hip-shoot on legal questions outside his experience without consulting with his cadre of brilliant young trial associates. But Barrington had been clear on that, if mysterious in his motivation: "No associates on this one, Kevin," he had said. "This matter is strictly *entre nous*. I'll explain it all when I see you in my office at twelve-thirty."

As Barrington's office clock announced the half hour, the handsome, superstar trial lawyer nodded a perfunctory greeting toward Miss Tarkenton and passed without waiting to be announced into the senior partner's main office area. He knew this violation of custom antagonized the secretary, who fixed him with the sour look of a teacher who hates children.

"Ah! Kevin," said Barrington, his voice friendly and ripe with anticipation. "Good. I have only a few minutes before I meet with the Plaintiffs' Coordinating Committee. Just give me the bottom line."

"It's not that simple, Austin. Who all will be there?" Stone asked, leaning his athletic frame against the doorjamb.

Barrington beckoned the younger man to be seated. "The full committee will be there: Olzeski, Katz, and Jake Wechsler. Among them they probably represent forty to fifty very ill ex-employees of the North American Chemical Company."

"Did all of the victims live in company housing at one time or other?"

"Yes, for at least five years."

"Just how sick are they?"

A quick shake of his head revealed Barrington's growing impatience. "Christ, Kevin, I came back here to get some answers, and I'm getting nothing but questions. As I told you, many of them are dying. I picked five victims at random for blood and tissue testing at Newkirk's lab. They're all full of chemicals—way beyond allowable safe limits. Now you know everything I know about the case. They're interviewing trial counsel to represent their clients. I think I can cut a good contingent fee agreement with them, but I've got to know enough about the applicable law to appear credible. They already know we're not personal injury lawyers."

"Okay, Austin." Kevin brushed a shock of blond hair off his forehead and focused his pale blue eyes on the older man. "Here's how it looks to me, but bear in mind that what I'm about to tell you hinges on a lot of things we don't know yet: the amount of toxic chemical contamination in the victims' drinking water and how much they've consumed. We don't even know whether we can tie any of their illnesses directly to chemicals from North American's dump site."

"The committee claims we can do all that," said the senior partner, lighting one of the ten cigarettes he permitted himself each day. "Let's assume we can. Do you agree the case has big verdict potential?"

"At the risk of sounding like a lawyer," said Kevin cautiously, "I must repeat that it all depends. To win these cases, the law as it now stands seems to require that we not only have to trace the chemicals from the toxic dump site into the well water these guys drank from, but also show that their specific injuries and illnesses were directly caused by the ingestion of a particular chemical."

"Have you found anything in the cases that suggests how others have done this in the past?"

"Christ, Austin, you gave me less than two hours, and it took me half that time just to remember where our library is—" Kevin started to laugh, revealing a line of even white teeth above a strong, cleft chin.

"Please," interrupted Barrington, rising abruptly and walking to the north side of his office. He stared silently for a moment out toward Marin County and the Golden Gate Bridge, then said, "Your humor is wasted at the moment, Kevin. Do these men have a case or don't they?"

Kevin read the impatience in Barrington's hardening tone and explained that expert witnesses were often unwilling to attribute specific internal injuries to a specific chemical ingestion. "Have there been any epidemiological studies or surveys?" he asked.

"What in God's name is an epidemiological survey?"

"Studying a specific group of exposed people and comparing their health conditions to the norm," Kevin said.

Barrington turned away from the window and began to pace back and forth behind his desk. "I doubt they've done one, but Olzeski says these guys all look like they're right off the Bataan death march. Some of them have already been diagnosed as having cancer of the liver, lungs, or kidneys. They're all depressed and suffering from various central nervous system disorders. Most of the men who worked nearest the dump have developed debilitating skin lesions."

"That's all well and good," said Kevin Stone, "but the issue is whether we can prove they got that way as a direct result of drinking well water contaminated with specific organic chemicals from North American's dump site. We won't have trouble coming up with legal grounds for a suit: negligence, trespass, and ultrahazardous activities, to name a few. The main problem will be causation."

Barrington took a worried drag on his Benson & Hedges, stopped behind his desk, and expelled the smoke as he leaned against the back of his chair with both elbows. "Maybe it doesn't matter if I'm late for this meeting. It doesn't sound good." Stone's silence increased the older partner's new pessimism.

"Maybe we could come up with an aggressive forensic expert who would make the connection for us," said Barrington, straightening. An imperious circling of his fist created a spontaneous smoke ring above his head. The unflattering backlighting of the sun as it sprayed through Barrington's east window emphasized deep lines like parentheses around the senior partner's rigid mouth. Kevin could hear a pleading intensity slip into Barrington's voice as he continued. "You know as well as I do that you can find an expert witness to say most anything if you look long enough and pay well enough. There's got to be *something* here,

Kevin. You're supposed to be the world's greatest trial lawyer; *come up with something!*''

Kevin had never seen Barrington quite like this; if he didn't know better, he would have thought Austin was approaching a state of desperation. Barrington the Great, the Unflappable One, our Leader, he thought as he weighed the risks of probing deeper. "Tell me something, Austin. Why this sudden desire to launch our staid old business firm into the personal injury business, particularly one as chancy as this seems to be?''

Barrington sank into his chair and ran a huge hand through his thick hair, then rested it palm down on the desk beside his other one. As he met Kevin's open gaze, it was obvious to the younger man that Austin Barrington was grappling with a decision more important than the abstract legal issues surrounding a prospective piece of litigation. Something's up, thought Kevin.

"All right," said Barrington, leaning toward the younger man. "Listen carefully. You know that we are not doing well financially, but you don't know how serious it is. I haven't got time to talk about it now, but take it on faith: If this case doesn't work out for us, we're finished." Kevin stared at the senior partner, who rubbed his eyes and suddenly looked every bit his age, heavy cheeks sagging into pale jowls. "In fact, it's even worse than that." Barrington crushed his cigarette into a bronze ashtray. "And only Gardner White, Adrian Fisher, and our outside auditors know what I'm about to tell you." He paused to swallow, then added in a quiet voice: "The firm is already technically insolvent, Kevin.''

"*What?* You can't be serious, Austin. What do you mean 'technically insolvent'?''

"I mean we are unable to meet our financial obligations. We're in trouble, just like Diamond and Pender and all the big firms that have been caught in this damnable recession, deregulation, and competition from New York firms opening branch offices here. I'm telling you all this so you will know why I'm considering this not inconsiderable shift in our professional direction. Also because you will be involved in the case if we get it; if we *want* it. They . . . they said they will want you to try the damn thing personally." From the way Austin spoke them, it was clear these last words were bitter in his mouth. "They want me too, of course," he added, straightening his shoulders, but the moment of rare vulnerability was not lost on the younger partner.

Now it was Kevin's turn to take a deep breath. Was Austin actually ready to bet the entire firm on what appeared to be a very dark horse? And expecting him to be the jockey? To put his own hard-earned ten-year victory string on the line for a long shot like this?

"I need not remind you, Austin, that I have never tried a personal injury case in my life. I—just like you and all the other partners in our firm—am a business litigator used to trying antitrust and securities cases, not who-got-in-the-intersection-first cases. I wouldn't know a whiplash from a compound fracture and all I know about 'emotional distress' is from spending weekends at home with my wife. Everything I know about personal injury work you could—"

"They want *you*!" said Barrington in a tone that broke through his obvious effort to keep a rein on his voice. "They *know* you haven't done any personal injury work, but they also know you've never lost a case in your life and probably never will. They've read your articles, they've seen your lectures, and they know your occasionally unorthodox techniques will apply to any kind of case. They want the best for their clients and they think that . . . well, dammit, they think you're the *best*."

Barrington rose quickly, took a few impatient steps toward his darkened conference area, then turned back and faced the younger partner. "Christ, Kevin, I'm trying to tell you that the bank has called our loan, and we've got to come up with something in a hurry or we're all finished!" He took a deep breath and exhaled noisily from billowed cheeks, then walked back and again rested both hands on his desk. Leaning toward Kevin, he said, "If I can get the damn case, you will try it with me, won't you? Bear in mind too that it's not just this one case. Consider for a moment the number of families living around the twenty thousand hazardous waste dump sites the Environmental Protection Agency admits now exist around the country. Olzeski claims that toxic waste litigation will dominate the United States courts throughout the 1980s and '90s, and he's right. *Money*, Kevin! *Big* money."

Kevin placed his own hands on the front of Barrington's desk, then absently fingered the brass top of a Mount Blanc lead-crystal inkwell. "I have nothing against money, Austin," he said. "With *my* wife, I can't afford not to have plenty around. But what I'm trying to tell you is that we may have a problem finding an expert who will make the causation connection *and* who will stand up on cross-examination. I'm just the messenger here, and I have to say it doesn't seem to have worked very often in the past. I wish I could be more enthusiastic, but . . . given the facts you've outlined, I'm sorry, Austin; I just don't like it. Too many cracks to fall into.''

Barrington scowled and started to frame a response, but the back of his clenched fingers smothered it. Then he rose from his chair and spoke again, now in a resigned voice. ''Kevin—I don't like it either, but unless you have a better idea, I would appreciate it if you would be a bit more positive about mine. As for cracks? Christ, we're already in one—a crevasse, actually—a financial black hole. There must be something we can do with this opportunity. Think, man, *think!*''

Barrington's plea generated nothing for the next minute but another unnerving silence while Kevin noticed the erratic tick-*tock,* tick-*tock* of Barrington's antique clock. An ambulance passed by far below them, breaking the delicate silence. Now it was his turn to pace, and he did so with stiff-legged steps and fingers laced tightly back behind his neck. An idea was trapped in the back of his mind, struggling to escape. *Yeah,* he thought finally as the notion began to find its voice, *it just might work.*

''It's still a five-to-one bet, Austin,'' Kevin said, ''but . . . do you remember *Molein* versus *Kaiser Foundation Hospitals*?''

''Vaguely,'' Barrington said. ''A leading case on traumatic neurosis, wasn't it?''

''Right. It came down from the California Supreme Court just last year. The court recognized that traumatically induced fear can constitute a disabling emotional injury justifying substantial money damages.''

''So?''

''So are these guys scared or what?'' Kevin asked rhetorically.

''Of course,'' Barrington said. ''They must be terrified. But didn't the court require more? Some kind of supporting, objective proof that the victim's fears were not merely imagined or contrived?''

''Exactly. And didn't you tell me—''

''Chemicals in the blood and tissue!'' said Barrington, interrupting. ''Of course!''

''Well, it's still five-to-one, but it might be worth a try if you're right about having nothing to lose and if we can convince the bank it's a viable theory. Your toxicologist, Newkirk or someone else, could conduct a study and testify that the exposure to these chemicals is known to increase the risk of getting various kinds of disease associated with a deterioration of the immune system. These guys have ingested those chemicals for years and are entitled to be righteously spooked. On top of that, they've already suffered an injury of sorts in that traceable chemicals have invaded their bodies. And Christ, Austin, this must make them all prime candidates for cellular pathology. The odds of escaping cancer for those who don't already have it maybe just jumped from three-to-one to ten-to-one against them . . . *and they know it*."

Kevin stopped talking but continued to pace, head down, and Barrington was silent, not moving a muscle, careful not to do anything that might inhibit the lava flow of ideas that had finally erupted.

"Next," continued Kevin, "we bring in a shrink to say that they're suffering quantum fear and emotional distress because they've become statistically high-risk candidates for cancer. Yes, yes. *That's it!* In this scenario—and remember, Austin, we're engaging in optimism here that would make Pollyanna look like a prophet of doom—we ask the jury to award big damages for emotional distress—call it 'cancerphobia' —*plus* a ton of money for each plaintiff to cover his ongoing periodic medical examinations in order to chart the progress of any possible malignancy." The young partner was excited now, his hands chopping the air, his voice gaining intensity. Kevin had paced all the way into the adjoining conference room so that Barrington had to raise his own voice.

"Are you saying that if we could prove these workers know they ingested contaminated water, we might recover just for the *fear* that they *might* get cancer?"

"It's possible, Austin, but only if the court will accept the presence of the chemicals in their bodies as the objective proof of genuineness."

Barrington rose from his chair with a sigh and turned toward the east window wall, gazing out toward a tanker as it began to slip under the San Francisco Bay Bridge. He spoke without turning toward Kevin. "You're telling me that we would be breaking new jurisprudential ground here."

"That's exactly what I'm telling you," said Kevin slowly, nodding his head.

"There are no California cases on the point?"

"I haven't heard of one."

Silence. The tanker was now lost from sight beneath a bank of fog stubbornly fighting a losing battle against the midday sun.

"Look, Austin," said Kevin finally, in a more reassuring tone, "if things are as bad as you say, we haven't a whole lot of choice but to spin the wheel. I just want to be sure that you and these guys you're about to meet with know they're signing on two commercial trial lawyers to try the toughest type of personal injury case there is—a case without strong support in either case-law precedent or the scientific community. It's possible that my cancerphobia theory, together with twenty cents, may buy us nothing more than a telephone call to our bankruptcy lawyers."

Barrington stretched and removed another of his ten-a-day cigarettes from a monogrammed gold case. He then turned back toward Kevin and fixed his dark wide-set eyes on the younger partner. "But you agree I should try to get the case?"

Kevin felt the disturbing power of Barrington's gaze, scrambling his own rationality, diluting his caution. The Unflappable One needed him.

"I'll support you," he said, finally, "in whatever decision you make."

Barrington's eyes softened with pleasure. "I knew I could count on you, good friend. Between us, by God, we'll do something with this sow's ear of a case. One more question: If we win—either on standard causation or your cancerphobia theory—can we hold it on appeal?"

"I'll believe it," said Kevin with a wry grin, "if you will."

Barrington's features continued to relax and Kevin thought for a moment the senior partner might actually smile. Instead, he brusquely rose to his feet and said, "Well, so be it. It's a time for taking risks."

Kevin, already beginning to wonder what he was getting into, watched Barrington move in long, powerful strides toward the doorway and his meeting with the Plaintiffs' Coordinating Committee.

THREE

∎

The next morning, in the first pale glint of the San Francisco dawn, the financial district seemed as inert as its dozing neighbors—Telegraph Hill to the north, Nob Hill to the west, the rugged Mission District to the south, and the Embarcadero to the east. The ubiquitous summer fog contributed to the illusion of stillness by allowing the first weak shafts of morning sun little purchase as they reached out to the damp sidewalks and buildings. Foghorn echoes mingled with the lonely whine of a garbage truck digesting what was left of the day before.

Slowly, daylight revealed several dark monolithic structures reluctantly separating themselves from a gray backdrop. While the skyline struggled to free itself from the fading grasp of night, a switch thrown on Wall Street three thousand miles away activated random sparks of light in many of the buildings. Inside, stockbrokers yawned over fresh coffee and blinked into desktop computer terminals.

As the morning sun took stronger hold, a massive structure emerged, older than the rest and higher than most, its upper levels still embedded in clouds of gray mist: the Imperial Building. Although hardly an edifice to fulfill Frank Lloyd Wright's challenge that architecture should "make spirits soar," this neoclassical concrete skyscraper gracefully held its ground against its younger glass and steel neighbors. Few lights here; not a stockbroker's building. But, barely visible at the penthouse level, light from within the northeast corner began to spill out against the darkness. Barrington's corner. The Eagle's Nest.

Within the soaring arched entrance below, the lobby directory informed visitors that an express elevator was available for floors thirty-eight up to the forty-second-floor penthouse, these five floors comprising the offices of Stafford, Parrish, and MacAllister.

"Restrained elegance" was how the interior architects had characterized the lawyers' efforts to personify their firm's image

27

on these floors. The partners at S.P.&M. had wanted the environment to exude strength, security, and success; not *démodé*, of course, but certainly not faddish, or even modern; no Knoll chairs or Herman Miller furniture, no high-tech, hard-edged styling for one of San Francisco's oldest law firms. Accordingly, traditional interior styling governed throughout.

The reception area of each floor was practically identical to all the others (including, upon their eight o'clock arrival, the receptionists themselves). Only at the penthouse level—the Eagle's Nest—were differences not only apparent, but obvious. There, a client would be greeted by a mounted Persian Armanibaf Bakhtiari rug, an antique reception desk carved of regal French oak, a lush carpet rimmed with dark-stained hardblock flooring, the faint aroma of a fine cigar, and a vaguely uncomfortable quiet.

Here, on the presiding partner's floor, police chiefs had been fired; mayors elected; reputations made and destroyed; history altered—all, of course, done quietly, tastefully. Entering the Eagle's Nest could be a disquieting experience.

But now, at dawn, while the upper floors of S.P.&M. remained dark, Austin Barrington sat alone behind a massive desk and barked sporadically against the morning's silence with precise, perfectly structured sentences—staccato prose that would require no editing or redrafting when Miss Tarkenton arrived at 7:30 A.M. to transcribe his dictation.

The senior partner's office was L-shaped, comprising two large rooms, the conference area off to his left, still in darkness. This room was furnished with an eight-foot antique Mediterranean table, surrounded by ten leather chairs and a small but efficient law library. A door behind a fully equipped wet bar led to a private bathroom with sauna and shower. Ten-foot-high ceilings in both rooms were broken by large skylights that, even on the darkest day, provided sufficient light to breathe saving life into dark oak walls and leather furnishings reminiscent of Dickens's bleakest prose.

The intrusive jangle of Barrington's private telephone was so unexpected that he glowered at the device through four rings before snatching the receiver from its cradle.

"*Yes?*"

"Austin! My *goodness*, do you have any idea what *time* it is?"

The woman's voice was no less piercing and intrusive than the unwelcomed ring of the telephone that had preceded it. Austin

Barrington scowled again and, holding the receiver like a radio-active bar he couldn't wait to drop, he began pacing around his desk, staring out his east window wall at the brightening horizon.

"Yes, Catherine, I know what time it is and I trust you do, too, since there is a clock on your bedstand no more than twelve inches from your hand at this moment."

"Don't be angry, dear; I just didn't hear you leave and I was worried."

"I'm perfectly all right, not that you should stop worrying."

"Oh, Austin, it can't be *that* bad."

"It's that bad," he said, and stared out the window as the silence lengthened. Just listening to her voice irritated him. Why couldn't she leave him alone?

"Well, I just know you'll find a way out, dear," came his wife's enthusiastic response. "Why, darling, S.P.&M. is one of the *biggest* law firms in San Francisco."

"Christ, Catherine, that's precisely why we're in trouble!" He felt his blood pressure soaring and told himself to calm down. Catherine could do this to him with the best of intentions. God knows he had tried to explain that it was the big firms like S.P.&M. with large overheads that were most vulnerable right now, but what was the use? "I didn't come down here at five o'clock in the morning to discuss law-firm economics with you on the telephone," he said finally.

"I'm sorry, dear. You know I would never have bothered you during business hours. I was just worried." The apology came with the internalized tolerance of that generation of southern women raised to understand the importance of commerce, if not its confusing details. Catherine Barrington knew that it would be better to interrupt her husband in illicit coitus—not that he had time for such things—than at his office when he was "busy." She recognized that the firm was his first love, his insatiable mistress, the all-consuming passion against which she had never tried to compete. Emboldened by his silence, however, she added, "You haven't forgotten tonight . . ."

"The symphony with the Paulsons? No, I haven't forgotten."

"And late supper after, at Trader Vic's?"

"I haven't forgotten," he repeated.

"I'll wear my new green dress if I can find a matching purse today. Would you like that, dear?"

"That would be lovely," he grunted, thinking *God help us, what crap we talk*. "And I didn't mean to be abrupt, dear," he added perfunctorily, "but I'm in the middle of something. I'll call later."

"I'll be here, Austin, dear. I *do* understand."

The senior partner replaced the receiver and poured himself a fresh cup of coffee. He tried to resume his dictation, to resuscitate his shattered concentration, but his eyes were now drawn to the latest accounting spread sheet: a mocking quagmire of numbers and bleak forecasts predicting that, barring a miracle, Stafford, Parrish, and MacAllister would be bankrupt in three months. Austin shivered and gratefully drained the hot cup, then poured himself another.

Later, as sunlight began to filter into his office, Barrington changed disks and once again continued his dictation:

> *So now the three of us must adopt a bold plan which will constitute a dramatic, indeed painful break with our tradition and reputation as blue-chip litigators handling only complex corporate disputes. I realize my proposal will offend some of our oldest clients and irreversibly alter our image within the professional community. I dwell on this because I know how much pardonable pride both of you take in our firm's culture. I share that esteem, but remind you that Athens had great and justifiable pride in its culture too—then came the Spartans. If we are to survive, we must abandon some of our traditional ways—no matter how cherished—for Gardner's bleak financial analysis is clear and his conclusions inescapable.*
> *Our situation is critical.*

Barrington's rugged features pinched in discomfort as he rose to stretch his arthritic left knee and poured more coffee. He looked again toward the east and stared without expression at the Mercurochrome spears of light the embryonic sun had begun to throw at the night. He inhaled deeply, then looked to his left, where the same beams could be seen at play on the variously angled windows of the fifty-two-story Bank of America headquarters, creating the appearance of a vertical garden of shimmering crystal.

But Barrington saw no beauty there either, only the stubborn gray clouds. He picked up his coffee cup, the contents of which were already cold and bitter. He drained the cup anyway, welcoming the assault to his senses as he reached for his dictaphone again.

An opportunity has arisen to represent a hundred or more personal injury plaintiffs suffering from various illnesses, including cancer, the result of ingestion of toxic chemicals in their drinking water. Details will follow, but locked in my safe are reports from the Newkirk Laboratory in San Rafael showing contaminated blood and tissue samples taken from five random victims which contain chemicals identical to those knowingly dumped in the vicinity of their drinking water by the plaintiffs' employer—our target defendant—North American Chemical Company.

The dictaphone loudly clicked off, then clicked again as Barrington continued:

I've asked Kevin Stone for a second opinion on the law and damages issues and he agrees with my rough estimates that potential jury awards or settlements from these cases could run into the high millions, our fees likewise. Accordingly, these are bankable cases. Kevin and I are convinced that our line of credit at the bank will not only be extended as to repayment date but increased in amount on the basis of signed contingent fee contracts with these plaintiffs. In short, our financial problems would be solved—for the time being, anyway.

In the process, I was able to solve another problem alluded to in our meeting at the club yesterday. Kevin's agreement to try the case eliminates our concern that he might leave and take our best people with him. As long as the case continues, Kevin will stay, and our firm will remain bonded together. And as long as we are together, there is hope. I don't have to tell you that Kevin's word is solid gold.

Despite all this, I can anticipate your resistance to taking on these personal injury cases but I urge that you not be so concerned about tarnishing our image. I for one would prefer to be known as a viable firm that occasionally handles P.I. work than a bankrupt firm that once handled only the most glamorous, complex, and exacting business litigation. And after all, we're not exactly chasing ambulances here. This case could well result in the largest verdict in history.

I believe that if I sign these first few people, another hundred will fall quickly into line. But we must move deci-

*sively, for the competition from traditional personal injury
plaintiffs' lawyers will increase with each day's delay. We
must act now.*

Barrington was finished. He removed the cassette and, for the
first time in weeks, smiled as he looked up at the oil portrait of
Whit Stafford across the room and toasted the founder with his
coffee cup. "Your problems were like cotillion intermissions
compared to mine, old boy," he said out loud. "But I'll get us
through this storm. You'll see."

FOUR

■

The young woman lies motionless on an oversize bed, its six oak
feet buried deep in Axminster carpet surrounded by silk-upholstered
walls on which are hung several bright Calder lithographs. At
her feet is a moiré satin comforter, carelessly thrown back in
reverence of summer.

A sudden gust off San Francisco Bay raises the curtain, allowing the morning sun to shoot through the briefly opened aperture.
A capsule of sunlight briefly illuminates golden-brown tufts of
glistening pubic hair pressed flat by her own slender left hand,
held willing hostage between shapely and well-tanned inner thighs.
Cast in alternating light and shadow, her knees straighten slightly,
while farther up the exquisite nude body, disheveled chestnut-
colored hair spills across the satin pillow and partly covers her
right hand and arm. Her security position.

Gamma sleep, now broken by gamma rays—Rachel Cannon's
daily beguine has begun.

She stirs at the sound of the multipitched foghorns ricocheting
off the Bay and its surrounding walls and buildings, including
her own Sausalito condominium. Turning over, she struggles to
hold on to a hauntingly erotic dream now turning to elusive
pieces, fragmenting like the wisps of white clouds fleeing before
the dawn just outside her window.

A tall nude man—Latin or very deeply tanned—is comforting her. She is either lost or has done something terribly wrong. Pearl-colored hair tumbles over his strong, lean shoulders. One arm gestures reassuringly—his palm facing her, iridescent fingertips pointing upward. His other hand incongruously strokes her vulva with a gentleness she has never experienced. He is speaking softly in a language she cannot understand though she knows she once did. She can almost recognize him.

Then he's gone.

Rachel Cannon reluctantly opens her eyes, turns toward the clock. *Damn!*

She knows that tardiness at Stafford, Parrish, and MacAllister is often fatal, particularly when the offender is a sixth-year female associate trying to break the gender barrier in the best but most conservative all-male law partnership in San Francisco. The seventh year at S.P.&M.—her next—is known to fellow associate attorneys as the *up-or-out* year: *up* to partnership or *out* on the street looking for a new job. She approaches this crucial year without grounds for optimism, and as she summons energy to attack the day, Rachel reflects on her lunch the day before with second-year associate and sidekick Jeffrey Johnstone.

"You worry too much about those guys, Rachel," Jeff had argued at Miyuki's restaurant. "Worry is waste; it has no redeeming social value." Rachel smiled at her young friend, wanting to say, *Jeff, dear Jeff, you should worry* more *about 'those guys.' You care too little about what you say, how you dress, and who is going to be your own savior when your time for partnership consideration arrives.* Jeff called it snobbery, but Rachel couldn't help her overly fastidious nature. Besides, Jeff's hayseed appearance and occasionally reckless candor was denying him the strong mentor relationship with a partner essential to survival in a big-city law firm. Ironically, even the assignment that had forever endeared him to Rachel had gotten him off on the wrong foot with most of the partners. She had asked him—then in his very first week at S.P.&M. following a one-year clerkship at the U.S. Supreme Court—to locate and obtain information from a missing witness crucial to a trial she was starting in just two days. Using an investigator, Jeff soon located the witness, but was chagrined to find him locked up in a jailhouse in the mountain community of Montezuma, population 283. Not long dismayed, Jeffrey flashed his business card, posed as the

witness's lawyer, and persuaded the sheriff to allow him an
interview. Unfortunately, the witness denied having a lawyer. Or
wanting one. Nonetheless, on the day before her trial, Rachel
had her information via a long distance call from the Montezuma
jail. *How did you get in?* she had asked. *No problem getting in,*
he had answered. *The rub is getting out.* Jeff was making his one
allowable call to a lawyer, for to gain access to the city jail, he
had awaited the approach of Montezuma's only beat cop, then
put on a drunken panhandler act that gained him face-to-face
contact with the sequestered witness.

The two had been close friends from that day forward, with
Rachel serving as Jeffrey's surrogate mentor despite her own
precarious position on the partnership track. Weekly lunches at
Miyuki's, often joined by Rachel's best friend Beth Abelson,
had provided a social respite, an opportunity to catch up on each
other's lives.

"So enough with the worry," Jeff had continued while Rachel
thoughtfully poked at a fried shrimp with one chopstick while
he, thick glasses fogging, renewed his attack on a bowl of ramen
soup. "You've made all the right moves and the timing is right.
They've just been waiting for the right woman to bring aboard.
You're it. Her. It's just common sense."

Rachel had flashed her wry, uneven smile and said, "Thank
you, Jeff, but so was the notion that the world was flat."

"That, my friend," replied Jeffrey, "is a hindsight exercise in
ad hockery unworthy of you. So relax already."

"While I'm busy relaxing, Jeffrey, please refresh my memory
as to just how many women have made it past their sixth year
during the seventy-year history of S.P.&M."

Jeff had laughed and shook his head, throwing his rust-colored
hair into motion in all directions. "Ah, yes, good ol' S.P.&M.
—'Stuffy, Patrician, and Male.' Let's see now. Four. The answer to your loaded, leading, and otherwise objectionable question
is 'four.' Before you and Beth Abelson that is."

"Now then, Mr. Johnstone, tell the jury how many of those
four women were elevated to partnership after their seventh
year?"

The ritual had been mechanically completed by Jeffrey:
"Roughly? Roughly none, counselor."

"Zero?"

"Zero."

"Will you agree that's not very many?"

"That's not very many, but be serious for a minute. None of them was a Rachel Cannon. I'm still just a rookie around here, but it's established lore that one of your female predecessors lasted six years only because she looked like Jessica Lange, and the other three, though plenty smart, reportedly chewed nails for breakfast. Rachel Cannon, on the other hand, is strong without being overly obnoxious about it and has a face that makes Jessica Lange look like a bag of antlers."

Rachel could not help but smile, saying, "Oh, Jeffrey P. Johnstone, you silver-tongued shit-slinger. How I love your hyperbole!"

They had laughed yesterday at Miyuki's, as they always did together, though down deep they knew that the recessionary slowdown had seriously jeopardized both their chances for partnership. Rachel also knew that women had received better treatment in Sam Peckinpah movies than at S.P.&M. As for the reasonably good looks that had always given her an advantage with men in the past, they now seemed to be a major impediment with the most important men in her life: the partners at Stafford, Parrish, and MacAllister. Rachel Cannon simply did not *look* like a lawyer. She tried, but as she glanced at herself in the restaurant's mirrored wall and appraised her typically restrained navy skirt and white silk blouse, she definitely did not see a lawyer looking back at her. Not even when she knitted her brow and thrust her jaw forward.

"About you," Jeffrey continued, "I speaketh not a grain of bullshit. About them, and their readiness for Rachel Cannon, well . . . we'll see. My bet is that you will have a two-window office and tenured power in about a year and a half."

"I don't want power over anybody, Jeff; just some control over my own destiny. There's already too little power to go around for that bunch."

"That's because Barrington has ninety-eight percent of it," said Jeff, savaging the last shrimp.

"That's not real power. That's control by intimidation."

"Well, whatever it is, he's damn good at it."

"Yes, but is the term 'mutual respect' too much to expect or too trite to stomach with Oriental food?"

"Neither. It's just irrelevant. This is Montgomery Street, Rachel, not Sesame Street. As for making partnership, don't look to me for sympathy. I'm just a common farm duck pecking around for a piece of the action at a time when all the big firms in town are hurting, probably including ours. But you're different, and you know it.''

"Oh, I'm different, all right—I'm a woman, I don't look like a lawyer, and to top it off, I'm older than all the rest of you, even older than some of the younger partners.''

Jeffrey had jabbed at her with a chopstick at that point: "Aha! There you have it! I charge you, Ms. Cannon, with six counts of gender incongruity, compounded by chronological asymmetry and two counts of marrying a horse in Cleveland.''

"Guilty as charged, your honor, but Justin Parks was more of a jackass than a horse and we were married in St. Louis, not Cleveland.''

Like many women in the professions, Rachel had started late. After the breakup of an ill-conceived two-year marriage, she had taken a job as a paralegal in a large San Francisco law firm. A year of sorting documents had persuaded her to resuscitate her lifelong dream to become a lawyer, and she gained admission to Hastings Law School.

She graduated high in her class in September 1975 at the age of 27, and joined S.P.&M. in 1977, after nearly two years as a winning prosecutor at the Alameda County district attorney's office. But time had been lost in the process and her age now placed yet another barrier in her path to partnership and the independence it represented. Moreover, her timing could not have been worse, for the recession of the eighties had hit just as the sexual revolution of the seventies was going out of style.

But this was no time to dwell on obstacles, nor could Rachel continue to languish in bed, listening to the early morning Sausalito sounds rolling off the Bay: ghostly voices and clunks and creaking from the herring fleet, mingled with the raucous, staccato pleas of the sea gulls and the occasional bark of a seal. She could not be late for the Tuesday morning trial staff meeting, where latecomers were notoriously unwelcome. There would be no run this morning and no cappuccino at Cafe Trieste.

She pulled herself out of bed and glanced out her bedroom window across the Bay, where in a few hours San Francisco's skyline would emerge, blinking across Alcatraz like a paroled prisoner, free from the white shroud of fog that had held it captive. She reluctantly turned away and moved toward her living room.

Rachel's walk was something between the purposeful stride of

a gymnast approaching the mat and the confident glide of a
fashion model. She had in fact worked in both commercial
photography and fashion as a sideline in college. No bra ads,
thank you—too small. No shoe ads either—too big. Hats were
her favorite then, but as she entered her living room this morning, she modeled nothing but a gold chain around her neck—a
birthday gift she had never removed, from a birthday—her
twelfth—she would never forget.

Rachel's father had missed her party—the Democratic Council
of Hutchinson, Kansas, was on the young congressional candidate's busy schedule that day—but Rachel was used to that. Jack
Cannon was a man for all seasons and all people. All Hutchinson
admired him; Rachel adored him.

He had arrived home that night in time to tuck her in and give
her the gold chain. It was the first time she had seen tears in his
eyes and he had never hugged her so tightly. She remembered
asking him if he remembered turning twelve and he had told her
grown-ups usually couldn't remember such occasions.

But Rachel would always remember her twelfth birthday because it was the last time she ever saw her father. The last time
she was held in his strong arms. The last time, in fact, she had
felt completely safe, thoroughly secure. And now, two decades
later, the thin gold chain accented the long line of a mature
woman's neck.

Rachel shot a worried glance at her mantel clock as she
padded through her living room, where sparse Herman Miller
furniture was arranged to feature the constantly changing view of
wildlife, scattered islands, and pleasure boats that combined to
make Sausalito one of the world's most beautiful waterfront
communities. Ignoring a mass of old magazines and newspapers
on the glass coffee table, she moved along the window-wall,
absorbed briefly in the awakening Bay, then entered her cluttered
kitchen.

Rachel never regretted pouring an unconscionably high per-
centage of her salary into her condo. It was her home, her
sanctuary. Nothing else provided her with a greater sense of
peace and general well-being. This was what she had worked so
hard for. Of course, a living space could not provide everything
in life she wanted, but it was a good start.

Still naked, Rachel stripped a banana and quickly blended her
fresh protein and yeast drink. She then returned to the bathroom
and flipped on the news while she showered. She sipped her

drink while she dried herself and attacked her snarled hair, then applied a light blush.

Rachel Cannon's face needed little makeup. Her skin glowed like a child's. Neither her prominent cheekbones nor her large gray-green eyes required cosmetic accent. Her full lips were naturally red, almost pouting when in repose, but turning up at the corners when animated, creating an illusion of innocence and youth. In reality, both were sure but somewhat distant memories for Rachel, but if a man should take pleasure in perceiving her as innocent, her face—though far from perfect—would do little to inhibit the fantasy.

She finished dressing, turned off the radio, and reluctantly left her tranquil apartment and the gentle pearl-haired stranger of her dream.

For all its wonders, San Francisco was an experience that had taken some getting used to, particularly for a young woman raised on unsullied air and warm summer evenings in Hutchinson, Kansas, where the hottest spot in town on a Saturday night was the local bowling alley.

San Francisco was undeniably exciting. "Everybody's Favorite City" meant the Geary Street theater district, Trader Vic's just up the street off Taylor (where Mike, the maître d'hotel, always knew who qualified for seating in the Captain's Cabin), the Superbowl champion 49ers, North Beach, the San Francisco Symphony, and a couple of offbeat discos that had recently sprung up in the resuscitated Haight-Ashbury district. Then of course there was Montgomery Street itself, offering a professional challenge with a raw quality you rode western style—not sidesaddle—if you wanted to stay up.

But Rachel acknowledged the city's negative aspects as well: seemingly endless fog, high-rise glass boxes thrown up by money-hungry developers, seismic anxieties, vacuum-packed tourists, and Chinatown shootouts, all set against a background of jarring, cacophonous traffic and perpetual construction. San Francisco had not been an ideal place for a young, recently divorced woman, particularly with an ex-husband living on Nob Hill just minutes from her Cow Hollow apartment. You never knew when Justin might turn up with some crazy new idea for something elaborate to do: helicopter skiing in Canada, flying down into the Grand Canyon in a Cessna 185, fresh Maine lobster . . . at a restaurant in Bangor. Rachel, who had lacked money for the previous decade, had been drawn as a college senior to Justin Parks's abundant supply of it—and his willingness to spend it on good times.

Rachel never was able to remember why she had married Justin. In part, it was probably because he could always smile in the face of her darkest moods, when her suppressed anger clouded her outlook and turned her bitter. "Why do you put up with me?" she had asked once after working herself into a rage over Justin's insistence on displaying a BAN-THE-BOMB bumper sticker on the front of his car and a NUKE-THE-BASTARDS on the back. "Well," he had replied with his childlike smile, "for one thing, you're a woman. I like that in a person." Rachel knew there was no point in asking him to be serious—or to take her seriously. She was no more able to reprimand her husband than she had been able, as a girl, to criticize her father. And Justin's wealth had spared him the need, or so he seemed to think, to be serious about anything, while Rachel viewed life as more than one long hedonistic spending spree. She had things to do.

In the second year of her marriage she realized that the differences in their personalities that had been attractive to her at first were now producing intolerable stress. Moreover, she had become stuck in an ironic and repetitive pattern: Fiercely competent and authoritative in dealing with the outside world, she was submissive and reticent with the man closest to her—at least until the day she packed her things and left.

Justin Parks would go through life wondering what on earth had gotten into her, and not until she moved to Sausalito did he believe that she was not coming back.

In San Francisco, Rachel belonged to others—her ex-husband, her clients, S.P.&M. In Sausalito, she belonged only to herself. Apart from this, Rachel knew it was both unfair and irrelevant to compare the village of Sausalito with the city of San Francisco, like comparing Monet with Lichtenstein, but on a bright morning like today she found it difficult to leave her peaceful harbor town and head toward the hot-wired city. To Rachel, Sausalito was a bangle hanging secretly in the ear of Mother Earth, shining bright on even the dullest day, with sea sounds to make Jack London weep. And what other town featured a Fourth of July parade led by a belly dancer astride the hood of a '52 Ford, followed by a marching band of children and senior citizens playing "She's a Grand Old Flag" on kazoos? Sausalito provided the kind of human and visual poetry that put things back in perspective—for a few minutes at least. *Hold this feeling,* she commanded herself as she approached San Francisco's manic-progressive downtown din. *Hold the feeling.*

Montgomery Street—the famed San Francisco financial district—with the ancient but prestigious Imperial Building coming into view. Rachel's place of work, designed in May 1922, symbolized the traditionalistic work ethic within. No Bauhaus in *our* house!

The squeal of the tires on her 1975 BMW echoed across the cold floor as she slalomed around a concrete column into her basement parking stall and leapt from her car. It was already 7:45 A.M.

"Morning, Rachel," Becky, the forty-second-floor receptionist greeted her. "You're late today."

"I just went out for lunch," Rachel said, smiling.

"You people sure put in crazy hours," said the receptionist, slowly shaking her head.

"It keeps us from worrying about how busy we are." With a wave, Rachel hurried past through the reception area toward her office.

"Crazy," repeated the receptionist, shaking her head and enviously studying Rachel's thin hips and legs—perhaps *too* thin. Besides, she consoled herself, men don't like aggressive women.

Rachel's unique physical appearance alone might have been sufficient to set her apart from the other women at S.P.&M., but although Becky the receptionist didn't realize it, there was more to it than looks: Call it a stubbornness to relinquish a youthful, virtuous charm that had yet to confront its own mortality; an effortless attitude that had now combined with the radiant bloom of self-possessed maturity to fashion a woman rich in complexity and promise. Too rich, perhaps, for the blood of her male peers, who seemed content to admire her from a distance.

Up till now.

FIVE

■

But *why* can't they send someone else?'' demanded Denise Stone, looking at her husband through narrowed eyes. ''Is this how the firm repays you? Are these the rewards that come with superstar status? Living out of a suitcase? Leaving your wife to run the house alone and tame the children single-handedly?''

Sarah, age nine, ran to the living room chair where her father was seated. ''Daddy! Are you going away *again*?''

Julie, two years older than her sister and, like Sarah, as blond as their father, looked up from her book, listening for the reply.

Kevin Stone pushed his hair out of his eyes with one hand and hugged his younger daughter with the other, then with a smile lifted her up on the chair beside him. Ignoring Denise's remarks, he addressed himself to Sarah's question, careful to involve Julie as he spoke. ''I'll be gone only a week or two at the longest. I have to take some depositions of some men who we think have been breaking the law. Now off to bed with both of you.''

''Are they bad men, Daddy?'' asked Sarah, absently poking at her father's leg with a sticky index finger.

Denise looked on silently, leaning against the massive oak mantel at the center of their pale gray living room. The furnishings were, by choice, eclectic in style and sparse in number. A younger Denise and Kevin Stone had collaborated to decorate their Victorian with a look that managed warmth without clutter, restraint without boredom. In happier days.

''No worse than most,'' said Kevin. ''Sometimes men who are successful in business get greedy and want to be even more successful. So they make secret arrangements with their competitors so they can charge higher prices to people like us.''

It sounds so simple, thought Kevin. And compared with the high-risk legal expedition Barrington had proposed two days before, a price-fixing case would be a breath of fresh air.

''I hope you get 'em good, Daddy,'' said Julie, a pale, tense

41

child, recently entering a difficult phase where her mother could do nothing right and her need for Kevin's love seemed much greater than he could provide.

"I'll try, sweetheart." Kevin enjoyed explaining his cases to the girls. He already held the hope that one or both would be drawn to the profession—though not necessarily to the trial bar, God help them—so he tried whenever possible to sweep away the dark veil of mystery surrounding the law, that foreboding aura that sometimes reminded Kevin of the Church, with its black-cloaked judges and tenacious remnants of Latin. Kevin Stone had been both a Catholic and a lawyer long enough to acknowledge the place for ritual in both, but mostly he enjoyed those moments in trial when all pretense and ceremony were cast aside. When the gloves were off and it was down to one on one: a flesh and blood witness in the box, the stalking cross-examiner on the hunt.

"Should you not add to your lucid explanation of antitrust price fixing," said Denise, her sarcasm accompanied as usual by an ingenuous smile, "the fact that after you win, your firm will be awarded fees that will amount to nearly as much money as your clients will receive?"

"Why, Denise," said Kevin, matching her mocking smile and verbal formality, "I never knew you to complain about the money generated by these unseemly efforts of mine—other than to say that it was insufficient to meet your not inconsiderable needs."

Kevin cautioned himself to exercise restraint. He hated quarreling in front of Julie and Sarah and knew how quickly these skirmishes with Denise could accelerate into open warfare, particularly during the past year or so. Besides, this trip had a particular potential for trouble and he knew he must be very careful.

He took a deep breath as he thoughtfully surveyed his wife. Even now, Kevin found himself momentarily caught by the seductive beauty of Denise's smile—the same sardonic smile that had nailed him twelve years earlier; a smile to charm King Kong. His rationalizing imagination had done the rest, ignoring and blocking out revealing messages during their brief courtship.

But Kevin had now long since abandoned his illusions about Denise and their relationship. Denise Mason Stone had always passionately shared her father's belief that she was one of "nature's treasured darlings"—blessed with both beauty and wit—

thus entitled, without further effort on her part, to the best of everything life could afford her. Just when it was that Kevin ceased to share that view he could not say, but he had to admit he had been in the slow reading group.

As a bright and handsome bachelor, he had always had his choice of women. He had also cherished the notion that there was a special woman out there somewhere with whom, and for whom, anything was possible. Yet he had jumped into marriage with Denise. Why?

Not for her mind, surely. He knew long before the wedding that Denise Mason was no rocket scientist. Not that she was dull; just not nearly as bright as she seemed. What had then passed for intelligence he now saw was an ability to neatly dramatize and articulate the occasional clever thoughts or ideas she did have. Her good sense of humor, fragile but alluring face, fine athletic figure, and excellent family pedigree convinced Kevin that he'd be a fool not to love her.

But then, there was her erratic disposition. How could he have been so easily duped, ignoring the early warning signals? He knew better than most that even the most circumspect people constantly betray their true natures to anyone willing to observe them objectively. Take, for instance, her rude treatment of waiters and other service people. Should he not have realized that she would someday be treating him similarly? But no, his well-stroked ego allowed his concerns about Denise's sharp tongue and critical nature to be fully allayed by her focused gentleness where he was concerned. His own self-centeredness had so dulled his judgment that he was shocked to find himself the principal target of her fury within weeks after their marriage. Everything he did seemed to irritate her: an inadvertently mismatched necktie, his choice of music, his commitment to the firm. And if he should by chance react angrily to her ridicule, Denise could explode into tears of hurt and resentment and might pout for hours or even days. He just couldn't figure how her mind worked.

Perhaps, he now realized, they had never really loved each other. How could they, when they had never really *known* each other? He saw clearly now that Denise had wanted a recklessly passionate love affair that would neither diminish in intensity nor penetrate beneath the skin. He remembered how her hard eyes had raked his face when he once tried to explain why he was not sexually responsive ten minutes after one of their bitter fights:

she—emotionally stimulated from the encounter; he—bruised from her passive violence and, though he didn't know it at the time, just beginning to hate her.

Yet, as he now stared at his pouting wife, Kevin had to concede that he had enjoyed the social prominence the marriage had bestowed on him and that he had liked being able to go places that had previously been denied him. Moreover, the fact that Denise's father was the chairman and largest stockholder in Mason, Inc., now one of the firm's largest clients, had provided even more luster to Kevin's status in S.P.&M.

Denise in turn had seemed to bask in Kevin's growing national prominence, and the illusion of independence from her wealthy parents that his excellent income now permitted.

And then there were Julie and Sarah, who provided Kevin's one haven of innocent, nonexploitive love. As his marriage to Denise had begun to drift aimlessly and her rare physical demands on him became a growing irritant, Kevin turned more to Julie and Sarah for solace in the scant and precious free time he had outside S.P.&M. There was nothing he would not do for them, he concluded, including staying with Denise.

How strange, he thought as he watched her plan her next combination of verbal punches, *I know every inch of that tall, thin body, her small breasts and rose nipples, her thin oval face with its slightly hawkish but decently turned nose, the pale cheeks, still smooth as glass, the shiny, thick black hair from which I have recently seen her executing maverick gray intruders, her dark eyebrows, perpetually tilted in an ironic skepticism. Yet, I can still be fooled for an instant by that chameleon smile. And the eyes, those disarmingly innocent, oak-colored eyes that could make an executioner weep.*

"That's not my point, and you know it," said Denise, abandoning her sarcastic tone, "I'm simply saying that it's your partners' greed that keeps you on the road all the time. You don't get one extra dime for trying all the toughest cases and living like an airline pilot in between. I think it's dreadfully unfair to us."

"To us?" said Kevin. "Or to you? I'm not complaining, Denise. It's my job and I do it."

The silence lasted only as long as it took Sarah—sweet sensitive Sarah, brimming with goodwill and wisdom—to change the subject. "What's a deposition, Daddy," she asked, "and where do you take it?"

"Do you take it for a walk?" said Julie, giggling.

Kevin laughed as he answered. "No, Julie, a deposition is where a witness—somebody who knows something important about an argument people are having—swears that he will tell the truth and is then asked a lot of questions under oath which are written down by a person we call a court reporter."

"Is it in a courtroom like the place you took us once?" asked Julie, abandoning her book.

"No, honey, it's in a lawyer's office. Nobody is there but the lawyers, the witness, and the court reporter."

"Why do you do a deposition, Daddy?" asked Sarah.

Kevin knew the girls were forestalling bedtime, but patiently continued to answer the girls' questions, until Julie asked, "Why do you have to go to New York to take a deposition, Daddy? Why can't they come here?"

"That's a *very* good question, Julie," interrupted Denise, with mock seriousness. "Mommy can answer that one. Daddy has to take the deposition in New York because that's where all the theaters, good restaurants, and fun nightclubs are. Isn't that right, Daddy?"

Kevin answered Julie as if Denise had not spoken, saying, "New York is where all the witnesses and defendants live, and where the trial will be if there is a trial. The law doesn't require them to come out here, so we have to go back there."

"*We?*" said Denise. "Which fun-loving partner or associate is going with you on this trip?"

Kevin cursed himself for the slip. It was the one thing he did not want to come out, particularly right now. He considered lying, justifying it on the grounds that the children were present and a truthful answer might be incendiary. Rejecting this, he processed alternative forms of evasion, then stifled a fleeting and perverse notion to answer her question with complete candor: *I'm going there with the most beautiful and fascinating woman I've ever known. And yes, Denise, I think I am in love with her.* Upon reflection, he resorted to a substantially glossed version of the truth.

"Barrington assigned Rachel Cannon to this case."

Denise straightened as if struck from behind. "You are going to New York with *Rachel Cannon*? I don't believe it! Of all of the more than seventy-five associates in the law firm, you just happen to be taking . . . *Rachel Cannon*?"

"Who is she, Daddy?" asked Sarah, staring up at her father while she toyed with her Raggedy Ann's hair.

"Rachel Cannon," continued Denise, "is a lonely young ex-model working as a lawyer while she looks for a new husband. She is also well known for her ability to work all day and dance all night. Have I described her accurately, Kevin?"

Kevin turned to Sarah again, as if Denise had said nothing. "Miss Cannon is a very fine lawyer who happens to be one of about twenty-five women lawyers we now have in the firm. She will be going to help organize all of the documents and to prepare questions for me to ask the witnesses at their depositions." With a sideways glance at Denise, he added, "She is also a dedicated lawyer who, as far as I can see, wants only one thing out of life: to be a good lawyer and to make partnership at Stafford, Parrish, and MacAllister."

"And just how badly," said Denise, "does she want to make partnership, Kevin?" That smile again, then: "Is there anything she wouldn't do?"

The new silence was more tense than before, and again it was Sarah who broke it. "But I'll miss you, Daddy," she said in a pouting voice. Kevin was pained by the anxiety he saw in Sarah as she extended chubby little legs over the edge of the chair and methodically clicked her heels together.

"I'll miss you too," said Kevin, again glancing at Julie to assure her that she was included. He fired an altogether different look at Denise, who had turned her back on all of them and was leaning with both hands against the mantelpiece. Kevin was struck by the image of a boxer between rounds, leaning against the ropes, planning the next round, generating new resolve.

Kevin's own thoughts ironically flew to happier days, when he and Denise had first purchased the old house on Broadway in Pacific Heights. Captivated by the view of San Francisco Bay, and comforted by the proximity to the Hamlin School—Denise was then pregnant with Julie—they had stretched their finances to acquire the once-regal Queen Anne Victorian which had deteriorated to a state that gave "fixer-upper" new meaning. Kevin had plunged in with all his energy, working sometimes until the early morning hours, welcoming the opportunity to use his hands instead of his mind. It had taken three years to restore the old house to her past glory, but when the work was finished, a shadow seemed to fall across their relationship. Julie was then nearly three, Sarah was almost one, and Kevin was finally

reaping the financial rewards of his ever-lengthening victory
string. At thirty-five years of age he had come to be regarded as
a rising star on the national legal horizon. Yet, something was
wrong. He was wealthy, successful, had two beautiful children,
was living in one of the most beautiful homes on one of the most
beautiful streets in one of the most beautiful cities in the world.

And he was desperately unhappy.

Now, seven years later, staring at Denise's back, he knew that
the end of the reconstruction had meant the beginning of a
recognition that they had nothing important left to say to each
other. An earlier reckoning had been held off by the creation of
children and a nest in which to raise them, but implacable reality
had stood waiting for them when their work was done.

Kevin lifted Sarah up and gave her a pat. "Go get ready for
bed now, sweetheart, and I'll come up and read to you for a few
minutes."

"If you're leaving in the morning, Daddy," said Julie, putting
her book down. "Can I stay up later tonight?"

"No, honey, you run along with Sarah. It's getting late."

"Will you come, too, Mommy?" said Julie, looking from
Denise to Kevin, then back to her mother.

"Yes, Julie, I'll come tuck you in later."

Kevin's heart ached as he saw Julie steal one last anxious
glance over her shoulder as she went up the stairs. He turned
back to Denise, his eyes narrowing as he said, "I would appreciate it, Denise, if you could reserve your suspicion and sarcasm
for a time when the children aren't around. Sarah was on the
verge of tears."

"Well, now. Isn't this just *wonderful*," said Denise, turning
from the fireplace mantel and folding her arms as she looked
down at the seated Kevin. "The concerned father has made one
of his rare cameo appearances at home to chastise the embittered
wife and mother concerning her selection of topics to be discussed in front of the children. Tell me, *Daddy,* just *when* am I
supposed to vent my 'suspicious sarcasm'? You drop in only for
meals, a change of clothes, and an occasional mandatory social
event. Perhaps when you return from your two weeks in Manhat-
tan with the fair Miss Cannon, you can fit me in for an hour to
talk with you."

Kevin blinked, then slowly shook his head from side to side.
"Just what do we really have to talk about, Denise?"

Denise said nothing, her anger apparently spent, and the two of them stared at each other, neither speaking further. Kevin could never tell whether Denise had become bored with the game or was afraid she had gone too far, since neither rational discussion nor apology ever followed their arguments. All he knew for sure is that it was getting worse. *We're chained together*, he thought, *by circumstance; by children, by parents, ambition, inertia . . .*

Kevin's legs felt heavy as he rose from his chair. "Let's make the best of it," he said in a voice laden with resignation. "We've given up the fantasy, Denise; let's at least try for some civility."

Denise Stone absently tugged at her lower lip, then clutched her sweater tight against her throat. Kevin watched the muscles in her cheeks dance to the grinding rhythm of her lower jaw and waited for her to speak. Instead, she snatched up Sarah's Raggedy Ann and walked out of the room without a word.

SIX

■

The following day Austin Barrington was having troubles of his own. "You *what*?" he shouted into the telephone. "You call that a minor technical error?"

A quavering, metallic voice responded in a rush of words. "Well, yes, Austin, I do. You must understand how many samples pass through this lab on any given day. We run hundreds of tests here and the error, well, it was made by a new technician, but it could have happened to anyone. It was simply a transposition of data on the three people involved. We rechecked all three, and they came out essentially negative. Dammit, Austin, this should be very good news for all three of them, although I realize it's somewhat disheartening from the standpoint of your case."

Barrington stalked back and forth behind his oak desk like a tethered horse. A swollen blue vein pounded visibly in his left temple, but he took a deep breath, then spoke into the receiver in a controlled voice that taxed his dwindling restraint: "Listen to me, Ray. Please don't be quite so cavalier about this. We filed a verified complaint against North American Chemical and the City of Lileton last week which specified the degree of injury of five of the toxic waste victims based on your test results, including the three you now tell me you were wrong about. In addition, we issued a press release that sets forth in even more specific detail the extent of the contamination your impeccable testing procedures had revealed. Now you call to talk about 'minor technical errors' and 'how it happens all the time.' Well, listen to me, Dr. Newkirk, we've been friends for forty years— ever since Dartmouth—but if what you're telling me is true, I'll have your goddamn license."

"Austin, I've rechecked this thing twenty-five times and—"

"Stop right there, Ray. The only thing I want you to tell me right now is what I'm supposed to say to Mr. Bernard Weisberg, a new client who is waiting in my reception room at the moment to press me for details on how fast we can get to trial and make him a millionaire. As you may recall, Weisberg is one of the three people whose tests your airhead assistant botched."

"Well . . . yes, Austin, Mr. Weisberg is one of the people tested who now shows essentially negative blood and tissue contamination. He's been poisoned out there, all right—no doubt about that—but the readings are extremely vague."

"Fine," said Barrington, his disgust unconcealed. "Just fine. Now, here's what you do, Ray: You keep checking and rechecking until you come up with those original answers you gave me; the answers on which I based my law firm's entire future. Meanwhile, I have to deal with Mr. Weisberg, but as soon as I can get rid of him, I'll be out to have a chat with you."

Barrington slammed down the receiver, took another deep breath, and instructed Miss Tarkenton to show Mr. Weisberg in.

Bernard Weisberg entered the massive office with appropriate humility, despite an incongruently confident, almost strident voice that announced at sonic-boom volume that he was "very extremely elated" to see the senior partner again and even more pleased with his fine work which, to be frank about it, represented the kind of professional dedication that made this country what it was today.

"Thank you, Mr. Weisberg," said Barrington as he shook the gloved hand thrust toward him and surveyed a man no more than five feet two inches tall and bald except for two white fringes of hair over each ear. Large brown eyes and a jovial, dimpled smile seemed to confirm the truth of Newkirk's revised diagnosis.

"Thank *you*, sir," said Weisberg. "I don't mind telling you I'm quite a hero out at Harrison House since that newspaper article came out. Would you believe that a car dealer even extended me credit? Is there a chance this thing could settle in the next few weeks? I'm very extremely eager to get out of Harrison House, and I've found a nice little garden studio—"

"Slow down, Mr. Weisberg," interrupted Barrington quietly. "As the saying goes, 'I have both good news and bad news.' The good news is that the testing laboratory has just informed me that they made an error in your case and that your blood and tissue samples do *not* indicate the level of toxic chemicals we initially thought was there."

Weisberg cocked his head to one side, furrowed his brow, and said, "You mean . . . are you saying that . . ."

"What I'm saying, Mr. Weisberg, is that you are not as seriously contaminated as we thought. On the other hand, your case—our cases—may have just gone out the window. As you know, we had initially agreed to take these cases primarily on the assurance of the Newkirk Laboratory that contaminants had demonstrably invaded your body. This would have provided the appropriate evidence to support your claim of emotional distress and fear of developing cancer. The bad news is that the revised results are apparently no longer strong enough to support that claim."

Weisberg lifted himself by placing both hands on one arm of the client chair and twisting sideways to his feet. He rubbed the backs of his hands as he aimlessly walked around the office for a full minute, digesting this new information.

"Are you all right, Mr. Weisberg?" asked Barrington.

The little man looked at Barrington as if the meaning of the question eluded him, then resumed his pacing. When he finally returned to face Barrington, his entire manner had changed. Gone was the jovial manner. Gone were the flashing dark eyes and ready smile. Bernard J. Weisberg had just been informed that his body was relatively free from poisonous contaminants; that his death sentence had just been commuted.

And Bernard J. Weisberg was angry.

"Now, see here, Mr. Barrington," he said finally, his booming voice fully recovered. "I signed and executed a binding contingency fee contract with you, and now I expect you to live up to it. If you don't, I'll go get another lawyer.''

"I understand your frustration, Mr. Weisberg, but try to understand our position too, and please be so good as to lower your voice. We relied upon a reputable testing laboratory which, it turns out, made a mistake. You should be relieved. As for the case, however, it is true that without the presence of strong, tangible evidence of contamination, there's really nothing we or *any* other lawyer could do for you.''

Mr. Weisberg thoughtfully pondered the senior partner's words. When he spoke again, it seemed more out of conviction than anger: "That's where you're wrong, Mr. Barrington. There are plenty of things you can do for me. To start with, you can take over the car payments for the 1980 de Ville I just signed for. Huh?'' He paused for a moment. "Better yet, you can go out and tell the schmuck who runs that testing lab that I'm going to sue him, too, if he doesn't stand by the original records.''

"To my discredit, Mr. Weisberg, I concede that I've already considered that possibility,'' said Barrington, his patience again challenged. *How*, he wondered, *could this be happening? Has my whole career been leading to this? To be standing here haggling with some pygmy sock merchant while my firm—my whole life—is slipping into a black hole?* The next voice he heard, however—his own—was reassuringly calm. "Unfortunately, Mr. Weisberg, the law requires that we must eventually subject you to blood, tissue, and other testing by the defense once this litigation gets under way. The defense medical team would perform the same tests on you that Newkirk Laboratory performed and would come to the very same conclusions that Newkirk has now come to.''

Bernard Weisberg was, for a minute at least, stunned into silence. He abruptly turned and walked quickly into the conference area, where he smacked a leather chair on each side with the palms of his hands. He then spun and said, "Well, then I'll go back out to the North American dump site and I'll *roll* in the goddamned stuff! And if that doesn't work, I'll eat it until my fucking eyes light up!''

"Mr. Weisberg. Again I must ask you to please lower your voice. Come sit down and relax for a moment. Committing suicide will do your case no good.''

Weisberg did not sit. Instead, he charged Barrington's desk and stretched his full five feet two inches across it, then glanced over his shoulder and lowered his voice to a whisper, saying, "I'm not talking about killing myself, for God's sake; give me a break, will you? Do I look *stupid*? I'm just talking about getting enough of the crap in my bloodstream to pass the defense doctor's tests. What the hell's the matter with *that*?"

Barrington appraised his client with new interest bordering on respect. Six months ago, Austin would have thrown Weisberg out of his office, but today he was actually intrigued by his client's total lack of scruples. Weisberg was obviously deeply frustrated and upset, yet he knew what he wanted. A little guy with very big balls, thought the senior partner as he slowly shook his head. "I'll tell you what's wrong with it, Mr. Weisberg. Your idea, though both courageous and creative, constitutes a fraud upon the North American Chemical Company, the city of Lileton, and the San Francisco Superior Court."

"Let's take those one at a time," said Weisberg, undaunted. "In the first place, I can't see you having a hell of a lot of sympathy for North American Chemical Company, who go around risking the lives of their employees—yours truly included—to line their own filthy pockets. Even if only two out of the five of us you picked turned out to have a high level of the stuff in our blood and tissues, it's no thanks to North American that we aren't all six feet under. Huh? I notice your lab doesn't deny I got poisoned from drinking that crap, which is one thing they got right because I did get poisoned, goddammit!" Weisberg wiped his nose with the back of his gloved hand, then continued. "As for the city of Lileton, I suggest you read your own press clippings, Mr. Barrington. You outright accuse them of looking the other way while North American did their thing. Hell, there was money going under the table all the time, and half the town knows about it!"

Despite his own dark mood, Barrington had to stifle a smile at Weisberg's dramatic rhetoric, thinking, *If this guy can't be a defendant, maybe we ought to make him a lawyer*.

"This brings us to your precious court," continued Weisberg, now erect, chest out, and pacing back and forth in front of Barrington's desk. "In the first place, the court doesn't have to know about it. In the second place, the court isn't down to one kidney the way I am, and the court doesn't have to wake up in its own vomit about three times a week the way I do, and the court doesn't have scars all over its hands and arms like I do. I talk to you about justice, Mr. Barrington, and you talk to me about *courts*! It's like I was talking to you about God and you keep talking to me about religion. So give me a break and let's quit playing games, Mr. Barrington. Do I go get myself a new lawyer and call a press conference to tell the world what dog-bite lawyers you are, or are you going to make good on your contract with me?''

Austin Barrington was no longer amused. The guy clearly was not bluffing and Barrington felt himself slipping into the alien grip of helpless confusion. Could it be that just a few hours earlier he had accepted accolades from the other Table of Three members for his ingenuity and resourcefulness in saving the firm? Had relished the front-page praise from all the major Bay Area newspapers (it had been a long time!) for his courage in taking on North American Chemical? Had graciously accepted new long-term financial relief from the firm's bank? Could it really be that all his genius and daring in saving the firm was to be derailed by a bungling pathologist and wrecked by a desperate, big-mouthed client?

"Well, Mr. Barrington," said Weisberg into the void created by the lawyer's self-reflection, "if I've got you figured right, there's something even more important than big bucks at stake here for you. Huh? You're the guy who has to face the press and explain why you shot yourself in the foot. So if you're that partial to humiliation, go right ahead, be my guest. But make no mistake about it: I've got nothing to lose and I'll blow the whistle on you if I have to.''

In a gesture apparently designed to allow his point to sink in, the client unbuttoned the coat of his dark-green leisure suit and plunked himself into a chair opposite the senior partner. "On the other hand," Weisberg continued, but now in a conspiratorial tone that made Austin wince with revulsion, "I'm willing to go out there and snort the goddamned stuff if that's what it takes. Are you hearing me? What the hell more could you ask already? Understand me, mister, I don't want to die or even get myself sicker. I'm sick enough, thank you. I just want your guy Newkirk to tell me how to take enough of this stuff to register on the tests, but not enough to hurt myself any more than necessary.''

Barrington slowly rose from his chair and walked over to his north window. He needed time to think. There must be a way out. Isn't there always? Think, he commanded himself, *think*.

But nothing came of it, and in the mean, empty silence that followed, he stood staring up at the Arcadia Building penthouse, wishing himself back into yesterday, when success and prosperity were his and he was sipping Glenlivet with a member of the Reagan cabinet in town for the day who thought *he* had problems. Well, maybe he did, but he also had plenty of places to hide, others to blame. *Not you, Bub, no siree. It's nut-cutting time and you're alone. All alone.* Weisberg, who had picked up a copy of *The Wall Street Journal,* looked up as Barrington suddenly began to shake his head violently from side to side. He started to say something to the senior partner, but thought better of it and returned his attention to the news. Barrington took a deep breath and shifted his gaze downward toward the street below littered with tiny crawling metal rectangles. Then, for the first time in his life, a nameless fear forced him back a step from the window, his heart frozen for two full beats by a clear mental image of himself falling . . . falling end over end, thinking his last thoughts, then splattering like a raw egg against the cold asphalt forty-two floors below. A laser shaft of heat sliced through his chest and into his groin. He turned away from the window and snatched a silk handkerchief from his lapel pocket, then dabbed his forehead and upper lip. He would have to shower and change shirts as soon as he got rid of Weisberg who, he was relieved to see, had been absorbed in the *Journal. How unfair,* thought Barrington, *that the little creep can sit there so self-assured because he has nothing to lose, where for me, everything I've ever achieved is on the line. How absurdly ironic that this disparity— his failures, my successes—should give him all the cards.*

Finally, the senior partner turned toward his client and fixed him with a look so hard that Weisberg recoiled. For the first time—without saying a word—Barrington had broken through the little man's defenses. Then, with the staccato coldness of a computer recording, he spoke: "You will do nothing today. You will talk to no one about this. I will call you within twenty-four hours. You will excuse me now."

Relieved to be dismissed, and smiling courteously again, Weisberg bid the senior partner good-bye and hastily withdrew from the office. By prearrangement, this was Miss Tarkenton's signal to have Barrington's car brought around for a trip across the Golden Gate to San Rafael, home of the Newkirk Laboratory.

For a full moment Raymond Newkirk waited for the laugh. Instead, Barrington's lips curled tightly the wrong way, and the toxicologist knew it was no joke.

"Do you have a better idea for remedying your dereliction, Ray?" It wasn't really a question.

"Austin . . . Christ, I couldn't feel worse about all this. But dammit, I can't alter the fact that those three old birds just aren't as contaminated as we first thought."

The two men sat alone in Newkirk's cluttered lab. His four technicians were at lunch and the door to the reception area was closed and locked. Newkirk had never seen Barrington like this and had never himself felt so uncomfortable. His mind was already fluttering around the room like a raised grouse pounding against a glass sky trap. His heart seemed to be invading his throat, cutting off air. He willed the phone to ring. A fire, even a small earthquake. Anything.

"Ray." That was all Barrington said, and it said it all. Just . . . *Ray*.

How could a person's name sound so obscene? thought Dr. Raymond Thomas Newkirk, who suddenly noticed that his chair needed some 3-in-One oil, which, in turn, somehow reminded him of the bottle of vodka in the cabinet just inches from his right knee.

"Ray," Barrington repeated, gravely shaking his head, "you gave us your professional assurance that all five were dangerously, indeed terminally, contaminated. My law firm relied on that professional assurance and committed itself to a multimillion-dollar lawsuit. It turns out now that one of your new kids made a mistake—just a little one, as you are fond of saying, but one that has created disastrous consequences. And you missed it, Ray. Were you too busy to check his work, or is it that you're drinking again?"

"Oh, hell no, Austin," responded Newkirk a bit too soon, he realized too late, so he added more casually, "Not for years."

"No matter the reason; it is the result we now must deal with. As Kevin Stone quite properly and emphatically pointed out to me as he left for New York, we've started the game; we can't just sit on the sidelines. I'm getting tired of lying to him and others about what's happened. You've got to make good on your first reports, Ray."

Barrington lit a cigarette. Newkirk licked his lips. Neither spoke for half a minute.

Barrington then leaned forward: "You'll agree you got us into this mess, won't you, Doctor?"

The doctor agreed he had.

"Now, if you have a better idea, Ray, let's hear it. But if you don't, then, goddammit, you'll do just as I say!"

He's gone barking mad, thought the toxicologist, trying to cope with the hypnotic force of those fierce, wide-set eyes. *What has he been through to have eyes like that? What's really at stake here that would drive Barrington this far? Falsify records? This can't be Austin Barrington. Arrogant, egocentric, overbearing, sure. But not crazy and never, never outside the letter of the law. And me—how did I get into this? More important, how do I get out?*

Newkirk somehow fought gravity to a standing position; it felt better looking down at the seated Barrington. "Slow down, Austin," Newkirk said. "Please, at least be practical. Even if I were willing to falsify my records, which, dammit all, I'm not, there's no way we could get away with it."

Just looking at Barrington's bloodless intensity caused an eruption of perspiration at Newkirk's hairline, but he went on, unable to stop explaining himself. "I know we're in a mess, Austin, and I agree I put us there. We're both professionally humiliated, perhaps even ruined. But, Christ, you're asking me to commit a crime! At least be practical—we'd be exposed the minute the defense toxicologist completed his own test results on the three of them. Then we'd *really* be in the soup."

At that, Barrington's anthracite features softened into the suggestion of a smile. "Not if they were really contaminated the way your report says they are."

"But they're not, Austin! That's the whole goddamn problem!"

"That can be handled, Ray. You know it can."

The words penetrated the toxicologist's brain with a force that knocked him back into his chair. *Oh, my God,* he thought . . . *My God, my God.* He considered trying to leave the room. *Just get up and walk right out.* Instead, he sunk even deeper into his chair, his right knee pushing hard against the cabinet. Against the Smirnoff.

"One of them—Bernie Weisberg—is not only a volunteer, Ray, he insists on it. He'll even come out here and take it. Or, if you prefer, I'll take it to him with directions from you."

"Oh, Christ, Austin, that's unthinkable. And anyway . . . it wouldn't solve the problem of the other two."

"I'll worry about the other two. You'll have nothing to do with it except for the preparation," continued Barrington quietly. "I'll administer it myself." Just like everything else, he thought to himself. *If you want something done right, do it yourself. Right, Bub?*

The last words caused Newkirk's mouth to drop open like a beached flounder. The toxicologist grasped the arms of his chair for renewed leverage and straightened slightly. He managed to raise his eyes to meet Barrington's; his jaw tightened and lifted almost imperceptibly. *This is insane,* he thought, but Barrington went on as casually as if he were ordering breakfast.

"It's not what it seems, Ray. All three of them are well over seventy years old, very ill, and are—according to your tests— suffering from some degree of contamination already. The artificial supplement, let's just call it 'A.S.,' will merely make their test results fall more in line with the allegations of our complaint. At the very worst, they may feel a bit worse, perhaps even die a month or two sooner, but at least they'll die rich and enjoy what's left while they're alive. I assure you that the other two would agree with Weisberg's plan in a minute if we but had the freedom to put the choice to them."

So this is why I went to medical school, thought Newkirk, *to be bullied into poisoning sick people I was trained to heal.* From a distant corner of Newkirk's youth crept a rumbling rage—no, *out*rage. It gathered momentum as it rushed into his consciousness, but once there, it found no voice. His mouth was as dry as a tray of zinc oxide. He wanted to say something, to get to his feet again, at least open a window. But the senior partner's presence paralyzed his intentions.

"You'll die a rich man, too, Ray," continued Barrington calmly. "Two million tax-free dollars, right off the top of the first settlement. Cash, of course."

The toxicologist was silent. Nothing in him moved now but a pounding heart, the beating wings of his mind now stilled.

When Newkirk finally opened his mouth, he was surprised at how easily the words came and the calm finality with which they reached up through the oily surface of his carefully crafted ambivalence.

"Let me think about it."

SEVEN

■

"Break out the Dom Perignon—we deserve some time off," said Kevin Stone as he and Rachel began to pack their briefcases and file boxes upon completing the last of the New York depositions—a Johnson Mills regional manager who admitted terminating a dealer who had threatened to expose the defendants' price-fixing conspiracy. It had been an exhausting but rewarding nine days for Rachel: up late each night organizing documents and preparing questions, then working with Kevin all day as he dug information out of witnesses they didn't even know they possessed. Mining gold from fools, Kevin had called it with an uncharacteristically cynical grin.

They were now the only lawyers left in the large conference room of their Park Avenue co-counsel's offices. She noticed how the sudden silence—the absence of contention—had transformed the room into an altogether different place; a pleasant place, actually. With the fighting over.

"Would you prefer gourmet food or a more vivacious atmosphere?" Kevin said, snapping his last trial bag shut.

"Both," Rachel responded, "but if forced to choose, put me down for fun over food."

"Then fun it will be," said Kevin, his fatigued face lifting into a smile.

This guy, thought Rachel, *is really something. He's handsome, smart, and competely charming. Also, dammit, completely married.*

Rachel recalled her excitement when she had first been assigned to work on the Johnson Mills case. An opportunity to work with S.P.&M.'s superstar was every associate's dream. She had also felt some trepidation, however, knowing that the assignment would require them to spend much time together during the next year, some of it on the road. Discreet though he was, Kevin lately had revealed a growing attraction to her—his

58

eyes sometimes lingering a second too long on hers, conveying a message easily understood. True, her last serious relationship had ended badly six months earlier, and while she was getting comfortable again with her aloneness, she recognized the warning lights of her own vulnerability in Kevin's blue eyes. And she knew that this one could lead to a world of trouble. And yet . . .

For better or for worse, the Johnson Mills assignment had offered no time to prepare herself; Rachel's very first project involved the New York trip. She had been concerned at first, picturing depositions of the defendant's key corporate officers by day, then just the two of them, alone together, in the Big Apple at night. She had always found the idea of an affair with a married man repugnant. Besides there was S.P.&M.'s unwritten but inviolate prohibition on intraoffice liaisons, for which punishment was always swift and harsh—and it was always the woman who was expelled in disgrace once the transgression came to light. The woman was always to blame.

Luckily, her honor and virtue were not immediately threatened and she was soon able to laugh at her grandiose fantasies. For one thing, the long working hours left neither time nor energy for mischief. At meals they were always joined by local counsel and/or client representatives. The only time she was alone with Kevin was during an occasional cab ride or on an elevator trip to their shared floor at the Helmsley Palace, at the end of which they would bid each other a tired good night and head for their respective rooms. All in all, Kevin seemed to be taking little notice of her, a discovery she greeted with relief mixed with— she had to admit—some disappointment. Meanwhile, she was chagrined to find herself taking considerable notice of him. Now, for example, as she glanced at his face and hands while he taped up the last box of exhibits, she was unable to suppress an electric twinge deep inside. She now knew from firsthand observation these past few days that those relaxed good looks belied an intense, encyclopedic mind that had made him one of the most feared and respected cross-examiners in the United States. After having watched him perform verbal surgery on four intelligent, hostile, and well-coached Johnson Mills Company senior officers, she understood how he had compiled his incredible record. Out of an unpromising tangle of inconsistent and confused facts, Kevin had, in just nine days of depositions, woven a tangible web of evidence that would support all their charges of antitrust violations and justify a seven-figure verdict in favor of their clients. For Dan Steadman, a dealer unlawfully terminated by Johnson Mills, it would mean a second chance, a new beginning, and she savored the satisfaction she felt in recognizing her own contribution to his victory.

But it had been Kevin's show and she had loved every minute of it. She had never seen a mind work like his: He was as fast as an IBM 360, capable of soothing a witness into a lulled state, then turning on him with the force of a battering ram. The questions she'd prepared had been helpful and well received, but she could see now that she still had much to learn.

"I'm still amazed that the regional manager admitted the threat to terminate," Rachel said, closing her trial bag. "Let's face it, Kevin. Our previous information on the point was on the flimsy side. Yet, bit by bit, he volunteered information that eventually killed him. Did you know he would self-destruct?"

"They usually do," he said, continuing to tape an exhibit box. "It's like the spider whose web is too flimsy to hold a large insect. If the unwilling guest simply sat tight, he'd soon fall out of the web of his own weight. But he panics and thrashes about, enmeshing himself deeper and getting more tired with each movement. Then it's killing time."

Rachel was surprised by the coldness of the parable and must have shown it, for Kevin suddenly laughed and added, "A bit morbid, huh? Sorry. Maybe I've been doing this too long."

Rachel smiled and inwardly shrugged off her first reaction. After all, she thought, didn't he deserve a lapse into the macabre after nine days of confrontation with hostile witnesses and their truculent lawyers? For all that, she still marveled at how youthful Kevin looked at forty-two years of age, particularly for a man who had lived on the precipice for the last sixteen of them, trying one major case after another . . . *and always winning*. Rachel had been a trial lawyer long enough to know the cruel price the courtroom extracted from its champions. She had watched high-tension lines begin to settle into her own forehead and around her eyes, and she wondered how Kevin stayed so young and fit. More specifically, she couldn't help but wonder what he thought of her, and whether the more prudent answer to his invitation might have been: *I think I'd better catch up on my sleep tonight, maybe call room service, do my nails, watch a little TV, make some phone calls* . . . The safe course. But safe from what? she asked herself. What is there to be afraid of?

Plenty.

Her relatively passive role during the days of actual interrogation had permitted her ample opportunity to observe Kevin, to study his features and movements as if through a one-way mirror. Quite suddenly, late one recent afternoon, while Kevin awaited an answer from one of the defendant's corporate officers, he had glanced in her direction and Rachel felt her heart stir with mingled joy and sadness at the sight of his tired, tense face. *My God, I'm falling in love with him,* she thought. Then, just as quickly, she dismissed the notion, the lawyer back in control.

After a drink at Harry's Bar downstairs, and another at P. J. Clarke's on Third Avenue, they were off to a raucous Italian restaurant called Il Vagabondo.

The step-down restaurant hummed with energy as they joined the three-deep crowd pressing toward a lone bartender. Traditional red-and-white checkered tablecloths, giant blown-up photographs of the staff, and a thoroughly Italian maître d' who looked straight out of central casting, all contributed to the convivial mood.

"Looks to me like we are in an Italian restaurant," shouted Kevin over his shoulder to Rachel as they crab-stepped their way through the crowd toward the tables.

"You mean this is not the Four Seasons?" replied Rachel.

Two drinks later they were seated and scanning the menu. "It's perfect, Kevin. I love it! May I order for both of us? I know exactly what the specialties are."

"Pardon my skepticism, but how does a woman on her first visit to a neighborhood Italian restaurant she thinks is the Four Seasons know what's good?"

"Order the veal-eggplant parmigiana. I guarantee it's the best you will ever taste."

"Rachel, I've never eaten veal-eggplant parmigiana, here or anywhere else."

"There, you see? You may pick the dessert."

"First, tell me how you know the veal-eggplant is so damn good."

"I have powers, Kevin. Irish voodoo . . ."

"Rachel . . ."

". . . plus, while you were paying the bar check, I asked the guy next to us what he was eating and he told me that's what all the locals order. I forgot to ask about dessert."

"Never mind. Without the aid of supernatural powers or

furtive consultations I will make the tough choice between the spumoni and the cheesecake—with the unerring precision of a coin toss.''

Their banter continued throughout a two-hour meal, covering topics ranging from politics to music; and the time seemed to evaporate as they talked. At first their discourse circled around their personal lives and touched only occasionally on their shared professional interests. Most surprising to Rachel was Kevin's detached and cynical attitude toward his status as a nationally famous trial lawyer.

"It's beginning to get to me," Kevin said. "You see, after my first five years of trying cases, I figured out that there's no real justice, only some lawyers who are better than others. A trial lawyer can win either side of almost any case if he's good enough and works hard enough. So he begins to take full responsibility for whether his client's case is won or lost—the ultimate arrogance. Pretty soon he's got himself convinced that the jury is judging him more than the facts of his case. And, incidentally, he's not far from wrong.

"Finally, he wakes up one morning and realizes he's burning himself out—more in fear of losing than for the satisfaction of seeing a 'just result' or even for the joy of winning.''

"But you always do win," Rachel replied, caught off balance by his candor.

"Yes, but when I do," he said slowly, "I feel only relief that I didn't lose.''

Rachel knew that Kevin had reached the age at which many fine trial lawyers begin to come unglued, depending more and more on pills or booze to find relief from the constant pressure of the courtroom. Moreover, Rachel had met Kevin's wife, and could see in an instant that the rumors were true: Denise Stone could not have cared less about how Kevin kept his miraculous record intact, nor the high price he paid to do it. She seemed to care only that he keep on doing it, that he be a winner, that he remain Number One. Rachel tried not to judge Denise harshly, but the fact that she seemed to have no life or strong interests of her own made it all the more surprising that she seemed to take so little interest in Kevin's. She remembered Kevin's look of discomfort at the Fishers's firm party that night a year ago when Rachel had asked Denise if she was relieved that the RMC antitrust trial was finally over. Smiling, Denise directed her response to Kevin: "I'll be most relieved when Kevin's modest share of the firm's fee arrives. The dear boy mangled my Canadian sable in our car door last night and a replacement is badly needed.'' "For me or the coat," Kevin had said, managing a self-ironic smile, but plainly embarrassed and angry at her tasteless remark.

Rachel remembered feeling danger at the moment, and found herself laughing too loudly along with the others in an effort to defuse the tension. Denise, never known for her restraint, settled for pointing her index finger—thumb up like a mock pistol—then wryly winking at her husband as she lowered the "hammer." The look they exchanged had made Rachel feel strangely sad, and oddly envious, for even in their hatred there was obviously a bond.

Now, a year later, it seemed to Rachel that the vertically creased brow between Kevin's blue eyes was the only visible hint of all those years of pressure, both in court and at home: two deep lines that plunged downward like a railroad track below tousled blond hair worn too long to satisfy either style or stereotype. At the lower end of his face, a slightly cleft, prominent chin created a Braque-like symmetry that, together with a strong, straight nose, lent strength to features sometimes almost feminine in their sensitivity.

As a second bottle of 1967 Barolo appeared ("It goes great with spumoni," Kevin assured her), Rachel matched Kevin's earlier candor by revealing her anxieties as an associate on the verge of "up or out," but Kevin deftly rechanneled the discussion to her family background. Rachel shifted uncomfortably as she reported that her father was dead—a lie she believed to be as close to reality as the only other alternative—and that her mother was in "poor health," a fair euphemism for alcoholism. Although she was flattered by Kevin's interest, her high spirits began to sink as he insistently probed for more personal information: "How did he die? Are you still close to your mother? How old were you when you lost him?" She felt a tightness in her throat and an uncomfortable heat spreading through her body as she gave vague and increasingly untruthful answers to his questions.

She felt defensive, as if his questions were attempts to pry her personal history loose from her—just as she had seen him do to others during the past nine days—to expose some vulnerability later to be exploited. After another minute, she excused herself as casually as she could, and walked quickly down the stairs toward the rest rooms. She rinsed her face and willed herself to relax, frustrated by her paranoid reaction. Kevin had asked friendly, normal questions, and probably would think no less of her if she were to tell him what it was like to turn twelve and suddenly find herself with no father, an alcoholic and promiscuous mother, and two frightened kid brothers. She had become the unwilling head of a family that had gone from riches to rags in one night and provided Hutchinson, Kansas, with enough gossip to drive her mother eventually into an institution and herself, rootless and frightened, out of town. Why, after all these years, was it still so damn humiliating?

She took a deep breath and applied a light blush. When she returned to the table, renewed, Kevin, seemingly unaware of her momentary distress, handed her a glass of wine, saying, "To the trip, to the partial dismantling of the defense, and . . . to us." For the first time—outside the safety of a large, well-attended law-firm meeting—their eyes met and held, their mutual admiration never more clear.

Dangerous ground.

"I ducked your comment about 'up or out,' Rachel," said Kevin, easing the tension. "Habit, I guess. But you needn't worry so much. You do good work."

"I had hoped you'd noticed," said Rachel, relieved that Kevin had chosen to pursue neither her family life nor the romantic implication so thinly veiled in his toast. But now a third topic, almost as sensitive as the other two, was on the table if she wanted to pick it up. She calculated the risks and decided that she would never have a better opportunity. Besides, outside the courtroom, Kevin was reputed to be both kind and fair, and since she had never been formally adopted by a mentor-partner, there had been no one else to approach concerning her future with the firm. Kevin's next comment would cue her direction.

"Everyone has noticed," he said.

"Thank you, Mr. Stone. I wasn't fishing for that, but I won't throw it back either."

"I'm listening."

Now or never, Rachel commanded herself. "I can assume, then, that you have opened the door to further interrogation on the point, counselor?"

"A bit, maybe," replied Kevin, his manner sobering, "although I should probably know better than to let a fast-lane camel like you get her nose under the tent. Go ahead. Fire away."

A frazzled waiter interrupted, slamming two desserts on the table. Rachel hesitated, wondered if their arrival should be construed as divine intervention. Kevin thoughtfully sipped his Barolo, waiting. "Well, are you going to shoot or not?" he asked, smiling.

"Well," said Rachel, straightening in her chair, "I can't tell you where the rumor started, but an informed source has hinted that there has never been a female partner at S.P.&M."

"As usual, Rachel, you're as subtle as a train wreck. At the risk of betraying defensiveness, I must point out that S.P.&M. is not the only all-male partnership in San Francisco."

"No," said Rachel, lifting her chin slightly, "but all the more reason to suspect there may be a grain of truth to the rumor. Anyway, you know what I'm getting at. To put it bluntly, Kevin, I'm wondering if I'm wasting my time." Rachel followed these last words with a large sip of wine and an unwanted bite of spumoni.

"Rachel, you were right about the veal-eggplant parmigiana," said Kevin, "but your Irish voodoo is wide of the mark on this one. I meant it when I said the entire partnership knows you are doing good work."

"I heard you, Kevin, but doing 'good work' does not seem to mean partnership at S.P.&M. if the person doing the good work happens to be a woman." *I've gone too far*, she thought, hating herself.

Kevin thoughtfully stared at her for a full moment and absently raised the back of his index finger to his lips. A waiter seemed to glare at her from across the room for no reason whatsoever. She raised a hand to her ear, unaccountably concerned that she had lost an earring. It was there, of course. Was it her imagination or had the entire restaurant gone silent?

"Look Rachel, you know I can't say more on this subject but . . . dammit, forget the past! You're different from the others." The reassuring words extinguished Rachel's emotional firestorm. "You know it and so do the partners," Kevin continued. "And . . . *so do I*." Again their eyes locked, and Rachel sensed that this time it would be up to her where the exchanged look took them.

"Okay," she said, taking a deep breath and putting on her most friendly, nonseductive smile. "End of harangue." *That was stupid of me*, she thought. *What had I expected to get out of him? What more could I expect him to say?* She tried to swallow her frustration along with another sip of wine. It was quite possible, after all, that Kevin was as much in the dark as she was. It took only two votes to defeat the entry of a new partner, and with the vote still seven months away, who could say what would happen? All in all, she realized, he had been superbly tactful. He had also been more than attentive in his last words and the way he had said them. She knew she must be even more careful now, for she couldn't remember a time in recent years when a man had looked at her *that* way when she had really wanted him to. Her self-imposed discipline was retreating in the face of the possibilities. *Keep it light,* she thought, then said, "Thanks for listening; meanwhile, I won't bet the ranch between now and the end of the year."

"You mean the ranch you grew up on in Hutchinson, Kansas?" Kevin asked, smiling.

"No, Kevin. It wasn't a ranch. Or a farm. And I didn't have a dog named Toto." She smiled too, trying to keep it casual, but he persisted.

"What *were* you like as a child?" he asked. "I still know nothing about you, except that your father was a lawyer. I'll bet you were the queen of Hutchinson."

Rachel's smile died in the face of Kevin's renewed probing and—for just a second—she again considered a resort to the truth. Not just "a lawyer," she would say. Jack Cannon was *the* lawyer in Hutchinson, probably in the entire state of Kansas. If he had stayed with it, he would have been a U.S. congressman at thirty-five and governor by forty. Everyone said it.

If he had stayed.

If he had not run away.

And no, Kevin, she would add, I was not the queen of Hutchinson, but I did feel like a princess. Not that I thought I was better than anyone else; I just grew up assuming that everybody had everything they wanted like I did. Then I turned twelve and had nothing. Then I really grew up.

Rachel fought back the ancient bitterness and managed a wry smile as she finally replied, "It was a nice place to live, but you wouldn't want to visit there." Actually, Hutchinson really *had* been a nice place to live until her father left, then it had become a grim, timeless prison. For one thing, they couldn't go anywhere. Rachel was too young to drive, of course, and her mother had lost her license soon after Jack Cannon's "departure." Virginia's first offense—driving while intoxicated—straight through

a vegetable market actually—had been "seen to" by Judge
Lambreau, one of Jack's former partners. Six weeks later, however, she was before him again, this time for driving her car into
an irrigation canal. She had been drinking, of course, and was
looking at herself in the rearview mirror at the time—hardly a
foundation around which to weave a strong defense. Fortunately
—as Virginia Cannon had never learned to swim—Kansas was
suffering a drought at the time, and the canal was bone dry. As it
turned out, losing her license meant nothing, for within a year
she had also lost the car. Ditto the house and everything else of
value. Then, the finale: Rachel was just fourteen when an aunt
she barely knew signed the commitment papers and took Virginia away to Topeka. It seemed Virginia had unaccountably
undressed herself at the Safeway, then held off her would-be
captors by pelting them with fresh produce.

Rachel's own confinement took the form of a Catholic high
school. She later learned that her mother had been released six
months later—dried out, introspective, and secure in the love of
Jesus—only to be recommitted a month later for assaulting a
young Methodist preacher's wife with a cast-iron frying pan.
Virginia claimed that the girl was stealing her youth with the
Devil's own help and pointed to the biblical entreaty to fight
Satan with "weapons of iron." This time Virginia didn't come
out, and, on the occasion of Rachel's last visit, accused her of
being secretly married to her father and living with him in Costa
Rica.

"I'd rather talk about you," said Rachel, shrugging off the
memory. "What made you the notorious winner you turned out
to be?"

"Mainly, as I've said, I think it was my fear of being a loser.
You see, I really *was* a country boy. Grew up in Lodi—my
dog's name was Warren, incidentally. I had a pretty dull and
decent, typically Valley childhood. Bicycles, Boy Scouts, Cam-
els at ten, Southern Comfort at fourteen, sports, girls, and, of
course, the movies and all the glitter, fast cars, and beautiful
women they brought into our provincial world. Somewhere along
the way, I guess I decided I wanted to have those things."

"And now you have them—partnership, money, success."

"I suppose so, but you know what they say about living by
bread alone. Besides, having a Ferrari now is not nearly as
exciting as it would have been to have a new three-speed Schwinn
when I was a kid."

He takes it all for granted, she thought. *It must seem so easy once you have it, and so easy to get it if you're a man.* A bread stick snapped in her fingers.

"My father was killed in the closing months of the war—" he continued. "Navy. Mop-up operations in the Pacific theater. Ironically, I was born on December 7, 1941."

"So you don't remember him at all?"

"He was off to war before I took my first step, and he never came back." Kevin smiled self-consciously, sipped some wine, and added, "But I had a decent sort of stepfather."

"You seem less than enthusiastic," Rachel said, reading Kevin's expression.

"He was," Kevin said thoughtfully, "a hard man to please. Actually, I loved the guy a lot, but I could come home with straight A grades and all he'd say was, 'Don't mow the lawn in squares. Do it in rows.' I'd be named captain of the basketball team and he'd say, 'Rows, not squares.' A very hard man to please, my stepfather." He paused. "And yet I miss him. In a way, I guess I'm still trying to please him. Impress him. You know, the father-approval thing."

"Ahh. So all those trial victories . . ."

"Right. All because I couldn't mow the goddamn lawn right."

Rachel laughed, saying, "I guess we're all lucky your family didn't have a gardener."

She finished her dessert and leaned back in her chair, feeling stuffed but relaxed again. The noise level was down a notch or two as tables had begun to empty. She enviously studied an elderly couple behind Kevin, holding hands and sipping anisette, oblivious to the activity around them.

"And your family had a lawyer," Kevin said.

Rachel looked into her wineglass, which she slowly rotated with the fingers of both hands. "He was a trial lawyer," she said quietly.

Kevin leaned forward with new interest. "A trial lawyer! So that's how we got you!"

"You're more right than you could know. You see, he actually referred a couple of California matters to S.P.&M. He used to rave about the firm."

"You're kidding! Why haven't I heard about this?"

"Nobody knows. It's unimportant, really. But I did grow up thinking that Stafford, Parrish, and MacAllister was the only law firm in the world outside of Hutchinson, Kansas."

"Well," said Kevin, beaming, "now you know you were right. So, tell me—"

"No," said Rachel, evading again. "You were telling *me* about *you*. What were you like as a kid?" she asked.

"Well, let me see. I guess I was your basic social klutz. If there was dog shit anywhere in the school yard, my shoes could find it during a five-minute recess."

"A real smoothy, huh?" She laughed.

"Afraid not." He paused. "But there was always the fantasy girl for whom I would risk everything and whose love would . . . well, validate all I would accomplish, validate *me*."

"That's a funny way to put it, like something done to a parking ticket. Did it work?"

Kevin smiled and slowly shook his head. "I'm afraid my ticket requires a lot of validation."

Rachel returned the smile. "Rows, not squares," she said.

Kevin nodded, but his mood turned serious. "Trial victories have eased the symptoms," he said. "Only the love of the right woman will cure the disease."

Rachel could see where this was going and, though tempted to let it run its course, decided to seek the refuge of humor. "You don't look sick to me, Mr. Stone," she said.

"That's because I've never felt healthier than I do this very minute, Ms. Cannon. You see, I think I've isolated the fantasy—I even know her name. Now I just have to convert the fantasy to reality. Does your Irish voodoo extend to alchemy, kissing frogs, that sort of thing?"

"I'm afraid I'm licensed to practice law, not alchemy," she said, surprised at Kevin's increasing candor.

"May I get you something else?" interrupted the waiter, much to Rachel's relief.

Kevin, without taking his eyes off Rachel's, said, "I'll take an alchemist, please."

"Sir?" said the waiter.

"Cappuccino," said Rachel, returning Kevin's gaze.

"Make it two," said Kevin as a roar of applause and laughter erupted from the rear of the restaurant, where a game of boccie was ending.

"Well?" said Kevin finally. "How about you? Any romantic fantasies?"

Rachel, determined to break the growing tension once and for all, said, "My passion is my work," then exploded in laughter, joined instantly by Kevin.

"Okay, fine," he said. "But where do we go from here?"

"You'll just laugh again," said Rachel.

"Never," replied Kevin.

"Well, I've been to New York half a dozen times, and I've never been to the Cafe Carlyle to hear Bobby Short."

Kevin did laugh again. "We could see him at the Venetian Room back in San Francisco, you know," said Kevin.

"We could, but don't you somehow doubt that we would?" replied Rachel, an unintended censure in her tone.

"No. I suppose you're right," said Kevin. "Look, Rachel—"

"No, Kevin, please. I'm sorry I said that. We're just two overworked country lawyers in the big city blowing off steam. Okay?"

Kevin managed a smile, saying, "Okay, counselor." He took care of the check while Rachel secured a taxi for them, starting off a long and late night in the pubs and smokey locales of New York City.

During their night out, Rachel enjoyed Kevin's ability to engage bartenders and other strangers in conversation on any subject, and his noncondescending kindness to the usual array of down-and-outers on the street. She was surprised at his knowledge and appreciation of music from punk to jazz and where to find it, his ability to have a good time without pretense, and, undeniably, his obvious pleasure in her company.

At a physical level, Rachel could find nothing to change in Kevin. His voice charmed her. His open, boyish smile and the way he moved quickened her heart and stirred her body. She now knew he wanted her, and she shuddered under the power of her own desire. At a comedy house in Chelsea, she drank two Irish coffees. *Am I trying to get even higher or building myself an excuse?* she asked herself, then ordered another.

Later, however, as the taxi slalomed its way through midtown New York toward the Helmsley Palace, their moods changed. They became silent, less relaxed. Her senses became attuned to every detail of the ride: the ripped plastic covers on the fold-up seats, the shattered Plexiglas window directly behind the driver's head, little signs and rules posted everywhere. She looked out at the endless rows of tiny shops now closed and protected with steel mesh screens: tap dancing studios for children, rug merchants, pizza and hero-sandwich parlors, palmistry, martial arts, used jewelry. The silence began to turn awkward as Rachel read and reread the unpronounceable name of the cab driver and mindlessly glanced again to her left at the silent gray sidewalks.

Kevin paid the fare and they entered the lobby of the hotel, approaching the elevators without enthusiasm, like prisoners boarding a boat to Devil's Island. As they waited, Rachel picked off an unhealthy frond hanging from a palm in a large brass planter next to the elevator doors.

"It was a nice evening," she said, but the stilted declaration just hung there. Kevin made no reply.

Both quiet now, they stepped into the elevator. Rachel watched the floor numbers as they flashed on and off, then found herself staring at one of Kevin's powerful hands. She traced the veins in her mind, then, looking down at her own hands, was surprised to see a leaf from the palm still clutched there.

"Thallus," she said abruptly.

"Pardon me?" said Kevin.

"Thallus. From the Greek. It describes plant bodies like leaves and roots. I learned it in college—during my Missouri period."

Kevin smiled, but seemed preoccupied.

Thallus, phallus, we're all alone in the Palace, she sang absurdly to herself, suddenly realizing how hard the drinks had hit her.

At last, their floor. They exited the elevator swiftly and were soon standing in front of her room. Rachel felt Kevin watching her as she began to open the door. She took a deep breath and tried to relax her shoulders, then turned her eyes toward his. "Thanks for tonight. It was," she added softly, "special." Still, Kevin said nothing, but as she turned to enter her room, he took her arm and gently turned her around to face him. They stood there, motionless. Kevin touched her face. His eyes were misting as they met hers, and a pang of excruciating sadness passed between them.

"Her name is Rachel," he said simply. She said nothing; instead, feeling suddenly weak, she leaned her head on his chest and put her arms around his hard waist. She could feel his strong, steady heart beating against her forehead and drew unexpected comfort from the fantasy that his heartbeat was hers and hers was his and that she would never be alone again. Yet, no sooner had Rachel experienced the feeling than she struggled to resist it. She knew what all this could lead to and, after allowing herself ten more heartbeats of intimacy, she quickly said good night, turned, and entered her room.

Once inside, Rachel's emotions ranged from self-congratulation to self-pity. She thought maybe she'd order food from room service. Then she considered a cold shower. She turned on the TV and immediately snapped it off. She was suddenly wide awake. She brushed her teeth; she stared out her window. *Thallus, phallus, I'm all alone in the Palace. Jesus!*

She undressed and slipped into her version of a negligee: a size small, but extra-long man's white cotton V-neck T-shirt. She sat on the edge of her bed, grabbed at the mint candy left by the night maid, then discarded it. She stared at her feet, hating them. She had always hated her feet and until recently had persisted in crowding her size eight-and-a-halfs into size eights. She remembered Hobie Adams, who called her "Bigfoot" in junior high school and proclaimed loudly at least once a week that she was supposed to wear the shoes not the boxes.

She stood up and paced some more, then brushed her teeth again without thinking, and washed her face. She began to feel more calm, and studied herself critically in the full-length bathroom mirror. "I'm starting to lose it," she said softly, running both hands along tan thighs and over her barely protruding stomach, then up to curved breasts threatening to escape through the V-neck opening, her nipples still erect.

Returning to the bed, her self-absorption was jolted by a heavy double rap on her door.

"Who is it?"

"It's me. Kevin. Open the door." It was a command, not a request, and she unlocked the door.

Kevin walked into the room and immediately they were in each other's arms. His lips were hot against her mouth, her throat, her shoulder. Their bodies pushed closer and closer against each other—fused and wanting. Kevin's feverish hands were everywhere, under her shirt, caressing her nipples as he pushed his erection hard against her. The tenderness was gone from him.

"Rachel" was all he said as he lifted her with passionate force into his arms and placed her on the bed, sweeping the T-shirt up around her shoulders. Passion compelled him, not insensitivity, and she fully shared the forceful urgency. Her decision, she now realized, had been made long before his, and as he entered her wetness, their eyes were fixed on each other's as if to affirm their mutual intent.

Minutes later, their tensions fully released, she said, "Tell me, Attila, have you ever heard of foreplay?"

"Foreplay?" he said, gentle again. "We've been engaging in that for the past two years."

EIGHT

■

The next day, PBA—Provincetown-Boston Airline—proudly proclaiming itself "America's Oldest Regional Airline," bounced its way out of LaGuardia right on schedule at 11:50 A.M., bound for Nantucket via New Bedford. A glowing—if somewhat subdued—pair of San Francisco lawyers shared the noisy twin-prop plane with a young couple from Minnesota and a third-generation Nantucket bicycle shop proprietor named Jesse T. Stuart.

Rachel suffered a mild attack of airsickness compounded by intermittent doubt concerning her decision to join Kevin. Smoother air and a Perrier calmed her stomach while she rationalized the trip with such lame bromides as "you only live once," bolstered by a recognition that the time to say no had already passed. Besides, she had always wanted to see Nantucket and was wildly in love. Also tired of New York and of saying no.

So after a beautiful Saturday morning together, in which Kevin established that he had indeed heard of foreplay, they checked out of the Helmsley Palace and caught a taxi to the airport. By the end of their roller coaster journey to the island, Jesse Stuart had offered Rachel and Kevin free time on a pair of his Mopeds and his secret guide to the best restaurants on the island. "Where are you staying?" asked the bicycle man, warming to his role as local sage.

"I suppose at the Jared Coffin House if we can get in," replied Kevin. The famous old hotel was the inevitable destination for first-timers to Nantucket and had justly earned its reputation as one of the finest guest houses in Massachusetts.

"May I make some suggestions?" asked Mr. Stuart rhetori-

cally. "In the first place, you can't get into the Jared right now
without reservations. In the second place, you kids look to be in
love and should stay somewhere special. Go to the House of
Orange over on twenty-five Orange Street and see if you can get
the loft apartment there. It overlooks the bay and has private
access to the widow's walk. Tell them Jesse T. Stuart sent you.
In the third place, where you eating tonight?"

"I give up," said Kevin, catching on. "Where are we eating
tonight?"

"Either Obadiah's, the Captain's Table, or the Boarding House.
Here's my card; tell them you know me. You may have to wait
awhile, but you won't need reservations."

"I heard the Mad Hatter's good," hazarded Kevin, betraying
his intended choice for the evening.

"It's good. But did you come three thousand miles for 'good'?
Go where I told you."

"Well, thank you, we—"

"Now, about tomorrow, do you know yet where you'll be
taking my Mopeds?"

"You haven't told us yet," Kevin said with a broad smile.

"Not bad, young fella. I like that. Gives rise to the debate
whether low humor beats no humor at all. If you're smart, you'll
visit Surfside on the south coast or, better yet, Siasconset over
on the east side. Check out Guidnet and Wauwinet too. Be here
a week or so?"

"How we wish," answered Rachel. "But we have to be back
at JFK early Monday morning, so we'll have to leave here
tomorrow evening."

"You're kidding! You don't come to Nantucket for just one
night!"

"Beats no nights at all," replied Kevin, more timid than
Rachel had ever seen him. "Doesn't it?"

"Barely," said the bicycle shop proprietor, scowling as if he
had been personally insulted. "Barely."

Kevin gently stroked Rachel's hand during this exchange and
Rachel realized that something about the presence of Mr. Stuart
gave Kevin's attentiveness special meaning. Then she realized
that the bicycle man's genial intrusion had provided a kind of
symbolic public acknowledgment that lent a brief solidity to their
fragile coupling. Jesse T. Stuart was their first and only friend.

Upon landing, Kevin and Rachel followed the old man's

instructions and luckily secured the little loft on Orange Street for the night.

"Oh, Kevin, it's wonderful," said Rachel, inspecting every closet and cupboard. Eclectic and colorful artwork was everywhere: oil paintings, stitchings, watercolors, and woven rugs, all crafted by the delightful hosts. "Let's never leave," she said, filling a copper pot with water.

"I bought one-way tickets," he said, smiling, and they fell into each other's arms, hungrily kissing as if they had been separated for days. The lovemaking that followed was almost a repeat of the first time, both of them starved and impatient.

Later, despite games they invented to try to slow the passage of time, the hours raced by. The House of Orange recommendation had confirmed their confidence in Jesse T. Stuart, so they broke away from their love-loft at mid-afternoon and went in search of his shop. They found the quaint, terrierlike man behind a counter in a large building jammed with no less than a hundred bicycles and at least half that many Mopeds. Side windows opened out to crowded wharves, where tourists pointed cameras at crusty fishermen who seemed not to notice them. Faces on some strangers' postcards, the locals seemed smug and superior, typical New Englanders.

Jesse T. Stuart provided Rachel and Kevin with maps and Mopeds, and pointed them in the direction of Siasconset. They then raced to Guidnet, where they made love under the summer sun on one of the long, lonely stretches of deserted beach there. Later, after hot cider and rum at a quaint tavern called the Atlantic City, they returned to the loft for a nap and immediately fell into deep, untroubled sleep in each other's arms.

They awoke in time to view the last of the sunset from atop the widow's walk. Holding hands, they scanned the horizon beyond the harbor, as had anxious sailors' wives in years past. Together, they read an inscription from a plaque fixed to a railing.

> He's not around to whisper words
> She thought she had to hear
> 'Til she learned the way
> That words could play
> Their own games with her ear.

> Yet as the lion waits in winter
> To taste the summer's sun
>   The sailor's wife
>   Stares out to sea
> 'Til her widow's walk is done.

The lovers watched the night close in, then changed and walked to the Boarding House for dinner, where they enjoyed a swordfish specialty cooked in almond sauce. After a delicate cheesecake, and a long stroll through the village, they returned to the loft.

Falling on the bed in the half light of a lone kerosene lamp, they explored each other with the passion of unfamiliarity and the desperation of people whose time is running out. The last vestiges of inhibition quickly dissolved before the fierce compulsion of their desire and the lovers became savage, immortal children at play, licking each other like animals, alternately stroking and seizing, soothing and scratching; whispering, raging, crying. Their glistening bodies writhed on the giant four-poster, until mingled cries of ecstatic protest finally signaled their surrender to the inevitable death-rapture of the moment. The faltering lantern projected primitive, surreal shadows onto the dark-paneled walls that surrounded them: profiles of arched torsos and heads pulled back.

After, there was neither sound nor the slightest movement. Rachel stared up at the flickering light on the ceiling, cradling Kevin's head on her shoulder. Secure in the dark warmth of her breast, he could not see the single tear glistening like a diamond on her flushed cheek in the dying light of the lantern.

The alarm shattered the Nantucket silence on Sunday morning, and they awoke, Kevin ice-cold in her arms. For a terrible instant she thought he might be dead, so chilled was his flesh, but then he said her name and clung hard to her. She lay holding him close and quiet for the next twenty minutes, trying to warm his shivering body and thinking insane thoughts: What would it be like to wake up together every morning? To make breakfast for Kevin, to see him off to work, then leisurely to plan the menu for a dinner party that night? She laughed to herself, for she knew that such a life was neither her fate nor her desire. Yet on this small island, lost in time, the fantasy seemed so innocent, so natural. *I must watch myself*, she thought, realizing that a seductive serpent was slipping almost unnoticed into the garden of her professional aspirations.

"What are you thinking?" Kevin asked, suddenly awake and watching her.

"Whether we have time for a walk along the waterfront," she answered.

They dressed quickly and walked along the wharves and beaches that last morning. They played among the derelict fishing boats washed ashore years before and sat for nearly an hour in one of them, holding hands and exchanging gentle words and kisses. Rachel noticed that the abandoned boat was ironically named *Faint Hopes* but did not call it to Kevin's attention. As they walked away from the relic, Rachel felt that something crucial was missing—like having an empty chair at a family dinner—but she couldn't put her finger on it.

They changed their flight reservations to later Sunday evening, then enjoyed a delicious supper at the Captain's Table. But there was a deep chill in the air now; their winter had come early. They had begun to evaluate the cost of the trip, as travelers often do near the end, and as lawyers, they understood that every contract—even one of short duration—has a quid pro quo. They fought melancholy by reviewing their day and sharing talk of favorite movies and books. But they made love no more, and it finally came to Rachel what had been missing after they had enjoyed their magic moment in the abandoned boat: a camera and a snapshot of the old derelict. The moment had been one for lovers to cherish, to enjoy in the years ahead. But their kind of love must feast on today, she thought, not forage for scraps of an uncertain future.

All in all, they had no regrets, and occasionally managed a smile as they were driven to the airfield.

It was time to go home.

NINE

■

Rachel returned mid-morning the next day to an office cluttered by ten days of mail and memoranda and a full calendar of meetings and court hearings. She surveyed the damage as she hung her jacket over the chair near her single, small "status window." Seniority in prestigious law firms tended to be manifested in office windows, or the lack thereof: Junior associates had no windows at all, senior associates one, partners two, and so on up the ladder of achievement. Out of her one senior associate window, Rachel could usually see nothing but another tall building, and today even that was smothered in San Francisco fog. She felt the need for a lift and was about to go for coffee when Jeffrey Johnstone appeared in her doorway, critically scanning the books and files piled all over her desk and floor.

"Welcome back. How was the Big Apple? And what the hell happened here? Did you get a license number?"

"Good morning, Jeffrey, thank you, how are you, and goodbye. New York was fine. We got what we wanted out of everybody we deposed. Details later. I will assume you are also fine because I haven't time for your reply if you aren't." She smiled briefly, but really wanted him to leave. "I've got an argument this afternoon in the Sorenson case, and I'm in a crunch, okay?"

"Okay, *okay*. And good luck today. As for your office, don't worry. I'll hose it down after you leave."

Rachel smiled, straightened a photograph on her picture wall, and picked up the draft of her brief. The photograph pictured her incoming associates class taken the year she joined the firm: nineteen of them then, less than half of them remained now, she and Beth Abelson the only women. Of the nine, only two or three would achieve the coveted mantle of partnership. Those who had already been eliminated from the race had moved on to some lesser firm or beat a hasty retreat to their hometowns to hang out a shingle. Others took government jobs, sold real estate, became stockbrokers, joined IBM, or just dropped out for a year or so to "reassess their futures." Rachel could not picture herself doing any of these things.

She started to study her brief for the afternoon hearing, but her thoughts kept turning to Kevin. She found herself staring at her telephone, wanting to dial Kevin's extension, just to hear his voice, to confirm that he was near. She even scribbled out some contrived questions but then buried the crumpled paper at the bottom of her wastebasket. She realized that even the idea of going for coffee was just an excuse to walk past his office. If he was there, should she just wave hello and pass on by? Did she dare pop in for a casual chat?

What she should do, she admonished herself, is give up coffee and quit acting like a silly, smitten schoolgirl. Rachel had never encouraged, much less dated, a married man, and she knew she must put her love for Kevin on hold for now. Time would reveal his intentions, just as it would soon make known her future in the firm, but neither event could be rushed no matter how much she wished it. And she must try not to worry about the fact that Kevin was a partner who held both her professional future and her heart in his hands. How stupid, how impossible, that it was with *him* she had violated the rule against office relationships, yet she rejoiced in the knowledge that the North American case would at least provide the ongoing contact with him she knew she now must have. She mused at the hypocrisy of it all and its diabolical catch-22 implications for women: Since it is a man's nature to attempt the seduction of women, he will inevitably try. If he fails, he is angered, for she has wounded his ego and frustrated his nature. So he withholds promotions and impartial reviews. If he succeeds, one of them must leave when they are eventually found out. And, of course, it is always the woman, as she is almost always the lower ranking of the two. How did all this come about? she wondered. Why must it be the woman who is at fault? Who pays?

Who bleeds.

Yet, as she tried to refocus her attention on the brief, she realized how much she missed Kevin and that the anger she had summoned was rote, impersonal, directed at the universal and convenient *them*, not at Kevin Stone. *How can I expect him to understand things about me that I'm only beginning to see myself*, she rationalized, and wished they were back in New York. A soft rap at her door sent her heart leaping. She looked up and was embarrassed at her considerable disappointment. Standing in her doorway was Beth Abelson. Not Kevin. Beth—looking pale as marble.

"Morning, Beth," said Rachel. But the woman said nothing, stood frozen in the doorway, apparently struggling for control. "Beth, what's wrong?"

"It's over, Rachel. I'm out."

The stark words hung grimly in the air, slowly gathering the density of reality as the two women stared at each other in silence.

Rachel finally spoke: "Barrington?" Beth, like Rachel, was a senior trial department associate. This meant that her dismissal would come straight from the top.

Beth nodded, fighting back tears beginning to form in the corners of her gentle brown eyes. "I knew it was coming when his secretary called at seven-thirty to tell me Barrington wanted to see me. Alone." Her slightly oversized chin quivered as she added, "He does it beautifully, Rachel, just like Audrey said. I even found myself babbling inanely to spare him any awkward silences. Can you believe it?"

"Have you told Jim?"

"Tonight," came the quiet response.

When it's my turn, thought Rachel, *who will be there to hold me, share my sorrow, bring me a flower . . .*

"You okay, Beth?"

"Sure. Other than being three months pregnant, miserable in my marriage, and now fired from my job. Hell, I couldn't be better." Beth choked out a feeble laugh under tear-filled eyes, then added, "In a way, I'm almost relieved that the shoe finally dropped." Rachel rose from behind her desk and Beth accepted the invitation to cry for a moment in her arms.

"Most of all, Rachel, I'll miss you. I was beginning to think that you and I would break new ground together. Now it's all up to you."

Rachel held Beth's wide shoulders at arm's length and took a deep breath. "I now hold little hope for me, Beth," she said. "Or for them either. They'll never change," she added, in a tone edged with anger. "But I will make it, Beth—if not here, then somewhere else. And so will you."

Rachel felt her friend's large frame tremble as she willed her wide mouth into a smile and straightened her coarse, burnt-umber hair with both hands. "I'll work on believing that tomorrow. Right now, all I want is to get good and ripped, which a pregnant woman can't do. So I guess all that's left is to get good and out."

Beth's smile slowly faded as there seemed nothing more to be said. The small pendulum clock on Rachel's wall seemed to double in volume. Beth took two halting steps toward the door, then turned and forced a laugh as she said, "At least now I won't have to go on the goddamn summer clerks' raft trip tomorrow!" The last word was barely audible as the second attempt at laughter broke into a deep sobbing lament that wrenched Rachel's heart. Beth fell against Rachel's breast again, this time giving in completely to her sorrow. "Oh, God, I tried so hard, so fucking hard . . . I gave so much. . . ."

"You're a good lawyer, Beth," Rachel whispered. "You know you are. Never stop believing it. It's them, not you."

Beth nodded her head as she sought to compose herself. Finally, she managed a game smile and walked slowly out of the office.

Rachel stared after her, already feeling a painful new sense of isolation and cruelly reminded of her own precarious position. Not that she was surprised. Rachel was accustomed to discrimination, chauvinism, and even sexual harassment. She had learned to discipline herself and had come to accept—or at least tolerate—the reality that she would have to work harder than the men around her just to stay even. And, so far at least, hard work and a positive attitude in the face of patent and pervasive discrimination had paid off. She had seized every opportunity to test her skills and she was still afloat, the only trial lawyer in the firm—other than Kevin Stone himself—who could lay claim to an almost perfect trial record. Before joining the firm, she had notched thirty-six consecutive trial victories at the Alameda County's blue-ribbon district attorney's office, and had scored three out of four civil trial verdicts in a row since joining S.P.&M. Her one loss had shaken her, because it was a case she should have won—factually complex, but winnable. She had been thrust into the unaccustomed role of supervising two other more junior associates and a team of paralegals. After the loss, she had been criticized for not taking a firmer rein on her people, for not taking charge. The criticism stung because it was true.

But didn't everybody have a flaw, a shortcoming, if you looked closely enough? Besides, in nonmanagement situations, she had proven that judges and juries didn't resent an attractive female trial lawyer as long as she was a *competent* attractive female trial lawyer. And though she secretly feared taking responsibility for controlling others, she was becoming notorious for her courage and success in facing adversaries.

But now she was alone: the last female six-year associate in a firm where a woman had never been allowed to climb the last rung to the top.

"Is Beth really out?" Jeffrey asked an hour later, his eyes popping like golf balls.

"She's out," said Rachel, the words coming easier now. Jeff was Rachel's fifth visitor since Beth had left to pack her personal things. Bad news travels fast.

"Any reason given?"

"Not really. Barrington made some reference to hard times and cutbacks. Beth didn't buy it and neither do I."

"How's she taking it?"

"Hard. How would *you* take it, Jeff?" Rachel's tone and mechanical cadence sounded a clear warning. "She's feeling hurt and powerless. She hasn't mobilized her anger yet. That will help." Jeffrey walked over to the window, turning his narrow back toward Rachel.

"It looks as if you've had no trouble mobilizing yours," he said quietly. "Plotting revenge?"

"Perceptive as usual, Jeff. It might be said that I'm spring-loaded to the pissed-off position, so don't be the one to pull the trigger," she warned.

Johnstone raised both hands with palms facing Rachel, but his tone conveyed no apology. "Look, sheriff. Shoot if you want, but you know where I stand. I only suggest that before you lead the unwashed masses into rebellion and get your own ass in a sling in the process, you might at least consider the economic realities underlying their side of the story."

Rachel slapped her pen flat on the desk and stared at Johnstone with a look of incredulity bordering on vexation.

"Let me guess, Jeffrey. You're about to tell me that 'economic facts' beyond the firm's control mean that the big boys at S.P.&M. have to fire all *women* associates at or before the end of their sixth year."

The young associate cocked his unkempt head and peered down at Rachel, then reached out and tentatively poked at one of her shoulders. "Hey. I'm just trying to fill the one tiny gap in your omniscient worldview."

Rachel shot Jeffrey a steel-edged look, but then shook her head abruptly. "I'm sorry," she muttered, attempting a smile. "I am definitely in a dark mood. An occupational hazard of sole survivors, I suppose. But frankly, Jeffrey, it sometimes irritates me the way you seem to buy into this bogus connection between the current recession and this firm's pattern of female sacrifices that dates back to the late sixties. Besides, S.P.&M. is one of the oldest and largest firms on the West Coast; they can't really be hurting that bad."

"Rachel, you know the arguments better than I do: The bigger a law firm is, the bigger it has to keep becoming to maintain that all-important, profit-yielding ratio of at least one and one-half productive associates to every partner. But that's hard to do in lean times when there's not enough work to do, so instead they just stop making new partners—as in you—and start firing rookie associates—as in *me*. Since you, in a more rational moment, were the one who explained all of this to me in the first place, I shouldn't have to tell you that we're *all* vulnerable. Audrey last month and now Beth—they were just the first."

"Well," said Rachel, sinking deep into her desk chair, "I'll believe that when I see that red, disheveled little porcupine head of yours get the ax, Jeffrey. And Frank Harris's, and Mike Martin's, and Irv Braun's, and Joseph Lloyd's—"

"Okay, okay. Enough already," interrupted Jeffrey.

". . . and Vic Cooper's, and . . ."

They smiled, and Rachel took a deep cleansing breath. "In a way," she continued, the hard edge gone from her voice, "it's our own damn fault. All half million of us. Just too damn many lawyers in the country right now. Someone should have pulled up the rope ladder long ago."

"What pisses me off," said Jeff, "is that most of them seem to be right here in San Francisco. Other than Washington, D.C., San Francisco has the highest ratio of normal people to lawyers anywhere. No wonder the big-firm partners are out hustling new business like life insurance salesmen, ripping off one another's clients and trying new specialties."

"Speaking of which, Jeff, what's been going on with the toxic water case?"

"Nothing. Not a peep the whole time you were gone. Did you pick up anything from Kevin?"

"He just said Barrington was 'taking care of it.' "

"Well," said Jeff, balancing on one leg as he buffed a brown wingtip shoe on the calf of the opposite leg, "he better be as smart as they say he is, 'cause from what I hear, it's one tough mother of a case."

"Tough causation issues," agreed Rachel. "It's hard to figure. Must be some very big dollars there somewhere."

"Rachel, your suspicious nature is showing. Give the partnership credit—they may be trying to do something worthwhile for once."

"Come now, Pollyanna," said Rachel, smiling, her black mood in full retreat but residual cynicism fighting a rearguard action. "Do you really believe for a moment that if they really follow through on that case, it's to make a better world? Uh-uh. I say it's strictly business and business as usual, although I'd like to be wrong."

"Perish the thought, Ms. Cannon. I must admit that the partnership's silence on the case since the press release has been reasonably deafening. Maybe they've figured out the case is simply unwinnable and are dumping the old guys."

"Now who's being the suspicious one?" said Rachel.

"Well, I hope I'm wrong, too, because in this economy, firms like S.P.&M. either have to find new sources of revenue or start laying off top-flight people. Like Rachel Cannon and Jeffrey Johnstone, for instance."

"What bothers me, Jeff, is that they seem to be doing *both*. These toxic cases would double the workload of everyone involved—so they respond by firing a good lawyer like Beth Abelson. And by the way, was it really just luck of the draw that it was Beth who went, not Frank Harris or Irv Braun?"

"Rachel, Rachel—you must understand that the partners at S.P.&M. are true gentlemen. Ladies always go first."

TEN

■

Rachel arrived at the Imperial Building the following Tuesday morning, trying gamely to hold the Sausalito feeling despite a sore throat and a one-hour traffic jam on the Golden Gate Bridge resulting from a head-on collision a few minutes ahead of her.

The annual weekend raft trip for visiting summer clerks had been a near disaster, with unseasonable freezing rain and high, rough water. It had been a long, nasty day with one associate and two clerks hospitalized for observation for pneumonia and hypothermia and Rachel declaring Monday her first sick day since her arrival at S.P.&M.

"Morning, Rachel!" The morning message center receptionist was standing at the coffee urn. "I hear you had a pretty wild raft trip Saturday. Pour you a cup?"

"Thanks, I need it. Yes, the trip was different this year. The river was on top of us instead of below us." The pungent aroma pleased her, and she gratefully took a sip of the hot coffee.

"Oh, did you get the message from Barrington?" the receptionist asked.

"Barrington! What message?"

"He rang you around seven-thirty or eight. But now he wants you to report to his office—alone—the minute Kevin Stone's nine o'clock seminar is over."

Rachel stared into the cup she now held in both hands. She and every other lawyer in the firm knew that Austin Barrington's policy as head of the firm was never to meet alone with associates except to inform them of their election to partnership or to fire them. He, and only he, did both.

Without saying another word, she turned and sleepwalked toward the stairway to the thirty-eighth floor conference room, trying to clear her mind. Outside, the rude two-note blare of an ambulance siren added to the hot confusion in Rachel's head.

She drew deeply on the coffee to avoid thinking, but succeeded only in burning her mouth and tongue.

Most of all now she needed privacy, time to think. She detoured into an empty conference room and closed the door. There she sat, head in hands, the message "report to his office . . . alone" rattling through her mind. Gradually, she began to relax. She took ten deep breaths, and held them before exhaling. *Two female firings within one week?* she thought. *Not even Barrington would try to pull that off.*

Would he?

Actually, nobody got "fired" at S.P.&M. Instead, an associate was discreetly informed by Barrington that the partnership had "determined that his or her potential might be better realized in a different environment." He would then graciously take responsibility for the partnership's failure in not ascertaining this earlier. He was known to be so good at it, he could almost make the dismissed associate feel sorry for him.

Relax, she repeated to herself, slowly bringing her runaway mind under control. She considered the possibility that she was overreacting: After all, she had been a model associate—unless, of course, her New York affair with Kevin only ten days earlier had somehow already come to light. This seemed unlikely, since she had told no one, and Kevin—a married partner—had much to lose also.

Kevin.

She had spoken to him but once since their return and even then not alone. Their exchange had been guarded and strained, as if they'd mutually agreed to protect their secret even from themselves. The weekend on Nantucket had already begun to achieve a dreamlike quality and her longing for him was becoming almost tolerable. Yet now her wretched soul needed him as never before and she had to bridle an impulse to slip into his office or call him up just to find out why this was happening. He had, after all, said he loved her—many times—and she had believed him then, given him her love in return. Wouldn't he want to be with her at a time as important as this?

Listen, Kevin, she would say. *You wanted to know about my father? And about the gold chain I always wear around my neck? Okay, I'll tell you. He ran off; left us high and dry and the chain is all I have left of him. I was twelve at the time and was left with a mother who went to bed every night with a bottle of bourbon. She even blamed me for his leaving. "You drove him away with your bossiness," she said, "and next you'll do it to me!" That absolutely terrified me.*

Next thing, Dad's law partner showed up and tried to make me feel better by reassuring me that the firm still expected me to be head secretary at Avery, Hargreave, and Cannon when I grew up. I remember saying "Thank you, Mr. Avery, but I think I'm going to be a lawyer instead." I can still see the patronizing old bastard managing a good-natured laugh and telling me that "girls don't become lawyers, Rachel" and then me flashing him my sweetest smile and saying, "Maybe girls don't, Mr. Avery . . . but women do."

Rachel would let the anecdote sink in; then she'd look Kevin straight in the eye and say: *Kevin, you knew how much partnership means to me and you must have known a purge was on. How could you not have told me?* And then he'd look straight back into her eyes and say: *How could I know, Rachel? I was in New York, busy falling in love with you.*

But I won't ask for his help or even an explanation, she realized, straightening in her chair as self-righteous anger began to gain a foothold. Why, dammit, *why*? Her thoughts began to race again, this time toward Barrington himself, and the few minor projects she had done for him. They had all gone well. There was another possible problem with Barrington, of course. Although he had been careful never to hazard a direct invitation, the senior partner had made his strong appreciation of Rachel's physical attributes clear on numerous occasions. More subtle than the rest, he had skillfully backhanded the ball into her court without even betraying the appearance of a game in progress. Barrington was the impeccable master of no-risk excursions: walking close to the line but never crossing over it.

She remembered seeing Austin Barrington for the first time at her first associates' orientation cocktail party. He effused power and energy with each step, and only his full mane of silver-streaked hair supported the possibility that he was into his mid-sixties. On the other hand, he was the kind of man hard to picture as a youth. If he ever was a kid, thought Rachel, he was the kind who could get into a fight and come away the winner with every hair perfectly in place.

Yes, her eyes had been drawn to him that first day as he joined a circle of other partners. She had been caught off guard when his eyes came to rest on hers with neither smile nor pretext, momentarily transfixing her with a gaze that carried sufficient energy to send a nuclear submarine under the polar ice cap.

Later, however, when they were introduced, he was gracious and genial, almost avuncular; yet she always felt somehow as if he was waiting for her to give him a sign and was mildly resenting her for not doing so. Even so, this hardly seemed grounds for termination, unless, of course, he knew how serious the thing between her and Kevin had become. But how could even Barrington know something she was only now discovering for herself? Reluctantly, Rachel left her sanctuary and headed slowly toward the conference area. The sickly bile of failure was spreading a sense of unworthiness through her body like a virus. She fought the feeling of dread welling up inside, and it seemed that heat now shot from every nerve ending. She needed to sit down again, but seeing no chair, she tried to find strength in thoughts of job alternatives and reassuring clichés: *It's not the end of the world, Rachel. They can't judge you unless you let them. Screw these guys. You're okay. You're a survivor. There are other firms, other cities, other partnerships.* And so on.

But nothing helped and, for the first time, she felt the need to cry. She continued along the hallway, maintaining equilibrium by running her hand along the cool wallboard. She passed a mirror and noticed that her normally high color had fled, leaving her as gray as the wall that framed her face in the glass.

Rachel reached the thirty-eighth floor and joined the throng of associates and younger partners who were crowding into the main library conference area. She studied the token handful of young female associates among the more than forty men now seating themselves in the large room. It struck her suddenly and with clarity that there was no end to the discrimination at S.P.&M.; to the false hopes and wasted years; to the humiliation and despair at the bottom of the slippery pole she had been clinging to.

Ironically, the law itself—her vocation and her hope—had turned its back on her. The Eleventh U.S. Circuit Court of Appeals had recently affirmed a lower court decision holding partnerships to be exempt from antidiscrimination legislation such as Title 7 of the Civil Rights Act. The court had dismissed a complaint of Atlanta lawyer Elizabeth Hishon alleging that her firing had been the result of sex discrimination and, although she was reportedly filing an appeal to the U.S. Supreme Court, the ruling now gave private partnerships the tacit license to sexually discriminate.

Rachel paused outside the conference room, her strength and resolve beginning to recover from the initial assault. *These guys have a ticket to ride,* she thought, *but I'll be damned if I'll give up my seat without a fight.* She silently committed herself to making this a conversation Barrington would never forget; then, still pale as death, she slipped into the seat Jeffrey Johnstone had saved for her.

"Jesus, Rachel," he whispered, "you look awful. What's wrong?"

She said nothing at first, then cleared her throat and spoke, staring straight ahead. "Barrington wants to see me after the staff meeting."

Jeffrey stared at Rachel's profile for a few seconds, then looked away.

"Look, Rachel," he said, still not facing her with real conviction, "with your trial record, could be they're making you a six-year partner."

Rachel managed a rueful smile. "Oh, I'm sure of it, Jeffrey. They're going to waive their seven-year minimum for the first time since Barrington himself made partner a hundred years ago—for a woman no less—and just as they're facing their big-firm financial crunch. What happened to your sky-is-falling economics? Where did Norman Vincent Peale come from all of a sudden? I think I liked you more as Adam Smith."

Jeff sat quietly, now also looking straight ahead, narrow shoulders hunched, his face as solemn as a pallbearer's.

Rachel touched him on the arm. "I'm sorry. My panic is showing. I do appreciate what you're trying to do, but it's time to face facts: Audrey Holzberg two months ago, Beth Abelson last Friday, and Rachel Cannon today."

"Look, Rachel," said Jeffrey with renewed conviction, "I know the firm's strategy with women lawyers: hire a few to keep the law schools off their back, work the good ones right up until time for partnership eligibility, then kiss their asses good-bye. But as a tactical matter they wouldn't dare take you and Beth out at the same time! The negative impact on morale would be devastating, not to mention what this could do to their recruitment program at the law schools. It would just be too damn obvious."

"You give these guys too much credit," Rachel said. "They

don't think or care about appearances. Why should they, with the Hishon case giving them the green light?''

Jeff's response was quicker this time. ''Elizabeth Hishon isn't finished yet and neither is Rachel Cannon. You'll see I'm right, Rachel.'' A door opened at the front of the conference room and Kevin entered the room. Jeff shook Rachel's arm as if trying to break a spell. ''Here comes our guru. I'd better go sit with my fellow rookies so you won't be accused of trying to sexually harass me. Now, put all this out of your mind for an hour; maybe there's a new trial trick or two even you haven't picked up yet.''

Rachel's voice in reply was dull, but her meaning was clear. ''I know what to do when I'm *in* trial, Jeff. It's this being *on* trial that's getting me down.''

ELEVEN

∎

The large conference room, jammed with more than sixty associates and a handful of partners, had gone quiet as Kevin Stone entered. He had that effect, thought Rachel: movie star looks, a Giorgio Armani suit cleanly tailored to his lean and erect six-foot frame, an aura of confidence as tangible and bright as a sunrise, combined with a wit and vulnerability that made him seem mortal to the young associates, even accessible.

Rachel had once seen Kevin's presence dominate a courtroom but even now could not say quite how or why. He was neither flamboyant nor overbearing. His manner in court with jurors and the courtroom staff was formal but never imperious. Even with adversaries and hostile witnesses, his style was rarely antagonistic. Yet Rachel had also seen firsthand how his righteous indignation—usually feigned—could turn men of the strongest resolve into stammering toads. In New York she had observed how cleverly he had manipulated witnesses into giving him what he wanted.

New York. Manipulation. Giving him what he wanted. Her

throat tightened. Maybe he had known all along. It seemed inconceivable, yet . . .

"Let's get started," began program chairman Mel Colvin, a member of Rachel's incoming associate class and the group's leading candidate for partnership. He was smart, productive, articulate, and male. Not even Rachel could deny that he deserved partnership, despite his meager trial record compared to her own and the fact that his certain elevation meant probably only one other available slot for the rest of them to fight over during the year and a half before their up-or-out date of January 1, 1984. Until today, Rachel had held hopes of getting the second one.

"Kevin is with us today to commence his annual trial tactics seminar," continued Colvin. "As you know, this opening session bears the somewhat intimidating title: 'The Right Stuff—Do You Have It?' Not to worry, gang; Red Cross CPR teams and career counselors will be on hand following the meeting." Nervous laughter rustled through the large, austerely decorated room. "Seriously," Colvin went on, "this six-part series is the high point of our in-house training program. Most of us here have been through it more than once and we keep coming back. I even see four or five partners lurking in the back of the room.

"I can assure you first-year associates that you will learn things here over the next few months that they don't teach in school and you won't find in any book or public seminar on trial tactics. Kevin will share courtroom secrets and techniques with us here that will blow away many of your cherished beliefs about how jurors' minds really work and what winning trial lawyers have to know—and do—to keep on winning in the courtroom, a place Kevin refers to as 'the theater of the real.' He may in fact even raise questions in your mind about whether your goal of being a trial lawyer is realistic; whether, indeed, you've got the 'right stuff.' As you know, S.P.&M. will always consider requests by litigators to transfer over to the business side, where you're sure to live a lot longer . . . unless, of course, you die of boredom."

A chorus of hisses and groans followed the facetious suggestion that any of them would abandon the courtroom glory trail for the more steady path of tax law, real estate syndications, or public securities offerings.

"My purpose here as a fellow associate is to urge you to get involved—this isn't law school and it's not a lecture. Kevin once described it as a participatory mental gang-bang. Like therapy, it works best when you jump right in. So don't be shy. Kevin also told us last year that he views the trial of lawsuits as an art form in which communication is the potter's wheel and information is the clay. Well, it can be said that we have with us today the master potter himself: Kevin Stone."

Kevin rose and took his usual position beside the lectern, not behind it. He never used notes, and seemed to be looking at everyone in the room at once as he started to speak in a voice that was resonant, yet low-pitched and conversational, as if he were simply replying to what Mel Colvin had just said. "As you know," he began, "no two ceramic bowls ever really turn out precisely the same, even when turned by the same potter, working with the very same wheel and clay. So it is that different approaches and styles of trial advocacy are natural and proper.

"But why is it that one lawyer can take a set of facts and present it in a manner that would charm the birds out of the trees, while another lawyer can take the same set of facts and present them with all the excitement of watching an automobile rust? That's what we're here to find out."

Rachel, in spite of her anguish, found herself already being drawn into Kevin's forensic snare. It had become so quiet, she wondered if everyone was still in the room. *How does he do it?* she wondered. Year after year, his enthusiasm never seemed to diminish even though—as he had confided to her in New York— only one, no more than two, of the fifty-odd brilliant young hopefuls sitting in this room would ever turn out to be truly expert trial lawyers. For that matter, fewer than a third of the people in the room would even be around in three years, persevering in the exhausting race to become partners, a status that only two or three out of twenty starters would achieve.

Partner. The word held such magic—perhaps even more for the stature and recognition it represented than for the financial success and independence partnership insured. The word represented the Olympic Gold of High Aspirations, and in the last ten years, the quest had somehow become as important and all-consuming to Rachel as the grail itself. Now, as she finally began to picture her life without either, she could feel involuntary tears begin to travel down her cheeks. She prayed no one would notice and let the few tears run their course, tasting their salty bitterness, then dried them while everyone's attention was fixed on Kevin.

"You learned nothing about any of this in law school," he continued, characteristically changing the pace of his delivery now into a rush of words, "first, because it would offend the cherished Socratic method for law professors to directly reveal any constructive information to a student, and second, because most law professors don't understand trial advocacy anyway.

"So let's be clear as to our goals over the next several weeks. Your sole reason for being here is to learn how to win . . . because to win is the advocate's sole reason for being. And, as we will see over the next few weeks, the only way to win is to know how to *take charge:* of your client, of your opponent, and, ultimately, the entire courtroom. To be able to do this, of course, you must be able first to take charge of your own life."

Is he talking to *me?* Rachel wondered as she felt a new pang of discomfort before realizing that everyone else, in his own way, was probably thinking the same thing. The room was dead silent. This was why they were all here. If they were to gain partnership, they would have to be successful in the courtroom. This meant they had to *win*, and keep on winning. And standing before them was a man who had handled every conceivable kind of complex case for over fifteen years—and had never lost. He had tried criminal cases, antitrust cases, securities cases, contract disputes, partnership dissolutions, and administrative law cases. He had argued before juries, judges, and arbitrators. He was known as the "Salvage Man" by insiders across the country because of his reputation for bailing out other lawyers at the last minute in cases they had failed to prepare properly or that simply had become too important or complex for their level of competence. Kevin Stone was a trial lawyer's trial lawyer, and today he was opening up his head for their inspection and scrutiny. It was obvious to Rachel that he relished his position and the burden that attached to it; that the approval of his own partners and associates was every bit as important to him as all the honors and press clippings he had garnered.

"We will be discussing techniques that lawyers who have been trying cases for years have never grasped. If you internalize them, you'll be able to defeat more experienced lawyers—*even when they have better facts on their side.*" Kevin paused to let this sink in, smiling and crossing to the other side of the lectern. "You see, my first principle is that there is no justice; there are only some lawyers who are better than others." Another challenging pause. Kevin watched the new lawyers steal furtive looks at one another and invited questions or comments. Immediately a hand shot up in the front of the room.

"Yes, sir?" said Kevin, pointing to a bespectacled, overweight young man, just in from Yale.

"If you are correct, Mr. Stone—in saying that there is no justice—what is it we swore as officers of the court to seek and uphold? Do you think we should try to gain an unfair advantage over our opponent and win at any cost? 'Our client right or wrong'?"

Kevin smiled almost maliciously. "A well-articulated, if somewhat naive question. *Of course* I think so. *Of course* your job is to do every legitimate thing you can do that will help you win. Never forget that you are the trial lawyer, not the judge or jury. It is *their* job to decide who is 'right' or 'wrong'; your job is to *win*, and to do anything you can ethically do to make that happen. If it takes tears to move the jury, start crying. If climbing the TransAmerica pyramid will get the jury's attention, go get some rope. Your question misconstrues both the nature of truth and the beauty of our adversary system. First, there are always two sides to an issue, but there is only one truth. Truth, as I will be using it, means nothing more, nor less, than reality; that is, what *really* happened, what was *really* intended, et cetera. Now, if you go about helping the jury to see both sides of the issue and your opponent skillfully presents only *his* side of the issue, your client will surely lose and you won't have learned a damn thing about 'truth.' This suggests a second principle: The system works only when lawyers for both sides put themselves completely in the service of their client's best interests and leave truth to the jury and philosophy to the philosophers. Oh, yes, and there's another pragmatic aspect: Losing lawyers don't always get paid."

Rachel saw Jeffrey Johnstone's arm shoot up.

"I understand that, Mr. Stone," said Jeff. Rachel was immediately anxious, momentarily forgetting her own plight, yet pleasantly surprised that Jeff's incongruously deep voice sounded so assured. "But so much confrontation and hostility is generated in the adversary process, well . . . maybe it's the system that needs overhauling. It seems to me that—"

"What's your name, sir?" Kevin's voice was courteous, but flint-edged.

"Johnstone, sir. Jeffrey P. Johnstone."

"Well, Mr. Johnstone. While you try to decide whether you

want to become a judge within the existing system, or to become a legislator so that you can change it, we have a roomful of folks here who just want to be trial lawyers. So let's assume that the adversary system, which has served us well for approximately two hundred years, is the one we will be working under for at least the next twenty and get on with it!''

Johnstone shook his head slowly, then bravely raised his arm again. Rachel saw a rare flicker of impatience in Kevin's eyes as he stared down at the skinny second-year associate. Rachel continued to feel protective, wishing Jeff's hair were less disheveled, his plaid suit less rumpled.

"With all respect, sir," said Jeffrey, "even our United States Supreme Court in *Leighton* versus *Pender* suggests at page one-eighteen that the adversary system need not and should not generate so much hostility."

"I know the case, Johnstone. And except for that particular quote, it's a scholarly opinion." Suddenly breaking into an amused smile, Kevin asked, "Do you always remember page numbers?"

"Well, no, sir. I guess it's because . . . well, I drafted that opinion when I was clerking at the Supreme Court the year before last." Kevin joined the explosion of laughter in the room, then explained with renewed patience how the system's primary function was to "re-create past reality—what really happened—out of conflicting and self-serving viewpoints."

"This is not easy to do," said Kevin, "since the reality we're after is usually so faded by time and twisted by motivations of self-interest that it's become little more than its own elusive shadow. Our adversarial system recognizes this and requires each party to designate its own champion to race backward into time in quest of support for its particular version of reality. This transfers the initiative from the emotionally charged principals into the hands of surrogate 'champions.' That's us, Johnstone. Okay so far?

"Now, while this transference helps prevent the principal litigants from killing each other over a five-hundred-dollar contract dispute, they're still packing around a lot of resentment. They still want blood, retribution, punishment. So we trial lawyers become their champions; we become surrogates to their violence—professionals to be sure, but only one step removed from our clients' hostility.

"Thus, to put it a bit dramatically, we trial lawyers take on our clients' anger and fight their battles until one emerges the winner, using verbal bullets to keep them from using real ones. And—lest we all get too righteous here—let's not forget that we do it for money. In fact, let's make that a third principle: Trial lawyers are the system's contract killers—its hired guns.''

Rachel watched the palpable and predictable wave of discomfort engulf several of the first-year associates and remembered her own first Kevin Stone session. Even with two years of real-world experience behind her as a prosecutor, she had been surprised and irritated by Kevin's iconoclastic words. Now, four years later, she reluctantly conceded that he had been right.

''If you don't take another thing away from this first session, Johnstone, try to remember this,'' said Kevin, whose delivery had become quiet, incongruously gentle, as if he were teaching a course in French cuisine. ''Because of its violent origins, a jury trial—whether we like it or not—is a buttoned-down alley fight; it's a barroom brawl in which you can get blindsided at any minute without warning. It's a street fight with an adversary who fears losing as much as you do and will go to any legitimate extreme to win. For all of these reasons, Mr. Johnstone, I regret to inform you that you could not have chosen a more hostile and demanding vocation if you had joined a Chicago SWAT team or the Pittsburgh Steelers.''

Another hand, this time belonging to one of the new young women associates. ''I haven't had all that many fights in my lifetime; well, none, actually.'' A ripple of supportive laughter broke the tension that had been building in the room. ''How do I cope with others who grew up playing football while I practiced synchronized swimming?''

''With great care,'' replied Kevin amiably. ''Remember that you *are* a woman. And don't hesitate to be one in the courtroom! If winning is important to you, then you'll use your femininity as you would use a sharp knife in an alley fight. Women can still get away with things that might earn a man a contempt citation— remember, most judges are still men. They may take you lightly— which I realize is an insult—but because of that they will go more than halfway with you, as long as you don't come on like Raymond Burr in drag.''

Kevin urged the women to refine the art that men had practiced for decades: making themselves attractive to jurors of the opposite sex while carefully avoiding threat or insult to those of the same gender.

"And remember that your superior intuitive nature—it *is* superior you know—will provide an advantage over a more contentious and experienced opponent. The point is to develop your masculine instincts without forgetting that you will still be stereotyped as a woman by your average jury if you reveal too much aggression. Don't think you should check your sexuality at the door. The jury doesn't want you to."

Yes, reflected Rachel, sex was indeed a powerful weapon—in or out of the courtroom—one that perhaps she had permitted to be turned on herself. Taking charge was something she just hadn't done; she had been responding to Kevin's agenda—and ignoring her own; letting pride in his attention and her own desire combine to control her actions. Suddenly she could see the irony in Kevin's urging of women to use their femininity on behalf of their clients, knowing that she would be instantly cast out of the firm—and perhaps was about to be—should it become known that she had used hers for her own satisfaction . . . and his.

As Kevin continued to talk, Rachel tuned out, her mind turning to her approaching confrontation with Barrington. Even the strident male chorus of sporadic applause now irritated her, though she knew that her frustration could not rationally be directed toward them. They were decent people, absorbed like herself in the bitter struggle to make partnership. Everyone knew that some would get trampled along the way. They had all been caught up in the same dance from the first day they walked in the door at S.P.&M.: *nineteen incoming associates racing down a burning pier toward a two-man lifeboat.*

She looked up at Kevin but no longer heard his words. She became feverish and felt a pounding in her temples. She tried to relax but the question smoldered in her brain: *Who were the two against me?*

Was it Gardner White, a close social friend of Alan Hancock, the prominent lawyer who she had beaten in a complex and bitterly contested case? It had been only her second case at S.P.&M., and Hancock had been humiliated by being defeated at the hands of a rookie—a *female* rookie at that! Then there was the Perkins case, her one trial defeat. Even Jeffrey had tried to warn her that her lack of assertiveness in dealing with her junior associates and paralegals could be detrimental to the outcome and perhaps he had been right. How was it, he had asked, that she could be so effective against an adversary, yet so incapable of dealing forcefully with her own people? Where was her famous discipline when she needed to discipline others? The issue was whether the partners had noticed the flaw. Until the summons by Barrington, she was sure they hadn't.

But most likely it was simply Barrington himself who had lost patience with her. Although Kevin had assured Rachel in Nantucket that the senior partner had never spoken ill of her, she knew better than Kevin what Barrington really wanted: an indication. The sign that would never be forthcoming. And Austin Barrington was not a man conditioned to being ignored.

When I get fired this morning, she mused bitterly, *will it be because I slept with Kevin or because I refused to sleep with Barrington?*

Time was running out.

Rachel checked her watch, anxious to get the confrontation with Barrington behind her, yet realizing this might well be the last time she would ever see Kevin in this milieu—a thought that clutched at the pit of her stomach. She thought, too, about how adroitly she had always exempted Kevin from her anger at the partnership. Irrational immunity conferred by love.

It also struck her that the firm was her only connection to Kevin, that she might conceivably be looking at him for the last time. The lens of her eye bypassed reason and began sending pictures of Kevin straight to her heart: here a look of mock surprise, now his quizzically compacted brow, then a spontaneous grin signifying tolerance to a befuddled associate. She knew that whatever was to become of her, she would treasure these images.

Kevin invited one last question to close out the session. A second-year female associate was on her feet behind Rachel: "Don't big-case trial lawyers usually have to become specialists in fields such as antitrust or tax litigation, just like business lawyers have done for years?"

Kevin answered quickly. "A mediocre trial lawyer who seeks refuge in some obscure specialty will be beaten every time by a good trial lawyer who has never worked in the field. And the world-class trial lawyer," he added, "like the frontier gambler, will turn up in *any* forum, in *any* kind of case, whenever the stakes are high enough."

"Would that include the North American Chemical case?" shouted a voice from somewhere in back. Mention of the case stirred Rachel from her distracted state.

"Well," replied Kevin, breaking into his boyish smile, "I hear the stakes are indeed high in that case." A ripple of excitement swept the room, for rumors had been rampant since the announcement two weeks earlier that the firm had accepted the North American Chemical case, followed by days of conspicuous silence. "Are we still in the North American case?" asked the same associate.

"Why shouldn't we be?" said Kevin casually, precipitating spontaneous applause and hurrahs.

"Will you be trying the case?" asked another.

"Don't you people have any work to do?" asked Kevin, smiling. "That will do it for today."

"Give us a break, Kevin!" shouted yet another anonymous voice to a chorus of applause. Kevin was obviously on the spot and seemed to be grappling with a decision. "All right. I can say this," he said finally. "First, we are indeed representing over one hundred ex-employees of North American Chemical who are all seriously ill, some near death, and yes, I will be trying the case."

Interruption for more cheering. This is sounding like a political convention, thought Rachel, now fatigued from anxiety and desperately wanting the session to end, wanting to get on with it.

"And," continued Kevin, "to illustrate my earlier point that the world-class trial lawyer will always turn up when the stakes are high enough, I can tell you that my co-lead trial counsel will be Austin Barrington."

Yet another outburst of applause greeted the announcement. Rachel saw looks of surprise mingled with delight that the best of two generations of trial lawyers were combining their efforts in the service of working people against the business establishment. But Rachel's alienation from the associates' elation was now souring into bitter anger. She saw herself—and Beth—as victims of S.P.&M.'s own brand of exploitation and resented the associates' naive acclaim.

"How about associate assignments? When will we know?" came another voice from the back of the room. Kevin smiled, looked at his watch, and held up both hands with palms facing the group: "How does one control this unruly mob? That's all for today." Cheering and more applause accompanied Kevin's exit.

Jeffrey caught up with Rachel in the crowded hallway. "So, Rachel, it's true! The mastodon is crawling out of the mud. It's hard to picture, I admit: our firm—champion of the common man!''

Our firm, thought Rachel. How easily he says it. He's just begun his career, yet he clearly sees his future. Glancing yet again at her watch, Rachel saw that it was nearly ten and began to walk faster. One did not keep Austin Barrington waiting, even for one's own execution, so she smiled a good-bye to Jeffrey and slipped through the crowd of excited associates. She felt estranged from the exhilarating din of their laughter—as if she were visiting someone else's high school reunion. Through the crowd, she caught a glimpse of Kevin's back as he walked down the hall, surrounded by admiring associates.

TWELVE

■

At ten sharp Rachel sat down just outside Austin Barrington's corner suite and stared hypnotically at Miss Tarkenton's blurred fingers as they blazed across her keyboard. In six years, Rachel had never seen Miss Tarkenton smile. To say she was plain in appearance did her too much justice. Her dried-paper skin defied makeup, giving her face a grainy Diane Arbus look. Her black eyes popped malice and seemed to warn oncoming traffic to move out of the way. Like so many of the older secretaries, Miss Tarkenton overtly resented Rachel's intrusion into a profession clearly reserved in her mind for men. For two decades, she had coveted her role as the most important woman in the firm. Female lawyers had changed all that. Rachel understood this and had always been charitable in the face of Miss Tarkenton's overt resentment, realizing that the firm was Miss Tarkenton's life too. Day and night, her total being was devoted to S.P.&M. and to Austin Barrington, in whose protection and reflected glory she felt secure and fulfilled.

The buzzer rang. Miss Tarkenton's birdlike body jolted as if it had absorbed 220 volts and she leapt to Barrington's door. Not more than forty-five years old, Margaret Tarkenton affected the clothing and hairstyle of a woman twenty years her senior: Red Cross shoes, black hair confined in a bun, and horn-rimmed glasses that hung on the beak of her sad, pinched face. She reemerged from Barrington's office and addressed Rachel through compressed lips: "Mr. Barrington will see you now."

For a moment fear crowded out anger and Rachel wondered if she would be able to say what she was feeling without—*God help me!*—crying. She entered the huge office and stiffly made her way to the chair to which Barrington beckoned her. She observed that he did not invite her to join him at his conference table but rather embraced the security of his massive desk: a magnificent fortress carved out of French oak, fully eight feet in width and four feet deep.

As Barrington lowered his giant frame into his high-backed leather chair, Rachel had to concede that he was indeed a formidable man. He looked no more than fifty years of age, was built as solidly as the oak desk between them, and possessed a mind no less complex and finely developed than the beautiful sculpted designs carved into the fine wood. She fought to maintain her resolve in the face of this restrained but awesome manifestation of power. She reminded herself he was still only a man.

"Coffee, Rachel?" asked Barrington, pouring himself a cup of a special blend made from beans grown on his own ranch on Kona, freshly ground at seven-thirty each morning by Miss Tarkenton. Rachel declined, determined to keep the confrontation formal. She hadn't been summoned to a coffee klatch. She felt her strength returning, her courage somehow fueled by the act of rejecting the proffered favor.

Barrington took a sip of his coffee, and looked over the top of the cup at the young associate. "Let me know if you change your mind. Coffee's a hobby with me, you know."

Rachel didn't know.

Barrington lit a cigarette and leaned back in his swivel chair as casually as if he were about to give dictation. "How did the staff meeting go? Kevin's usual flawless exhibition, I trust?" Rachel thought she detected a touch of sarcasm in his choice of words and tone of voice.

"It was excellent," she replied, switching her pronoun from "he" at the last second.

"Do you like . . . working with Stone?" asked Barrington, engaging her eyes for the first time.

"He's an excellent teacher," said Rachel. She was striving to match Barrington's nonchalance, but realized that she was nervously fingering a button on her blouse. "His techniques have informed much of my own style."

"Then I shall allow myself a modicum of satisfaction, as I'm sure I informed much of his. He has been my most . . . notoriously successful protégé. The press dotes on him," Barrington said, then added with an insincere half smile, "All well deserved, of course."

Rachel gave a quick, noncommittal nod, and the senior partner continued. "I regret that you and I have never had an opportunity to work together." He rose slowly from behind his desk, looked above her auburn head, and exhaled smoke at the ceiling. His hand swept upward in an imperial arc, as he added, "This administrative crap keeps me out of the courtroom now."

Rachel decided not to mention Kevin's public disclosure of Barrington's trial commitment in the North American case. Meanwhile, Barrington seemed to be enjoying a momentary tense silence and Rachel's captive attention. She studied his face for a sign, but then quickly turned away to avoid being misunderstood. There was still no mistaking the intention behind his eyes, however. Yes, Austin Barrington wanted her, but as a man wants a woman, not as a senior partner wants a new junior partner. The realization rekindled her commitment to go out like a lioness.

"You wanted to see me, sir?"

"Yes, indeed. But because of the seriousness of the matter before us, I've decided to have Kevin Stone present for this conversation. Before he arrives, I must ask you—more specifically, perhaps—how did you and Kevin get on in New York? You were together a full week, I believe?" *My God*, thought Rachel. *He knows.*

"Nine days," she said, an uncomfortable heat again invading her rigid body. This was not to be the usual good-bye-and-good-luck termination speech. She was on trial. Perhaps Kevin as well.

Barrington smiled and turned toward his intercom system, saying, "I don't mean to pry, but it's important that you tell me the truth." He pushed a button near his telephone.

"Yes, Mr. Barrington?" chirped Miss Tarkenton.

"Where in the hell is Stone?"

"He's walking in your door right now, sir."

"Ah, so he is. Hello, Kevin. Sit down there right next to Rachel if you will. Coffee? Here you are."

Rachel could detect nothing from Kevin's customary smile and quick nod of his head. He took his seat beside her while Barrington ominously removed a thin file from a drawer in his desk. Rachel looked at Kevin, who looked at Barrington, who turned his gaze back to Rachel, who now longed for nothing but to be done with this business; to get on with her day, her life.

"You have been exceedingly patient, Rachel, and for that I am grateful. I will now get right to the point. As you well know, Kevin has been heavily occupied since our filing in the North American Chemical case. Now that he's back, it's time to get moving. I—Kevin and I—have decided to bring you aboard as the senior associate on the trial team. He and I will share lead counsel duties, which means you're going to have to put up with both of us . . ."

Rachel barely heard the rest. She half turned toward Kevin as Barrington's voice droned on, saw that he was smiling calmly toward her. She tried to assimilate this jarring shift in her fortunes: from certain rejection and denial of her heart's desire to active participation in the richest lawsuit in the United States, perhaps in the history of American jurisprudence! More important, the litigation could carry well past the end of her seventh year, which could mean only that the partners' present intention was for her to go up, not out! She tried to concentrate on Barrington's words: ". . . and Ray Stein will be the head junior associate team member reporting to you and Kevin. Stu Wallach will personally handle the paralegal and document management team, under your direct supervision, of course. I'll handle the medical workups. Other team assignments will be announced soon."

"Before I forget," Kevin interrupted, addressing Barrington and seeming oblivious to Rachel's immobilizing joy, "there's a squirrelly kid named Johnstone here somewhere, Austin. He was at the seminar this morning. I like his tenacity and guts. I'd like to see him assigned to Rachel's research team. Okay, Rachel?" Rachel managed an enthusiastic nod.

"Johnstone. Johnstone," said Barrington thoughtfully. "Oh, yes. He's under Jackson Miller—second year, I think. Bright kid, number one in his class at Northwestern, I believe, then a year on the Supreme Court. A bit overzealous, I've heard. Can't place his face."

"Look for a ballsy little squirt right out of *American Graffiti:* horn-rimmed glasses and hayseed sticking out of both ears," replied Kevin. "The kid looks like a surplus broomstick, but I suspect he knows the law."

"Miss Tarkenton," said Barrington into his intercom, "add a Mr. Johnstone to the research team. Have him report to Miss Cannon later this week." Then, turning back to Rachel, he said, "The extent of your own actual involvement at trial will be determined as we go along. Meanwhile, you will soon be directing four or five associates and another ten to fifteen paralegals. I expect you to be tough. This won't be a popularity contest and I'll expect you to keep them in line and on target. Any questions?"

Rachel shook off a twinge of anxiety, then heard herself saying, "How soon can I get started?"

"How about yesterday?" replied Barrington with a smile, and handed her a brown-jacketed file with her name already typed across the tab. "Study this and we will resume here tomorrow at seven A.M. Our meetings with expert witnesses will start no later than two weeks from today. It's all in there. As you will see, this case presents some extremely challenging problems. We are counting on you." Barrington stood up to signal the end of the meeting. Then, without taking his eyes off Rachel's, he added, "Please stay on for a moment, Kevin, will you?"

Rachel arose on unsteady legs and left the room, clutching the North American Chemical file to her body as a starving person would hold a loaf of bread in a mob.

Within twenty minutes Kevin surged into Rachel's office with a proffered handshake and a smile he had to turn sideways to get through the door. "Did I just witness the unflappable Ms. Cannon in a rare moment of discombobulation?"

"Understated as usual, Mr. Stone. Try totally disoriented with both socks knocked off," said Rachel, beaming. "I've never been so surprised, elated, or relieved."

"Relieved?" asked Kevin.

"Yes, relieved, particularly after what happened to Beth on Friday. When I received Captain Queeg's summons, I assumed it was my turn off the plank. Besides, I didn't exactly distinguish myself in the Perkins case as the best staff manager in town."

Kevin held on to her hand and smiled at her in a way that made her feel fourteen and in love for the first time. "A minor flaw in an otherwise perfect picture," he said. "Remember when we were in New York and I told you the partners regarded you as someone special?'' Then, lifting her hand to his lips, he added, ''Our feelings for you are stronger than ever.''

The gesture immersed Rachel's eyes in an emerald mist, though a caution light blinked uncomfortably in the distance. ''I guess I'm still a bit overwhelmed, Kevin. Thank you for your part in it. I hope—I mean I'm sure that you didn't . . .''

''I did nothing, actually, but confirm to Austin that you were the best we had and that I thought we could all work well together. This has been his show from the beginning. I'm just happy you're happy.''

Kevin's eyes locked on hers. He put his free hand around her waist and moved closer. *Please don't*, Rachel thought, *not here of all places.* Kevin seemed to read her qualms and he hesitated, saying simply, ''I've missed you.''

''And I you,'' she said, then smiled and walked behind her desk, adding, ''Want to sit for a moment? I have legitimate grounds for detaining you.''

''Legitimate? Oh, well, I'll stay anyway. Shoot.''

''Well. I've only perused the file, but unless I'm missing something, this thing looks like it could go a couple of hundred million dollars. The only thing that puzzles me is the firm's two-week silence after filing the complaint and holding the press conference. Sure, the case has some tough causation problems, but . . . is there something I'm missing?''

''Not at all.'' Kevin lowered himself into one of her client chairs and resumed his professional manner. ''But what I'm about to tell you must go no farther than this room. Okay?''

''Of course.''

Kevin ran a hand through his soft, unruly hair, lowered his voice, and began. ''It's all quite absurd in retrospect, but I guess it had the Table of Three in a panic for a while. I didn't know what was really going on myself until it was already resolved. At first, Austin fudged with me, told me that Adrian Fisher and Gardner White were having their usual old-boy second thoughts about taking on the establishment, plus the plaintiffs'-personal-injury-firm image the initial publicity had generated. As I learned later, the truth was that Dr. Raymond Newkirk, Barrington's toxicologist friend who owns a testing lab in Marin County, thought that he had made an error in his lab analysis on some of the first five potential plaintiffs Barrington had taken up there.''

"This was the testing done in Newkirk's lab before we committed to take the cases?" Rachel asked.

"Yes. Barrington wanted one hundred percent certainty that these North American ex-employees were not only hurting, but that they were hurting specifically from ingestion of toxic water contaminated by North American's dump site."

"Since that's what we ultimately will have to prove, that makes good sense," Rachel said.

"Right—though I have a wild backup theory on how we might get around the need to prove specific causation. Anyway, everything checked out fine at first—you saw some pretty specific allegations in the complaint and newspapers—but three days after the press release, Newkirk called Austin and told him a technician had misread some data, resulting in a quantum exaggeration of contamination levels in some of the five men tested."

"How could he have made such a mistake?"

"Hold on, I'm not finished. I know Newkirk, incidentally. Used him on a drunk driving defense I tried once as a favor for a client. He's an M.D. who never practiced medicine and a pathologist who never performed an autopsy. As a toxicologist, though, he's okay—no Louis Pasteur certainly, but competent enough to administer and interpret blood serum tests for toxicity."

"So you thought."

"So we thought. Well, here I am surrounded by press and nosy associates and I don't know what to tell them. After about a week of this I began to get a bit pissed and told Austin it was time to make a go or no-go decision. He agreed, of course, and told me he'd force the Table to a decision. What he really did—as he admitted to me when you and I got back from New York—was visit the lab, interview all the technicians, and walk them through the whole process again step by step. He even took the five old guys back out there again."

"Let me guess," interrupted Rachel. "He found that the only error was in assuming there had been an error."

"Right as usual, Ms. Cannon. Newkirk has confirmed that all of them are just as contaminated as he had first told us. That was now about a week ago, but Barrington wouldn't let me announce it until yesterday. I guess he checked and rechecked Newkirk's work a dozen times before he was sufficiently certain to stick his neck out again."

"I would hate to have been in Newkirk's shoes. Our leader is rather intolerant of sloppiness."

"True, but it all worked out. You have to give Austin credit. One way or the other," Kevin said, "he gets the job done."

THIRTEEN

∎

Meanwhile, across town, in a gunmetal-gray, fiberboard-partitioned cubicle on the ground floor of City Hall, a different kind of case against North American Chemical was under discussion. Two plainclothes homicide inspectors quietly argued across stacks of files, photographs, and reports, piled precariously high on a metal desk with a broken leg. A thick treatise on criminal forensics supported the deficient corner, failure of which would precipitate an avalanche of paper that could bury the entire floor.

The larger man was standing. He looked more like an off-duty wrestler than an on-duty cop as he watched and listened to the younger man who sat behind the ancient desk, staring at a four-page list of North American's stockholders.

"So does this support my theory or what?" said Lieutenant Dan Conti as he sprang from his chair and slapped the document with the back of his hand. Once on his feet, the wiry homicide inspector appeared taller than his five feet eight inches, at least until he stood beside Cleveland Roberts, a one-time 49er defensive end. Roberts shook his head as he peered unhappily at the list Conti had thrust in front of him.

"You're smokin' wacko weed, Dan," said the black police sergeant. "It ain't illegal to own stock in a chemical company. Some of my best friends own stock in chemical—"

"Cleve. Be serious." Dan Conti's voice was neither deep nor resonant, but carried the unwavering intensity of a surgeon's scalpel. Born in the Italian North Beach area of San Francisco, Conti had been raised tough and had stayed that way. After three years at the University of San Francisco, two of them on a boxing scholarship, he joined the S.F.P.D. and quickly worked his way back into plainclothes while finishing college at night school. He amassed a department record both for number of arrests made and most physical beatings absorbed. Conti had become a legend in a few short years, but reached a point where he was no longer fooling anyone on the streets. He had run out of effective disguises. Department legend had it that when he made formal application for plastic surgery, that did it. The captain brought him inside, promoting him to inspector rank partly to keep him from killing himself.

Whether the story was apocryphal or not, it was clear that Conti's overzealous nature and simplistic morality had created jealousy and resentment among many of his fellow officers and detectives. Most mistook his fanatical dedication for blind ambition, an understandable reaction; the mainspring that drove Dan Conti was not the kind of thing he revealed to strangers, and he had few friends. He was respected and feared, but not loved— the profile of a loner.

"This is the breakthrough I've waited for, Cleve. The mob owns the North American Chemical Company! Look at their chairman of the board of directors, for Christ's sake: Joseph Lucca, known to us as 'Las Vegas' Lucca, a group chief who goes all the way back to Jimmy Fratiano when Fratiano was the Mafia's chief West Coast enforcer. Murder is just business-as-usual to these guys, Cleve. Lucca was even at the Appalachian 1957 grand council meeting. Now he's in Lileton, California. Doesn't that mean anything to you?"

Sergeant Roberts just turned around, looked up at the ceiling, and smiled sadly, the back of his thick neck and bald head becoming a washboard. "Sure it does, Dan. It means you're outside your jurisdiction. It also means you're going hunting without a license again, Dan, and *that* means Captain Mahan will soon be hangin' your white ass out to dry, maybe for the last time. You keep feeding on that Mafia myth, Lieutenant, and you're gonna end up with a mental ulcer."

Conti snatched the papers back from Roberts, more out of impatience than anger, then moved swiftly back to his seat with the athletic grace of an ex-Golden Gloves boxing champion who had managed to stay in fighting shape despite his thirty-seven years.

"I'll need help," he said finally, his dark brown eyes reaching out to hold the sergeant's gaze. "We can't expect the New York U.S. attorney's office to clean up the whole damn mob alone.

They're *here*, Cleve, right here in our own backyard. Under the 1970 racketeering act, all we need to prove is two predicate acts of extortion, fraud, or whatever by Lucca or North American, and we can take their whole fucking family down!''

The big man shook his head again as he said, ''Apart from the fact that you're just generally crazier than a runover dog, Dan, I got to remind you that you ain't *got* two predicate acts. You ain't even got one.''

''That may be true at this moment, Cleve, but I tell you my instincts are very strong on this one,'' said Conti after a brief silence, during which he began to stroke his prominent nose and seemed to withdraw within himself.

Roberts smiled good-naturedly and said, ''Then why is it that the captain's instincts haven't led him to the same conclusion?''

Conti's full lips formed themselves into an ironic smile, though his eyes remained sad and hooded by impassive, down-sloping lids. ''The captain doesn't trust instincts, Cleve. Considers them un-American. He wouldn't accept a collect call from his instincts.''

Roberts laughed and held up hands as big as suitcases: ''Well, sir, you might consider getting an unlisted number yourself. As for me? Sorry, Lieutenant. I *need* this job.''

Conti entered his small, sparsely furnished Russian Hill apartment at seven that night and grabbed a beer from the refrigerator. He heated up some lasagna from the night before and turned on the TV just as Dan Rather was hailing *Columbia*, the first spacecraft ever to be relaunched, then relaunched again. The spicy smell of the warming pasta kindled his hunger and he devoured dinner ten minutes into a *Kojak* rerun, then clattered the dishes into the sink and tried to decide what to do next. Maybe a drink at Prego or Perry's, he thought as he walked into his tiny bathroom for a quick shower. He then went to his bedroom and slid open a mirrored closet door, revealing his one material treasure: a wardrobe that an Italian count would envy. Conti surveyed his cache with satisfaction, then laid out a new pair of gray slacks from Brioni's and a blue silk shirt fresh from the cleaners. He knew that downtown they called him everything from a clothes horse to ''Dan-dy,'' but he didn't mind. Dandies wore polyester suits that changed colors when they turned sideways and sported pencil-thin mustaches. Dan Conti had taste. Sure, he made a crummy $1,460 a month take-home and had only $2,000 in savings. But he had a dozen pair of

Ferragamo shoes that said he was something special. Not just
another cop.

He dressed, then returned to the bathroom to brush his teeth,
shave, and brush back his thinning black hair. Looking out at
him from the mirror was a weary but reasonably attractive
second-generation Italian-American. Married: once (and, unlike
the *Columbia*, not likely to be relaunched) to the beautiful Lila
Evans Conti (still the love of his life), alias Baby, who, upon
wearying of Dan's misplaced passion for law enforcement, was
last seen three years earlier headed for Jakarta of all places with
a promising young soft-drink executive for Christ's sake who
had replaced her Sears wedding band with a two-carat stone that
had crushed Conti's heart. Children: none. Baby had said that to
bring up children with an absentee police inspector as a father
would be a crime. Baby knew how to make a point. Hard
feelings: none, but no forgetting either. Occupation: homicide
cop. Preoccupation: death. Not just murder, and not just his own
death. Conti indiscriminately hated all death. He was a universal
death-despiser who had even become an outspoken opponent of
the gas chamber—a position hardly calculated to win promotions
and friends in the police department. Which maybe explained
why he had so few. Friends. Promotions were no problem
despite frequent skirmishes with S.F.P.D. Captain Fred Mahan
and notwithstanding his alleged overzealousness, unorthodox methods, aloofness, and perceived cockiness. Promotions came because he was, for all his faults, the best there was, and because
he worked tirelessly and *did* accept collect calls from his instincts. He didn't care that others regarded him as single-
dimensional, for didn't he love photography, art, and music—both
jazz and opera? He even liked to cook when there was time for
it, and he loved good films. Also red wine and now—after too
many nights of mourning the loss of Baby—women.

Baby.

Looking back, he could see that the thing with Baby had
probably all worked out for the best. She had not been right for
him. Dan could see it clearly now. Now that the blinding hurt
and anger were behind him. Now that the longing had subsided.

Lately, he had even begun to wonder what his relationship
with Baby revealed about himself. For under discussion here is a
woman who thought that Boston was in the state of Washington.
Who spread peanut butter on her ham sandwich. Who was
openly flirtatious with his best friends and whose idea of a real

man was Rod Stewart. Who had not worked a day since they were married although she claimed to have been a bank teller for a year after dropping out of Marin Community College in order to follow the first U.S. tour of the Spider's Webb in the intimate company of a Swedish lead guitar player whom she had met one night at the Sweetwater in Mill Valley. It was hard to picture Baby as a bank teller but she *was* good at numbers. Dan knew, because she had done one on him.

Baby had been nineteen, far too young, he realized far too late. She was also too tall, too pretty, and too full of expectations. She also made him feel old, which, at thirty, is not a welcome experience. He knew he bored her. For one thing, she had lost all interest in his work once she found out that his reality was not as exciting as the afternoon TV, which soon became her chief passion—after Rod Stewart, of course. For another thing, they had run out of conversation. She had as little interest in the law as he did in rock and roll. They communicated best in the dark.

Following two years of heroic emotional handstands, Dan more or less gave up and sank back into a routine not unlike his life had been before Baby. She, in turn, tempered her real-life dreams and withdrew more and more into a world of television, interrupted only by two or three attempts at getting a job—the last of which was as assistant bookkeeper in a soft-drink manufacturing company. Locating Boston was apparently not on the screening exam, because she got the job.

Despite all of this, Dan had loved Baby with all his heart, and a part of him always would. Never mind that they had no social friends—other women were naturally uncomfortable around Baby's innocent and seductive beauty—and forget that she could do nothing in the kitchen but put together a fairly decent tuna fish casserole. Or that she read only *People* magazine and the entertainment section of the morning *Chronicle*. Their mutual disillusionment was forgotten at night, where they celebrated an inexplicably unsullied physical connection that possessed for Conti the addictive power of heroin. Then, one day, he learned why Baby had gotten that job with the soft-drink company.

But that was behind him and now he understood what happened when you gave your heart. What happened was you got what you deserved.

Now he was enjoying women again.

But tonight, the face in the mirror was lined with fatigue and pleading for a night in. Besides, sitting on the kitchen table that served as a desk was the file he had put together on North American and the city of Lileton. He traded his silk shirt for a terry-cloth bathrobe and started through the file, becoming more energized with each page. Jimmy Fratiano. Joseph "Las Vegas" Lucca. He began unconsciously to stroke his nose and hum "The Battle Hymn of the Republic."

Carmine Romano, Guido Luciani, the list went on.

The inspector was doing what he loved most of all.

PART TWO

■

THE CATALYST

■

WINTER, 1982

Tempt not a desperate man.

—William Shakespeare

FOURTEEN

■

Rachel and Jeff escaped the tide of bustling last-minute Christmas shoppers into the relative warmth of the Imperial Building lobby, recently transformed into a forest of holiday greenery. Holly and pine boughs hung from every wall, surrounding a traditional twenty-foot-high Christmas tree, resplendent in multi-colored lights which glanced off the soaring brownstone walls of the huge foyer, then leaped even higher, emphasizing the height of the buttressed ceiling. To Rachel, the Imperial Building was not just a place of work, but a work of art, now enhanced by mountain scents and kaleidoscopic colors.

"Finish your shopping yet?" Rachel asked Jeff, loosening her scarf and entering the S.P.&M. express elevator.

"Let's see. Three days left, right? I'll start any day now. I did manage to get off a package to my folks. This hasn't been my most relaxed holiday season. As a matter of fact, I've had exactly two weekends off since June, when we took on the North American case."

Six months, thought Rachel. It had gone by so fast, her time and energy dominated by typical early legal maneuvering and document exchanges with the defendants, then helping Kevin when she could on his New York antitrust case.

Kevin. New York. Not a day had gone by since then when she hadn't thought about him. They would never again be separate in her mind. Nor would her mind ever be far separated from his, though they had slept together only once since Nantucket—a crazy and beautiful two hours at her apartment after Newkirk's mid-October deposition in San Rafael.

Kevin had offered to drop her off in Sausalito and she had offered him coffee and later they had laughed themselves sick when they found the cold, untouched cups still on the kitchen counter. Then he had dressed to go home to his wife and children and Rachel had stopped laughing herself sick. The painful week that followed had left her empty and convinced that in making love with Kevin her body was writing checks her heart couldn't cash. She must not let it happen again. She must fight the craziness. Kevin was married—a subject they pointedly avoided—and she was in the fishbowl existence of her up-or-out year at S.P.&M., another taboo subject. Until these issues were resolved, her feelings for Kevin had to be reined in, disciplined, perhaps sublimated to the attainment of partnership, her other heart's desire.

"Hey, up there! Are you listening? Earth to Rachel, Earth to Rachel."

"I heard you, Jeff. Cheer up. Another weekend is almost upon us."

"Swell," said Jeff, "Scrooge Barrington's definition of a weekend is only two more working days till Monday."

"I'm sure your year-end bonus will reflect the firm's eternal gratitude for your sacrifice," said Rachel, smiling.

The two stepped off the elevator at the Eagle's Nest and the receptionist informed them that Professor Childhouse had just arrived and was with Mr. Barrington. As Rachel and Jeff headed toward the northeast corner office, she said, "It's a wonder Austin has time to meet with an expert witness considering all the senior trial associates he's had to fire this week."

Jeff gently took her arm, saying, "I know what you're thinking, but a year from now it will be Rachel Cannon: partner-elect. Sure, they made only three partners this year, but if they make only *one* next year, it—she—will be Rachel Cannon." Rachel smiled as he added, "And then you'll probably no longer lower yourself to join this humble junior associate for our weekly lunch at Miyuki's."

"Of course I won't," said Rachel. "Why eat with you when I won't even be speaking to you?"

"Thank you, Rachel. That remark just shortened my Christmas list. So," Jeff added in a lower voice that snapped her back to reality, "I get to meet the great Professor Desmond Childhouse at last. By the way, is it my imagination, or are you a bit on edge?"

Rachel had been responsible for surveying the available field of forensic experts in a number of scientific disciplines the North American case would call into play: toxicology, water mechanics, molecular genetics, immunology, pathology, chemistry, medicine, and economics. Professor Childhouse had been easy to find. He had first caught the attention of the press as a champion for the beleaguered residents of Love Canal in Niagara, New York, and as a frequent witness before congressional committees considering the cleanup of toxic waste dumps. When Childhouse turned against the administration and became the first reputable professional to denounce the EPA's mishandling of its charter under the so-called "Superfund," he became an instant media darling.

The professor spoke with authority. During his twenty-five years as a full professor at the University of California Medical Center, Childhouse had written the definitive text on molecular genetics, two books on toxicology, and dozens of articles on the correlation between organic chemicals and pathology. Rachel knew that in complex cases such as the North American case, the testimony of experts could be even more important than the testimony of the parties or the skill of the trial lawyers. Good experts could make or break any case, and Rachel had spent a substantial amount of the past half year making sure she had found the best in each field.

"I've got a lot riding on the professor today," she said quietly.

"Do you have any doubts about him? He sounds like the Kevin Stone of forensics."

"No," said Rachel without hesitation. "It's just that he has never testified in a jury trial and he knows so much that he can be, well, obscure at times."

"I assume you've worked him over on the importance of keeping it simple and to the point."

"Endlessly, but if he flunks today, so do I."

"He'll do fine. How does he look?"

"Well, that's another problem. Strictly a matter of first impression, of course. He's brilliant, but he's not your Barrington kind of guy."

Margaret Tarkenton stopped them with her usual inquiry: "Is Mr. Barrington expecting you?"

"Yes," they said in unison, exchanging glances as she picked up the intercom phone, then waved them on with the cool indifference of a customs agent.

Seated in the conference wing at one end of the table was Barrington; at the other end, Professor Childhouse. Kevin occupied one of the chairs in the middle, and Barrington beckoned Rachel and Jeff to two chairs opposite Kevin. Introductions and small talk were quickly dispatched as Barrington called the meeting to order and turned to Professor Childhouse. "Well, sir. As I said, we are most pleased to have you aboard. How—in general, of course—does it look so far?"

All eyes shifted expectantly to the expert witness. To Rachel, he was, in most respects, the perfect forensic expert. His appearance would neither inspire women nor threaten men. He had a pink-skinned face, as round as a bowling ball, which glowed with an innocent energy that belied his fifty-eight years of age. His youthful looks were balanced by thinning gray hair, a sign of erudition to most jurors—an impression corroborated by glasses that looked thick enough to enable him to study cells without a microscope and that gave his enlarged eyes an owl-like appearance. Rachel wished him taller, a little less paunchy, but she knew that once he was seated in the witness box his physical stature would diminish in importance. She wondered what Barrington was thinking and whether Kevin would test him for tolerance to pressure during this first interview.

"It's an interesting case," said Childhouse in a high but authoritative voice.

"How so?" asked Barrington, leaning forward and picking up a pencil.

"Well, unlike the problems I ran into in Love Canal, Miami, and New Orleans, I have found here some rather clear correlations—using the gas chromatograph–mass spectrometer—between samples of dioxin, benzene, and trichloroethylene, and samples taken from North America's dump." Rachel and Jeffrey exchanged troubled looks, but Childhouse did not pause even to breathe. "These correlations were augmented by a high instance of comparability with epidemiological surveys and toxicologic studies on microtus which demonstrated that neurotoxins had produced injuries to the peripheral nervous system, including demyelination of the myelin sheath with concurrent slowing of nerve conduction velocity and trauma to the nerve axon itself."

Kevin Stone began to stare at the ceiling, while Barrington abandoned his attempt at taking notes. "Those tests," continued the professor, "were performed at Stanford and also detected DNA strand breaks and unscheduled DNA synthesis in lymphocytes, if you can imagine that!"

"No, sir," said Kevin in a courteous tone, "I can't."

"Pardon me, Mr. Stone?"

"Put bluntly, sir, I *can't* imagine it—and neither will the jury—because I haven't understood one thing you've said. Now, I'd like you to start over, and forget those five-dollar words for God's sake.''

Don't sugar-coat it, Kevin, thought Rachel, studying the concerned face of the diminutive professor, who took a deep breath and exhaled, saying, "It's a problem I have. I appreciate your directness.''

"No problem," said Kevin reassuringly, glancing at his notes. "But let's start over. What, for example, is microtus?"

Childhouse appeared embarrassed. "Well, counselor, I'm afraid you've just made your point. 'Microtus' is a . . . mouse.''

"Mouse," said Kevin, staring into the expert witness's enlarged eyes for what seemed to Rachel an eternity. "Mouse," he repeated. "All right, Professor, let's try it again.''

The expert witness self-consciously removed his pipe from a coat pocket and placed it on the table in front of him, then slowly began to summarize his findings. "It is," he concluded, "as bad as what we found at Love Canal.''

"You're referring to the construction of housing at Love Canal in proximity to a toxic waste dump site?" asked Barrington.

"Not just houses, Mr. Barrington. They built an elementary school right on top of it.''

"What did you find there?" asked Kevin.

"You name it. Lindane, benzene, dioxin—some of the very same chemicals you have in the North American dump site—toxins that attack the central nervous system and cause convulsions and epileptic seizures.''

Jeff, still the student, involuntarily raised a hand before he asked, "Isn't benzene a solvent known to cause leukemia in humans?''

"Indeed it is," said the expert witness, cocking his head toward the young associate. "It can also cause everything from simple fatigue to chromosomal damage—at levels of less than ten parts per million. It can take paint right off walls, but one of its favorite targets is bone marrow.''

"And we've got that at North American, you say?" asked Barrington, leaning forward. "I take it benzene is about as toxic as a chemical can get?''

"Unfortunately, there's something even worse: dioxin. Your ground mechanics expert, Saul Franks, found high levels of that as well, both in the dump site at North American and in the aquifer that feeds the water wells servicing the workers' quarters at the company's housing facility.

"Dioxin," continued Professor Childhouse, knitting his fingers together, "is known as the 'doomsday chemical.' Only pure botulism and tetanus toxins are more deadly. The chemical is two thousand times stronger than strychnine, one hundred fifty thousand times more deadly than cyanide. Yet it's all around us and we still produce it in vast quantities. It can be absorbed through the skin, inhaled with dust, or swallowed in water, and is the most potent promoter of cancer known to exist. It also causes symptoms of headaches, weight loss, fatigue, memory loss, depression, blood clots, hepatitis, and, in severe cases, chloracne."

"Professor," said Kevin in a discouraged tone. "It is obvious that you know your field inside and out. What is not so obvious is whether you will make sense to lay people. I'll be candid with you, sir: If you can't, your knowledge cannot directly help our clients. Now please tell us what you mean by 'chloracne' or whatever you called it."

Rachel's heart sank. Kevin was right, of course, but must he be so harsh? She concluded that he was also testing the expert for his tolerance to confrontation. It was clear, too, that her own success or failure in her first major North American case assignment was riding on the little professor. Why hadn't she been more aggressive with Childhouse?

"I again apologize, Mr. Stone," said Childhouse without defensiveness. "Chloracne is a condition of the skin. Much like severe acne."

"Your students thank you, Professor," said Kevin, smiling, apparently appeased. "Now what's dioxin used for?"

"It's primarily found in a weed killer. It's a contaminant of the herbicide known as 245-T or Agent Orange, with which we tried to defoliate Vietnam between 1962 and 1971."

"Could you give us a rough idea of how much dioxin was found in the well that services the defendant's housing facility?" asked Rachel.

"The preliminary tests showed concentrations as high as five hundred parts per billion, roughly the same as at Times Beach and Newark, New Jersey."

"Per *billion*?" exclaimed Barrington. "Still, that's so infinitesimal it's difficult to imagine it being harmful." As he spoke he looked at Rachel rather than Childhouse. Though his face was expressionless, Rachel felt herself reddening, caught herself nervously fingering the top button of her blouse. *This was not going well.*

"It is, however, sufficient to be deadly," answered the professor. "Indeed, just *one* part per billion is considered to be a chemical time bomb. Concentrations as small as five parts per *trillion* can kill a young guinea pig and have caused significant increases in cancer in tests performed on rats and monkeys. Dioxin also attacks the central nervous and immune systems in humans and is a primary cause of liver disease, cancer, and birth defects. You show me someone exposed to this chemical and I'll show you a victim of demyelination!"

Kevin abruptly rose from the table and fastened Dr. Childhouse with an icy stare. "It's show-and-tell, is it, Professor? Well, let me tell *you* something: You show me a plaintiffs' expert who can't communicate with a jury and I'll show you a defense verdict."

Rachel looked from Kevin to Barrington to the obviously shaken expert witness. Something was happening inside her stomach as she realized that Kevin was having to be too harsh because she had been too gentle. He had called it "a minor flaw," in the context of the Perkins case, but she now knew better. Dammit! Why hadn't she grilled him!

The expert witness removed his pipe from his pocket again and this time jammed it into his mouth. "Yes," he said, "I know I've done it again. I'm assuming too much and not getting my point across." Childhouse put the pipe back into his pocket and returned Kevin's hard gaze. "Well, let me try to explain it this way: Just three *ounces* of 2,3,7,8–tetrachlorodibenzoparadioxin evenly distributed and subsequently ingested by a million people may very well kill every blessed one of them."

"Yes, *yes!*" said Kevin, throwing his arms in the air. "*Now* you've gotten your point across. Technical words are fine to establish your authority as long as you explain what the hell they mean and then describe their effects in a way we can all understand. A multisyllable word might impress jurors, but it won't *scare* them. But tell them that just three ounces of dioxin would *kill* them—along with the rest of the entire population of San Francisco—and you've got their full attention!"

"Now," continued Kevin, who, to everyone's relief, resumed his seat, "why and how was North American dumping this stuff?"

"That's simple. They produce herbicides and solvents. Most of the toxic waste from their products appears to have been dumped in barrels which, for some indeterminate time, have been leaking as a result of rust and deterioration. In some cases, they just dumped the stuff in a large trench they had prepared for the purpose and covered it up."

"You say 'indeterminate period of time,' " said Barrington. "How long does it take for these contaminants to cause illness and physical damage?"

"Some of these chemicals—EDB for example—can kill on the spot," Childhouse replied, cleaning his thick round glasses with vigor and authority. "Several weeks ago, EDB killed one man instantly and decomposed the vital organs of another worker, who died two days after inhaling it while cleaning out a tank at the Occidental plant in Bakersfield."

An eerie, thoughtful quiet filled the room, interrupted only by the scratching of pens on paper. The professor took advantage of the opportunity to chew on his pipe for a few seconds before Kevin broke the silence. "Professor, how does a chemical like that find its way into the organs of a victim?"

"With an eagerness bordering on lust." Childhouse's round eyes blinked rapidly as he tapped imaginary tobacco from the bowl of his pipe into his hand. "Approximately seventy-five to eighty percent of the human body is composed of water, which in turn provides the fluid for cellular protoplasm. Unfortunately, neither the body's fluids nor the tissues they supply can discriminate between essential and alien chemicals, presenting a hospitable matrix for disease."

"You've seen the Newkirk Lab blood and tissue testing results, Professor. What are the most common diseases that result, once those chemicals invade the body?" asked Kevin. "You mentioned attacks on the central nervous system and the immune system?"

"Yes, these are the most common. Since your workers were all men, they were at least spared the fate of pregnant women in their final year at Love Canal: fourteen pregnancies and only two normal births. One child was born with his diaphragm and intestines outside his body. One had extra toes. One had three ears. Some had club feet. It might even be said that the lucky ones were those who miscarried altogether."

Another respectful silence blanketed the room as each lawyer screened the professor's data through his or her own emotional filters. Rachel had seen the pictures; the photographs had brought tears to her eyes. Jeffrey just stared at the expert witness in silence. Kevin again rose from his seat, this time nodding his head in satisfaction, stretched, and walked over to the east window. Even Barrington appeared to be affected by the expert's words. "Love Canal seems an ironic name for that project," he said quietly.

"It does seem to be the wrong four-letter word," said Childhouse, who then turned to Kevin Stone. "Am I doing any better?"

"You're going to be dynamite," said Kevin, smiling. "Pure, uncut dynamite."

Desmond Childhouse beamed his relief and Rachel resumed normal breathing.

"Well, Rachel," said Barrington, "where do we go from here? Do we still need this Saul Franks fellow?"

"Yes," said Rachel without hesitation. "We need a groundwater consultant to provide the jury with the mechanics of how the chemicals got from the dump site into the aquifer, then into the plaintiffs' well water. Dr. Newkirk will provide his analysis of the chemicals and correlate them with his findings derived from the plaintiffs' blood and fatty tissue samples. Professor Childhouse will be able to tie it all together and can also provide a perspective on how really serious the problem is nationwide, the government's apathy, how industry is getting away with . . ."

Rachel's concentration was broken by the staccato tapping of Barrington's pencil on the conference table. The senior partner scowled as he pushed his massive frame away from the table, saying, "Try to remember, Rachel, that we are here to try to win a case for our clients, not save the world. We have angered enough of our established clients as it is without turning this thing into a national crusade. Besides, government apathy, other than that exhibited by the city of Lileton, is totally irrelevant in this case."

The reproach both surprised and angered Rachel. She had discussed this strategy with Kevin and had assumed that Barrington agreed that the national issues were too hot to ignore. Despite a warning glance from Kevin, she started to speak: "Austin. The case—"

But it was Professor Childhouse who interrupted Rachel this time. "Please, Mr. Barrington," he said, "the fault is entirely mine. Over the course of my three meetings with your associate,

I fear I have successfully infected her with my own global anxiety and frustration.''

"Thank you, Professor,'' said Rachel, rising to pour herself a cup of coffee, ''but I would rather take responsibility for my own zeal than to be irresponsibly lacking in it. Coffee, anyone?'' Barrington shot Rachel a hard look, but Kevin moved in quickly.

"Thanks, Rachel, I'll have a cup,'' he said. ''Perhaps, Austin, a middle ground will evolve as we gain more information. It just might turn out that a little flag-waving would work to our advantage.''

The professor replaced his pipe in his pocket and resumed cleaning his glasses wearily. ''With all respect, Mr. Barrington, and I don't mean to kick a dead horse, but Ms. Cannon has every right to be concerned when Anne Gorsuch—the chief administrator of the national agency in charge of cleaning the poison from the nation's drinking water—was recently cited by Congress for contempt. We should *all* be worried.''

Barrington addressed Dr. Childhouse, but looked straight at Kevin. ''Professor''—his voice now hard-edged—''I'm worried *only* about winning this case, and when we gather for our next session, I will expect all of us to focus all our concerns *on this case*. I do not demean your personally held global concerns, but I'm a lawyer battling a tough case here, so let's save our clients first, then move on to the rest of the world.''

Professor Childhouse regarded the comment in the same manner as he had all the other comments and questions—with unperturbed patience—then gave his shoulders a slight shrug, and said, ''With all respect, Mr. Barrington, in my view the fates of your clients and the rest of the world are inexorably bound. It may be presumptuous of me to say it to you, sir, but when you and your firm enlisted in the battle, you became involved in the war.''

Rachel saw Kevin suppress a smile, while Barrington scowled, then recovered his conciliatory tone. ''Perhaps you are right, sir,'' said Barrington. ''But whether it be the battle or the war, let's fight it together, one day at a time.''

At that moment Rachel, glancing once more from Barrington to Kevin, decided there would be many more such battles before the real war began.

FIFTEEN

∎

Stefan, the President's Club head waiter, always knew what to bring each member of the Table of Three, and when to bring it: Perrier with extra lime for Adrian Fisher; vodka and tonic tall for Gardner White; and for Austin Barrington, a small brandy snifter of Glenlivet, neat. Approximately fifteen minutes after drinks were served, the movement of a single Barrington finger would signal Stefan to take lunch orders. There would be two more trips during the course of the luncheon: serving the appetizer, then later the entree, and that was it. A large pot of very hot coffee would be left with the entree, and the dishes would not be removed until the Table of Three's departure.

Serving the Table of Three was both stressful and rewarding. Stressful, because any violation of the rigid routine could result in a waiter's transfer to the kitchen; yet rewarding, for there was really little to do, and the Christmas check at the end of the year was three times larger than that for any other table. But on this early spring lunchtime in 1983, Stefan would somehow miss the subtle elevation of that imperial index finger—a summons for a never-before-requested second pot of coffee.

"Stefan," Barrington admonished the waiter, "I believe you've gone blind as a cave shrimp. Have you had your eyes examined lately?" Stefan blushed, humiliated in front of his peers and several members within hearing distance.

Barrington's mood was indeed foul that March day, for he was encountering rare and strenuous resistance at the Table. Things had gone well enough through the cocktail period and appetizer course. Gardner White had reported continuing good relations with the bank as a result of the North American case, then turned to a recommendation that S.P.&M. begin making plans to establish a branch office in Hong Kong to service the predicted increased commerce with Communist China by the mid and late 1980s. Other routine matters had been handled smoothly until, midway through the entree course, the subject had turned to "Project Salvation," a euphemism for the Barrington-Newkirk conspiracy that made discussion of the subject no less delicate.

Gardner White and Adrian Fisher had been predictably shocked five months earlier when Barrington had revealed the truth about Newkirk's bungling and the measures that he, Barrington, had been forced to take in order to rectify the problems Newkirk's error had created. Both had grudgingly accepted his explanation— that there was no possible alternative and that no appreciable additional damage had resulted to the three men to whom he and Newkirk had administered the "artificial supplement"—but only after an incendiary three-hour meeting in Barrington's office during which White had variously threatened to call the police, quietly resign from the partnership, and leap from the top of the Imperial Building. "Let's face it, Gardner," Fisher had said finally as he paced back and forth in Barrington's conference area, his limp never more pronounced, "what's done is done whether we like it or not, and, dammit, both the firm and our one hundred forty-seven clients are saved."

Thus was coined the phrase "Project Salvation," after which White, the color drained from his usually pink round face, angrily fell into line. After all, *he* hadn't even known about the deed till it was too late, and at this point, he rationalized, what could he do? Blow the whistle on his partners and spend his retirement years in a welfare hotel in Oakland? Hardly.

It had been risky, involving Fisher and particularly White, but Austin Barrington's unerring instincts told him that he would need the Table's unequivocal support before this thorny operation was concluded. He had failed, however, to anticipate the stone wall of resistance he faced today as he unfolded the next step in his plan to consolidate his power and "assure the success of Project Salvation."

He had led the Table into the subject with a brief and glowing description of Desmond Childhouse and his progress in trying to connect specific chemicals to specific injury.

"Have you detected any suspicion at all on the part of Professor Childhouse or any of our other experts?" asked White, lowering his voice.

"None whatsoever, so far at least," said Austin. "Fortunately, this environmental field appears to be a new and imprecise science."

"Thank God for mankind's small steps forward in this area at least," said Adrian Fisher, "but I am much more concerned about Kevin's suspicions than I am about some outsider's. Kevin will have to be as close to this as you are, Austin—coffee?"

"You're quite right, Adrian, and that's why," said Barrington, taking full advantage of the perfect opening, "I have decided we must bring Kevin into it."

Fisher stopped pouring coffee in midstream. White nearly choked on a piece of turbot. Neither spoke, but their incredulity was clear. This, of course, was no surprise to Barrington. From the very beginning he had known that he would eventually have to involve his moralistic younger partner and that the Table would resist it. He paused again, but seeing that his two fellow senior partners were too stunned to speak, continued, saying, "You already know that Kevin will play an essential part in this project; in fact, we were able to nail down these cases only by committing that Kevin would try them with me. I have tried to divide our major responsibilities so that he would handle the liability and causation issues and I would handle the extent-of-injury and money-damages aspects. I hoped by this division of labor to keep the medical records entirely to myself."

"And it has worked," said White with an unsuccessful effort at demonstrating calmness. "Has it not?"

"So far, yes. The problem now, however, is that the issues of causation and damages have intersected. Kevin must have access to the medical data to show that the injuries were caused by chemicals from the North American dump site. I assure you, gentlemen, that much as I dislike the notion myself—Kevin and I are having our share of disagreements—there is simply no alternative."

"Can't you just give him the revised records without telling him about Newkirk's bungling?" asked Fisher.

"Even if it worked, Adrian, it would solve only part of the problem. If we don't open up to Kevin, he'll be no help to me in keeping the defense experts and our own people in the dark."

Fisher poked at his untouched plate and, in a voice pinched with displeasure, surprised Barrington by saying, "You'll never convince me, Austin. Quite frankly, this is an ugly business altogether, and going outside the Table is just more than we bargained for. I'm opposed to it."

White irritably pushed his unfinished plate away and grabbed the coffeepot in a manner that demonstrated his concurrence with Fisher's view.

"Adrian. Gardner. Look, I can understand your views and your frustration. I like this even less than you can imagine. But if Project Salvation is going to succeed, we've got to match our resolve with an equal amount of flexibility. If we do, we'll save our firm and—incidentally—make more money individually than we ever dreamed of. But you *must* let me run with this problem."

Gardner White leaned back in his chair and rubbed his blood-red eyes, telltale badges of a tax lawyer only six weeks from April fifteenth. He looked ten years older than he had ten minutes before. A note of despair crept into his voice and he said, "I understand your situation, Austin, but I agree with Adrian. I would personally rather run the risk of one of the medical experts discovering our secret than to voluntarily expose it to an outsider."

"Gardner," said Barrington through lips tightening with impatience, "Kevin Stone is hardly an outsider. He's your partner; he's on our side. In fact, he will probably sit at this Table someday. Someday soon. Not only that, but he's co-lead counsel in the lawsuit as well. I can't conceal medical records from lead counsel, now, can I? Adrian. Please. Explain to Gardner how difficult that would be!"

White appeared to have stopped listening. He studied the backs of his hands, then flicked something off his cuff. "And remember, Gardner," Barrington continued, "it's not just our own experts, it's the defense experts as well. It's going to take both of our best efforts to control all of the people who will ultimately see the medical records. Kevin has got to be brought in!"

"He's got to be brought *down*," said White under his breath.

"What?"

"Nothing, Austin," said White, looking up suddenly, as if an alarm had gone off. "I was just thinking about what you were saying."

Barrington leaned closer to White, saying, "I'm trying to be patient, Gardner, because I know these principles are little understood in your end of the law. But you must trust our judgment on this litigation matter, and remember, I'm the one living with Project Salvation hour by hour, day by day. You may have to hear about it once or twice a week when I come to you with a specific problem, *but I'm on the firing line every damn minute every day, risking my neck trying to keep the firm solvent!*"

White glared back at Barrington and responded with equal

intensity. "Listen, Austin, you're a trial lawyer by choice, so don't expect me to give you either applause or sympathy. And I'll thank you not to patronize me because I'm a business lawyer. My judgment is as good as yours when it comes to issues that may well expose us to criminal charges."

Fisher touched White on the shoulder, saying, "Come on, Gard, Austin was just—"

White spun toward Fisher. " 'Come on,' yourself, Adrian! Look at what the glamour world of the trial courts has done for you. You've got a liver like a tire iron. Trial pressures almost destroyed both you and your marriage. Where's the good judgment in that? Well, you righteous litigators shoved this thing down my throat in the first place—now you can damn well pull it off without me. Maybe I'm just a drab little tax lawyer in your eyes, but as long as I'm at this table, my vote is no and it stays no and that's that!"

"Gardner, Gardner," said Fisher in a rapidly tiring voice, "I am every bit as concerned about this new development as you are, but I do believe you're being a bit overly sensitive and that we're all losing our focus here. Austin does not intend to demean business lawyers in general, and certainly not you in particular."

"Of course I don't," said Barrington, addressing Fisher as if to encourage his mediation efforts. "I am only urging Gardner to give some consideration to the fact that you and I are naturally more familiar with the difficulties involved in keeping Kevin in the dark."

"And there, Gardner," said Fisher, "I find myself reluctantly swinging toward Austin's view. I think we are just going to have to trust Kevin Stone. Believe me, it will be impossible for Austin to keep such an essential element of proof from his co-lead counsel. If we were personal injury lawyers, we might have anticipated this problem, not that it would have changed anything. Quite frankly," he added, turning to Barrington, "I don't even know how you'll be able to keep Rachel Cannon in the dark."

"Well, that's another bird I think we can kill with one stone," said Barrington, his pun wasted on the still-fuming tax partner. "Once Kevin understands what's going on and is fully co-opted, he'll be better able to control Rachel."

"How can Kevin control Rachel better than you can?" said Gardner White in a whining tone. "You're the senior trial partner, for God's sake."

Barrington's voice grew noticeably irritated as he said, "Let's just say that Kevin definitely has her attention."

"I have heard a rumor or two to that effect myself," remarked Fisher, "but it doesn't bother me as much as it seems to bother you, Austin."

"Adrian," said Barrington, more in disgust than anger, "sometimes you can be the world's biggest asshole."

"So I've been told."

White looked confused, but said nothing further as Barrington turned impatiently and began signaling in vain for Stefan. "I take nothing away from Kevin," he said, changing the subject as if everything had been resolved, "but when you and I were trying cases regularly, Adrian, things were a hell of a lot tougher. It's a different arena, now: computer support, swarms of paralegals digesting voluminous depositions taken by brilliant and overpaid associates; a damned different game than the lonely one we used to play."

Fisher nodded sadly. White yawned, but not from boredom. Barrington caught Stefan's eye.

"I'm reluctant to interrupt this moment of nostalgia," said White finally, "but I think that we should bring this matter to a conclusion one way or the other. To sum up my view, I think we've already taken too many risks and I'm opposed to taking any more. I vote no. This whole damn adventure was a mistake. We could have solved our financial problems by lowering our costs, cutting the fat out of our operation, getting more lean and mean."

"Oh, God, Gardner. You talk like we're running a mom and pop butcher shop here," said Barrington, despairing that he would ever understand how White's mind worked. "Anyway, there's no turning back now and—"

"Austin," interrupted White in a quiet but intense voice, "perhaps we should consider doing just that."

That did it. Barrington's eyes smoldered as they probed the tax lawyer's face. His pupils sharpened into coral specks and he seemed poised to assault the pudgy White physically. "Are you *serious*?" he asked, momentarily shifting his burning gaze to Fisher, who would not meet his stare, then looking back at White's averted eyes. "And just what would you like me to tell our clients, Mr. White? 'We regret any inconvenience our poisoning you may have caused but—' "

"Austin, please!" said White, recoiling at Barrington's explosive reaction. "I'm just suggesting that we . . . keep all avenues open."

"There *are* no 'avenues'!" said Barrington, maintaining his fierce hold on White's eyes. "There is only a one-way street, and dammit we are on it to the end! *Is that understood?*"

White, exhausted by the exchange, betrayed a tremor as he gulped down the dregs of his coffee and looked hopefully over at Fisher, but Fisher's perusal of the dessert menu told the tax lawyer that his mutiny had collapsed. He was alone.

Barrington broke the moment of silence that followed by addressing Adrian Fisher, his voice still tense. "Are you planning to order dessert today, Adrian?"

"No," said Fisher quietly, abandoning his shield, "and for the record, I'm changing my vote to yes. I share your concerns, Gardner. Sometimes I wake up at night and think I'm dreaming all this. God knows I'll be glad when it's over, but until it is, we just have to let Austin run with it."

"All right," said Gardner White, his hands clasped together, his shoulders thrust forward and rounded, his eyes fixed on the center of the table. "I've had my say, but promise me one thing, Austin."

"Let's hear it," said Barrington, disciplining his voice into a more conciliatory tone.

"I want your word that you have stopped administering the supplement. Using it with Weisberg—when he insisted upon it—was bad enough. Using it on the others was dangerous and, in my opinion, inexcusable. I pray it has not gone further. I must have your assurance that it has stopped, and that it will not be repeated."

Fisher and White both stared at the inscrutable face of their partner and awaited his response. Barrington stared down at his fresh cup of coffee, savoring the strong aroma as he said, "There were a few weak spots to be patched here and there, now that you mention it."

This time it was Adrian Fisher who nearly rose out of his chair, saying, "Jesus, Austin, I thought that our strongest theory of recovery now was the justified *fear* of getting cancer—cancerphobia—not proof that they had it! Why in God's name do you have to keep poisoning these people?"

"You are wrong, Adrian," said Barrington, gathering himself to quell yet another rebellion, "and also unfairly pejorative. The so-called 'cancerphobia' theory is a theory, without precedent at

the moment, which originated in the creative mind of your young
hero Kevin Stone. While it is undeniably logical, no California
court has held it to be the law. If the judge refuses to adopt it,
we've got to be ready to do it the hard way: by establishing
cause and effect—a specific chemical resulting in a specific
illness.''

"I thought—"

"Let me finish," said Barrington, blocking Fisher's attempt to
interrupt. "Even Stone's theory, if we are able to assert it,
requires at the very least the presence of alien chemicals in the
body, the existence of a so-called 'subclinical biologic injury' to
convince the judge that the plaintiffs' claimed fear is genuine,
serious, and reasonable." Barrington paused to sip his coffee,
though he was clearly not finished. "I have done nothing more
than provide that. The modest amount of chemicals I have
introduced into the bodies of these plaintiffs will not in any way
hasten the development of serious pathology. It will simply
provide their cases with the credibility they need to obtain unprecedented monetary verdicts and thus be able to live out their
lives in relative affluence—which, by the way, you two will do
as well.''

Barrington shot out the last words with a relentless, withering
glance at the fatigued tax lawyer, who, after an expectant silence, responded in a barely audible monotone: "I'll continue to
do my part, Austin, but that doesn't mean I like it. And, while
parliamentary issues are hardly appropriate now, I want to record
my no vote to your inclusion of Kevin. I also repeat my request
for your commitment that no more A.S. will be used.''

"Austin," said Fisher in a pleading tone. "Haven't we got
enough?''

"All right," said the senior partner with a gentleness he did
not feel. *Why wouldn't they just let him handle it?* "If it will
make Gardner feel better, he has my word on it.''

"Satisfactory, Gardner?" asked Fisher.

"Well, all right. Sure. What else can I say? I trust you will
give us Kevin's reaction, Austin. Do you have a backup plan in
the event he threatens to blow the whistle?''

Barrington dabbed at his mouth with his handkerchief, folded
it neatly, and slid his chair back to signal the end of the meeting.
"Our gifted superstar may be a bit virtuous, but he's not immune
to the call of Mammon," he said. "No backup plan is required,
I assure you. I can, and will, control Kevin Stone.''

SIXTEEN

■

"How's our damage case looking, Rachel?" asked Kevin, entering Rachel's unusually cluttered office later the same afternoon. Books, both legal and scientific, were stacked along the walls. Her desk was piled high with research memos, copies of pleadings from other cases currently in litigation, Lexis printouts of newspaper and magazine reports. Notes and paper everywhere. "That *is* you behind that wall of paper, is it not?"

"It is indeed," said Rachel, "and from behind the great wall I bring good news and bad news on the damage issues. We're now solid on the history of our clients' exposure to the chemicals and we've got Childhouse's animal studies tied in by computer to the North American chemicals found in the well water. The so-called 'dose response' in animals is clearly correlatable."

"Ah, so it's you behind there, Professor Childhouse! Disguising yourself as the lovely Rachel Cannon. But your obscure diction gives you away!"

Rachel laughed. "Get with the vernacular, counselor," she said, in a way that gracefully finessed Kevin's tacit invitation to be less than businesslike. She was making progress and wanted to hold her ground.

"Dose response," she continued, "simply means you lace a mouse's diet with dioxin and his drinking days are over—no more liver. That's the good news—not for the mouse, of course—but the bad news is the difficulty in extrapolating this to humans and tying specific toxic chemicals to specific disorders. Even Childhouse thinks that we're going to run into big trouble here."

"It doesn't sound encouraging. By the way, when do I meet our other expert—the groundwater consultant?"

"Franks. Saul Franks," answered Rachel. "Whenever you want. I had my first meeting with him yesterday, and he's prepared to draw and quarter the city of Lileton, its department of health, and all its councilmen together with their spouses, children, and pets.''

"Has he got the balls to stay in the building if it catches fire?''

"What do you mean?'' Rachel asked.

"Can he take the heat? Austin has heard rumors to the effect that a Mafia family out of Las Vegas owns North American Chemical.''

"That's funny," said Rachel. "Saul told me the same thing. He told me that a guy named Joe Lucca runs North American *and* the city of Lileton.''

"So he knows what he might be getting into, I guess. Blowing the whistle on the local scene could make him a prime target for Lucca's mafiosi cousins if he starts cutting too close to the bone.''

"He knows the whole story, and he's a tough guy. He'll hold up.''

"Sounds good,'' said Kevin, starting for the door.

Rachel returned to her work, then looked up after a few seconds to see Kevin still standing there, staring at her.

"There is something else I need to talk to you about,'' he said quietly, drawing the door closed behind him.

"Yes?''

"I want to talk about us.''

Rachel was not surprised. For weeks now they had lived with the unspoken agreement that their romance had to be placed on hold. But love, she knew, demanded care and feeding; it must grow or die. Yet the fact that Kevin seemed about to confront their dilemma head-on sent a wave of apprehension racing through her. *I can't think about this now,* insisted a voice in the back of her head. Yes, their relationship was far from ideal, but it was all she could manage right now, and despite her own mixed feelings, she prayed that Kevin would not say anything to disrupt the delicate balance. Every ounce of her rational being told her she had to maintain control, not lose it. Not now.

"Yes?'' she said.

Kevin looked suddenly youthful, almost awkward to Rachel as he thrust his hands deep into his pockets and groped for the words he wanted. "Well, it would help if you put your pen down for a second—''

Kevin turned suddenly as Stu Wallach came flying unannounced through the door. "Rachel! I've got something here . . . oh! Sorry, Kevin, I didn't see you.''

"It's okay, Stu," said Kevin somewhat irritably. "I've been wanting to talk to you anyway. Can't you move your coders faster? The defendants' production and inspection records are coming in faster than we can get them computerized by trial category."

"I'll have a schedule ready for your approval by Monday morning, Kevin," Wallach said, apparently unperturbed. Part of his job as head of the Computer Litigation Support Department was to suffer the anxiety manifestations of trial lawyers. A deep inner security spared him from personalizing these barbs: He was the best at what he did, and it was evident that he knew it.

"Okay, Stu." Kevin mustered a conciliatory smile. "Thanks," he added, and slumped heavily into the client chair beside Rachel's desk as Wallach closed the door behind him.

"Are you sure you feel like talking?" she asked. "You look exhausted."

"I'm whipped," said Kevin. "The New York case we worked on comes to trial next month, and I'm beginning to feel like a one-armed juggler with six plates in the air."

"You look like you could use some sleep."

"I'm trying to quit," said Kevin, managing a smile. "I'll be fine, and I do want to talk." Kevin closed Rachel's office door again, then added, "It's not just sleep I need, Rachel."

There was no mistaking the hunger in his voice. Rachel flushed as the heat of crossed emotions rose within her: wanting, fearing, resenting. Above all, just the fact that she had misgivings convinced her that the time was not right. She walked toward the door to reopen it, but Kevin took her gently by the hand and turned her toward him. "It's you I need, Rachel. You, you—"

They kissed long and deeply before Rachel forced herself back to reality: They were in the Imperial Building—the law offices of Stafford, Parrish, and MacAllister—not the Helmsley Palace, not Nantucket. She reluctantly pulled away. "Kevin," she said, "I—we—can't do this. Barrington . . . anybody could walk through that door at any moment."

"I know. You're right, of course, but . . . please. Just listen to me. I'll stay for just a minute."

Rachel's face softened into a smile, and she returned to her seat behind the desk. "You can stay, but on your side of the desk."

Kevin seated himself, looking to Rachel like a man struggling to solve a puzzle with too many moving parts. Rachel wondered how she had allowed herself to fall in love with him. Could she, *should* she have used her head in New York? What had she been thinking about that night? After New York she had tried a new date or two and concluded she'd just as soon be working or watching a movie with a girlfriend. So, with plenty to occupy her time, she had drifted into a state of passive celibacy. Reason had won over passion—with occasional lapses here and there. That's how she preferred to characterize it, at least, avoiding more harsh self-portrayals, such as faithful-mistress-to-an-unfaithful-husband. At year's end, when she was either elected to partnership or ejected to the streets, the matter with Kevin would also be resolved. Until then she would endure the loneliness and live with her uncertainty.

Now, as she examined Kevin's tense face, it struck her for the first time that his love for her had become yet another pressure in his life, a life already stressed to the maximum; that he was hurting even more than she.

Kevin leaned forward across the desk, touching her lightly on the back of her hand, where his eyes remained fixed as he spoke. "I have something I must tell you, even though I know it's the worst of all possible times. The only thing worse than telling you would be to keep holding it in, something I just can't do.

"From the moment we left Nantucket, I've not gone a day without wanting you. I think now that I must have loved you long before New York. Since then, with the exception of a few relapses, I think I've played my role and kept my distance pretty well. But you've played your role so well I'm beginning to fear it's not a role for you at all." Saying this, Kevin took a deep breath and paused.

"I'm a good actress too," Rachel said.

Kevin exhaled and smiled with evident relief. He took her hand in his and said, "Then I must tell you one more thing. I know now that Denise and I will be separating. . . ." Rachel involuntarily withdrew her hand. "Let me finish, Rachel. I'm not asking anything of you; I just wanted you to know. What happens after I do is up to you. Okay?"

"I don't know what to say, Kevin. Of course I'm pleased, yet also sorry about the pain ahead for you. I know how hard it will be on you and the kids." Rachel stopped, got up, and slowly paced around behind where Kevin was seated. She felt cautious, yet intoxicated with new hope. What she really wanted to say was *When, darling? How soon?* She also wanted to touch him, but something held her back. She chose to keep it light. "I hope it all works out. Meanwhile, I'll not be going anywhere—I understand there's some work to be done around here."

Kevin smiled and the stress melted from his face. "You're telling Noah about the flood," he said.

"Kevin," said Rachel, turning serious, "promise me you'll take better care of yourself. I've never seen you look so tired."

"You're right. I think it's all catching up with me. I may be a little younger than most burnouts, but I had tried more than fifty cases by the time I was in my early thirties. In the last ten years the cases have gotten bigger and the pressure to keep winning has grown stronger. I'm even beginning to look forward to getting kicked upstairs into administration—just like Adrian Fisher did, then Barrington after him. This trial business, darling, the stress is so . . . relentless: high-pressure confrontation all day, preparation all night—after a while, well, I'm getting tired, Rachel. Sometimes I . . ."

Rachel saw that Kevin's eyes were moistening with tears. She wanted to hold him in her arms, to console him, as he continued, choking out the words: "For years, all I thought about was winning, being the best. Now that I've done it all, I'm beginning to feel the pain that must have been there all the time. Now it's like being a stunt diver, diving into a shallow pool, only after each case I win they raise the diving platform a little higher."

"I understand, Kevin," said Rachel. She did understand that Kevin was reaching out to her to bring some peace and stability to his chaotic world. Another quiet warning sound went off somewhere deep inside. She took Kevin's hands in hers. "Kevin. Just know that I'm here and that when the time comes, we'll both know what to do. Meanwhile, there's so much to be done . . ."

"All right," said Kevin, nodding slowly, then rising to leave. "But the time will come soon. I promise you."

She walked him to the door, but instead of opening it, Kevin leaned his weight against it, then took her in his arms and kissed her deeply. Hands still at her side, she returned his kiss and was astonished at the immediate exchange of passionate heat between them. A sense of exquisite addiction seized her. She felt her legs go weak, and offered no resistance as Kevin reached up, opened the top button of her blouse, and caressed her bare breasts, his mouth never leaving hers. Somewhere in the distance, she heard a sound—like a telephone ringing—her telephone. Ignoring it, she answered Kevin's embrace instead.

Later that day, Gardner White impatiently rocked back and forth on his heels at the front door of Adrian Fisher's Piedmont mansion. He jammed the doorbell a second time, suddenly resenting the fact that he was being observed on a closed circuit TV scanner.

"*Gard-ner,*" came the musical voice from behind the closed door even before it was opened, and the pudgy tax lawyer found himself in the warm, if somewhat awkward, embrace of Florence Fisher, a full eight inches taller than he. "Where have you been, you brilliant little devil, and what on earth brings you all the way across the Bay?"

Florence Fisher's blanket of goodwill smothered White's best intentions to remain stern. "Flo, my dear, you are a sight for sore eyes. The old guy must be treating you all right after all."

"Oh, when I see him he does, Gardner. Actually, I guess I've been a bit of a bear myself lately. He has probably told you that I've launched one of my more vicious campaigns to persuade him to retire before they have to cart the old bastard out of S.P.&M. in a wooden box." The last words were incongruently followed by a peal of her raucous laughter as she removed White's topcoat and hung it in an entryway closet. "I know, Gardner, you don't have to say it. He would wither up in six months without that snake pit you fellows call home." Florence Fisher then turned serious, bending her six-foot, large-boned frame downward so that her head was almost on a level with White's. "It's just that I don't think he really enjoys it anymore. He's been more edgy during the last few months than I can ever remember, even worse than when he finally went off the demon rum; and you know how bad that was."

"I haven't been a cuddly pussycat lately myself, Flo," said White. "Stress seems to be in the air this year."

"It's going around, all right," she agreed. "If you hear of a cure, let me know. Meanwhile, the grand master is expecting you. He's waiting at the pool bar. I know he'll be happy to have company. You know the way; I'll join you later."

Gardner walked swiftly through the living room and down the hallway that led to the pool and tennis court area. Darkness was closing in on the Fishers' private forest as Adrian Fisher rose to greet his partner.

"Hi, Gard. You must have a powerful thirst having traversed the mighty San Francisco Bay. What can I get you?"

"I'll have Perrier, just like you."

"Sounds serious, but then I gathered that much from the tone of your voice on the telephone."

"I'll get right to the point, Adrian," the younger partner said, before even sitting down. "I know it's bad form, at least unusual, to caucus privately like this, but this is not a usual situation. No matter how many times I try to understand Austin's decision to reveal Project Salvation to Kevin Stone, it comes out bad. Frankly, I'm here to lobby you to change your vote."

"I know your concern, Gardner, and I share it," said Fisher in a conciliatory tone, offering the drink to White. "But Austin's right when he says we're in it now for better or for worse, and that we have no choice but to let him run with the ball. I thought we pretty much settled that at lunch today."

Gardner White twirled the ice in the glass he had half emptied already, regretting his gesture in foregoing a real drink, and already beginning to see he was wasting his time. "I know how you feel about Austin, Adrian, but I feel I have a right to speak my mind. He's wrong on this one. He could make Project Salvation work without bringing Kevin in if he really wanted to."

"I don't agree with you," said Fisher, throwing his head from side to side with the stubborn authority that is the exclusive perquisite of old age. "Don't you think Austin would have avoided this if he thought he could?"

"Adrian," said White, rising to his feet, "I just *told* you what I think. You must see that Austin is more envious of Kevin than either of us has realized. I know I sound like a street-corner psychiatrist, but my personal view is that down deep he actually hates Kevin."

"Why, for God's sake?"

"Because Kevin has everything that Austin no longer has: uninterrupted victories, high national profile, high energy, creativity, and most of all, youth. Throw in his undeniable good looks and the fact that Rachel Cannon is probably nuts about him, and you've got a guy just too goddamn perfect for his own good."

Fisher clipped a long cigar and thrust it into his mouth. "Just what are you getting at, Gardner? And what the hell has Rachel Cannon got to do with any of this?"

"Come on, Adrian. You may be old, but you're not that old. There's not a partner in the firm that hasn't had a crush on her at one time or another, and I include our friend Austin. I'm not suggesting anything serious, only that she's part of the piece."

"You'll have to be more specific. What piece?"

"I am suggesting that Austin can tolerate Kevin only if he can find a flaw in him. If he can't find one, he'll create one by co-opting him in our conspiracy, then controlling him as he said he would."

Adrian exploded with laughter. "Christ, Gardner, I always knew you should have been a psychiatrist instead of a lawyer. Sure, Austin envies Kevin. Who doesn't? And sure, Austin's a controller. But to say that his main motivation in opening up to Kevin is to despoil his morality . . . Oh, come on, Gard, have a real drink. It won't bother me. Hardly anything does anymore."

Gardner White said nothing for a moment. *I've lost it,* he thought. *I'm all alone in this cursed nightmare.* "There's just no end to it," he muttered under his breath.

"What?" asked Fisher irritably. "Speak up, Gardner. There's no end to *what*?"

White rose to his feet and looked down at his partner. "Nothing, Adrian. Sorry. If you change your mind, call me tonight before it's too late. I can't win this one alone."

"You're worrying way too much, Gard, but I bet you won't shy away from the pay table when those big verdicts start rolling in. Eh? Come on now, cheer up. By next spring we will have tried the first fifteen plaintiffs and have settled over one hundred more. Then this whole mess will be forgotten. That'll put the lie to Orwell's bleak forecast for 1984, eh? The firm will be alive and well again, and so will you and I, Gardner. And we'll both be richer than God."

Hands crammed into his suit-coat pockets, White stared at the seated Fisher, and said, "We'll see," and left through a garden gate.

Florence Fisher entered the patio a few minutes later bearing a tray of appetizers. "Where's Gardner?" she demanded. "I have his very favorite red caviar and blinis."

"He had to get back to the office for a dinner meeting," said Fisher offhandedly, relighting his cigar. "He said to tell you good-bye."

Florence Fisher pulled a chair up to her husband. She took one of his huge hands in hers and said, "Gardner's upset about something, and so are you. No one would know, but I know. And it's not because he left without his overcoat. Now tell me.''

"There's nothing to tell. Go on in and cook us some dinner. Maybe I'll take you to an early movie.''

"You only offer to do that when you're trying to distract me. Why can't we talk about this? You've not been yourself for the last six months. Now Gardner shows up looking like death warmed over. What in the hell is going on over there at the office?''

"My darling Florence,'' said Fisher, touching her curly gray hair, "you know I never discuss office matters at home, but I will tell you this: We are encountering some difficult financial tensions, all of which we shall overcome in due course.''

"And then,'' said Florence, preparing a blini for her husband, "there will be something else. You are past retirement age, Adrian Fisher. I need not remind you that neither of us is getting any younger. Let's get out while we can still enjoy ourselves. If you insist on having something to do, we can build matchstick castles, buy a hardware store in Cupertino, *anything* but what you are doing.''

"What,'' said Fisher, staring across the pool toward the darkened and unused tennis court, "do you think is on at the movies tonight?''

SEVENTEEN

■

"So tell me the latest dirt from the Eagle's Nest,'' said Beth Abelson, settling in her chair across from Rachel at a restaurant near the Alameda County Courthouse.

"Boring, all boring,'' said Rachel, twisting out of the coat and scarf she had worn for protection against the chilly winds that had nearly blown her car off the San Francisco Bay Bridge as she crossed into Oakland. "But I came to get information, not give it. Tell me about the baby! And your new job.'' Rachel found it delightful and relaxing to be in the company of someone who knew—and cared—about her, but who didn't expect anything beyond the unselfish honesty of friendship in return.

"Eliza's great—almost three months old now. As for the job, well," she added wistfully, "it's not the major leagues, but it's a living." Beth was now a deputy district attorney. "Actually, I just won a complex fraud case and sent a pair of white-collar bozos 'up the river'—as we law and order folks like to say."

"Congratulations! Actually, I read about it last week. The headline, as I recall, was quite classy: 'Deputy D.A. Demolishes Dastardly Duo.' "

Beth seemed to enjoy the laugh at her own expense. "It was bad, but not that bad. The main thing is that it's great to be back in court again. I tried seven cases in four months before my maternity leave and now I've got a first-degree murder going out next Monday."

"Beth, that's wonderful!" It was hard to believe that Beth had been gone from S.P.&M. for almost a year. Rachel studied her friend's face and wondered if Beth had always looked so tired, so much older than her thirty years. Had childbirth sapped her vibrancy? Had Barrington? Breaking into a new job? Her face was pretty when she took care of it, but she didn't seem to bother any more, and her skin looked more drawn than Rachel remembered. Deep crow's-feet extended outward from her intelligent brown eyes. Beth's ongoing battle with the calorie seemed well under control, but her shoulder-length, thick umber hair looked lifeless and disheveled—the wind perhaps—and her ready smile now turned down at the corners of her wide mouth, hinting at a resigned irony. But beneath, Rachel could see that the old spark persisted. "Still," Beth continued, "my heart remains with complex business litigation. I guess that's why I enjoyed this embezzlement case so much; I got to tear apart the defense's expert CPA. Speaking of expert witnesses, how is the North American Chemical case shaping up? I hear there's a Mafia angle."

Rachel updated her friend on the case, including the rumor that a Mafia family out of Las Vegas owned most of the stock of North American Chemical. Beth confirmed the rumor and added some information of her own, concluding that by virtue of the Mafia's controlling interest in the chemical company—which in turn was providing most of the jobs and therefore the tax base of Lileton—they also controlled the Lileton city council and police force. She also had heard that company president Joseph Lucca was fronting for a mob family whose *capo mafioso*—Carmine Romano—was trying to go legit, Frank Costello style.

"But why chemicals?" asked Rachel. "I've heard of casinos, pool halls, racetracks, even hotels. But a chemical company?"

Beth leaned forward and said, "One of our senior prosecutors is informally helping a San Francisco police lieutenant named Dan Conti put together a possible RICO—racketeering act—case against the Romano family. Conti claims that one of the biggest cost factors in the chemical industry these days—among reputable companies anyway—is waste disposal. If you don't care how sloppily it's done, and you're willing to take the risk that you may get caught—a small risk given the puny state and federal enforcement staffs—the profit margin soars. Quantum bucks!"

"Particularly," Rachel said, nodding her head slowly, "if you hedge your bets by controlling the city health department and its enforcement powers—and, all humility aside, it might have worked, except for our lawsuit."

A shadow of concern crossed Beth's face. "Don't take them lightly, Rachel. I could tell you stories you wouldn't believe."

"Please, not during lunch. And enough shop talk. What's it like at home with Eliza?"

"That's a different story," said Beth. "Let's just say that with a new baby and a new job, I could definitely use a wife."

Rachel laughed, and before long the friends dropped the courtroom topics and turned to the men in each other's life. Beth's domestic life had not gone well since leaving S.P.&M.; she had recently discovered that her husband was having an affair.

"Do you still love him?" Rachel asked after hearing the lurid details.

Beth spread her hands, palms up, and looked hopelessly puzzled, as if the question had never occurred to her. "My God, Rachel," she said at last, her eyes moist, "I haven't the slightest fucking idea." With that, both women broke out laughing, so hard that heads turned around four booths away.

"What about you, Rachel?" said Beth, removing a tissue from her purse. "Open up! Can you top getting fired, a new baby, and an old husband with a new girlfriend all in one year?"

"I certainly hope not," said Rachel. For a moment, she felt an urgent need to confide in Beth, in someone, but she quickly cast the thought aside and steered the conversation back to Beth, saying, "For what it's worth, I'm really glad you're back trying cases. You are incredibly good, you know." And she was—

better than any of the men Rachel had worked with at S.P.&M. Besides Kevin, of course.

"I'm feeling good about myself right now, Rachel, although it scares me that my work has become so important to me: it's really all I have right now—other than Eliza, of course. I guess I needed this verdict to remind me that I really *am* good. Those bastards across the water did all they could to convince me that I wasn't. But it sounds like they have come to wisdom, albeit late, and are ready to make an exception for you."

Rachel slowly nodded her head and paused as the waiter delivered their check. "It seems to meet their present purposes, but a lot can happen in the next few months. My performance on the North American case will decide it."

"But they can't *possibly* mean to throw you out," said Beth. "It looks to me like you've got it wired—unless, of course, you get drunk at the Christmas party and get caught messing around with a partner or something."

Beth's attempt at humor fell flat. Rachel could not mask her discomfort. Beth seized her friend's hands. "Oh, Rachel, I'm sorry. I've struck a nerve, haven't I? It must be Kevin. Is it? I knew there was some reason you wouldn't talk about the New York trip! Don't worry. You know you can trust me to keep my mouth shut. And God knows every one of us had a mad crush on him at one time or another."

"It's gone beyond a crush," said Rachel, returning Beth's warm grasp with a bittersweet smile. Then: "Oh, God, I guess I've got to tell somebody . . . I love him, Beth."

Beth put her cup down, her eyes glistening with interest. "And Kevin? Does he know? How does *he* feel?"

Rachel picked up the check and her handbag, suddenly determined to end the conversation. Yet there was unabated joy in her face as she finally replied, "We love each other, Beth."

Beth's own face brightened with excitement. "My God, Rachel, you're serious. Have you . . . done anything about it?"

Rachel fished a bill from her wallet to cover the check, then smiled at her friend, saying, "I must object to that question, counselor, on the grounds that it's overly broad, vague, and ambiguous. Also gauche and beneath you."

"Objection sustained," said Beth, laughing, much to Rachel's relief.

"I have to run," she said, then, "To tell you the truth, I don't feel comfortable talking about it yet. Besides, I have to attend a meeting with our chief expert witness in thirty minutes."

"Oh, well. All right, I guess," said Beth, finishing her coffee while Rachel paid the check, "but only because I have to be in court myself. Remember, I'm coming over next week, and I expect a full report. Meanwhile, I don't have to tell you—of all people—that you couldn't have picked a worse year in your professional career to start consorting with a partner. You've got to be careful, babe, really careful. If they even begin to suspect—"

"Then I'll be back here in Oakland where I started, working for you this time," said Rachel with an ironic smile.

But Beth wasn't smiling. "I'm not kidding, Rachel, and you know it. The bastards are looking for an excuse, and once they get it, they'll get you."

Austin Barrington was in no mood for pleasantries. "I have a police commission meeting at three o'clock," he said, staring pointedly at Desmond Childhouse, "so let's get right to the point: From what you have seen so far, are you able to say whether these plaintiffs' injuries are the result of North American's toxic by-products?"

"At the risk of sounding like a lawyer," said Childhouse, "the answer is yes and no. If you look at these charts prepared by Saul Franks, I can explain where we're going."

Childhouse walked to an easel, upon which were several three-by-four-foot mounted charts. "This first graphic represents a cutaway view of the earth's surface out at North American and shows the downward movement of water and waste material from a toxic dump into the aquifer below. It also shows how chemical wastes tend to run horizontally along the surface, then migrate downward in the form of leachate into the underground aquifer."

The professor deftly removed the chart from the easel, revealing another exhibit that depicted the area from above, showing the position of the water well in reference to the dump site, the plant, and the underlying aquifer.

"What I *can* say with reasonable certainty is that the samples of the dioxin, benzene, et cetera, from North American's dump site are qualitatively identical with samples from the aquifer and the water well that supplied your clients' drinking water. I can also say that the various illnesses and dysfunctions suffered by the one hundred and twelve plaintiffs I have tested—cirrhosis of the liver, central nervous system disorders, kidney lesions, and so forth—are medically consistent with exposure to the various chemicals found in the dump site, the underlying aquifer, and the victims' drinking water.'' Childhouse went on to explain the studies he had done to come to those findings, as Barrington, Rachel, and Jeffrey Johnstone listened.

"Finally," Childhouse said, "I will testify that a causal connection is further corroborated by blood serum and fatty tissue test findings, which reveal the presence of many of these identical chemicals in several plaintiffs who were tested by your Dr. Newkirk.''

"Before we pop the champagne corks, Desmond," said Kevin, "you apparently *cannot* say that—''

"No, Kevin," said Childhouse, ruefully shaking his head, "I know what you're going to say. I cannot directly tie specific chemicals to each specific plaintiff's specific injury or illness. You will have to do that with a combination of overwhelming circumstantial evidence and your undeniably silver tongue.''

"Let's not forget cancerphobia," said Kevin.

Barrington laughed disdainfully, then addressed the expert witness: "Please ignore my younger partner's active imagination, Desmond. I've been trying to convince Kevin lately that we should forget cancerphobia. I concede it looked good at first, but we've found no law to support the theory and meanwhile we've developed, as you just put it, 'overwhelming circumstantial evidence' to make our traditional causation case. So let's forget your shotgun approach, Kevin; we're going to have to get these verdicts the old-fashioned way; we're going to have to *earn* them.''

No smiles greeted Austin Barrington's attempt at humor as he turned back to the trial team. Rachel glanced at Kevin and saw ultramarine ice instead of his soft blue eyes.

"Austin and I have differing views on trial strategy, Desmond," Kevin said finally in a tone sufficiently casual to conceal his annoyance from everyone but Rachel, "but it would be inappropriate to burden you with our internecine spats.'' Austin acknowledged the reproof by arching a prominent eyebrow. It suddenly hit Rachel that she was seeing the tip of a large and dangerous iceberg. What was going on between these two?

But Barrington had resumed talking to Childhouse as though the antagonistic exchange had not occurred. "We're used to tough challenges," he said, "and we're going to pull this one off. When we do, I predict a total damage award of over four hundred million dollars. I tell you this so you won't hold back on any testing needed to make the correlations, no matter the cost. Is that clear?''

As Barrington lectured his witness, Rachel noticed that Kevin continued to examine the last diagram, apparently troubled by something other than Barrington's stubborn adherence to ''the old-fashioned way.'' He has reason to worry, thought Rachel. He knows that it's ultimately up to him not only to make this turkey fly but to lay golden eggs as well. Her commiserative thoughts were broken as Kevin leapt to his feet, grabbed a marking pen and with short, slashing motions began drawing arrows in the pale blue area depicting the underground aquifer on Childhouse's chart.

''What in the hell are you doing, Kevin?'' exclaimed Barrington.

Ignoring him, Kevin addressed Childhouse: ''Isn't this building over here a semiconductor plant?'' He indicated a small square approximately two thousand yards south of the North American water well.

''Yes,'' replied Childhouse. ''That is the Lawton-Pacific semiconductor plant.''

''And isn't it a fact that Lawton-Pacific generates many of the same chemical waste products also generated by North American?'' Rachel had rarely seen Kevin so intense. He was not just testing the professor's forensic skills under pressure this time; he was testing the very foundation of their case.

''Yes, indeed they do.'' The professor's voice remained calm, though he absently reached into his pocket for his pipe and began chewing on the stem.

Kevin pointed to the small arrows he had drawn in the area of the underground aquifer. Each new arrow pointed toward—fed into—the incriminated North American water well, but not from the direction of North American's own dump site; rather from the south—*from the Lawton-Pacific Semiconductor Company*. ''Isn't it just as likely that the chemicals—or some of them— which have injured our plaintiffs came from Lawton-Pacific or even perhaps some other plant?'' The professor chewed on his pipe in silence as Kevin continued. ''Proving causation is tough enough, Desmond, but if North American is going to be able to point the finger at another possible source for the toxins, it's going to be even tougher. Lawton-Pacific and God knows how many other plants within the area are all located above, and seem to be connected to the same damn underground aquifer that feeds the North American water well!''

''Jesus,'' Jeffrey whispered. Rachel glanced at a suddenly pale Austin Barrington.

Professor Childhouse carefully balanced his pipe on the table, removed his thick round glasses, and rubbed his eyes. As the silence spread tension throughout the room, the expert witness again approached the chart. ''Very observant, Mr. Stone,'' he said. ''I took the precaution, however, of checking that very issue by having Saul Franks test the aquifer at various points on either side of the North American well. Look. See these small green dots? They represent these secondary test drills, which showed that the density of the contaminants found in the well rapidly diminished as his test drills moved farther southward— away from the North American dump site. Conversely, they grew stronger as they moved *toward* the North American dump site. This, combined with the fact that not a single chemical was found in the North American well that was not also found in abundance at the North American dump site, will permit me to testify with sufficient certainty that the chemicals we found— both in the well and the victims themselves—indeed came from the North American dump, none other.''

All eyes anxiously turned toward Kevin, the suspense building as he considered Childhouse's response. Then slowly, like a chilled glass fracturing under heat, a broad smile broke across Kevin's face. Finally, he looked at Barrington and said, ''We may get the bastards yet.''

After Childhouse had been excused, Barrington asked Kevin for his estimate of time to trial.

''We've been filed about eight months now, and based on the last time I checked the jury calendar, I would guess about another year and a half.''

''Sir?'' interrupted Jeff quietly.

''Maybe longer.''

''Sir?'' said Jeff again.

''Yes? What is it, Jeff?''

''The California Code of Civil Procedure permits plaintiffs over seventy years of age to have their cases advanced for trial.''

The group sat staring at the young associate for a few seconds before Rachel leapt from her chair and grabbed a copy of the code from Barrington's bookcase. Indeed, it was just as he had said: Section 36(a). "Good point, Jeff," she said. "But wouldn't the section provide the same relief for all our other plaintiffs as well if we can show that good cause exists? If so, why not select fifteen or twenty from our total client group—at least half of whom are in the senior category and the other half potentially terminal—and go for an early trial for this entire subgroup on a motion to advance?"

Rachel looked at Kevin, read encouragement, and continued. "The other advantage is that we could bring our biggest potential damage cases up to bat first so that their large verdicts would provide precedential value for settlements in the other cases."

"I like it," said Barrington instantly, nodding at Rachel appreciatively. "Anything wrong with that, Kevin?"

"Nothing, other than that you and I didn't think of it first," said Kevin, smiling. "You two got any more rabbits in your hats?"

"Well, sir, I might have a wild hare or two," Jeffrey said.

"Shoot."

With gathering confidence Jeffrey outlined his idea for several recently uncovered "long-shot" theories: a private nuisance allegation to eliminate North American's "reasonable care" defense and to justify punitive damages; even an assault and battery theory to avoid the necessity for proving an injury.

Barrington regarded the young associate with new respect, then turned to Rachel. "What do you say, Rachel?"

"I see no downside to amending our complaint to include these theories, Austin," she affirmed, mindful that the "ultra-hazardous activity" doctrine—which holds defendants who conduct certain dangerous functions to a standard of strict liability no matter how much care they exercised—had yet to be applied to a toxic chemical case in California. "Nuisance and battery are long shots to be sure," she added, "but they just might overcome North American's primary defense: their claim that they exercised reasonable care, given the level of scientific knowledge at the time most of their disposal work was accomplished."

Barrington looked at Kevin, who gave an almost imperceptible nod of affirmation. "Draft the amendment," said Barrington. "We'll take a look at it."

"What I think is evolving, here," said Rachel, now addressing both Barrington and Kevin, "is a broad approach that will attempt, first, to show that North American failed to exercise reasonable care, and second, to establish that North American's chemicals caused our clients' specific injuries. As there is neither settled law on the first problem nor medical certainty on the second, it seems to me we must be as aggressively creative as possible.''

Rachel glanced at Kevin, expecting to see the admiration or even the professional respect she had hoped for; but instead he met her eyes with an undeniable look of love. She found herself blushing and wondered, as she always did, if their feelings in these meetings were as transparent as she feared. But if Barrington noticed, he concealed it well as he smiled broadly and said, ''It would appear that we will not lack for creativity. Good job, both of you. Now let's go set a record.''

That evening, Kevin and Denise Stone were finishing their monthly obligatory dinner at the Barringtons' Hillsborough home. Kevin had considered phoning regrets but thought better of it, recalling Barrington's rather pointed remarks following the afternoon meeting concerning Rachel's vitality and how well the two of them seemed to be working together. He was probably being overly sensitive, Kevin realized, but this was no time to encourage any suspicions.

Denise lived up to his worst expectations by consuming more than her share of wine during the meal and dominating the table talk with boorish complaints and mindless chatter. By the time dessert was served, her taunting of Kevin had become so pointed that Barrington had signaled Catherine to lure her into the kitchen while the men repaired to the living room to pour brandies.

''That meal was delicious, Catherine!'' said Denise, her mood instantly improved. ''How and where did you find your new cook?'' she whispered as if importuning a Russian ambassador to defect to the West.

''How, my dear? With great difficulty and care. Where? I'll *never* tell. Isn't she *marvelous*?'' The stout woman was glowing with pride. ''I don't know how I ever managed without her.''

Catherine was leading the way into the living room with coffee, Brie, and Carr's wafers. ''Let's not have any more office talk now, gentlemen,'' she said, putting the tray down with a clunk to emphasize her admonition.

''Well, what would *you* like to talk about, Catherine?'' Barrington's tone suggested a lack of optimism concerning the quality of her response.

''Well, let's see now,'' she said, everlastingly oblivious to her husband's subtle ridicule. "Isn't that funny. I can't think of a thing. What would *you* like to talk about, Denise?"

Denise's sour mood had sweetened somewhat as she'd chatted with Catherine in the kitchen. Now, it returned as she snatched up her brandy and passed the ball along. "I don't know, Catherine. What would you like to talk about, Kevin?"

Kevin disapproved of Denise's tacit collaboration with Barrington in taunting Catherine, a decent but naive soul, but responded with apparent good humor. "Oh, well, if you insist, my first choice would be the Forty-niners' Superbowl victory last month. Okay?"

"No, I'm with you boys and your office talk," said Denise, plopping down beside Barrington. "Let's see now. Let's start with a personnel report. How is Rachel Cannon doing? In her legal activities, I mean."

Kevin could not conceal his look of disbelief. How much could she know? Was he in the grip of gossip or paranoia? *I must not appear defensive in front of Austin,* he admonished himself, but it was Barrington himself who interceded.

"She's doing quite well, as a matter of fact. But I agree with my good wife," he added with an avuncular pat on Denise's thigh. "Let's not bring our work home with us, tonight at least."

Denise was not to be diverted. "I can't understand why you men don't like to talk about the office with us ladies, do you, Catherine? I think it's just wonderful, for example, that Kevin doesn't have to go on those long trips to New York all alone. Like last summer, Kevin. Having Rachel along must have been like having your own stewardess, only you didn't have to leave her at the airplane."

Kevin put down his drink, turned to Catherine, and, with apparent calm, said, "Thank you both for a lovely evening. The meal was superb. You truly outdid yourself. . . ."

"I think Kevin feels that I'm outdoing myself also," said Denise, giggling foolishly as she put down her drained snifter, then rose unsteadily and picked up Kevin's untouched cognac.

Barrington also got to his feet, poured a fresh cognac, and handed it to Kevin, saying, "Come on, lad. Denise is just having a little fun with us. If you need a witness to your moral character, I'll be happy to oblige."

Did Kevin detect a mocking tone in Barrington's voice? A wink? And wasn't he overdoing the genial-host routine a bit?

"You, Austin?" Denise was saying with mocking sternness. "That's like asking Errol Flynn to attest to Warren Beatty's virginity!"

While Barrington was trying to figure out whether to be flattered or insulted, Catherine took her turn at changing the subject. "I'm so *glad* you enjoyed the meal, Kevin, but all the credit goes to Lucille, who is simply—"

"Oh, hell, Catherine," said Barrington, turning sullen, "Kevin doesn't give a damn about your cook."

"You're *wrong* about that, dear. Why, just a few moments ago—"

"In the old days, Denise," said Barrington, ignoring Catherine and perversely skating on the edge of the delicate subject, "you would have had nothing to complain about, because a trial lawyer did it all by himself. Now'days, a lawyer needs someone on the road with him just to help carry all the damn deposition transcripts and computer runs."

"That explains," said Denise, abandoning all subtlety, "why Kevin chose a big, strong associate like Rachel Cannon to carry all those big, heavy transcripts all the way to New York."

"Austin—Catherine," said Kevin abruptly, "I have a long and very strenuous day tomorrow that starts in about seven hours."

"Oh, stick around, Kevin," laughed Barrington. "We all know that Rachel is too serious about making partnership to risk it all for a moment of reckless passion with a toad like you."

Kevin needed no further proof that Austin and Denise had formed a spontaneous alliance. *Denise is just fishing,* he thought grimly, *but Austin is pretty sure. I've got to break out of this.*

"Good night, Catherine . . ."

"You're not going anywhere," Barrington interrupted in a tone both friendly and mischievous, "until you've finished the last drop of that fine VSOP I just poured you."

"And you haven't *touched* the nice Brie, Kevin," added Catherine earnestly.

Kevin met Barrington's taunting look straight on, then, without breaking eye contact with the senior partner or saying a word, snatched the brandy snifter and gulped the contents in a single swallow, all pretense of good humor gone. "I'm leaving, Denise," he said with quiet intensity. "You can come with me now or take a cab."

Denise jumped to her feet in mock surprise. "Well, darling,

why didn't you say you were ready to leave?" Catherine also rose, seeming confused by their sudden departure. Denise gave her a society hug and Barrington a kiss and a wink good night.

"Nicaragua," said Catherine.

"It's too late for conversation topics now, Catherine," said Barrington wearily.

"A Central American country," said Denise. "What do I win?"

"That's where I got her," said Catherine. "My cook. I *knew* you'd get it out of me."

As soon as they were in the car, Denise leapt to the offensive. "Aren't you a little old for chug-a-lugging cognac, Kevin? That little scene certainly succeeded in putting Austin in his place. Too bad he was not only our host, but a good friend who also happens to be the most influential man in the law firm. You have probably just thrown away any hopes of becoming his successor someday."

"That's bullshit, and you know it," said Kevin. "You need not worry about Austin. As you put it, he's indeed my 'good friend.' "

"What I meant, counselor, is that he is *my* good friend. You, he merely tolerates because it's in his best interest. Catherine tells me he calls you 'Mr. Perfect' behind your back. Did you know that? She's so goddamn naive she passed it on to me thinking it was a compliment."

"I'm not interested in this conversation, Denise."

"Well, you should be, Mr. Perfect, because the truth is that your hero, Austin Barrington, hates your guts. What's more, as much as he needs you now, he'll drop you like a used condom when it suits him."

For the first time, Kevin looked sideways at his wife. "You're drunk."

"I may be drunk, but you, Mr. Perfect, are blind. Have you ever stopped to consider how Austin feels now that you, not he, get all the headlines? When people who once sought his advice now come openly to you instead? Open your eyes, for Christ's sake!"

"I don't want to argue with you anymore, Denise, and certainly not about who is going to be Austin Barrington's successor."

"Then just what in the hell have we worked for all this time?"

Denise demanded. She stared straight ahead at the slowly oscillating windshield wipers.

"I wish I knew. It certainly wasn't to spend an evening like this."

"The evening would have been perfectly nice if you hadn't been so damn defensive. You must be insane to get so upset over nothing."

Kevin jammed on the brakes and whipped the car off the road onto the shoulder. Denise clutched the dashboard for stability as the car skidded to a stop, and she started to shout something at Kevin, but his withering glare silenced her. His hatred for her was a tangible presence, like the swirls of dirt the hot tires had stirred up around them. "Denise," he said in a sandpaper voice, "listen to me. Your passive violence doesn't work anymore. Do you *hear*? I give you two choices, and warn you that only one of them involves you staying in this car. Your choices are to walk home or to shut your fucking mouth."

"That's fine; that's just fine, Mr. Perfect. I have nothing to say to you anyway."

"You never did," said Kevin, snapping on the radio.

EIGHTEEN

■

March can be San Francisco's meanest month, as any local will attest. March marks an annual invasion of biting winds that glance off a chilling moat formed by the surrounding waters of the Pacific Ocean and San Francisco Bay, and then race like street gangs down Montgomery Street, stinging faces, upending displays, and eviscerating umbrellas. March in San Francisco is a time to visit friends in Arizona.

The forty-second floor of the Imperial Building often swings like an inverted pendulum during these winds—as much as ten feet at the top—but neither that nor his hangover from the Barringtons' dinner evening and the three drinks later in his study accounted for the vertigo Kevin Stone now experienced as he sat dumbstruck in the senior partner's office, staring vacantly across the room into Barrington's stern face. A small desk lamp gave Barrington's head a masklike glow which lent a surreal quality to the words he had just spoken. *This can't be happening,* Kevin thought; yet there was nothing illusory in Barrington's unambiguous gaze or in the words that ricocheted through Kevin's head like night tracer bullets in a dark tunnel. *Weisberg demanded it . . . he had every right to it, Kevin . . . everything was at stake . . . artificial supplement . . . thought you should know . . . no risk of detection . . . all behind us now . . .*

Since law school days, Kevin had experienced nightmares in which a paralysis of his vocal cords had prevented him from making an objection during a trial. It was like that now, only worse, partly because he knew he was awake, partly because he knew that no words could change what he had just heard.

He pulled himself to his feet, walked over to the north window, and looked out toward the darkening bay in a hopeless bid for clarity. When he finally spoke, he seemed to be talking to himself. "That's why you've been so protective of the medical records."

"Of course," said Barrington in a conversational tone, "not only to protect their contents, but to protect all of you from potentially incriminating knowledge—in the unlikely event Project Salvation had come to light."

"You mean if you got caught."

"Have it your way. Our post hoc descriptions are as pointless as concerns over being 'caught.' It's over now and all that *is* relevant is that our clients and our firm have been spared a terrible embarrassment and the loss of millions of dollars to which they are justly entitled."

Kevin began to feel the first rough saw-teeth of anger cutting through the shock Barrington's disclosure had caused. He faced the senior partner and said simply, "You're serious, aren't you?" then rubbed his face roughly with both hands and shook his head violently. "Austin," he continued, "you must be *insane.* Don't you see what you've done? Nothing can justify poisoning your own clients."

Barrington swiveled his chair around and faced Kevin with a withering look. "Before you get too far astride your white horse, Kevin, please listen more carefully to what I'm trying to tell you. Weisberg asked, indeed *demanded,* that I do this for him. He went out to Newkirk's *by himself* and drank the mixture that

Newkirk had prepared solely because the little bastard insisted upon it and threatened to sue us all if we did not comply with his demand.''

"You're telling me that you didn't commit a felony on Weisberg, that you've merely defrauded the defendants and Superior Court of the State of California," said Kevin through clenched teeth. "That will be a great defense at your disbarment proceedings. And what about the other poor devils you poisoned who *didn't* ask for it? Who don't even *know* about it!" Kevin ran his fingers through his hair, wondered why he was having this conversation when he should be calling the police. *Christ,* he thought, *they probably won't even believe me.*

"I can understand your concern, Kevin," Austin continued, seemingly unperturbed. "Perhaps I was wrong in administering it to the others. Time will tell. But I resent the suggestion that I literally poisoned these men. I merely introduced a controlled amount of chemicals into their bodies to qualify them under *your* harebrained cancerphobia theory before I realized how improbable it was. There you have it. That's it.''

Kevin turned toward the door, saying, "You realize I have to report this to the police, Austin?"

"Do what you think best, Kevin. But hear me out first. Come. Sit for just a minute, then I will detain you no longer."

"I'll stand right here, thank you."

"Very well." Barrington methodically lit a cigarette and inhaled deeply as he loudly clicked his lighter shut. "It was my misfortune to choose victims for initial testing who were not nearly as affected as many of the other plaintiffs have since turned out to be. Oh, they were sick, all right, but had much lower toxin ratings than Newkirk's initial report indicated. Newkirk discovered his error only after we had filed our complaint and issued an unfortunately detailed press release. You know now, Kevin, that had the truth come out, we would have been bankrupt in two months and the laughingstock of the entire legal community. God knows the case was already difficult enough. This would have killed it. I had no choice but to bring the initially tested plaintiffs into line with all the others. Don't you see, Kevin: They are all old; they're all going to die anyway—at the very worst I advanced their demise by a modest number of days. As a matter of fact, the dosages we gave them probably won't even make them appreciably more ill than they already were. But now, dammit, the stuff will show up in their blood and tissue tests and qualify them all for millionaire status! Don't you see, Kevin? I've done nothing more than provide them a far better life than they would have had without my mild tampering. That was my mission and I've achieved it. You've got to believe me, Kevin, that if any one of them had been given a choice in the matter, they would have chosen the very same thing that Weisberg did.''

''And just who are you,'' said Kevin, his tone streaked with anger, ''to make that choice for them? With Weisberg, you may have just defrauded the court. With the others, you also are guilty of attempted murder with intent to commit great bodily injury.''

''Will you stop being a lawyer for five minutes and listen to me, for Christ's sake?'' asked Barrington, his face reddening but his voice still calm. ''Aren't you forgetting our other one-hundred-plus clients whose cases and monetary recoveries will be out the window if this thing comes to light now? Think long and hard about this, Kevin, because what it comes down to is that you can't help anyone now. All you can accomplish by the exercise of some distorted sense of morality now is to *hurt everyone:* your clients, the firm, Adrian and Gardner—''

''*They* know about this?''

The first glint of white teeth broke the shadow across Barrington's face in the dim light. ''Of course they know about it. I hope you don't think I would undertake such an activity without the full support of the management committee of the firm.''

Kevin stared at Barrington, unbelieving. ''You can't be serious. Adrian might have gone along with it because he's too old to fight you, but Gardner would never have accepted this.''

Barrington reached over and lifted the receiver off the hook, extending it toward Kevin. ''Which one of them would you like to dial first?''

Kevin moved toward Barrington's desk, hesitated, then sank into a chair. Barrington rose and walked over to his bar, where he poured a vodka for Kevin and Glenlivet for himself. ''You know how Adrian feels about you, Kevin. You're like a son to him. And,'' he added, extending the drink to Kevin, ''you've been like a kid brother to me.''

Kevin stared at the glass, wanting its contents, but aware that sharing a drink with Barrington now would be tantamount to a handshake. He took the glass but conspicuously put it down on the desk without drinking from it.

"You really expect me to go along with this, don't you?"

"I know you will, Kevin, because you know that the adverse publicity could ruin not only the firm, but the cases of the other one hundred forty-four innocent clients who had nothing to do with any of this. Your silence and support on the other hand will ensure that they all receive the kind of money that will give them the best treatment available and, eventually, a death with dignity."

Kevin's mind raced to cope with the logic of Barrington's rationalization but came up against a brick wall: Adrian in jail, the plaintiffs thrown out of court, S.P.&M. in ruins, no money to buy off Denise, losing Rachel. He felt tired, very tired, but forced himself to think.

"Suppose," he said, regarding the senior partner through lowered eyelids, "that your 'mission' demanded further administrations of the concoction?"

"It won't. There is absolutely no need for further dosages. It's finished. You have my word on it. My limited supplementation has now solved our problem; our clients' problem. I repeat, Kevin: Your intervention now can only undo all that and put Adrian, Gardner, and me behind bars just for doing what we thought was best for all our clients—the greater good for the greater number."

Forty-two floors below, the sound of a police siren split the silence as Kevin now stared fully into the crystalline dark eyes of the senior partner.

"You bastard," he whispered.

"I'll excuse that, Kevin, although I would have expected more grace from you, even in the circumstances. It tends to confirm suspicions that have been growing in my mind about—well, about your mental state."

Barrington's words dug into Kevin's brain and set themselves like fishhooks. The younger man slowly rotated his pounding head back and forth on sagging shoulders, until a look of ironic amusement began to spread across his lined face. "You are really something, Austin," he said finally. "You tell me that you and two other members of the firm have defrauded the court and committed felonies on our own clients—and then you say that *you* have suspicions about *me*! Well, I don't know who you are anymore, Austin, but I'll tell you this: I don't give a rat's ass about your suspicions."

Barrington's eyes flickered and he started to speak, then rose, took a deep breath, and walked around his desk to where Kevin was starting to rise. The malice melted from Barrington's face as he gently rested his hand on Kevin's shoulder. Despite his intentions, Kevin could not bring himself to turn out of the grasp of the senior partner, nor to tune out his sonorous voice, now more consoling than explanatory. "You misunderstood me. My suspicions are born of concern, not criticism. I simply see in you what I saw in Adrian Fisher twenty years ago and what I saw in myself ten years ago."

Barrington paused for a moment and squeezed Kevin's shoulder reassuringly. "You're tired, Kevin," he continued in a tranquilizing tone. "Bone tired. You may be fooling the rest, but I know better. You have tried more cases than anyone in this city. And each one gets harder, the pressure greater, because you never lose. Am I right?"

Kevin sat silent, the point beyond argument. "You, Kevin, like all the great trial lawyers, are being ground down by the existential dread of contingency, that black and hopeless inability to foresee and forestall every problem that might erupt during a trial, yet driven by the determination to try." Barrington walked over to his bookcase, picked out a volume, and smiled benignly at Kevin. "I greatly admire Bugental's analogy of the ship-wrecked sailor stranded on a desert island who spends his life building a rock wall against a tidal wave, the direction and height of which he cannot know. Indeed, all he does know is that it may never come at all. Yet the poor bloke will spend the last futile years of his life piling rock upon rock."

The book snapped shut with a sound like a shot.

"Isn't that the way it is, Kevin? Aren't you tempted now to settle a case you would have taken all the way to the World Court at The Hague five or ten years ago? Doesn't it take more time and energy to memorize those depositions, charts, and accounting records than before? Doesn't your soul yearn for other, different challenges and opportunities? A more reflective life-style?"

Kevin remained silent, his frayed mind searching vainly for a flaw in Barrington's logic.

"Then let's get this case behind us," Barrington said with fresh enthusiasm. "When it's over, you and I as trial counsel will share multimillion-dollar bonuses over and above all the others—Gardner and Adrian have already volunteered that." Barrington replaced the vodka in Kevin's hand. "Then," he added with a smile laden with goodwill, "it will be time to enjoy the fruits of your labors."

Barrington saluted Kevin with his glass, then turned solemn again and said, "Kevin, it's time to come in out of the cold."

NINETEEN

■

"Sure do appreciate you coming here, Ms. Cannon," said Emmett Dixon, as he held the door of his cottage open for Rachel. "I can't even find a doctor who'll make a house call these days."

"I'm happy to do it, Mr. Dixon, but sorry to hear you're not well today."

Emmett Dixon was one of the most gravely ill plaintiffs, his vital organs ravaged by years of exposure to toxic waste at North American. He was too ill, in fact, to travel downtown to Rachel's office for his first predeposition preparation session.

"All the same, you better be careful, young lady," said Dixon, sinking quickly into a chair, "before you begin to give your profession a good name."

Rachel laughed as she scanned the client's tiny cottage. It was meticulously neat, but in a self-conscious way, like a humble village that has exerted itself in preparation for a visit from the king. The small living room was dimly lit by two untrustworthy-looking floor lamps with necrosed shades and frayed wiring. One lamp illuminated a photograph of a used-up-looking woman Rachel took to be Dixon's wife—the records had revealed him to be a widower—and the other brightened a nearly finished jigsaw puzzle showing Buckingham Palace at the Changing of the Guard. There were piles of old newspapers, some already yellowing, with gaping holes where things had been cut out, and nonfiction paperbacks dealing with politics and travel, all neatly stacked on the top shelf of an incongruously modern teak bookcase. The bottom shelf doubled as a wine rack, but Rachel could not identify the three dusty bottles there. On one side of the bookcase was an emaciated philodendron, the plastic pot still wrapped in colored foil; on the other side sat Dixon in an overstuffed armchair with upholstery gone bald with age. Rachel sat across from him, choosing a straight-back chair over a chesterfield sofa covered with a beautifully crocheted afghan that provided a strange contrast to the large Sears TV that loomed behind it.

Emmett Dixon was as neat as his house: his thin white hair freshly shampooed and a full-length corduroy bathrobe covering a flannel shirt and unnecessary trousers, worn in observance of modesty. Deep lines crafted by years of suffering gave his face a hard look in repose, but his undefeated eyes and ready smile refuted any impression of bitterness.

"Would you like some coffee or beer?" he asked.

"Not right now, thank you," said Rachel, instantly drawn to this white-haired little man. Her file indicated he had just turned seventy-nine.

"So what's a pretty young lady like you doing with a brief-case? I expected some guy with greasy hair and a shifty eye."

Rachel's full lips formed a smile. "You seem to have a low opinion of lawyers."

"That, my dear, is an understatement. Do you know how to tell the difference between a lawyer and a snake lying in the middle of the road?"

"I give up," said Rachel.

"The snake is the one with skid marks in front of him. Do you know what's black and brown and looks good on a lawyer?"

"What?" said Rachel, still smiling.

"A Doberman pinscher."

Rachel laughed courteously. "We will try to improve upon your impression of us, Mr. Dixon."

"You already have, Miss Cannon. Those teeth of yours are as even and unnaturally white as a row of piano keys."

Rachel laughed. "Mr. Dixon, you are obviously not as sick as the nurse said you were."

"Feeling better every minute. A woman pretty as you must have some Irish in her, right?"

"Right you are," said Rachel. "I had a grandfather who looked a great deal like you, as a matter of fact."

"I'll take that as a compliment, since any kin of yours had to be good-lookin'."

Dixon wore his loneliness as openly as the scars on his hands, and it was clear to Rachel that this old man would talk as long as she would listen. And listen she did. Down deep, she suspected that providing companionship might be more important to the old man than winning him a big money judgment that could come too late anyway. It bothered her that this could be said for most of the plaintiffs. A fat fee for the firm; a share of the courtroom triumph for herself; and for the clients? Money—assuming they lived to see it. Money they would be too old and sick to spend, and without even children to leave it to. *Christ, am I a lawyer here or a social worker? Both*, she concluded.

They continued to visit for another thirty minutes, interrupted twice when Dixon excused himself. "I guess you know the bladder is shot," he had said the second time, with a look of acute embarrassment that broke Rachel's heart. Finally, he sighed and said, "Well, now, what are you going to do to me?"

"First, I think I'll make you answer some routine questions. I understand you worked at North American Chemical for twenty-five years."

"That's right. My wife passed away when I was fifty-five, so I lived at the company's low-cost housing during my last ten years there."

"What was it like living there?" asked Rachel.

"It was all right. My main problem was I missed Shirlee. On top of that, they wouldn't let me play my saw."

"Your saw?"

"Sure. When I was a kid, I was one of the best fiddlers in the state of Washington. When I lost a finger on my left hand in 1920 working as a lumberjack, I took up the musical saw. I got good at it, been on the radio three or four times."

"What kind of work did you do at North American?"

"I transported open drums of chemical waste material to the dump site using a forklift. Pretty dumb, huh? I guess you could say I dumped the stuff all day, then ran back to my room and drank it all night, laced, of course, with plenty of Old Crow, which I unfairly blamed the next morning for my shakes and jingles."

"When did you first realize that it was the water, not the booze?"

"I never did know till the word got around that some lawyers were working up a case. Oh, I already knew I was a goner; the doc had said not to make any plans more than a year or two off, but I never knew what had caused it. Now I think back on all those years of sores on my arms and hands and coughing myself to sleep every night, slowly coming unglued and not knowing why." The old man said this more with regret than bitterness, and Rachel's heart ached for him.

"We're going to try to do something about it," said Rachel, knowing her words were hopelessly inadequate even as she said them.

"Oh, it could be a lot worse, young lady," said Dixon, slapping scarred and liver-spotted hands to knees like chicken bones and forcing his craggy features into a smile. "I've always wanted to travel, and now it looks like that poor water is going to make me a rich man."

"So," said Rachel, leaning forward and trying to play to Emmett Dixon's brave facade, "where are you going to go with all your money?"

"That's easy," said Dixon without hesitation. "Ireland. And if it's everything I hear it is, I might just stay there. Oh, I'll also take a look at Scotland and maybe spend a night in one of those fancy castles that sit right on a loch. There's one I've heard about near Fort William I'd like to try, and then I'd like to see Edinburgh. If I don't run out of money, then I'll probably visit Paris—they're reputed to have some pretty women there." Dixon's mood turned serious as he added, "Now tell me: what's this deposition all about?"

Rachel explained, as gently and clearly as she knew how, what would be required of Dixon when his deposition was taken.

"That's askin' a lot of this old man," he said when she was done. "Talkin' is about all I can do anymore. It also sounds pretty darn dull."

"Exciting or dull, we're going to give you the best representation we can," said Rachel.

"And you look to be just the man—woman—who can do it," said Dixon with a wink.

Rachel smiled and touched the old man's weathered hand, saying, "Well, Emmett, as the one-time mayor of Ottawa, Canada, once said: 'A woman has to do things twice as well as a man to gain recognition—but fortunately, that's easy.' Now, Mr. Dixon, let's get to work."

Rachel returned to the Imperial Building with bittersweet feelings about her meeting with Emmett Dixon and a renewed resolve to give him her best. She also reminded herself to maintain a professional distance from this instantly lovable old man, for Barrington had told her that Dixon had little more than a year to live.

Rachel's next stop was Kevin's office for a scheduled meeting. She had been looking forward to seeing him, but could see in an instant that he was in a foul mood. His usually light complexion seemed darker than the bleak sky outside, his eyes bloodshot with tension and fatigue. She noticed that his coat had been thrown in the corner and lay crumpled on the floor with several volumes of the *California Reporter* series.

"I'm sorry I'm late, Kevin," she said tentatively. "I just got back from a meeting with Emmett Dixon.'"

Kevin grunted something incomprehensible and continued straightening books and papers on his desk without looking up. The piles were in such complete disarray Rachel suspected that Kevin had just scooped them up in a bundle from the floor, where a broken ashtray still rested. Kevin's drawn face touched her deeply, and she fought off the urge to put her arms around him. Finally, he looked up at her, his features instantly softening.

"I am . . . having a difficult day."

"Is it the North American case?"

"It's a lot of things," Kevin said as he rose and turned toward his window in an apparent effort to compose himself.

"How is your prep going in the Jamison case? It seems like an awful time to be going off to New York on another major trial. How long do you think it will take to try it?"

"I don't know," said Kevin in a flat tone. "Five weeks, seven weeks. Who the hell knows?"

Rachel walked over to Kevin and tentatively touched his shoulder. "Hey. Cheer up! We'll hold the fort back here, and you will return to a well-prepared case. Just keep thinking of what you'll do with your share of all the money we're going to get out of those guys."

Kevin turned around to face her, an alien look on his face as he said, "Over three million dollars, as a matter of fact, and I already know what I'm going to do with it: pay off Denise, put the rest in high-yield stocks and bonds, then tell these bastards to take this job and shove it."

Rachel looked uncertainly into Kevin's troubled eyes. "Should I come back later? We can discuss the motion to advance tomorrow if you'd prefer."

"I'd prefer," said Kevin, sullen again.

Rachel turned slowly, then headed for the door.

"Rachel, wait! I'm sorry," said Kevin, stretching his head from side to side and grimacing from apparent tension and discomfort in his neck. "A ton of things are coming down on me right now and of all the people in the world I don't want to take it out on, it's you. I'm sorry, Rachel—sweet Rachel. Forgive me?"

"Only if you let me help you on Jamison. I know I can't go with you, but if there's anything I can do here, just tell me. I'd like to see you still in one piece when you get back. I'm worried about you, Kevin. You look exhausted."

"I'll be okay. How about you?"

"If our motion to advance the trial date is granted, it will be rough—you know: 'Be careful what you want—you just might get it.' But we'll make it somehow. When do you leave for New York?"

"Next week," said Kevin glumly, "and I accept your condition." His eyes reached out longingly toward Rachel's as he added, "It won't be the same this trip. Without you."

"I know. I'll be thinking of you too."

"Rachel," said Kevin, putting his hands around her shoulders, "you're the reason I know I'll get through these next months. God, how I love you."

Rachel read a desperation in Kevin's voice she had never heard before and willingly responded. "I love you, too, Kevin." She reached up and touched his face, then his lips. "I'll be right here," she added, her mouth turned up at the corners in a half smile, her emerald eyes fogged in tears. "But now, sir, please unhand me, before Austin walks through the door and . . ."

Rachel felt Kevin's hands stiffen on her shoulders, then drop to his side at the mention of the senior partner's name. "Kevin? Is something wrong? I was just—"

"No, of course not. I just remembered some work I owe him."

"You too? One of the things I'll miss during the next few weeks is your role as a buffer between Austin and me. Any words of advice?"

"You'll do fine," said Kevin. "Just try not to push his button on the global issues. You can't win that battle alone. Remember, S.P.&M. is still the establishment's darling, riding the white horse in this case only because that's where the money is."

"Not to worry, Kevin. I have nothing against money and I'll do whatever it takes to help win this case."

Kevin looked at her oddly and said, "Good. You might have to."

TWENTY

■

Gardner White hurried through the elevator doors at the Arcadia Building's fifty-eighth floor and entered the lobby of the President's Club. His round face and flat features were still glowing from the stinging March winds outside. Pumping his pudgy arms for momentum, he dashed straight toward the main dining area, ignoring the posh surroundings.

Josef, the polished maître d', greeted him by name and informed him that Mr. Barrington and Mr. Fisher were already inside at the table. *As if I didn't know that,* thought White, glancing at his watch and continuing down the hall toward the main dining room.

"Greetings, Gard," said Adrian Fisher, sliding Gardner's chair back for him.

"Hello, Adrian, Austin," he said, still panting from exertion. "I'm sorry to be late and even sorrier about the reason why."

"Have a sip of your drink. Slow down," said Barrington.

"I just came from the bank," the tax lawyer said in a rush. "They've had a management turnover and just reviewed our loan portfolio."

Fisher and Barrington leaned forward. "And?"

"And we are in deep trouble. The bastards have frozen our line of credit. They now say they won't even advance next month's loan funds without a specific repayment plan commitment."

"Christ," muttered Fisher. "Here we go again!"

"What did you tell them?" asked Barrington casually, signaling Stefan that they were ready to order.

"I told them they were being goddamned unreasonable! First they cut us off, then they see our press release and say everything will be fine. 'How much do you want?' they ask. 'Sky's the limit.' Now all of a sudden the new loan committee thinks our North American case looks problematical—possibly even a loser—and they cut us off again. What was I supposed to tell them?'' White took several deep breaths and, when neither of his partners spoke, plunged on. "So, here we are on March 15, 1983, right back where we were on May 28, 1982. The question now is, what the hell do we do? Because of this North American case, we didn't cut any associates, as I'd suggested, but plowed right ahead and made three new partners at the start of the year. We've also sunk a ton of money in expert witnesses, investigation, and medical testing. So, what do I tell the bank?''

"Tell them nothing," said Barrington, sipping his Glenlivet. "I'll have a talk with them."

"You'll have a talk with them," White repeated in a tone that was half mockery, half disbelief. He picked up his drink, rattling the melting ice cubes in his glass.

"I believe I just said that," said Barrington calmly.

"Yes, well, you had better be ready to do more than that. I tell you, the bastards are intransigent, and what's worse, maybe they're right. Frankly, Austin, you know I've never liked this thing you've gotten us into—even before I knew about that blasted supplementing you say you had to do, and then bringing Kevin in. We should have just cut our associate staff in half and, if necessary, our own partners' draws as well. We didn't need to bet the whole damn ranch on this kind of long shot."

"Who—other than the bank's in-house toadies—characterizes the North American case as a 'long shot'?" asked Barrington, coolly sipping his scotch.

"Your co-lead counsel, Kevin Stone, that's who," snapped White. "I talked to him just last week."

Adrian Fisher leaned forward suddenly. "Is that true, Austin? Does Kevin think we've got problems?"

Austin Barrington silently cursed Kevin as he retreated within himself to review the situation. He could cope with Gardner's ineffectual rebelliousness, even the bank's vacillation, but he could not have Kevin feeding Adrian Fisher's anxiety.

"Kevin has supported my decision from the beginning."

"But he *does* think it's a long shot, doesn't he?" said White, pressing his advantage and casting a sideways glance at a concerned-looking Adrian Fisher, who now cleared his voice and began to speak in a quiet, courteous tone.

"I must confess, Austin, that several partners have recently suggested rather strongly to me that you—that we—have overstepped our bounds. Perhaps it's time to review our position and at least consider Gardner's more conservative solution to the firm's problems. This case is sucking up more money than any of us dreamed and the bank may just have a point. Maybe it's time to stack rifles, Austin," the older man finished.

Barrington's eyes flashed for just a moment. *'Stack rifles' my ass,* he thought, but responded in a calm, emotionless voice. "That's where you are all wrong. I intend to inform our vacillating bankers that one week from today the Superior Court will grant our motion to advance the trial of the first fifteen plaintiffs, and that before this very year is out we will have won verdicts well into the hundreds of millions."

"Of *course*," said Fisher slowly, the light dawning. "Advance the damn thing for trial. That's the ticket!"

"Is there a remote possibility," asked Gardner cautiously, "that this motion could fail?"

"I think 'remote possibility' is precisely the way to characterize it," Barrington assured him. "Should the bank remain stubborn, of course, and insist on reneging on their prior commitment, I would have no choice but to have S.P.&M. stop representing them as general counsel."

"Come on, Austin," chided White. "That poses no threat to them at all. Every firm in town wants to represent that bank. We wouldn't gain a thing and we'd lose another big client in the process. What's the point?"

Barrington delayed his response a moment while the appetizers arrived, then said, "Because of the conflict of interest which would result when we file our complaint next week, suing them for one hundred million dollars, our anticipated fee in the case, as damages for breach of their earlier agreement to fund the North American case to completion."

Fisher began to smile. Gardner White looked skeptical. "You'd do that?"

"In a minute," Barrington said quietly.

"Would we win?" White asked.

"In a minute," Barrington said. White looked at Fisher, who knitted his brow, then nodded his tentative agreement.

For ten full seconds White and Fisher looked at Barrington, their faces relaxing. Finally, Fisher broke into laughter, and White followed, shaking his head back and forth, saying, "You trial horses never cease to amaze me. No wonder you view me the way a race driver looks at his mechanic.''

"If it's any consolation, Gardner,'' said Fisher, "mechanics live a lot longer than race drivers. You'll still be around to probate the wills of trial lawyers twenty years younger than yourself.''

"Then here's to mechanics and long life,'' said Gardner, smiling.

"And to insure adequate cash flow during your golden years, Gardner,'' said Barrington, "I am meeting after lunch with yet another forensic expert who will play a lead role in the success of our venture: a water mechanics engineer, of all things. Meanwhile, don't worry about the bank, Gardner; I'll see to them later this afternoon.''

"I'm seeing a water mechanics expert myself this afternoon,'' said Fisher, his withered but still handsome face cracking into a wry smile. "Damn kidneys acting up again. This new quack specialist has me pissing every color in the rainbow and in between he's got his finger up my ass.''

"If he's got small fingers, I want his name,'' said White, scanning the choice of entrees. "My prostate is killing me, and now he tells me I've got the gout besides.''

"Getting old is a bitch,'' confirmed Adrian Fisher.

"But,'' said Barrington, finishing the ancient line, "it beats the only other alternative. I must say, you two are a real barrel of chuckles today. Why don't you ditch your ladies tonight? The Warriors are in town and Catherine has a class, a yoga class for God's sake.''

"Who are they losing to tonight?'' asked Gardner.

"Portland,'' said Adrian.

"Well, you'd better count me out,'' said Gardner. "Tax season, you know.''

"Which do you think is most boring,'' said Barrington, winking at Adrian, "practicing yoga, or practicing tax law?''

"I'll tell you what's most boring,'' said Adrian Fisher. "Watching the Warriors lose again, but count me in.''

"So, Mr. Franks, welcome to the team.'' Barrington's voice lacked conviction, and his disappointment in Franks's physical presence was evident to Rachel. She was not surprised, for Franks stood at five feet one, even shorter than Professor Childhouse, and she guessed his weight at little more than one hundred pounds. Even Jeff had dropped a few unkind asides to Rachel as Kevin and Barrington poured coffee in the conference area of his office before the formal meeting began. "Where did you find this one—riding in the fifth race at Golden Gate Fields?" Jeff had said. "I hope there's not a high wind on the day he's due in court."

"He's not *that* short, Jeff."

"Whatever you say, Snow White."

Franks also appeared at least ten years younger than his thirty-three years. His skin shone pink and his eyes glittered with innocence as he walked into Barrington's conference area. Only a prematurely receding hairline created the impression that this might—just might—be a grown man.

Rachel glanced at Kevin and was relieved to see that he at least seemed to be withholding judgment. She liked that in Kevin—though handsome himself, he neither seemed aware of it, nor did he seem to attach too much value to it. Austin, on the other hand, who could still turn heads in a room upon entering, seemed annoyed with anyone whose physical presence was less than commanding.

"Let's get right to it, Mr. Franks," said Barrington in a tone lacking his customary charm. "I understand you are an expert in state water quality regulations that apply to cities like the defendant Lileton. I understand further from your *curriculum vitae* that you hold an engineering degree in water mechanics, that you worked for the state of California for the last few years, and that you are now a groundwater consultant."

Franks quickly reviewed his educational background and his experience with the pesticides unit of the state Division of Occupational Safety and Health, then recounted direct experience with North American's meretricious claims of exemption from state monitoring laws and its success in "persuading" hearing officers of their innocence.

"So," said Barrington, "North American will claim they disposed of such small amounts, they were exempt from the statutes and therefore not in violation. Lileton will corroborate this, because if North American was exempt, the city can't be charged with a failure of its duty of enforcement."

"Exactly," said Kevin. "One defendant will bootstrap the other."

"We've got this problem all around us," said Franks. "Plenty of laws, but inadequate enforcement."

"You seem as gloomy about all this pollution business as Professor Childhouse," said Barrington.

Saul Franks drained his soft drink and smiled, saying, "I consider that a real compliment, Mr. Barrington." He continued staring at the empty container as if trying to find an encouraging word, but finally just shrugged his shoulders and said, "Picture the earth's four billion six hundred million years as just one month. On this scale we humans have been here for only a minute or so. In that flicker of time we've squandered the six basic elements necessary to life: carbon, hydrogen, oxygen, nitrogen, sulphur, and phosphorus. We're destroying our forests, killing our animals, and polluting the air we breathe, the food we eat, and the water we drink. Our factories belch sulphur dioxide into the air and it comes back down as acid rain. Our industrial molecules are threatening the ozone that shields the earth's surface from ultraviolet radiation. Meanwhile, we add thirty million people a year to the planet to share our rapidly depleting resources. In summary, folks, we're blowing it."

Franks drew a breath and turned to Kevin, seated at the opposite end of the table from Barrington. "You're on your way to New York City to try a case, Mr. Stone," he continued. "If you walk the streets for one full day while you are there, you will breathe in the toxic equivalent of two packs of cigarettes. And if you go out to Long Island or New Jersey, I strongly urge you to drink Perrier water."

"Yes," said Barrington, pointedly looking at his watch. "Sound advice, I'm sure, but let's stick to our case and let Congress's Superfund clean up the other problems."

Franks laughed and said, "Pardon me, sir, but the Superfund is nothing more than a super joke. After two years' time, perhaps the EPA can claim—though it's debatable—to have cleaned up *six* out of the twenty thousand hazardous waste dump sites they now admit exist. Meanwhile, an estimated two hundred sixty-five million *tons* of toxic waste are being generated nationwide every year. That's more than a *ton* of toxic waste for every man, woman, and child in the United States—according to the conservative EPA's own figures."

Rachel saw Barrington stifle a yawn, but urged Franks to continue.

"The EPA now admits that around two thousand five hundred forty-six sites require immediate handling, and that they now need at least forty billion dollars! The one-point-six-billion-dollar

Superfund won't even pay for the paperwork involved!'' The little engineer then gave Barrington a direct, almost challenging look as he said, ''We have created a situation here as foolhardy and dangerous as nuclear energy and more immediate than Russian missiles—a national disaster, and there is no prospect of sufficient money to salvage it. I believe that if the jury can be made to see this, Mr. Barrington, they will make an example of North American.''

''Or,'' said Barrington with a cool authority that conveyed to Franks that he had gone beyond his area of expertise, ''they may feel that North American's conduct is relatively venial when compared with what's going on elsewhere.''

''I disagree,'' said Kevin, causing Barrington's left eyebrow to shoot up. ''I think we should shovel in all the national peril material the court will allow. Saul is right—we've got to get this jury angry—and to do that we must first get them involved.''

Barrington maintained an outward calm, but for what must have been the third time this month, Rachel saw bitter tension between the two partners. The senior partner closed debate, however, as he rose abruptly and walked toward the coffee urn. ''We don't need to debate this now, Kevin,'' he said. ''Continue, please, Mr. Franks.''

Picking up the subterranean antagonism between the two lawyers, Saul Franks shifted to an explanation of how the contaminants in the North American dump site had been able to leach into the underlying soil and penetrate the aquifer, forming a poisonous plume capable of moving over seventy feet a year, ''as silent and invisible as nerve gas, except that it doesn't blow away.''

''How long does it take to dissipate?'' Kevin asked.

''It doesn't,'' Franks answered. ''The underground reservoir is contaminated for geologic time. So you can see that our country—our entire world—is in grave—''

''Mr. Franks,'' interrupted Barrington as he shook his head and pointedly glanced at his watch. ''This is all very interesting, and your grasp of facts and figures is impressive. You are certainly well-informed, if not entirely responsive.'' The senior partner noisily tapped the table three times with his pen, then added, ''Do you follow football, Mr. Franks?''

''Football? Well, sure, I occasionally watch it.''

''You've heard, then, of the two-minute warning?''

''Yes, sir.''

"And of the two-minute drill?"

"I believe that's when the team that's behind in the last two minutes runs its plays quickly and without a huddle in order to avoid wasting any time."

"Exactly," said Barrington, smiling wryly. "Now, I feel that this meeting has been somewhat lacking in focus so far, and I must leave soon. May I suggest that you and Rachel think of yourselves as a team that is indeed behind and about to engage in a two-minute drill. Cover only the essential parts of your testimony, but cover it all. I will time you."

Saul Franks, obviously unsure whether Barrington was serious, looked at Rachel, who, knowing Barrington was always serious, was lost in her own speculation.

Two minutes, she thought. *The bastard. He spent more time than that just greeting everyone this afternoon. He knows we can't sum up four months of work in two minutes.* She wondered if he was embarrassing her to get back at Kevin somehow. If so, this might mean he had suspicions about the two of them. A feeling of dismay swept through her as she saw Barrington's hard, dark eyes on her, waiting. *Maybe he just wants me to fail.*

Rachel rose to her feet, took a position behind her chair, and spoke to Franks in a voice that concealed both her anger and her anxiety. "I am going to ask you some questions now, Saul, and I would like you to answer them as you would if you were in court, but keep your answers brief. I'll skip your qualifications as an expert and just hit the major points for now."

Franks nodded his agreement as Barrington pointed out that the second hand on the clock over the wet bar was almost at the twelve o'clock position. *"Go!"* he said as it reached the top.

"First, Mr. Franks, did you, at our request, perform a series of test drills at the site of the North American Chemical Company?"

The engineer straightened in his chair, mirroring Rachel's new formality, and answered, "I did."

"And does the report I now show you accurately present the findings from these test drills?"

"It does."

"Was the work done in connection with these test drills accomplished either by you or under your direct supervision?"

"It was."

"How many test drills did you complete?"

"Eight in all."

"What was the purpose of these test drills?"

"To extract samples from the aquifer that provides water to the wells that have serviced the employees of the North American Chemical Company."

"Tell the jury what an aquifer is."

"An underground water reservoir. The way it works is . . ."

Christ! thought Rachel, glancing at the clock. *Thirty seconds gone and I haven't even begun to get the toxins into our plaintiffs.*

"Just tell us what you were looking for," said Rachel, interrupting.

"Chemicals," said Franks simply, catching Rachel's sense of urgency.

"Did you perform any other kinds of testing at the other sites?"

"Yes. I took samples from the toxic waste dump site at the North American Chemical Company and from the well that services the housing facility at North American."

"Did you at our request perform a qualitative analysis to compare the samples taken from the toxic dump and well water with the samples taken from your site test drills?"

"I did indeed."

Good, Saul, thought Rachel. *That's it. Keep it short.*

"What, if anything, did you find?"

"I found almost an exact correlation between toxic chemicals taken from the toxic dump and those found in my test drill samples."

What am I forgetting? thought Rachel, her mind in high gear. *Ah, yes—get the chemicals into the well!*

"Did you also compare your test drill samples from the aquifer with the well-water samples?"

"I did, and I found the same kind of correlation there too. Same chemicals filtering through the whole system. Silent. Lethal."

"What, if anything, do you conclude from the results of these comparisons?"

All eyes were on the sweep hand of the clock as it reached twelve again—their time was half gone.

"One minute!" said Barrington smugly.

Meanwhile, Saul Franks's words began to come faster and even more clipped as he said, "I conclude that the toxins from the North American dump site permeated the porous ground surface beneath the dump site, worked their way into the aquifer that underlies the North American site, then created a poisonous plume that moved underground to a point directly under the water well that services the housing facility. The chemicals then were drawn up into the well, poisoning the drinking water of the plaintiffs here.''

"Did the concentration of these toxic chemicals exceed safety standards?"

"By far."

"Are you familiar with the standards that apply to these chemicals in terms of safety tolerance?"

"I am, having spent years drafting regulations and then, as a state investigator, trying to enforce them."

Rachel glanced at the clock. *Twenty-five seconds left.* "Which chemicals did you find in the plaintiffs' drinking water that were both traceable to the North American dump site and in amounts that exceeded safe tolerance levels?"

Franks answered in a torrent of words: "I found benzene, lindane, carbon tetrachloride, chlorobenzene, toluene, chloroform, dioxin, PBBs, PCBs, TCEs." He gasped a lungful of air as all five sets of eyes now watched the second hand. Only fifteen seconds left. "I also found several dangerous metals, such as nickel, chromium, lead, and cadmium—all in amounts well in excess of established safe levels."

"What do you mean by 'safe levels'?"

"I mean the level above which people over time and in significant quantities will manifest a variety of pathologic symptomatology, such as damage to their vital organs, and," finished Franks just as the second hand hit twelve straight up, *"even death."*

The senior partner grudgingly smiled while Rachel said to herself, *In your face, Barrington.* What she said out loud was, "In rough summary, Austin, there it is."

"Very good," Barrington said with an appreciative nod at both Rachel and the engineer. "Thank you for indulging me in this little exercise. Give yourself a touchdown and the game ball."

It was obvious that his initial reservations about Saul Franks—and Rachel's judgment in retaining him—had been largely dispelled.

"Thank you, sir, but the credit goes to my quarterback," said Franks. Rachel smiled and shook the expert's icy hand. She noticed Kevin's own relieved smile, but wondered how long she could go on ducking Barrington's bullets before one of them connected.

TWENTY-ONE

∎

"All rise!" shouted the bailiff the next day. "The Superior Court of the City and County of San Francisco is now in session, Judge Mathew Bainbridge presiding!" Rachel, Jeffrey, and Alan Hancock rose in unison along with the handful of courtroom observers and other lawyers with motions on the afternoon calendar. As usual, the bailiff's cry, like a coxswain's shouted orders to his crew, accelerated Rachel's heartbeat a few beats per minute. She watched Judge Bainbridge sweep up the steps to the bench with a quickness that belied his sixty-seven years and inactive judicial status. His back was as straight as a tree. His black robe neatly concealed a protruding stomach and provided sharp color contrast to a shock of white hair. It occurred to Rachel that Mathew Bainbridge probably never looked better than when judicially attired, just as another man might look his best in a tuxedo. He had been a defense attorney in private practice, a fact that had initially alarmed the S.P.&M. team when they heard the judge had been specially assigned to hear all matters and, eventually, to preside at trial. So far, however, he had been fair, but this would be Rachel's first appearance before him and her adrenaline was flowing. The judge nodded a greeting to counsel and immediately set to work scanning the thick North American file before him.

"Be seated, please," the bailiff said mechanically. *Showtime,* thought Rachel as she glanced past Jeffrey at Alan Hancock who, not surprisingly, was already smiling a greeting to the bailiff and winking at the court reporter. Hancock's temerity in taking such liberties amazed Rachel, as did the fact that the court attachés never seemed to resent it. Hancock had elevated brass and bluster to a new level: state-of-the-art chutzpah.

Judge Bainbridge continued to flip through his court file, then finally announced, "Action number eight two dash one six two eight, *Weisberg, et al.,* versus *North American Chemical Company and the city of Lileton.*

176

"Good afternoon, gentlemen . . . and lady," said the judge. Was this a subtle gibe? Rachel wondered. *Will he be calling me "honey" next?*—as one county judge had just last month. Her investigation had revealed Bainbridge's credentials and reputation to be beyond reproach. Two of S.P.&M.'s partners had tried cases before him when he was on active status and had found him to be eminently fair, though conservative in his leanings.

I'll soon find out, thought Rachel, momentarily wondering if she and Jeff had created a monster with the idea for this motion to advance the trial date of the first fifteen plaintiffs. For reasons she could not fathom, Austin Barrington's initial reaction to the idea—"It can't hurt to try"—had subsequently taken on a fierce, almost desperate intensity. "You *must* deliver on this, Rachel," he had told her last night, only hours after she had passed the Saul Franks test. "Don't let me down on this one." It was unlike Barrington to personalize his demands on his staff. Could it really be so important? Or just another bullet to duck?

"Please excuse me, Ms. Cannon," continued the judge, "we didn't see many ladies as trial counsel during my more active tenure on the bench, but I guarantee I'll have this under control by the time the jury is in the box."

"No apologies necessary, your honor. But if I am as successful in this motion today as I hope to be, you won't have much time to practice up."

The judge smiled tolerantly and said, "All right, Ms. Cannon. Tell me why I should grant your motion."

Rachel went straight to the point. "First, your honor, justice delayed in this case is clearly justice denied. Hardly any of these plaintiffs—mostly aged and terminally ill bachelors and widowers who took advantage of North American's low-cost housing—have any heirs or successors."

Judge Bainbridge removed his glasses and peered down at Rachel with bloodhound eyes under bushy dark eyebrows raised high in mock astonishment. "Let's be careful about these 'aged' clients of yours, Ms. Cannon. I note from the complaint that at least six of them are younger than I am."

Rachel joined the courtroom in laughter, then said, "If our clients were in as good a condition as the Court appears to be, we would not have to be out here today." The judge gallantly bowed his acknowledgment while Rachel continued. "Unfortunately, this is not the case."

Rachel then reviewed her doctors' sworn declarations, setting forth the plaintiffs' deteriorating conditions and the applicable rules of law. *So far, so good,* thought Rachel. *He tolerates flattery well.* Then it was Hancock's turn, and he came out fighting.

"Your honor and I both know that just outside these courtroom walls, thousands upon thousands of litigants are patiently waiting for their day in court. I'm not talking about big corporations or people with big claims like these plaintiffs. I am talking about the little people who *don't* have the resources of a Stafford, Parrish, and MacAllister behind them. These little people are abiding by the system; they aren't trying to cut in front of someone else in line as Ms. Cannon's gate-crashers want to do." Hancock's voice gradually took on more intensity as he urged the Court to "exercise its own discretion in the matter and instruct Ms. Cannon to be patient—though that trait may not come easy to her."

Rachel was surprised at Hancock's vehemence as he continued his personal attack. "Ms. Cannon has forgotten that justice serves defendants as well as plaintiffs. Let's call a spade a spade, your honor: Her firm's strategy is to file a multibillion-dollar lawsuit, then deprive us of adequate time in which to prepare to defend against it.

"She has a perfect right to bring this outrageous suit, of course. But we have the right to fully analyze and resist her specious claims. She would like to deny us this right because, I believe, deep in her heart she knows that if given a fair and sufficient amount of time"—Hancock's voice was now booming with righteousness—*"we will prevail."*

Rachel stirred in her seat uncomfortably. How quickly Hancock had swung the pendulum back in his direction. *I better stick it straight to the judge and stop with the good-guy–bad-guy stuff.*

"Any further remarks, counsel?" asked Judge Bainbridge, looking over Rachel's head at the clock on the wall, the universal expression of judicial impatience.

"Just this, if it please the Court," said Rachel. "I'll not waste time on counsel's vision of thousands of patient people gnashing their teeth on the courthouse steps. The fact is that our legislature had determined that people seventy and over, or those who can show good cause, are entitled to precedence. It is not for Mr. Hancock or me, or—with all respect—even this Court, to dispute it. It happens to be the law, and this Court is bound to uphold it. It may have been the plaintiffs who initiated this lawsuit, but it was the defendants who, as the complaint alleges and the evidence will show, initiated the willful and reckless contamination of the drinking water of their captive employees, with full knowledge of what they were doing. Having concealed the danger, and having nearly killed many of their own employees, it hardly becomes them to complain when their victims seek to obtain redress while they are still alive. Thank you, your honor.''

Hancock started to rise, but the Court silenced him. "I have heard more than enough, counsel. The motion to advance as to all fifteen plaintiffs in the first group is granted if plaintiffs will accept a date somewhat beyond the one-hundred-twenty-day statutory period. I see that both sides estimate approximately seven to nine weeks of trial. Do we have a courtroom around August of this year, Mr. Clerk?''

"Your honor!" said Hancock, again leaping to his feet. "That's only five months from now.''

"That's strange," said the judge, unsmiling. "That's exactly what my calendar says.''

"The earliest date we have, your honor, is September," replied the court clerk.

Hancock rose, scanning his appointment book. "Your honor, I have a serious problem with September. My calendar shows two cases of relatively short duration that month, but then—if I may throw myself on the mercy of the Court—I had planned to take my family on a brief vacation. Couldn't we start in October?''

Hancock's voice was pleading, and the judge peered at the calendar, murmuring a low "hmmmm.''

Johnstone whispered into Rachel's ear, "The bastard's buying more time! I can see his calendar from where I'm sitting, and there's not a damn thing on it in September. He's looking at *blank pages*!''

"Not to worry, Jeffrey," said Rachel.

"All right, Mr. Hancock. I have never denied a busy lawyer a chance to relax with his family. Set this trial down for the first week in October, Mr. Clerk.''

Rachel rose to her feet. "Your honor, as much as it cuts against my best interests, I must say that my calendar in October is in exactly the same state as Mr. Hancock's in September.''

"The entire month?" asked Judge Bainbridge.

Johnstone squirmed in his chair, knowing that Rachel had no commitments in October, and certainly no vacation plans.

"I'm afraid I may have to join with Mr. Hancock in delaying

the commencement of the trial into late October or early November, your honor.'' Jeffrey groaned softly and covered his face with both hands.

"All right, what's fair for one is fair for another. I am setting a date for commencement of the first fifteen plaintiffs on Monday, November 7, 1983, and I'll hear no further discussion. Thank you, counsel, and good day,'' he added, rising and heading for his chambers.

"All rise!'' cried the bailiff. Rachel quickly packed her files, gave Hancock a quiet courtesy handshake, and was out the door with Jeffrey in hot pursuit.

"Rachel! Have you gone totally bananas? You could have had this thing on for trial by early October if you had pushed the judge. And then you gave up another month for no reason at all!''

Rachel strode purposely toward the taxi stand with the casual but elongated stride of a thief leaving the scene of a crime. *"Au contraire,* my friend. I got exactly what I wanted.''

"The earliest possible trial date?''

"No, but he wasn't going to give us September anyway, so what's the next best thing? Figure it out, Jeffrey. If the trial takes seven weeks and it starts on November the seventh, when does the jury start deliberating the issue of how much money they're going to award these poor old victims?''

Jeffrey stopped dead in his tracks and broke into a giant smile. "You wily broad,'' he said admiringly. "You got yourself a Christmas verdict!''

Rachel smiled while waving down a cab. "Strange, that's what *my* calendar says.'' Both broke out laughing as they piled into the taxi. Jeffrey gave Rachel a victory slap of the hand as they settled themselves in, then suddenly turned serious.

"There's just one thing, Rachel. Can it be that the highly moral—the *previously* highly moral—Ms. Cannon stretched the truth a tad with a judge of the Superior Court concerning a proposed vacation in October?''

"Maybe Hancock did, but I didn't. All I said was that my calendar in October was in exactly the same state as Hancock's in September. You had already told me that Hancock's calendar for September was blank; well . . . so is mine.''

Jeff shook his head in wonder. "You *are* a piece of work, Ms. Cannon. Did you take Hancock's wallet while you were at it?''

The lawyers laughed again and exchanged another congratulatory slapping of hands.

"Do either one of you mouthpieces want to tell me where you'd like to go," asked the cabbie good-naturedly, "or shall I just join your patty-cake game?"

"The Imperial Building, please," said Rachel. Then, glancing at her watch and seeing that it was after five o'clock, said, "Strike that, driver. Make it the Washington Square Bar & Grill. Who would deny us a mini-celebration party?"

Rachel leaned back against the seat and took a deep breath. Another bullet ducked.

TWENTY-TWO

■

The next morning, as Kevin packed his bags for New York, Denise was making a rare and unsuccessful attempt to be nice to her husband. Kevin was unmoved, recognizing her sudden affection as a sign of her momentary insecurity concerning the state of their marriage. Something had snapped deep inside him that night at the Barringtons' and Denise was clever enough to know that it might have been the sound of the last link breaking in a weakened marital chain. For the first time, Kevin saw rampant fear in his wife's eyes, eyes that must see that his customary resilience was gone, his apparently inexhaustible willingness to forgive and forget suddenly exhausted. He had changed; had he cared enough to pursue their marital struggle, he would have sensed the victory. But something had happened, and her perception of this new distance between them was apparent to Kevin in the sound in her pleading voice as she said, "Kevin, dear, must you go? Why must it always be you? Why can't somebody else go try that stupid little case?"

Kevin's head jerked no more than half an inch—as if he had been annoyed by an insect—as the demeaning words stung his ear. *Is she trying to engage my emotions?* he thought, realizing

how easily she could do it. He knew now that he hated her, ye
they remained joined together emotionally at the hip.

"That 'stupid little case' involves the loss of my client's life's
work, Denise. It's also an opportunity for me to try an antitrust
case on the plaintiff's side, which I've never done. The answer is
yes, I must go."

Denise leaned her body at a provocative angle against the
four-poster, positioning herself so that the early morning sunlight
struck her sheer silk nightgown in a way that revealed a perfectly
proportioned body that had somehow escaped the ravages of
thirty-eight years and two childbirths. Kevin did not notice.

Denise sighed, then slipped out of her seductress role and into
a terry-cloth robe. "So how long will it take the white knight to
save this downtrodden victim of corporate America?" she said
with a slight tremor in her voice, lighting a long brown cigarette.

Kevin stopped packing for a moment, straightened, and started
to say something, then resumed his packing. "You're not sucking me in this morning, Denise," he said as he impatiently
walked to the dresser, removed six sets of underwear and socks
and stuffed them into a suitcase. He paused for a moment,
leaned against the dresser, and met Denise's eyes reflected in the
mirror above it. He felt that he was seeing Denise, really seeing
her, for the first time. Now temporarily in control of his own
reactive anger, he was able to view Denise as a consummate
actress in a one-woman show, able to play any part demanded by
her rapacious ego. Even now, with the show obviously closing.
"A week or two, maybe more," he added. "Would you please
go see why Sarah is screaming bloody murder?"

"Ah, the concerned father," said Denise through compressed
lips. Gone the seductress; gone the mother. Enter the sarcastic
bitch, always her finest performance. "Yes, master, I'll tell
them not to disturb Daddy while he's preparing to run off to slay
yet another dragon—to return at his pleasure bearing riches from
the East."

"I've never known you to complain about the money before,"
said Kevin, returning to his packing. Without a trace of rancor.
he added, "I recall, in fact, that my 'prospects' were quite
instrumental in both your decision to marry me and your father's
decision to permit it. Now, will you go see what's happening to
Sarah or must I?"

"What's happening with Sarah," said Denise, her thin mem-
brane of civility now thoroughly punctured by Kevin's refusal to

be engaged in their usual war games, "is what happens with Sarah at least four times a day when you're not around. Sarah taunts Julie, thinking that Julie will not dare to retaliate out of fear that you will punish her when—if—you get home. Julie finally loses patience and pushes or slaps Sarah. Then Sarah cries bloody murder. If you care so goddamn much about our children, why don't you stick around sometime and get to know them? Let your hero Austin Barrington go try a case for once. Or maybe it's time to dust off the legendary Adrian Fisher."

Kevin took in a deep breath—the air in their bedroom had the sharp, obnoxious pungency of stale cigarettes—then turned to face Denise, who had moved over to the dressing table and now sat with legs crossed, arms stretched out behind her on the dressing table. "Let's not do this, Denise. There's no one else to try this particular case, and I have committed to do so. As you well know, Austin is knee-deep in administration now, and Adrian no longer remembers where the courthouse is."

"There's that to be thankful for I suppose. But mark my words: You'll bleed to death in the trenches before they let *you* get 'knee-deep in administration.' "

"I'll have my turn when it's time."

"And just when will that be?"

Kevin noisily secured the zipper on the main compartment of his bag. "I don't know," he said, then added quietly, "soon, I hope."

"Well, I *do* know," said Denise. "They'll kick you upstairs when they've had your very last drop of blood. And not a minute before."

"You don't know a fucking thing about it, Denise," said Kevin quietly. Then he added in a resigned tone, "Besides, they've already had my last drop of blood."

"Oh, bullshit," said Denise, her face twisted as the torrent of bitter words spewed like vomit. "You *love* going out there and being the hero. You can't pack your bag fast enough to run off to New York again with your little bitch Rachel. As for your downtrodden client, I pity the poor bastard if he thinks he's going to have the benefit of *your* full libido with that slut around, holding your briefcase in one hand and your cock in the other!"

Kevin snapped his trial bag shut and turned to stare at his wife. *So that's it,* he thought. *She knows. Or is she still on a fishing expedition?* He considered, then quickly rejected the urge to tell her everything, to get it over with. But now was not the time. Too much going on. *Get North American behind you,* he admonished himself. *Hold on for a few more months.*

"I won't even dignify that comment," said Kevin coldly, "except to say that Rachel is too tied up in North American to try the case with me. I'll be taking a younger associate."

"Ahhh," said Denise, smiling through drawn lips, "time to trade in the aging Miss Cannon for someone younger. What's the new lucky girl's name?"

Kevin shook his head in disgust and met her smoldering eyes. "Larry Atkinson."

"How *typically* clever!" said Denise, not to be denied, flinging both arms in the air. "That should spare dear Rachel any jealousy. Good thinking, Don Juan."

"Thinking—*before* you shoot off your mouth—is something you might work on while I'm gone, Denise." Kevin, retaining outward calm, was surprised at the internal violence of his reactions to his wife's barbs. She had become a prison he longed to escape.

"Oh, really? I think that I think pretty damn well, thank you. I think, for example, that you don't give a damn about me *or* the girls, or you'd give us more than just the dregs of your time."

Kevin lifted his bag off the bed and dropped it noisily on the floor. "And just what would you and I do," he asked, matching her disdainful tone, "with more time together? Play Scrabble? Pull the wings off moths? Let's face it, Denise," he added, quickly understating his emotions, "we just don't get along."

"We used to," said Denise, showing a flash of fear again, but too resentful now to resume her coquettish manner, "when you brought more . . . vitality home."

"Meaning what?"

"Meaning you're losing it, old boy. Well, now, maybe you're better with secretaries and girl lawyers, but your wife hasn't seen you in bed for many moons. I also haven't seen you in court in a while, but my guess is that it's showing up there too. And if you think you're kidding anybody with that breath spray, forget it. That perfume smell of vodka precedes you before you even open the door. I'm getting sick and tired of hearing you stumble in here late every night, stiff as a board, except, of course, between your legs." She laughed at her own wit. "I guess I think you're no longer so goddamn perfect, Mr. Perfect."

Kevin started to pick up his bags, then paused, and in a flat tone said, "What do you really want, Denise? What do you want from me? Do you want a divorce?"

"What do I want?" she snapped, ignoring his last words. "I want you to come back from New York and start being a father to your children and a husband to me. I want you to stop drinking so much and get ahold of yourself. I want you to see my point of view on things once in a while and stop being such a fucking *lawyer* when you do get home." Denise defiantly threw her mane of black hair back with one hand and added in a cracking voice that betrayed imminent tears of frustration, "Most of all . . . goddamn you . . . I want you to make me *happy* again!"

Denise stormed from the room and slammed the door, leaving Kevin staring after her, wondering how it could have taken him so long to really get to know his wife.

TWENTY-THREE

■

The Dodge black-and-white carefully threaded itself through the cataract eye of mist-enshrouded foliage, the *tic tic tic* of its engine amplified by the still and moonless night. A spotlight occasionally shot from the patrol car, probing the bushy darkness like a bird dog, turning the fog into an alien glow. But no muggers, rapists, or even consenting adults were flushed from cover this quiet night in San Francisco's Golden Gate Park.

The police car came to rest in front of the Manfred Hopkins Marine Life Center, and a new shaft of light from the vehicle pierced the massive glass front door, disappearing into the dark interior beyond. There was no sign of the caretaker within, nothing but more darkness.

Rookie police officer McFadden was reluctant to leave the warm comfort of his car, for the summer fog had turned to a cold drizzle and the sight of the huge, dark building made him feel strangely uneasy.

He considered calling for backup, but dismissed the thought and walked stiffly toward the entrance, flashlight in hand.

"Hey, McFadden!" the night sergeant had growled thirty minutes earlier. "Run over to Fish City and see what's with the night watchman over there. His name's Weisberg. We've had three calls from a friend of his who thinks something's wrong."

"Why not just call him on the telephone, Sarge?" asked the young police officer, already wishing he hadn't.

"Jesus, McFadden, now, why didn't I think of that! Then if there wasn't any answer, I might have even thought to check out the telephone to make sure it was not out of order. Who knows? I might even have double-checked the watchman's schedule to make sure that I was not wasting the time of someone as important as Patrolman Stanley W. McFadden." Although spoken in deadpan, the sergeant's smiling eyes betrayed his affection for the young rookie. *Was there ever a moment in my life*, thought the sergeant wistfully, *when I was so innocent?* Everybody loved McFadden.

"I'll get right out there, Sergeant," said the embarrassed officer, gratefully exiting, his face as red as his short-clipped hair.

"You do that, Officer," replied the sergeant more gently, like a good father who knows that some children must be treated differently from others, but that all must be loved.

Patrol Officer McFadden approached the ten-foot-high main door and found it unlocked. He applied his two hundred pounds against the heavy brass door, and it opened an inch. He then stopped and pressed his ear to the opening. Nothing.

As he entered the tomblike Marine Life Center, he unsnapped the holster at his side without thinking. The moonlight slicing into the entryway behind him provided the only illumination. Where are the darned lights? he wondered, feeling as if he must be looking in all the wrong places. Foolish, this nervousness, he thought—who's going to steal a bunch of fish? Yet, there was no sign of the night man.

Patrolman McFadden looked wistfully back at his patrol car, again considered backup, but dismissed the notion as he reflected on the teasing he could suffer back at headquarters. It would not take long for handwritten signs like "Rookie Savaged by Giant Goldfish" to spring up in the locker room. He didn't need that.

What he needed to do was to get the lights on, then to find Weisberg. The blackness was definitely getting to him now, inflicting him with vertigo. He leaned on his light beam for support while he wiped beads of cold dampness from his forehead. As he continued to scan the walls, the piercing sound of a telephone stopped his heartbeat for a full second. McFadden whirled in the direction of the sound, wielding his flashlight like a gun. It came to rest on a telephone next to an empty table and chair, apparently the caretaker's station.

"Officer McFadden," he said into the receiver, surprised at the resonance of his voice in the huge entry hall.

"Thank God you're there, Officer. May I speak to Bernie? This is his roommate, Aaron Harris. I'm the one who made the report. Is everything okay?" The anxiety in the caller's voice paradoxically calmed the rookie.

"I just arrived, Mr. Harris. Mr. Weisberg must be on his rounds somewhere. He's not here at his station."

"Will you have him call home the minute you find him?" asked Harris anxiously. "I've been worried all night."

"Certainly, sir," said McFadden. "I'm sure there's nothing to worry about. I'll have him call you the minute I find him."

McFadden hung up, bolstered by the residual echo of his own voice, and followed his flashlight beam toward the room that housed the main tanks. He passed through a wide corridor flanked on either side by eye-level aquariums containing a dazzling array of tropical specimens, all bathed in the eerie but welcome glow of underwater lighting.

But entering the main tank room, he was again plunged into total darkness, save for the beam from his own flashlight. "Mr. Weisberg?" called McFadden. "Mr. Weisberg!" The only reply was the thrashing sound of broken water at or below floor level. McFadden spun around and pointed his light in the direction of the noise. For one horrible second he thought he had found Mr. Weisberg, but closer inspection revealed a crocodile slithering into the floor-level reptile pond opposite the main tanks.

McFadden resumed his movement across the room toward the main exhibition tanks. The gurgling symphony of the smaller aquarium tanks began to recede relative to the pounding of his own heart. He began to walk faster, his flashlight slashing at the layers of darkness like a swordsman, his free hand instinctively moving toward his holster. *Where was the night watchman?*

Straight ahead he saw three interconnected main tanks, each thirty feet long and twenty feet wide, forming a continuous viewing window eight feet in height and ninety feet in total length. Each of the three tanks was separated by a solid wall, separating the sea lions, swordfish, and other specimens housed there. As he walked around to the rear of the tanks, he tried to ignore the agitated thrashings of the killer sharks he knew occupied the center tank.

Returning to the front of the tanks, he again called out the caretaker's name: "Mr. Weisberg, sir? Mr. Bernard Weisberg!" No answer.

He decided to return to the entryway to make another effort to locate the light switches and check in with the sergeant. As he turned, he scanned the three tanks with his flashlight and saw something bumping against the glass of the middle tank no more than a few feet away, floating just below the surface. He moved closer and directed the beam into the tank. There, clearly now in the bright light and no more than two feet from his face, McFadden saw the shredded remains of a human body—its one remaining eye staring straight into the policeman's own bloodless face.

McFadden had found the night watchman.

Officer McFadden felt the bile of fear and revulsion in his throat as he dialed headquarters. While waiting for the ring, his spotlight fell at last on the light switch panel.

"Emergency," came the mechanical voice of a young woman at the other end.

"Give me Sergeant Daniels. Quick." As he waited, McFadden involuntarily kept turning the flashlight toward the entrance to the tank room. He realized he was strangling the phone as if it were his only tangible link to reality.

"Daniels here."

"Sergeant, this is McFadden at the aquarium. I have found the night watchman, sir, Mr. Bernard Weisberg, or . . . at least what's left of him."

"*What?*"

"He either fell or was pushed into the shark tank. They didn't leave much. Can you hold on a minute, Sergeant, I think I've found the main light panel."

The patrolman rushed to the corner of the room and threw the switch, exploding the room into bright, welcome light. As he walked back to the telephone, he spotted an envelope centered in the middle of the desk. "I'm back, Sergeant. There's an envelope here on Weisberg's desk. Do you want me to open it?"

"Go ahead," replied the sergeant. "Protect for prints."

The admonition irritated McFadden despite the fact that he was about to forget to do so. He picked up the envelope by the edges, carefully opened it with trembling fingers, and removed the contents: a three-by-five card with meticulous handwriting crammed onto both sides. McFadden quickly read it to himself.

"Hold it, Sergeant. I think this explains everything. It's long but I'll read it to you:

> Everybody knows that cancer means pain. I have learned that it also means the day by day humiliation of your spirit and the destruction of your soul.
>
> Pills help the pain but they turn me into someone else I don't know and don't like. The more pills I take, the more I change. Every day now I need more of them.
>
> I would prefer the pain, except that it grows too strong for me to bear so that I weaken and take the drugs and become someone else again. I have tried them all. It's always the same.
>
> I am rambling a bit. The point is, what kind of life is this? I hurt physically without the pills. I suffer even more emotionally when I take the pills. And the Grim Reaper is always there in the wings waiting for me.
>
> The answer is: It's no kind of life at all and I'm sorry, but you can have it.

"Okay, McFadden," said the sergeant after a moment, "I'll send the morgue crew out. Leave everything the way it is and start your report. I'll get the foundation director and the morgue crew right down there."

"Anything else, Sergeant?" asked McFadden, trying to keep his voice steady.

"No, that does it. Just make sure the place is secure before you leave." The sergeant sensed that the rookie needed to talk. "What a way to go, huh?"

"You should see him, Sergeant. It's like he got run twice through a meat grinder."

"You'll see a lot of things you won't like before you're on this end of the telephone. Talk to you later."

Officer McFadden only dimly perceived that he had been paid a very encouraging compliment. Right now, however, a lifetime of bagging groceries or collecting bridge tolls appealed to him more than working his way up to desk sergeant.

He went back into the main tank area, seeing it in the light for the first time. Nothing appeared to be out of order, except, of course, for the peripherally observed shadowy mass, still bobbing against the curved viewing glass. A few hours ago, McFadden reflected, that shredded mop was a human being just like me, drinking coffee, watching TV, capable of speech, action . . . suicide.

He noted that the sharks—a half dozen or more averaging five or six feet in length—seemed to intentionally avoid Weisberg's sparse remains as they circled the large tank. Almost like they're embarrassed, he thought. McFadden was suddenly tired of being alone, wishing someone would show up. He began to kill time by checking out other corridors and exhibition areas, but found nothing unusual. Finally, fifty years later by the rookie's reckoning, the morgue staff appeared.

"He's in the center main tank," said McFadden, casually pointing to his rear, summoning new energy.

"Okay," replied the man in charge. "But we just got the word on radio that we're to hold up until Inspector Conti shows up."

"Conti?" asked Officer McFadden. "What's the homicide department doing on a suicide case?"

"Beats me. I guess he overheard the sergeant instructing me to report over here, then came on the telephone when he heard what had happened. He told me his shift was ending and he was going to stop by here on the way home just to look around. I asked him whether there was anything wrong and he just said, 'This suicide story sounds fishy to me.' "

"Under the circumstances, that's not very funny," said McFadden righteously.

"But shit, Officer, let's face it: If you list the ten worst ways to check out of this world, jumping into a shark tank has got to be close to the top. That's enough to get any homicide inspector suspicious, and Dan Conti can smell murder before it's even been committed."

"Don't you think that a murderer would realize that?" replied McFadden, eager to have someone to talk to. "If you are going to phony-up a suicide note, you just drown your victim, you don't create suspicion by feeding him to sharks. I read the note and my view—if the note's his, of course—is that the guy was so zapped on pills when he took the dive, he couldn't tell a shark tank from his own bathtub."

"I'm not arguing with you, Officer. I just drive a meat wagon and do what I'm told. Here's the lieutenant now; that must be the director with him."

McFadden had seen Conti only once before, when the famed detective was teaching a three-hour crime detection course at San Francisco State. Conti had built a national reputation as a man at war with crime. One of the jokes around the squad room was that Conti's only fear in life was that at the rate he was solving murders, he would run out of them before his pension accrued. Now, here he was in the flesh, moving toward McFadden with the heel-toe-bounce walk of an athlete. The detective was followed by a tall, elderly man. Both wore civilian clothing.

"Are you McFadden?"

"Yes, sir," replied the patrolman, suddenly feeling uneasy again. At six feet two, McFadden was inches taller than the inspector, yet the rookie felt small in the shorter man's dynamic presence.

"Is everything just the way you found it?" Conti asked him, his large brown eyes locked onto McFadden's. The question was innocent enough, asked in the perfunctory manner of a family doctor inquiring when his flu patient's symptoms had started. The inspector's full mouth was even half smiling, as if he knew concessions had to be made. Nonetheless, McFadden felt another icy dampness creep over him and inexplicably imagined himself assigned for life to the intersection of Stockton and Geary— condemned like Sisyphus to endure an endless mountain of crazed drivers.

"Exactly, sir, except for the note on the desk which I was careful not to smudge." Conti walked to the desk and carefully picked up the note by its edges. He was clad in loafers, slacks, white linen shirt, and sport coat, but in this case, clothes did not make the man casual. Dan Conti was the kind of man who would look fiercely intense dressed in a tutu.

He glared at the note from under heavily hooded lids with such concentration that McFadden would not have been surprised to see it burst into flames. Everything the inspector did, every move he made, conveyed a feeling of conviction and intensity. As he watched and waited, the rookie was struck by the ridiculous notion that Conti—through a combination of his suspicious nature and his indomitable will—was capable of converting a true suicide into an actual homicide. He imagined investigations, crime lab reports, lineups, even a trial, complete with innocent defendant, of course. The lieutenant would simply will away the existence of a suicide note and the apparent absence of any motive to kill an aged victim who was dying as fast as he could anyway. And ultimately, of course, the innocent defendant would be won over to Conti's side and confess.

In reality, McFadden and every other cop on the force knew that Conti was not merely quick and creative, but possessed sound instincts tempered by a logical and disciplined mind. In truth, the bedrock of Conti's success was his conviction that the potential for homicide lay buried in the heart of every man and woman, awaiting only the final thrusts of a mean world's pick and shovel to unearth it.

It was clear to the rookie as he watched Conti continue to scrutinize the words on the note that the detective deeply mistrusted them. The three-by-five card was tilted and turned over and over again, as if it were one of those little toy puzzles with holes into which you try to maneuver tiny steel balls. In the respectful silence, McFadden studied the intense face of the inspector. He noticed that the renowned crime-smelling nose angled slightly to the left—reputedly the concerted achievement of a University of Pacific boxer with a good left hook and a U.S.F. team physician with bad eyesight. The dark-complexioned features were otherwise unmarked and his short black hair was completely dry, despite the drizzle he had just passed through. The hands that rotated the three-by-five card were small, almost delicate—not at all like a fighter's.

"All right," Conti said at last. "Let's have a look inside. This is Professor Ames. He runs the place. Is this the caretaker's station?" asked Conti, gesturing toward the nearby desk and chair.

"Yes, Detective Conti, his—"

"Inspector," interrupted Conti. "They don't call us detectives anymore in San Francisco."

"Excuse me, Inspector. This is my first experience with your department. Anyway, yes, it is," replied the tall, white-bearded director, looking professorial even in the corduroy pants, pullover sweater, and running shoes he had hastily donned upon being awakened by the desk sergeant. "His rounds are made from this station, but ninety percent of his time is spent right here at this desk, at least on the graveyard shift."

"Twelve to eight?" asked Conti.

"No. Mr. Weisberg is . . . was . . . in our part-time senior employees program. His shift this month was from eleven to four A.M."

"What were his duties here?" asked Conti, beginning to stroll in the direction of the main tank area. The others followed him like pilot fish.

"Our night caretakers are here more to monitor tank temperature control and lighting than to guard against burglary or vandalism. People don't seem much interested in stealing fish—although some of them are quite valuable."

"And these overhead lights are left on all night?" asked Conti just as they began to enter the main tank room.

"Excuse me, sir," interrupted McFadden. "That reminds me of something else that was different when I arrived. All of the overhead lights were out."

"Tell me, Professor Ames," said Conti without seeming to have heard McFadden, "is the light switch near the entry door the only control for the overhead lights in the entry room and main tank area?"

"Yes. It's all on one switch," replied the curator. "Well, here we are at the main tanks. Oh, my God!"

The director averted his eyes from the mutilated body still bobbing gently against the glass. Conti also appeared uninterested in viewing Weisberg's remains and instead began to walk in small, mincing steps around the entire perimeter of the tanks. There was an awkward stillness of sound and motion, like the respectful silence before the start of a funeral service as the director, McFadden, and the two morgue attendants watched Conti disappear through the Employees Only door behind the main tanks and emerge at the other end a half minute later.

When he had completed his walk around the tanks, he stroked the length of his generous, skewed nose, and his manner suddenly became brisk. "Officer McFadden. Return to the caretaker's station, pick up the telephone, dial the night sergeant, and give him the following message: 'This is Rookie Patrol Officer McFadden. Please disregard my premature assessment of this matter as a suicide and, at Inspector Conti's request, send the crime lab team on the double.' You got that straight, kid?"

"Yes, sir, but—"

"On the double!"

"Yes, sir."

"Now, Professor Ames, please tell me if you see anything out of the ordinary here other than the fact that your night man has fed the sharks in an unorthodox manner.''

"I most certainly do, Inspector. In the first place, what you are looking at is the largest and finest captive collection of black-tip reef sharks—*cacharhinus melanopterus*—anywhere in the world. Although they are cartilaginous omnivores, and have been known to attack swimmers in shallow water under some circumstances, they are generally not considered to be dangerous to humans. In fact, our staff divers often swim among them during exhibitions.''

"They seem to have forgotten their manners on this occasion," said Conti dryly. "This is where you had the great white for a while.''

"Yes. We set a record before we lost him. . . .''

"I remember. He looked like an Oldsmobile with its hood open. How would Mr. Weisberg have gotten into the tank?''

"He would have reached the center tank by the stairway you saw at the rear of the tanks. That leads to a metal catwalk that runs the length of the tanks. Then all he did was lower himself into the water two feet below.''

"You apparently assume that he voluntarily dropped himself into a tank full of sharks. Is that because you believe he was under the influence of the drugs he mentions in his note?''

"Not necessarily. Bernie knew those fish are normally harmless and that they would, in all probability, tend to avoid him. Once he decided to drown himself, he would logically choose them rather than being mauled by sea lions in the west tank or prodded by swordfish and eel in the east tank.''

"But you mentioned that this type of shark *has* been known to attack humans under some circumstances. What circumstances?''

"The carnage we see here could be the result only of what we call a 'feeding frenzy.' This phenomenon—about which surprisingly little is known—can be initiated in the case of black-tips either by a victim retreating in fear or by the sharks' uncanny sensory perception of blood.''

"Blood from a head wound, for example?" asked Conti.

"I know what you're getting at, Inspector, but it could be anything: a nick from shaving, even bleeding gums. A shark's olfacto-gustatory sense can detect blood at just one part dissolved in up to a hundred million parts of seawater. In this confined space it would take very little to excite an attacker. And once one of them makes a move, the frenzy is on.''

The lieutenant paced impatiently during this last answer, as if he had asked for the time and been told how to build a Swiss waterclock.

"Look, Professor. I can guess that you'd be reluctant to have a murder investigation out here. But level with me: in view of what you've just said, doesn't it look like he was first wounded, *then* dumped in the tank?"

"I'm not being evasive, Inspector. I'm merely trying to explain that you should not rely too heavily on that theory. Remember, sharks *are* predators and . . ."

"Well, Professor. My own guess is that Weisberg's death was caused by a different kind of predator."

"Perhaps so, but there's yet another problem with your theory, Inspector Conti. I did not know Bernie well, but I can tell you that he was terminally ill and did not have an enemy in the world."

"Do you have Mr. Weisberg's address and telephone?" asked Conti, turning back toward the entry room. "I want to run out after breakfast and break the news to the victim's roommate—the guy who reported a possible problem. I want to have a little chat with him."

Officer McFadden came back at a half trot.

"The crime lab is on the way, sir," said the rookie, his eyes downcast. As soon as Professor Ames got out of earshot, he whispered, "May I ask what I missed, sir?"

Conti took a deep breath, shrugged his shoulders, then exhaled. "How did the late Mr. Weisberg get to the tank area?"

"He either walked or was carried," replied McFadden.

"If he was all alone and getting ready to take a dive, as you assumed, how did he get to the tank area?"

"He would have walked over to the rear of the east tank of his own accord," replied McFadden.

"In the dark?" asked Conti, turning toward the young officer with his arms extended, his palms upward. "The lights were out when you arrived. After Weisberg took his dip, who turned them *out*? It certainly wasn't Mr. Weisberg."

"*Jesus,*" exclaimed McFadden, pounding his fist against his forehead.

"I doubt that it was Jesus either. Got any other suspects?" asked Conti.

"Well," McFadden ventured, "I guess it would be pretty

stupid to assume that Weisberg turned out all the lights and then made his way to the tank using a flashlight?''

"Okay, let's assume for a minute that our Mr. Weisberg had a flair for the dramatic. What became of his flashlight?''

McFadden's fair skin turned crimson again. He was beginning to blink on and off like a roadway safety light. "I don't know.''

"I don't either. But I looked carefully, and since I couldn't find one on the bottom of any of the tanks or anywhere in the exterior vicinity of the tanks, I'm sure that you will find it in a desk drawer back at the caretaker's desk. And while you are there, call in and get yourself some backup to make sure that nothing is changed or touched until the crime lab people finish up here.''

The director returned with Harris's address. Conti thanked him and told him that the morgue people would clean up what was left of the victim after the crime lab finished. He also inquired as to opening hours.

"Ten o'clock A.M.,'' replied Professor Ames.

"Our lab people will be gone before then, but no employees will be allowed in here until the crime people finish their work. Officer McFadden will see to that. Right, McFadden?''

"Yes, sir.'' McFadden snapped to, as if awakening from a bad dream. Conti knew the young officer had suffered a confidence crisis but also knew it would be futile to patronize him.

"When the lab boys get here, I want both rooms dusted and vacuumed. Then I want any shred from what's left of Weisberg's clothing checked for hairs or fibers. You,'' said Conti, turning to the head of the morgue crew, "when the lab people leave, take what's left of the body to Pathology. Tell them I want to know if there is any evidence of bruising from a heavy instrument and, if they can find a big enough piece of lung for analysis, whether he drowned or bled to death.''

"We'll take care of it, sir,'' said McFadden. "You must be ready for some sleep, sir. You're way past the end of your shift.''

"Sleep?'' replied Conti, looking at the rookie as if trying to catch on to a poorly told joke. "Don't you see there's been a murder committed here tonight?''

TWENTY-FOUR

■

Dan Conti's conversation with Aaron Harris was unexpectedly difficult and unsettling.

Shock had produced a lethargy in the tall, large-boned man that made him an unwilling participant in the emotional autopsy of his friend and roommate. Moreover, when the lieutenant did get answers, they were not the ones he wanted to hear. Conti now stared icily up into the sallow, flabby features of the over-weight old man, fighting a growing feeling of unreasoning irritation.

"I tell you," said Harris, in a dazed mumble, "Bernie had no enemies. And no, he didn't have any insurance other than a ten-thousand-dollar retirement policy."

"Who was the beneficiary?" asked the inspector with the frayed impatience of a man confronting a dead-end street while attempting a shortcut.

"Bernie's beneficiary was an older brother who disappeared years ago. I told him he should change it because the money would all go to the state. I think he would have taken my advice when his time grew closer, assuming he hadn't made contact with his brother."

Ten measly grand to a beneficiary nobody can find—great fucking motive for murder! thought Conti. Doubt began to spread through him with an uncomfortable damp heat. What if the kid—McFadden—was right? He felt as if he were coming down with something. He suddenly needed to go home and get some sleep.

"Do you know his handwriting?" asked Conti in a tone that betrayed his fatigue and anxiety.

"Of course," said the phlegmatic Harris, grunting his words in a barely audible voice. "We shared this dump for three years."

Conti removed a Xerox copy of the note which had been

delivered to him by McFadden an hour before. He handed it over to Aaron Harris. "Is this Bernard Weisberg's handwriting?" asked Conti.

"Sure looks like it to me," replied Harris, lazily surveying the paper.

"Study it," insisted Conti irritably, jumping to his feet and thrusting his hands deep into the pockets of his Ralph Lauren sport coat. "Compare it with other notes and calendar entries you must have somewhere here around the house. I need you to be absolutely certain."

The sternness of the detective's command was like a gentle slap in Harris's face. He seemed to awaken for the first time. "If you say so, Inspector," said Harris, moving over to the desk and silently scanning the words. "Ah, here's something," he said finally. "Look here; look at the way he makes his p's and l's. Nobody could forge Bernie Weisberg's handwriting. Nobody but me could even read it, let alone duplicate it."

Conti considered himself a reasonably competent handwriting analyst and quickly spotted three or four other similarities. There could be no doubt: Bernard Weisberg had indeed penned his own suicide note. *"Shit!"* he muttered through clenched teeth, leaning on the desk, head buried in his shoulders.

The expletive hung in the ensuing silence. A living room clock became audible, until it was drowned out by the sound of crumpling paper as Conti discarded the Xerox copy of the note in the wastebasket. Then he straightened abruptly and walked to the door, saying, "Thanks for your help" over his shoulder.

"I just wish I could have been of more help to Bernie," said Harris sadly. "I had no idea he'd do this. I knew he was suffering, but with all that money now within reach . . ."

Conti released the doorknob as if it were white hot: "Money? What do you mean? *What money?*"

"Bernie had filed a lawsuit along with several others against the North American Chemical Company and the city of Lileton; you know, the toxic water case that's been in all of the newspapers."

"Is that why Weisberg was dying?" asked Conti.

"Sure. He had taken in so much chemical contamination, he glowed in the dark. He had been given less than a year to live."

"Did Bernie ever tell you how much money he thought he would get as a result of this lawsuit?"

"All I know is what his lawyers told him. They were talking two million dollars."

Conti's downward-sloping eyes awoke to new possibilities. He took a deep breath and resumed his seat, leaning close to Harris.

"When was he coming up for trial?"

"Probably no more than a few months is what they told him. His group—the first fifteen—were the ones who were most seriously poisoned," replied Harris. "I think the lawyers' theory was to get huge verdicts for them, then start settling the rest."

"Was he employed at the North American Chemical Company?"

"For eighteen years. He also lived there in company housing the whole time, like most of them did. The lawyers told him that the water well that serviced the people out there was contaminated by a chemical waste dump site less than a mile away, right on the same property."

"Now, listen carefully, Mr. Harris, and think before you answer. Did Mr. Weisberg really seem to be any more emotionally dejected lately than he was five or six months ago?"

"Oh, yes, and it was getting worse all the time. I sometimes wondered how he held on this long. They told him there was no cure and he was in pain all the time. What he says there in the note is true. He had a terrible reaction to any kind of painkiller. That's why I kept an eye on him, even when he was at work."

"But had he ever actually mentioned suicide?"

"He never talked about it. But I guess if I were in his shoes, at our age, I would have considered it myself. And I know one thing for sure, Inspector: That's Bernie's handwriting."

"I heard you the first time," snapped Conti, rising and walking toward the front door again. "I'm sorry, Mr. Harris," he added, half-turning. "I'm a little tired. Thanks again for your help." Conti and Harris had exchanged moods: Harris's earlier state of immobilizing languor was now Conti's; Conti's initial alertness was now manifest in Harris's strong voice.

"Inspector, if you don't mind my saying so, it don't matter now to Bernie how he died. Why is it so important to you?"

The inspector paused in the open doorway for a few seconds, then closed the door and left.

"Here they are, Lieutenant," said the deputy county clerk: *"Dixon, et al.,* versus *North American Chemical Company, city of Lileton, et al.,* a complaint filed June 4, 1982—a little over a year ago now. Three files full of legal gobbledegook."

Conti had gotten to bed at last, but it was too late for sleep—he was far too tired. Besides, Harris's last question, ignored at the door, was being broadcast from his pillow in several frequencies. Finally, he leapt up, half in frustration, half in relief. A hot shower and a shave would help him follow up on the one last thin lead.

Conti now walked over to a stand-up reading table and began to study the voluminous contents of the clerk's file. First, he carefully read the allegations of the complaint, pronouncing each word to himself. Even the arcane legalese was massaged word by word, for the inspector knew that when the words of this file ran out, so also did his last hope for proving his hastily reached and widely trumpeted murder hypothesis.

It was all boilerplate. Words. Lawyer talk. There in the caption, however, was indeed the name of Bernard J. Weisberg—one of the fifteen plaintiffs in the first grouping of ex-North American Chemical Company employees and residents, allegedly the victims of the various offenses perpetrated by North American, resulting in

> . . . shock and injury to the nervous system of said plaintiffs as a result of the ingestion of the aforesaid organic chemicals . . .

Conti nibbled at each word of the complaint, but then it was over. At the end was a standard prayer for damages—three million dollars in compensatory damages and six million dollars in punitive damages for Weisberg's case alone. Conti knew these amounts far exceeded what the lawyers actually hoped to get, but Harris had not been wrong when he forecast great wealth for Weisberg had he lived; at least one million dollars could be expected in a case like this even if only half of what the lawyers said was true.

Conti also knew about North American's Mafia ties and its alleged control over the Lileton city police. The chief executive officer and three directors had been indicted three years before by the grand jury on racketeering charges, but one key witness had been excused from testifying because of a long-standing heart condition, while the other was found floating in San Francisco Bay. But though contracts for murder were let out over far less than a million dollars, thought Conti, not even North American's eastern cousins would tackle the elimination of all fifteen plaintiffs, knowing there was at least a hundred more to follow the first group. Nothing could be so big as to warrant that kind of mass slaughter. Nothing made sense.

After an hour Conti had come to the end of the file: a paper shower of routine notices, issuances of summonses, motions and countermotions, interrogatories and answers to interrogatories. He had already started back to the clerk's counter as he began to scan the last document, a short, two-page pleading, entitled "Dismissal," dated just two days earlier. Something there caught his attention, stopping him in his tracks.

Reading more quickly now, he saw that it had been filed on behalf of another of the fifteen plaintiffs who had also died after the filing of the complaint. Since the decedent apparently had no heirs to succeed to his alleged damages, his case had been dismissed. An attached declaration stated that the particular plaintiff had been the victim of an automobile accident in Santa Cruz County. His name was listed as Charles V. Hallinan.

Conti touched the tip of his angled nose and considered the blossoming possibilities. Two plaintiffs out of the first group of fifteen, slightly less than fifteen percent of the batch. He wondered what the odds were of not just one, but two plaintiffs in the same case meeting death within five weeks of each other? One on a Santa Cruz highway on June 11, 1983. Another in San Francisco on July 19, 1983. He turned back to the clerk, a dry smile now crossing his pale face. "Where's your telephone?"

The deputy clerk tipped up the hinged counterboard, beckoned him through, and handed him a telephone.

"Operator, I want the number for the Santa Cruz County sheriff's department."

One receptionist, one secretary, and one deputy sheriff later, Conti was finally referred to Sheriff "Bull" Mattson, whose deep, rough voice sounded true to his name.

"Are you positive, Sheriff?" Conti said after listening to several minutes of homespun non sequiturs. "Doesn't it seem like more than coincidence that two plaintiffs with no heirs, both standing to gain multimillion-dollar verdicts in the same case, have died within five weeks of each other?"

Silence leaked from the receiver in Conti's hand. He pressed on: "Wasn't there *any* hint of suspicious circumstances in the death of Charles Hallinan?"

"None whatsoever, Lieutenant Conti," came the response—a slow Southern drawl, but each word assured and precise.

Conti could almost picture the man at the other end. Big, obviously. Overweight, probably, judging by the coarse bourbon voice. A hedonist's voice. Probably a smoker too. Cigars, maybe. Wears glasses, guessed Conti from the sheriff's delay in reading from a report he claimed to be holding in his hand. What kind had he been reaching for? Steel-rimmed, possibly. So ran Dan Conti's mind as he waited for the voice to reveal new secrets concerning its speaker.

"I assure you, Lieutenant, that if there had been anything irregular, we would have spotted it and built a complete file. Hallinan was an old fart, it turns out, riddled with cancer and blind in one eye. He shouldn't have been on the road at all. Seems he was on his way to a religious retreat and lost control of his car. Unfortunately, the point he picked to do it at was where there was no right shoulder guardrail, so he went all the way down. Couple a hundred feet or so."

"Anything funny about the car?"

"Nothing much *left* of the car. The gas tank blew. The old man was blown to bits."

"Anybody see him go?"

"Nobody." The sheriff replied too quickly, it seemed to Conti. "Well, there was one kid whose elevator don't go all the way to the top, if you know what I mean. And he didn't see really anything unusual, anyway. I'm sorry I can't help you, Lieutenant, but this is just one of twenty accidents we average up there on highway seventeen every month, year in and year out. That stretch of road can blow the dots off the dice of better drivers than that old guy was."

"Okay, Sheriff. Thanks for your time," said the inspector in the most casual tone he could affect. "I appreciate it. Say, listen, Sheriff—I see here that I'll be in your neighborhood tomorrow. Mind if I drop by and say hello?"

Conti was not surprised by the delay at the other end of the line. He knew that Sheriff Mattson would resent his intrusion, no matter how tactfully orchestrated. If the sheriff's investigation had been incomplete or an erroneous conclusion drawn—as Conti was beginning to suspect—he could expect an inhospitable welcome. The lengthening silence was beginning to lend support to this hypothesis, so he decided to take the lead. "Well, fine, then; would around two in the afternoon be okay?"

"Well . . . ummm, I'm going—"

"Great then, Sheriff. See you tomorrow afternoon."

Dan Conti hung up and stared in silence at the complaint and dismissal in his hand. At least he had a lead now—a link between the two victims: their law firm. He was familiar with the firm—one of the big ones—headed by a member of the San Francisco Police Commission. That might help. He looked at the top of the recently filed dismissal for the names and telephone numbers of the lawyers handling the case and picked up the phone again.

TWENTY-FIVE

■

Deputy Sheriff Ralph Stinson could feel his side of the argument slipping away. This came as no surprise; in fact, he had grown accustomed to losing these arguments with the sheriff and usually accepted his routine defeats with quiet dignity. After all, any deputy who challenged the boss had a lock on second place. Last place.

But this was different. It rankled him that this thing was getting swept under the rug; for he knew he had been right and he knew Sheriff Bull Mattson knew it too. *He was afraid to take this one to the coroner*, thought Ralph.

"Do you think I was afraid to take this one to the coroner, Ralph?"

"Hell no, Bull. I know you ain't afraid." While Ralph generally honored the truth, he held his own ass in even higher regard. The call from the San Francisco homicide inspector had created a dilemma for Deputy Stinson by reinforcing his own strong suspicion that Charles V. Hallinan, retired chemical plant foreman, had been forced off highway 17 to his death five weeks earlier. Now, with the inspector due to arrive at headquarters in less than an hour, Stinson saw this as their last chance to file an official homicide report—one that could avoid embarrassment if San Francisco P.D. knew more than they did.

"You want to file a report, Ralph? You go right ahead, *Deputy*. Be my guest." As he said this, the sheriff's tiny eyes flashed through fatty slits, belying everything his mouth had just said.

Bull Mattson was a truly ugly man. His huge, flat nose sprawled beneath tiny round eyes, filling out that part of his face not already occupied by a cavernous mouth, filled with doglike teeth, usually clamped around a half-smoked cigar. A massive jaw pyramided into his chest without stopping anywhere for a neck. Forty-six years of living behind those features had embittered him, had made him a dangerous man who hated every living soul better-looking than himself, which in Bull Mattson's case included just about everybody on the planet.

"No, Bull . . . hell, it ain't that big a deal. It's just that the kid, the witness, seemed pretty damned straight—"

"Ralph," interrupted the sheriff, his irritation growing as he leaned as close to the deputy as his girth would permit. "Where do you get these crazy goddamn ideas? Your problem is we let you walk the Santa Cruz Pacific Mall beat too long. Your idea of a straight kid is anyone who can stay awake for five minutes without a toot. Shit, Ralph, that kid's pilot light blew out years ago."

The deputy felt a coldness growing under his arms. He had to bat his eyes to clear a hypertensive blurring of the sheriff's gross features. *Back off, cowboy*, he warned himself.

"And even if he *was* straight," continued the sheriff, leaning back now and adopting a more conciliatory tone, "are you gonna buy his rank speculation that the old fart was bumped off highway seventeen by a goddamn pickup truck, when the kid admits in the next breath that he was coming off a tight curve at the time with his girlfriend all over him like a wet rag? Hell, it's a miracle *they* didn't go off the road, too, with him at the wheel and her on his gear shift. On top of that, the punk admits that he didn't see any actual contact between this phantom pickup and the old guy's Impala."

Ralph Stinson snaked his lanky six-foot-three-inch frame even deeper in his chair. It was no time to be sitting taller than the sheriff of Santa Cruz County. "It's not just what he saw, Bull, but where he saw it. There's no more than two or three short breaks in that right shoulder guardrail between the summit and St. John's Retreat, where he was headed. It seems like one hell of a coincidence that it's right at one of these breaks that the kid sees the old man getting rammed by that yellow pickup.''

"*Thinks* he sees, Ralph. *Thinks* he sees," snapped the sheriff. "Am I right?"

The deputy agreed he was, silently cursing himself for giving Mattson the opening.

"And will you also agree there's a difference, Deputy?" he asked rhetorically, in full control now. "Christ, sometimes you talk like a man down a post hole." Bull Mattson's jaw relaxed, allowing his thick lower lip to flap open like a landing craft hitting the beach. Ralph Stinson involuntarily stared at the flabby mouth, knowing that in a minute the outer edges of the sheriff's thick tongue would begin to slowly sprawl out of the corners of his gaping lips, the tip securely anchored to the back of his upper teeth. This unconscious mannerism signaled "checkmate" to those who knew Mattson. Deputy Stinson suddenly mused that in Bull Mattson's fifty years of life, no one had ever cared enough about him to tell him how ugly he looked when he did that.

"As for your goddamn 'coincidence,' Sherlock," continued the sheriff, now fully on the offensive, "I suppose you would say it's a big 'coincidence' every time somebody goes through a break in those guardrails. Well, Ralph, that's just totally bullshit logic. That old man ain't the first to go through a gap in the rails and God help us he won't be the last. Christ, Ralph, we wouldn't even be having this stupid fuckin' conversation if he hadn't gone through a gap in the guardrails 'cause he wouldn't be dead now! By your lights, *every* death through the rails is too big a coincidence and should be assumed to be homicide! I swear, you talk like you've been smokin' that shit in the evidence locker!''

"You're right, Bull," said Deputy Stinson in full retreat, unable to follow, let alone refute, the sheriff's syllogistic reasoning. His head was beginning to hurt.

"You're damned right I'm right!" shouted Mattson, staring at the deputy with disdain.

Why am I doing this? thought Stinson. *I don't get paid one extra red cent for going through this shit.* But what came out of the deputy's mouth was this: "Okay, Bull, let's forget what the kid *thought* he saw. He *was* sure the truck was yellow though, and I think we got to take his word for that much at least."

The ponderous sheriff demonstrated one of his rare attempts at self-control. *"Sooo whaaat?"* he said at last with exaggerated tolerance.

"Well, the damage to the old man's left rear bumper and fender showed a lot of yellow paint. You agreed I should check with the guy who lent Hallinan the Impala and he says that there was no yellow paint, in fact no damage at all to the left fender or bumper when Hallinan took off for St. John's."

"Yeah, I agreed you should check it out, Ralph, and do you want to know why?" Stinson heard a distant rumbling—a storm was approaching. "I said 'go check it out' just to see if you would really do it; just to see if you would actually fuck away good taxpayers' dollars to confirm the obvious: that nobody in the world who has ever lent his car to somebody is going to be dumb enough to blow part of a total loss insurance claim by admitting there was previous damage within the deductible. Can you follow that, *Deputy?* You didn't prove a goddamn thing, Ralph, except that you might just have a few lights out in your own marquee."

Stinson averted his eyes. *This ain't going right,* he thought. Ralph Stinson was a man who was aware of his limitations and comfortable with the subordinate role life had dealt him. Moreover, he was also a practical man, who realized they would never find that old yellow pickup truck and, without a description or a license number, the affair would undoubtedly go into the books as another unsolved murder—just what Bull Mattson didn't need right now with elections coming up. Yet Stinson knew there had been some kind of foul play out there on highway 17—a manslaughter at least, and probably worse, for it to have attracted the attention of a San Francisco homicide inspector. The deputy steeled himself for one last try. After all, the skid marks started, stopped, went sideways at sharp angles— they just didn't act like the skid marks of a lone car losing control. *Besides,* thought the deputy, *if you've got the presence of mind to brake as much as the victim obviously did, why steer yourself right through a break in the right shoulder safety barrier?* It was murder, all right, and if there was going to be a coverup, he didn't want it on his head.

"Bull, you saw the skid marks." Stinson knew he was on dangerous ground now—openly challenging the sheriff. "Murder is written all over the highway up there."

Mattson exploded. "Oh Christ, that really cooks it! I say fuck your goddamn skid marks, Stinson! Jesus!" Turning as red as his socks, the massive sheriff jerked forward out of his chair, shooting it backward into the scarred wall behind him. To Stinson's relief, Mattson then whirled and turned his back on the deputy, as if to dismiss him. Stinson started to unfold himself from his chair while the sheriff began fumbling with his file cabinet, which jammed. He slammed his palm hard into it and spun around again, his face trembling. "And fuck you, too, *Deputy*, if you think your Dick Tracy theories are going to knock the wheels off my campaign for reelection!" Stinson could think of nothing to say, which was probably divine intervention, as the sheriff was just getting started.

"Let me spell it out for you once and for all." Mattson leaned forward again, his upper body connected by giant arms to the desk—hands and knuckles in a football lineman's stance.

"What we've got here is an old guy in bad health who probably had a nip or two and lost control of his car. Happens all the time."

"Hallinan's blood alcohol content was zero," Stinson said quietly, unable to resist calling Mattson on his first clear-cut mistake.

"Okay, Kojak, you've got an answer for everything. Answer this: Drunk or sober, is it or is it not a fact that Hallinan was totally blind in one eye?"

"Yes, sir. At least that's what the owner of the car said."

"And Hallinan was also dying of cancer, wasn't he?"

"Yep. That's why he was going to St. John's Retreat."

"Now, did your famous fucking investigation disclose whether he had a single enemy in the whole goddamn free world?"

"He had no enemies."

"Did the old fart have so much as a dollar of insurance?"

"No."

"Did he have any heirs to collect his insurance even if he did have any?"

"No."

"Have you come up with a single suspect, anywhere in the entire fucking *universe*, who would have wanted Charley Hallinan dead?"

"Not that I know of."

"And didn't that guy who lent Hallinan the car also tell you that Hallinan had less than a year to live?"

"Yes."

"Well then, Deputy. Has your wild-ass imagination found any

reason whatsoever why anyone would take the trouble to murder an old uninsured one-eyed fart without enemies who was busy dying anyway?''

"No," said Stinson, who could feel the glare of Mattson's eyes burning into his own lowered eyelids, "but this Inspector Conti ain't coming all this way unless he thinks somebody did.''

The sheriff pulled his chair back from the wall and slowly lowered himself into it, shaking his head from side to side. "Well now, Ralph, don't you worry your head about some big-city snoop coming into *my* jurisdiction. He's gonna get zilch for his trouble. As for you, can we assume that this fucking conversation is over, once and for all?''

Silence. The lower lip and tongue again. Checkmate.

"You're the boss, Bull.''

"Well, thank you, Deputy," said Mattson, grabbing a report in one hand and reaching for his glasses with the other, "I'd appreciate it if you would remember that the next time you order up a skid mark analysis from the criminal lab on an obvious one-driver negligence case.''

Jesus Christ, thought Stinson, *the fat bastard sure does get around.*

"Sorry, Bull.''

"Sorry *shit*, Ralph! Sometimes you act like you *want* me to lose the election! We've got enough trouble in this county with real crime—drug addicts and gay grab-ass on downtown street corners—without you inventing more of it! If you want a coroner's investigation, you better bring me more than some funny skid marks and the word of some kid coming off a tight curve with a taut pecker.''

"You've heard all I've got, Bull. I'm satisfied if you are.''

"Well, Ralph," Bull replied, gently now. "If you're sure you're satisfied, just take a minute to close your file and then run on over to Felton. I'm getting some complaints that Nort Hawkins has opened up his garage casino again.''

"Okay, Bull, if you don't need me for the meeting," said the deputy, untangling himself from the battered chair.

"I don't think you'll be missed, Ralph. You sure you're satisfied now?" repeated the sheriff as Stinson reached the door. Bull Mattson was always graceful in victory.

"Yeah, sure. Thanks for listening, Bull. Sorry about the lab report.''

"Forget it, Ralph. The whole thing is dead and forgotten.''

*   *   *

As a weary Dan Conti lowered himself into the same battered chair thirty minutes later, he remarked on the beauty of the drive over the summit, then segued straight to the point, asking the sheriff to confirm the place where Hallinan left the highway. Mattson replied that he was glad the lieutenant had enjoyed the ride, because identifying the point of the vehicle's departure was about all he could do for him.

"But the CHP report references some skid marks," said Conti. "Did you check them out? Do any friction studies?"

The sheriff responded to the question with an amused smile. "Lieutenant, if we called in the eggheads from Forensics every time we lost somebody up on highway seventeen, we'd be broke in six months. We're just country folk out here, Lieutenant, doing the best we can."

"Well," said Conti, unsmiling, "what about the yellow pickup seen by the eyewitness?"

Mattson laughed out loud, more in amazement then derision. "Do you have any idea how many pickups we have in Santa Cruz County? There's hardly a family without one in the mountains. Besides," he added with a lascivious smile, "the witness was busy violating the penal code with his girlfriend at the time."

"Did she corroborate him?"

The sheriff gave Conti an obscene wink. "I've never heard it called *that* before. Fact is, she was under the young man's dashboard at the time . . . probing for oral evidence."

Ten minutes later Dan Conti was back on the road with nothing but a copy of a routine accident report, a continuing suspicion that Mattson was either stonewalling or hopelessly incompetent, and a general feeling of disgust. As he passed the point where Hallinan's car left the road, he confirmed his earlier impression that there was less than a handful of openings in the right shoulder barriers all the way to the summit. If it wasn't murder, he thought, it was a cruel and unlikely coincidence that Hallinan should plunge through one of those narrow openings to his death, hundreds of feet below.

As he approached the summit, he breathed deeply, as if the clean air might purge the lingering presence of Bull Mattson's leering face from his consciousness. He spotted a deer, then later an acorn woodpecker and a host of stellar jays, as he surveyed the trees on both sides of the road, taller now, more lush and green. Occasionally, there was a giant sequoia redwood tree. *Sempervirens*—a remnant of that ancient species of conifers that once proliferated throughout the northern hemisphere—majestic survivors, interspersed with dense manzanita and sagebrush as impenetrable as barbed wire. Which brought him back to the inscrutable sheriff and the growing tangle of evidence leading nowhere.

Hallinan and Weisberg. Same age, once employed by the same company, both killed within a period of five weeks.

Why?

As he crested the summit and started down the hill leading back to San Jose and San Francisco, he had to admit that his trip had been a waste of time. He suddenly felt tired and began to regret a dinner date he had made the day before with a secretary from City Hall, a definite airhead, but possessed of great legs and a receptive sensuality. Maybe, he thought, she would settle for a couple of drinks and a visit to the Manfred Hopkins Marine Life Center.

"Yes, Lieutenant, I know it's your day off," came the strident voice of Captain Fred Mahan the next morning. "I'm calling to make sure you know it too. *Okay?*"

Dan Conti stretched the telephone cord so far that the end of the receiver began to rotate out of its precariously cradled position between his shoulder and neck. A herculean effort notwithstanding, he was unable to prevent his intended eggs over easy from becoming a pair soft-scrambled. "Captain. Can I call you back? I'm in the middle of screwing up my breakfast."

"Don't worry, I'll be brief," came the curt reply. "I know of at least two calls you've already made this morning to my already overtaxed crime lab. Okay?"

"Actually, I've made four calls to the boys at Criminalistics, plus one to Pathology," interrupted the inspector, his dark eyebrows spiking into a scowl as the toaster jammed.

"Well, I want you to stop it right now, for Christ's sake!"

"I can't, Captain. The eggs are already scrambled. Why don't you join me? I'll burn an extra piece of toast for you."

"Funny, Dan. I do appreciate your ability to laugh in the face of disaster."

"Only you, Captain Mahan, would call burnt toast a disaster."

"Conti, listen to me. The disaster is that you've intimidated my boys at Criminalistics to where they are putting your fantasy world ahead of my actual homicide projects. *Okay?* You not only have violated department procedures, you've managed to . . .''

Conti gently placed the receiver on the counter while he devoured the last of his breakfast and poured a second cup of coffee. He spotted a woman's silk scarf flung over the back of his couch and unhappily realized that a return trip to City Hall would be required. Once had been more than enough.

Conti turned back to the telephone, which continued to blare a loud reproach: ''. . . and I won't have it, Dan! I've defended your trigger-happy excursions into the Mission District. I've put up with your bizarre costumes and disguises. I saved your ass— your very *ass*, okay?—with the mayor's committee by denying you had left your badge on your desk before you 'went hunting' as you put it for Billy Starker up in Marin, for Christ's sake, I . . . are you there, Conti?''

''Yeah. I'm here,'' said Conti, picking up the receiver, ''and I'm enjoying every moment. But while you're catching your breath, let me repeat that this *is* an actual homicide. I could *smell* murder in that aquarium, Captain, and my nose has never been wrong. You know that. Besides, it won't take Becker five minutes to dust that phony suicide note for prints and as for the pathology lab, they *had* to jump on the lung work right away or it would have been too late.'' He could not resist adding: *''Okay?''*

The captain's anger was palpable now, and his voice filled Dan's kitchen with a strident, metallic sound. ''Just where in God's name do you get off, putting your fucking nose ahead of logic and common sense? It's that goddamn Mafia crusade again, isn't it? Huh? I've got a nose, too, you know. Well? Am I right?''

Dan added his dish and silverware to the crowded sink. ''There may be a connection.''

''Oh, Christ, I knew it! Well, listen to this, Conti, and listen good: I just talked to the crime lab and they found prints on the note all right. Guess whose? The goddamn victim's, of course. *Okay?* Now, how can I convince you to stick to solving the murders we already have before inventing some we don't need?'' His anger nearly spent, the captain's tone softened. ''Dante. Why the hell can't you stop trying to be everywhere at once?''

Dan knew that Mahan loved to ask questions that had no answers. So from Conti he neither expected a reply nor received one. Besides, Mahan knew the answer even better than Conti, for Mahan had been a police officer in the mid-fifties when

Dan's father was killed that day in a random robbery-murder at his North Beach grocery store. Dante was then only eleven years old, and Fred Mahan a much younger police sergeant who had astutely seen a lust for vengeance burning in the boy's eyes and, like a surrogate father, had convinced Dan to join a young police cadet program. As much as the blustering captain now frustrated him, Dan knew how much he owed the older man, for that eleven-year-old boy—overwhelmed by guilt and despair—had indeed intended to kill Washington Jones, Jr., the day—the very hour—Jones was released from Juvenile Hall. Mahan later confessed to Dan that he had told his sergeant that if they failed to turn young Dante into a cop, he was going to end up a killer. "Do what you want," the sergeant had grunted, "but my guess is he'll turn out to be both."

Dan Conti drained his cup, mistakenly judging the captain to be finished, then poured himself more coffee to enjoy up on his apartment building's small rooftop deck. Nobody else used the roof, and it had become his private hideaway; one of the few places he felt completely relaxed. He glanced out of the north window toward the Bay to be sure the weather was still holding and was relieved to see more than a hundred newly launched white and multicolored sails. Only a handful of splintering clouds marred the light blue curtain above the shimmering water.

"So let's get it straight, once and for all," continued the captain. "You will not waste one more minute of your time or the department's time on either your mob fantasy or this current folly of yours. *There was no murder!* Get it?"

Silence. Dan sipped his coffee, noticed that a race had started out from the St. Francis Yacht Club.

"*And one more thing,*" Mahan added with a steely insistence that signified he had at least two or three more things, "I would like to settle once and for all who is running the San Francisco Police Department. *Okay?* The next time you want . . ."

Dan gently replaced the receiver on the table and stared into his coffee, wondering how the murderer had managed to get Weisberg's prints on the note.

PART THREE

■

THE CRISIS

■

SUMMER, 1983

For this is the true strength of kings, when
they corrupt the souls of those they rule.

—MATTHEW ARNOLD

TWENTY-SIX

∎

Later the same week, Kevin Stone, pale lips clamped tight, broke through Miss Tarkenton's usual barricade of bureaucratic sputtering and dropped a stack of pleadings noisily on Austin Barrington's desk. The papers came perilously close to a plate of fine china bearing a bacon, lettuce, and tomato sandwich on wheat toast.

"What's this?" grunted the senior partner, dabbing his lips with a linen napkin bearing the logo of the President's Club. "Motion to strike by the defense?"

"Exactly," said Kevin in a hoarse voice. "They were served on us twenty minutes ago."

"You sound terrible and look like you've been hit by a truck," said Barrington. "Are you ill?"

"Temporary, Austin, temporary. I assure you those papers are causing me far more grief than my hangover. The defense has moved to strike our cancerphobia theory."

Barrington just smiled up at Kevin and handed the papers back without looking at them, saying, "Don't you mean *your* cancer-phobia theory, Kevin?"

"This is no time for one of our petty disputes about strategy, Austin. You liked the cancerphobia theory well enough at the beginning when you were desperate, and you would do well to recognize that it may still be our only real chance. Hancock does, for Christ's sake, which is why he's put together a damn good argument for eliminating it from the case!"

"I shouldn't wonder he has," said Barrington coolly. "It's simply not the American way to hand out money to people who claim they're afraid of getting a disease without having to prove they've actually got it. I'm not even sure I disagree with Hancock."

"Then you disagree with *Molein* and *Ayers* versus *Jackson Township* as well," said Kevin, his face flushed with frustration, his head beginning to pound. *God, you're loving this, you sanctimonious bastard*, thought Kevin. *You'll see me wrong about cancerphobia even if it costs us the whole fucking case!*

"Not at all, Kevin; I simply disagree with *you*," said Barrington in a bored tone as he picked up a segment of his BLT and resumed eating, his signal that the meeting was ending. *"Molein* is a California case that has not been extended to permit recovery for emotional distress from fear of getting toxic diseases. *Jackson Township has* been so extended, but it's a New Jersey case not recognized in California. Am I right?"

Kevin felt blood pounding in his temples and ran his tongue over dry lips. It occurred to him that people were at their ugliest when yawning or eating and that not even the fastidious Austin Barrington could gracefully subdue a triple-decker sandwich in public. *I've got to get out of here,* he thought, feeling suddenly nauseated. Instead, he walked into the conference area and gathered himself for another approach. He could tell that Barrington had been souring on cancerphobia, placing more and more reliance on Professor Childhouse to make the difficult causation linkage between each chemical and each injury, but surely this was no reason to take such apparent glee in Hancock's motion to strike the fear-of-cancer damage theory from their complaint. Puzzled, he stared at the blasé senior partner, who had begun to peruse *The Wall Street Journal* as he ate. Kevin knew he was being insulted but could not figure out why. None of it made sense. Where had their relationship gone off track? What was he up to? Kevin had always admired—even tried to emulate—the senior partner's cunning nature; at least until the recent evening at the Barringtons', when Kevin had himself become the target of his host's disingenuous games. *Is Denise right? Does Austin really hate me?*

"Austin," he said, walking back to the senior partner's desk, "at least you must agree we're far better off with cancerphobia in the case than without it."

"No," said Barrington without looking up and in the manner of one speaking on the telephone to an investment fund salesman. *(He's got that one down, too,* thought Kevin.) "I'm trying to tell you I *don't* agree. If cancerphobia is in the case, we will continue to depend upon it and unconsciously slacken our efforts to prove traditional, direct causation. Then if the judge later rejects your little notion at trial, which you admit he might, we're caught somewhere between the two approaches. No, Kevin, I don't agree at all. As a matter of fact," Barrington added, pausing first to wipe his mouth with a linen-hooded index finger, then to fold the napkin beside the plate in a manner that said his meal could not continue until Kevin's intrusion ended, "it's time for all of us to awaken ourselves from your creative pipe dream and get back down to basics. Go oppose it if you will—it was your idea, remember?—but don't look to me for help."

"But that's exactly what I *am* doing, Austin," said Kevin angrily, leaning across the desk and purposefully putting his hand down over *The Wall Street Journal*. "I admit it's a tough one, but Judge Bainbridge might listen to you: similar ages, both World War Two vets, same club. Rachel and I will prepare the papers, but this one could use some of your old-boy clout, Austin, if only to preserve the threat of cancerphobia for settlement purposes. I'm asking you to argue it yourself, Austin." Kevin heard a supplicatory note creep into his voice. Was he still debating or had he begun to beg?

Barrington's eyes stared down at the younger partner's hand covering the newspaper, and Kevin could swear he felt the back of his hand growing hot. He withdrew it, and, as if there had been a string connected to Barrington's chin, the senior partner's huge head simultaneously rolled up to face Kevin. Then, in a distracted, almost musical drawl, Barrington said, "Oh, come now, Kevin. I'm sure you'll do just fine."

There was plainly nothing more to be said. Kevin stood staring and wordless as Barrington moved a hand slowly across his desk, then, with surgical care, planted a finger upon a lone crumb of toast that had escaped the confines of the gleaming plate.

"Yes," he repeated, smiling as he flicked the fugitive particle onto the china, "you will do just fine."

Kevin did not do fine at all.

The plaintiffs' opposing papers were reasonably persuasive, but the argument went badly. Kevin was prepared, but unwell, and as hard as he tried to take charge, it was Hancock who controlled the courtroom that day, pounding relentlessly on the same refrain: that to allow monetary recovery to people who had ingested toxins, but who could not connect specific injuries to a specific chemical, would be an open invitation to everyone with "gout, boils, ulcers, or hemorrhoids" to seek recovery from suppliers and manufacturers all over the country. "According to Mr. Stone's experts, your honor, almost every American is consuming toxins every day in our drinking water. We are, therefore, *all* prospective plaintiffs! It is not hyperbole to suggest that Mr. Stone would have this court make a precedent that would cripple our entire free enterprise system!''

Kevin responded that the New Jersey *Ayers* case had required reasonable proof of objective reliability and that such evidence was present in the North American case by virtue of the Newkirk blood and tissue body burden tests. But Judge Bainbridge, who had been specially assigned to handle all aspects of the case all the way through the trial, seemed more swayed by the absence of direct California precedent, and it was evident to Kevin that the judge's pioneering days were behind him. The case was slipping away.

"The motion to strike the so-called cancerphobia allegations," the judge said wearily, cutting off argument after Hancock's rebuttal, "will be granted. Next matter, Mr. Clerk."

Adrian Fisher and Gardner White found Kevin standing alone in his darkened office three hours and four double vodkas later, his tie open, hands shoved deep in pockets, staring through Levelor blinds at the summer fog. The strident chanting of Iranian students on the streets below filled the strained silence in the room.

"We heard the news, Kevin," said Fisher finally. "Tough break."

"Yep," said Kevin, an ironic smile on his face, "tough break."

"I read your papers. They were excellent. Our facts presented a logical case for the extension of the *Molein* doctrine and adoption of *Ayers* in California. We were dead right on the law."

"Thanks, Adrian. But now we're just dead."

"Do you mean that, Kevin?" asked Gardner, propelled two steps forward by the nervous energy behind his question. "Does this kill the case?"

Kevin turned to face the two older men for the first time. He saw dark lines of concern grooved in both Adrian Fisher's kind face and Gardner White's pinched features. He was reminded of his father's funeral, and the sad-faced uncles there he barely knew, impotent to stem his young boy's grief. All the ingredients were now present for another wake, except for a corpse and his mother's occasional whimpering to break the awkward silence. Trust the Iranians to provide that.

"It doesn't help the case at all," he said inadequately, wondering why he had even returned to the office. To face the music? To escape the consolation of the Washington Street Bar & Grill while he could still walk? To seek reassurance from Rachel, the only S.P.&M. witness to his lackluster performance?

"What are the odds of winning now? Without cancerphobia," demanded White. "Give it to us straight."

Kevin shrugged his shoulders and said, "Call it twenty percent."

"That's exactly what I thought! Let's call a spade a spade, Kevin," continued the pudgy tax partner while Adrian Fisher—deep in thought—limped randomly around the large office. "You're in this now as deep as the rest of us, and probably don't like it any better than we do. Isn't it time to cut our losses and protect our asses at the same time? Shouldn't we dismiss this damn case right now and hope that we can bury Project Salvation in the wreckage?"

It was Fisher who turned and answered. "You don't just abandon your clients, Gardner, even if the court would permit it, which it won't. The best we might hope for would be to substitute out of the case in favor of another firm."

"Then you agree with me, Adrian, that we should at least look into it?"

"Let's just say I'm open to the idea, if Kevin tells me the case is now a loser."

"Well, Kevin?" asked Gardner, sensing that he was finally gaining some ground with his objections.

Kevin said nothing. He knew he should be more concerned about the whole affair, but felt consumed by a morbid lethargy. The numbing taste of bitter defeat mixed with straight vodka still stung his tongue as he inwardly agreed that the case would be difficult now, perhaps even impossible to win. The thought of losing a high profile jury case to Alan Hancock and seeing his winning streak—possibly his career—so ingloriously ended cut through his protective stupor like a knife. On the other hand, the consequences of quitting now were unthinkable. Everything would go down the drain. The bank would pull its line of credit and the firm, despite Gardner White's optimistic cost-cutting strategy, would surely fail. His own hopes for someday joining the Table of Three and Rachel's partnership would, of course, die along with the firm. And instead of the hoped-for three or four million dollars in his own bank account, he would now be personally accountable, along with the other partners, for repayment of the current bank loan. Kevin peered outside into a suddenly thickening fog. The demonstrators had moved on, their angry voices giving way now to honking commuters.

"I don't know," he said finally.

"You don't know what?" said White.

"I just don't know."

TWENTY-SEVEN

■

Three days later Austin Barrington called to order a special meeting of the S.P.&M. partnership, displaying an outward calm that did little to disguise his anger. A quick head count told him that about fifty of the sixty-eight partners were present—a surprising turnout for a meeting called on such short notice. Barrington also grimly noted that it was the first special meeting ever called without his advance approval. Worse than that, it had been called over his protest—and by a member of his own Table of Three!

Barrington still did not know how Gardner White had successfully lobbied several key senior partners to agree to a full partnership debate on whether to continue or abandon the North American case in favor of substitute counsel. Adrian Fisher had been the first to tell Barrington that White, fuming over Barrington's orders that all available cash flow now be channeled into the North American case, had broken ranks and persuaded several partners that the case was leading the firm deeper into financial ruin. White's secondary objective, the elderly Fisher had reported to Barrington, was to minimize the revelation of the Table's role in Project Salvation by ending the firm's involvement in the case. He had even engaged in informal (and totally unauthorized!) negotiations with a "reputable and able" firm, who had indicated a willingness to substitute into the case and to pay S.P.&M. costs incurred to date, plus a ten percent referral fee if they were successful in settlement or at trial. Barrington's first reaction was to dismiss White's defection with an imperious grunt, and to draw an unfavorable comparison between the tax partner's brain and a navy surplus toilet float. His complacency was quickly erased, however, when Fisher himself caved in and agreed to a special meeting on the issue. Barrington had barely had time to put his own not inconsiderable skills in partnership politics to work in garnering at least twenty advance votes in support of his cause and—most importantly—in persuading Adrian Fisher to at least hold to a neutral position at the meeting.

Thus armed, Barrington prepared to do battle.

His most formidable opponents would be White, of course, and Tasker James, a senior litigator with outspoken designs on Barrington's job as presiding partner. He was also concerned about Kevin Stone, whose lack of optimism concerning the trial had not improved since Barrington's recent refusal to reopen the argument about the cancerphobia issue in front of Judge Bainbridge. Barrington feared that such a motion would antagonize the judge and only highlight their failure to the detriment of the firm's morale, already at a low ebb. Besides, he thought, it wouldn't hurt the firm to see their wonder boy wrong once in a while. "Best to let sleeping dogs lie, Kevin," he had counseled, feeling a perverse kind of pleasure in viewing the lines of defeat in Kevin's face.

But Kevin now had cards to play, and all Barrington had been able to extract from the younger partner just prior to the meeting was his assurance of objectivity. "I'll be as loyal to you and the case as my duty to the partnership permits," he had said with unaccustomed vagueness. Kevin was clearly the wild card in a deck Barrington now had no choice but to deal.

"Order, gentlemen, order," Barrington said in a strong voice carefully devoid of the bitterness he felt as he stared down the table at men who, but for his courage and resourcefulness one year earlier, would now be foraging for jobs in a glutted, recessionary market. The table was set with ingratitude, even disdain.

"Let us begin. We are here, as you know, to consider the motion of Tasker James, seconded by several of you, calling for our withdrawal from the North American case, subject, of course, to recruiting substitute counsel satisfactory to our clients and to gaining the court's approval."

Without shame or apology Barrington exploited the advantage of the Chair and proceeded to present his case first, eloquently explaining to the partnership how the case had prevented the firm's financial ruin. Most of the partners were hearing details of their near-brush with disaster for the first time and the senior partner could see that his words were evoking the anticipated response of shock and gratitude. He warned them that a typical referral fee arrangement with substitute counsel would satisfy neither the banks nor the firm's financial needs. He then reviewed the case in a favorable but ostensibly objective light, and, after a harsh glance at Gardner White, reminded the partners that if they but "stayed with the ship," they would ultimately win a verdict of "unprecedented magnitude." He closed with an inspired plea for "renewed dedication to those shattered men who have entrusted their lives to our care, relying upon the professional integrity of our commitment."

The opposing speeches by Gardner White and Tasker James were dry and clinical by comparison, thought Barrington smugly. White focused on the huge financial drain imposed by the case and the recent ruling against Kevin's cancerphobia theory. He then argued that the firm should turn to a cost-cutting alternative rather than to a "continued investment of their hopes and limited funds in this insane adventure." Barrington smiled, for these final words had come across as gross hyperbole, since only White, Fisher, Barrington, and Kevin Stone could know just how "insane" the adventure had really become.

Tasker James spoke next—at unnecessary length, thought Barrington—emphasizing the "stark departure from our firm's renowned commitment to complex corporate and quality securities litigation" and dramatically intoning that although his personal embarrassment resulting from the firm's entry into the "mud wrestling" world of personal injury work was not at issue, "the loss of corporate business from a disillusioned establishment most certainly was."

Barrington was astonished when this last comment provoked a chorus of approval from many partners, and he rose with a swift rejoinder that heaped shame on any who would demean his decision to place the firm at the service of needy people who had not had the advantages of "most in this room." All was fair now. Never mind that his rhetoric trod dangerously close to overt hypocrisy—he was now in battle; this was Barrington the Advocate at his best.

This was also Barrington the Realist, who knew that this was it, that he would never make a more important argument in the life—or death—of *Dixon* versus *North American, et al.* When he finished his second grand peroration, championing the downtrodden and espousing the loftiest motives for S.P.&M., he smugly thought that even his ass of a father might actually find cause to praise him. Then, in an effort to end the debate advantageously, he asked, "Are we not ready for the question, gentlemen?"

The gentlemen were not.

"Is it true, Austin," asked the semi-retired Tipton Olney, "that the police suspect foul play in the recent deaths of two of our clients and are paying us a visit tomorrow? I would hate to see us drawn into messy publicity."

Barrington had to raise his voice to be heard over the hum of surprised voices. "That's ridiculous, Tipton. Yes, we're being 'paid a visit,' but, as a member of the Police Commission, I've been assured it is entirely routine. One death was a vehicular accident, the other a suicide—with a note left in the decedent's own handwriting following a period of acute depression."

"Let's hear from Kevin Stone," interjected Tasker James. "Can we win this damnable case, Kevin?"

In the quiet that followed, as all eyes turned toward the younger partner, Barrington added to himself what he knew James had really intended saying: . . . *since we can no longer trust Austin's judgment in the matter.* Barrington's leadership had never been so openly flouted, and he silently vowed that when this battle was behind him and a vote of confidence recorded, Tasker James would be asked—forced, if necessary—to leave the partnership.

"The case is not without some problems," said Kevin slowly, "but I agree with Austin's monetary recovery assessment. Assuming we win the first group's case on liability, the verdict and subsequent settlements should exceed two or three hundred million dollars, plus punitive damages."

Gardner White leaned forward and aimed a pudgy finger at Kevin, saying, "But tell them what you told me after Judge Bainbridge dismissed your cancerphobia theory."

I should have considered this, Barrington thought, suddenly worried. *Kevin has himself become a liability, carousing around town at night, fighting me at every turn, disrupting my leadership behind my back . . .*

The room went silent, for Kevin Stone's answer to White's question would not just determine the destiny of the case. Many partners now knew that it could also decide the life or death of the firm *and* Austin Barrington—for not even his detractors doubted they had become one and the same. Kevin stared in silence at a pencil in his hand and in the suspense of the moment Barrington, though unaware of it, had stopped breathing. "Without cancerphobia in the case," Kevin said finally, then paused for what seemed like minutes to clear his throat, "we could have trouble."

Gardner White was on his feet, his cherubic features now blotched red with intensity. "Yes, yes, but tell them exactly what you told me, Kevin," he said in a crackling voice. "Tell them what the odds are now—without cancerphobia in the case."

For the first time Kevin glanced up the table to briefly meet the burning eyes of Austin Barrington, then returned his gaze to the empty notepad in front of him. "Twenty percent," he said quietly.

The room roared its astonishment—or so it sounded to the betrayed senior partner, who had heard everything now but the crow of a cock. He knew how to read a room and he knew he had lost. It was over. He'd be lucky to garner ten votes—loyalty votes at that—and only half that number in a secret ballot.

"Call for the question, Austin," said a gloating Tasker James. "Let's vote and get back to work."

Damn you all, thought Barrington. *Time! I must have time!* "This is a matter of great consequence, Tasker," he said, no longer concealing his anger, "and I'll not cut off debate so quickly. Does anyone else wish to be heard?" Barrington hated the pleading note that had crept into his last words.

The room fell silent for an eternal moment. Barrington glanced outside and saw darkness closing in. The seconds ticked noisily by on the giant grandfather clock behind him, and he knew that he must call for the vote, that he could delay no longer. Then, just as he began to speak, Adrian Fisher slowly rose from his position at Barrington's right. "I have a word, Mr. Chairman, if you please." All eyes were instantly riveted on the eldest partner, whose solemn gaze in turn remained fixed on Barrington. "It is with great difficulty that I tell you, Austin, that when faced with the question, I will have to vote against you and in support of the motion to withdraw from the case."

Barrington looked up in disbelief at the gaunt and spindly Fisher—once his mentor and his oldest friend in the firm—now driving the final nail in the coffin of his hope. Adrian had been the one who taught him that loyalty to one's partners was the unique hallmark of S.P.&M. And now this. A cold dampness spread across his back now and the alien taste of defeat filled his mouth.

"However," continued Fisher, stretching a gangling rope of an arm up to scratch the back of his elegant head, "I do not expect to be faced with this dilemma, not today at least. I assume that our Messrs. Barrington and Stone will be filing a motion for reconsideration on the cancerphobia issue?"

Gardner White intervened quickly. "Kevin has already informed me that it was considered but rejected by Austin, who felt it had no chance for success."

Barrington shifted in his seat and shot another searing look at Kevin. *My friend, Kevin Stone,* he thought bitterly, *key witness for the prosecution.*

"Not surprising," said Adrian Fisher, undaunted and smiling amiably across the table at White. "But not particularly relevant, either. My amendment to the motion now before us is simple and, I believe, worthy of your unanimous assent: I move that no action be taken on our withdrawal from the case until a motion to reconsider the cancerphobia ruling has been filed, argued, and denied. We owe at least this modest delay to our clients and to our presiding partner, who has moved heaven and earth in his unstinting efforts to save our firm. Would you care to second the motion, Gardner?"

My God, thought Barrington as Fisher took his seat, *what a piece of work! I didn't think the old bird still had it in him.*

Gardner White's capitulation was a foregone conclusion, the vote to delay unanimous. *The old man stood by me,* thought Barrington, temporarily reassured. *And for what it's worth, I've got another two, maybe three more weeks.*

Time to think. *"You lucked out, Bub,"* an ancient voice chided in the back of his head.

It was business as usual—on the surface at least—at the weekly trial team leaders' meeting the next afternoon. Only a puffiness around the eyes betrayed one of Barrington's infrequent sleepless nights. He had dozed only long enough to suffer his one recurring nightmare, the one in which he appeared for a law school class at Harvard only to find to his surprise that final exams were scheduled for that day. He was both completely unprepared and totally nude. Panicked, he takes his seat, then sees that the professor is his own father—W.W. II—laughing down at him from the lectern. *Don't worry, Bub*, he says, patronizing his son. *I'll see that you pass!*

They agreed that the motion for reconsideration would be filed the next day, with hearing and argument, by Barrington personally, scheduled in ten days. Because the special partnership meeting had been cloaked in security, Rachel openly evidenced her surprise at Barrington's reversal on filing the motion. "I'm happy to help, Austin," she said, "but I'm not sure what we can do. We put our best arguments before Judge Bainbridge and didn't even come close."

"Then come up with some new ones, dammit," snapped Barrington. "I want cancerphobia back in the case at all costs."

"Ease up, Austin," said Kevin in an uncharacteristic tone of admonishment. "You know we'll give it our best shot. Rachel just remembers what you told us last week, when *I* was the one arguing in favor of giving it a try."

Rachel was embarrassed by Kevin's intercession, but felt grateful to him for it nonetheless. She watched as the partners exchanged hostile looks; it was clear to Rachel that the Barrington-Stone relationship was deteriorating by the week.

She also noticed that though Barrington seemed tired, Kevin looked totally spent, even ill. His kinetic eyes were now redrimmed and flat. His fair skin, once glowing, was pallid and tattooed with red confetti specks. Even his voice had lost its calm resonance as he turned to Rachel, saying, "Okay. We'll start tonight. Is your schedule clear, Rachel?" Rachel hardly had time to answer yes before Barrington moved on to the next item on his agenda.

"As you all know, we lost Charley Hallinan last month in that traffic accident in the Santa Cruz mountains. Charley's death unfortunately has serious implications for our case, since he was one of our first fifteen, and probably our most seriously injured plaintiff to boot. As you know, the old fellow left no heirs to carry on a wrongful death action in his behalf, so we had no choice but to dismiss his case.

"Well, Rachel," he continued, "it's time to get out your dismissal forms again. As you know, Bernard Weisberg took his own life three nights ago at the Hopkins Marine Life Center. And, I'm sorry to say, that Weisberg, like Hallinan, left no heirs—at least none willing to continue his lawsuit. He is survived by a half-sister, but she hasn't seen him in years, received no support from him, and therefore has nothing to gain in pursuing the matter. We also had to tell her, of course, that Weisberg's monetary damage case died with him.''

A thoughtful silence embraced the room while the lawyers considered Barrington's words. ''I'm speculating, sir,'' said Jeffrey finally, ''because I haven't seen the medical files, but haven't we just lost our two biggest cases?''

''Quite right, Jeff. Only Hallinan himself was more seriously ill than Bernard Weisberg. In a space of exactly five weeks, we have lost our two biggest potential verdicts and, therefore, our two largest potential fees.'' He paused for a moment. ''And now, to complicate our lives further, these back-to-back misfortunes have provoked an imminent visit from a San Francisco Police Department homicide inspector.''

''What?'' demanded Rachel in a surprised tone.

''Nothing to be disturbed about,'' Barrington assured them. ''He apparently thinks there's some connection between the two deaths because both victims were plaintiffs about to go to trial in a highly publicized case. Now, if he speaks to any of you, I want you to be as cooperative as possible; after all, we are the big financial losers here if he turns out to be right. On the other hand, I remind you of your solemn commitment to protect the attorney/client privilege, an obligation that transcends any duty to assist in his informal inquiry. You may tell this inspector— Conti, Dan Conti is his name—only what is already a matter of public record. I don't know what he's looking for,'' continued Barrington, ''but remember, any inquiries pertaining to the plaintiffs' medical condition—whether from the police, the press, opposing counsel, or even the clients themselves—are to be referred to me and to me alone. It is my nature to be a bit overprotective in these matters, so these medical records will continue to be kept under my personal lock and key until the Court requires that they be revealed to defense counsel. Is that clear?'' Expecting no response and getting none, Barrington continued. ''I would also like you, Rachel, to begin helping Kevin build the monetary-damages part of the case, starting as soon as the motion to reconsider is filed.'' Rachel nodded her agreement.

Kevin, however, was now staring out the window, seemingly oblivious to what Barrington was saying. ''All right, Kevin?'' Barrington asked, overly solicitous.

''Sure,'' said Kevin in a flat tone.

''Good, then it's settled,'' said Barrington. ''We'll spare no effort to turn Judge Bainbridge around. Let's get together tomorrow at ten-thirty to see what you've got." He snapped his memo pad shut, and with a nod, dismissed the group.

Rachel looked at her watch, and saw that it was almost five o'clock. "I'll start reviewing our earlier brief on cancerphobia. Want to shoot for a bite around six-thirty?" she asked Kevin.

"Sounds fine," he answered without enthusiasm, then walked off without another word.

"What's eating Kevin?" asked Jeff as he walked with Rachel toward her office.

"He's just tired, I guess. The antitrust case in New York turned out to be a killer, even though he won. Now he has to come back to a bad ruling on his pet theory and crank up all over again."

"There's more to it than that," said Jeffrey. "Our star looks a bit unhinged if you ask me, which may explain Barrington's Captain Queeg behavior today."

"Don't worry about Kevin," said Rachel. "When the bell rings, he'll be there."

TWENTY-EIGHT

■

The Washington Square Bar & Grill was relatively quiet for a summer night. Rachel glanced at the bar to her left as she and Kevin entered and saw the usual eclectic sprinkling of tourists, neighborhood habitués, journalists, artists, stockbrokers, and middle-aged singles.

They chose a table in the main dining room, far from the cacophony of the honky-tonk piano and the ebullient voices at the bar. "Vodka rocks," said Kevin in a voice barely audible over the convivial din, his glazed, unhappy eyes sharply contrasting with the festival mood. "Start me with a double."

"I'll have a glass of the Mondavi chardonnay," said Rachel, studying Kevin's face. She then looked around and added, "Seems a bit slow here tonight."

"Slow," echoed Kevin, then lapsed into silence for the next five minutes.

"Do you feel like talking about it?" Rachel said finally.

"Talking about what?" Kevin said, scanning the room with vacant eyes.

"Whatever it is that's turned my lovable prince into a wordless and melancholy frog. Is it Bainbridge's ruling? Afterburn from the New York trial?"

"Keep going," said Kevin. "But don't forget to throw in Barrington and Denise and this desperation motion we're supposed to put together, not to mention the everyday insults one must endure as the price for participation in the great panorama of life." Kevin downed his vodka and ordered another.

"It can't be that bad, Kevin," said Rachel, touching his hand. "As for the motion, maybe we can beat the odds."

"What the hell, it's worth a try," sniffed Kevin, "since losing it would start a chain reaction that will rain death and destruction on our brave little world."

"Isn't that a bit bleak? We could still win the case," said Rachel.

"We'll never know," said Kevin, staring into his empty glass.

Rachel's heart ached as she saw the distress in Kevin's face, but decided not to press him for clarification of his obscure remarks. Their desultory conversation throughout dinner centered on the motion and was conspicuously devoid of the flirtatious banter and intimate glances that had electrified their first meal together in New York City—just over a year before. That electricity had survived somehow all these months, but now Rachel felt it dimming as she watched Kevin consume two more doubles before dinner, then polish off a half bottle of wine during the meal, all without apparent effect. He seemed bent on getting drunk, but unable to do so. Rachel decided once more to try and bring him out.

"Kevin, you're troubled about something. I don't mean to pry, but I'd like to help if you feel like talking about it."

"Nothing to be said," said Kevin, loosening his tie and raising his eyebrows in amused irony. "There's already more than enough talk in this world. Remember Camus's characterization of lawyers in *The Fall*?" he added in a mock stage voice: " 'Are we not all alike, constantly talking and to no one, forever up against the same questions although we know the answers in advance?' ''

"No, Kevin, I don't. And frankly, I'm far more interested in figuring out how to get the right answers from Judge Bainbridge.''

"Simple. We don't.''

"Then why bother?'' Rachel asked, losing patience with the game.

"Why not? Nurse!'' shouted Kevin to a passing waitress. "More plasma.''

While Rachel considered Kevin's current elliptical response, Don Amis—a lawyer and mutual friend—stopped at their table. "So what brings the Stafford, Parrish, and MacAllister brain trust out our way? I didn't think you guys took time out to eat.''

"We eat once a week whether we need it or not, Don,'' said Rachel, smiling. "But we don't want it to get around.''

"Your secret's safe with me,'' said Amis. Kevin merely delivered up his hand like a spectator at a ball game passing a hot dog to a stranger. Don Amis exchanged a quick look with Rachel. "Well. Don't let me interrupt you,'' he said pointedly. "Congratulations on your New York case, Kevin. I read about it in the paper last month and meant to call you.''

"No big deal,'' said Kevin, maintaining his ironic tone, his eyes focusing with some effort on Amis for the first time. "Just another small step in mankind's inexorable evolution toward perfect justice.''

"Well, I don't know if I would go that far, but I would be happy to be able to knock off a multimillion-dollar verdict in six weeks' work. See you guys later.''

"Good-bye, Don,'' said Rachel brightly, trying to cover for Kevin's apathy.

A moment or two of silence followed Amis's departure. Rachel looked out the window and allowed herself a moment of nostalgia as she gazed across Columbus Avenue at couples strolling in Washington Square. She envied them, and a sadness enveloped her. She tried to picture Kevin and herself walking arm in arm, but the image eluded her. Why? Was it the suffocating cloak of secrecy that had been dropped over their love? Or the horde of other obstacles—the case, partnership, Denise—that now blocked her romantic illusions, obstacles that only time and patience could eliminate. She still felt that she could wait, but now it was Kevin who worried her. Though she had reacted defensively at the time, Jeffrey was right: Kevin did seem to be coming unhinged during the past several weeks.

"You seemed very upset about Weisberg today," she said.

"Why shouldn't I be?" he said with surprising intensity. "It's not every day you have a client feed himself to sharks five weeks after another client drives himself off a cliff."

"You think there's a connection?" she asked.

"Of course there is," he said, flashing unexpected anger as he sipped his new drink. "Weisberg was fed too much lindane, went bonkers, and fed himself to the fishes. It's not surprising that anything that strong also made Hallinan inattentive on a twisting road."

"But, Kevin," she said gently, "we've known all along about the deadly consequences of these chemicals—that's why we got involved."

"We're involved, all right," he said bitterly, ignoring her eyes.

Puzzled, Rachel stared at the sullen Kevin as he sat hunched over elbows spread dangerously wide on the cluttered table. It saddened her to see that the once-faint vertical lines between his eyes had become deep crevasses traversing a pinched brow.

"Kevin," she said, her voice beginning to reveal her impatience, "we're doing everything we can. We've advanced the case for trial, our preparation is going nicely, and Christmas will fall either at the end or in the middle of our case. With the thirteen plaintiffs who remain, we still have a solid case. What more can our clients ask? What more can we do?"

Kevin's irritation was obvious as he scanned the room for their waiter. "Nothing," he said. "Not one goddamn thing. So let's just forget it, all right?"

"Kevin," said Rachel, momentarily stunned by the vehemence in his voice, "I was only—'"

"You were only ruining the possibility of a relatively relaxed meal with your constant questions. Now, can you let it go or not?"

Rachel felt heat spreading to her face as heads turned toward Kevin's rising voice. The man she loved—and thought she knew—was suddenly a stranger shouting at her in a public restaurant. She was embarrassed, even angry, but mainly disappointed. With less volume, but equal intensity, she said, "Yes, Kevin, I can let it go. I don't have to sit here while you rudely ignore Don

Amis, disturb the people around us, and put down all my attempts to cheer you out of your cynical pout."

"Well, then," said Kevin, lowering his voice, "why don't
you just go over and sit with Don Amis. I noticed that *you* didn't
ignore him."

Rachel started to rise, fighting back tears of anger, then took a
deep breath, exhaled audibly, and said, "Kevin, you won't like
this, but here it is anyway. I don't know what's eating you, but
whatever it is, it's changing you and not for the better. Don't
worry about any further attempts by me to snap you out of it;
you can just stay inside your little protective sphere of self-pity.
But we have a job to do and I'll do my part. I just hope when I
see you back at the office tomorrow morning, you'll be ready to
do yours."

As Rachel rose to her feet, she saw that Kevin was really
looking at her for the first time that evening. His eyes were
bloodshot and burning with intensity. When he finally spoke, his
voice had a pleading and gentle quality. "Wait . . . please sit
down. I just . . . you're right. I'm having a bad time right now,
Rachel. I don't know what's gotten into me. I'm just so . . .
damn tired. I'm sorry. I'm really sorry."

Rachel took her seat. "It's all right," she said, her anger
cooled by the black despair in Kevin's voice. "Why not go
home and get some rest? I'll go back to the office and get a first
draft ready for you to look at first thing tomorrow and—"

"Not on your life, Ms. Cannon," said Kevin, changing moods
again and rising to his feet somewhat unsteadily. "There's too
much to be done. We've got to get this business behind us!"
Kevin's insistence reminded Rachel of a drunk claiming to be
capable of driving his own car, and her concern deepened as she
followed Kevin out of the restaurant and onto the sidewalk on
Powell Street. He stood uncertainly, hands thrust deep into his
pockets, swaying slightly. Rachel suggested that they walk back
to the office up Grant Avenue to Montgomery Street, perhaps
with a stop at Enrico's for cappuccino. Kevin could obviously
use some coffee, and Rachel recognized that her own psyche was
in need of a jump start. The meal had thoroughly depressed her.

The lawyers walked in the silence of their own thoughts, and
Rachel began to feel better as she experienced the rich blend of
sights and smells of the coffeehouses, boutiques, and head shops
of North Beach. They turned left onto glittery Broadway, where
a sleazy-looking young man invited them to view a "live sex

act," then passed the frenetic horde of tourists lining up for the next show of female impersonators at Finocchio's. At Enrico's, Rachel's disappointment returned as Kevin ordered an Irish coffee and sank back into his anxiety and irritation. It had been a bad idea. They finished their drinks quickly and Rachel called for the check.

By the time they reached the Imperial Building again, it was nearing nine o'clock and Kevin had somehow regained his equilibrium. They worked separately for three hours before combining their efforts into a working draft. "Well, what do you think?" asked Rachel.

"It's as good as it can get," said Kevin. "The problem is we haven't given the judge anything dramatically new. There's nothing here to change his mind."

"I agree. I was hoping to be wrong," she said, reaching for a telephone to call a taxi.

"Didn't you drive in today, Rachel?" asked Kevin.

"No, it was so beautiful I took the ferry in."

"Hang up. I'll run you across. It's only fifteen minutes."

Kevin drove his Jaguar across the Golden Gate Bridge in less time than that and in almost complete silence. Kevin seemed back in control, but his shifting moods made Rachel wary, and she felt eager for the tranquility and solitude of home. They pulled up in front, and Rachel gave Kevin a friendly squeeze of his hand, saying, "Good night, and thanks for the ride."

She began to open the passenger door, but Kevin pulled her back toward him, then moved closer and kissed her. Surprised by his swift insistence, she neither resisted nor responded. Her mind simply slipped into neutral, not wanting to acknowledge either to him or herself that his kiss was simply not welcome tonight.

Sensing her distance, Kevin apologized, then sunk back in the driver's seat. "I don't know what's happening to me lately. I always thought I could juggle six or seven balls in the air at once, but life just isn't working for me anymore. Winning in New York was mostly good luck combined with a good case. A trained seal could have won it with those depositions we got last year. Remember? But last month my mind just wasn't with it. All I could really concentrate on was you. Can you believe that I even stayed at the Helmsley Palace? The second week I was able to move into the room we shared that night. I started to call you fifty times."

"Oh, Kevin," Rachel said, warmed by his words and taking one of his hands in both of her own. *Words,* she thought, *I've missed just talking to him as much as anything.* They had really had so few real conversations, none really since Nantucket. The looks across a crowded room, the occasional mad petting in forbidden places; how long could this sustain them? With no words, no sharing of ideas and feelings.

"I've tried everything to take my mind off you," he continued. "Just seeing you walk down the hallway still affects me like the first day of a trial; you know, heart pounding like a trip-hammer. It's like watching one of Degas's ballerinas, the way your beauty is so concretely here and now, yet triggers anticipation of something beyond the moment, something unforeseen. Tell me, Rachel Cannon, am I sounding crazy?"

"You're sounding wonderfully romantic and, *God,* how I hate being practical and ending it, but, really, Kevin, I'm completely whipped and tomorrow brings its own unforeseen events. We'll need to be rested to deal with them."

"You're right, of course, but it's killing me, Rachel—this being together but not being close."

"Kevin, it's only a few more months until the case is behind us and then we can—"

"A few more months! That's like Bainbridge sentencing that poor old bastard to eighty consecutive years last month. Remember? The old guy says, 'Judge, I can't do eighty years.' Remember what the judge said?"

"I do," said Rachel, smiling in spite of herself. "He said, 'Well, just do the best you can.' And that, dear Kevin, is what we're going to have to do."

"But I'm trying to tell you I can't do it 'a few more months'!" Kevin exclaimed. "I've tried hard work. I've tried hard play. I can't forget you for a minute. I know part of it is that things have become so damn miserable with Denise." He shook his head and looked down at his hands, which now clenched the steering wheel. "Facing her at the end of a chaotic day is more than I can handle. Then there's Barrington and this fucking case that's . . . that's . . . oh, Christ—enough with the self-pity! It's just that I'm dancing as fast as I can and pleasing no one, certainly not myself. All I know for sure now is that spending the rest of my life with you is more important than bleeding away the rest of my life in a courtroom or growing old at the Table of Three." Kevin took a deep breath and fixed her with misting eyes.

"Rachel, darling, I'll do whatever it takes for us to be together. I can't wait a few more months. I need you *now. Tonight.*"

Rachel was moved by his sincerity, but still somehow felt distant, troubled, as if she were a spectator to his obvious need. Why? Was it her own fatigue? His insistent attitude? The fact that these were not words of love, but of need—demanding words that were falling on her like stones, threatening to crush her own weary spirit? *I can't handle any more of this tonight,* she thought, looking out the passenger window at the fog sliding down toward the Bay.

She then turned her head back to face Kevin's insistent eyes; infrared eyes that split the darkness, burning into her resistance. "Kevin," she said in a hollow voice that echoed unpleasantly in her own ear. "I'm tired, too, and juggling a few balls of my own. You must know that I worry about you, too, whether you might somehow work things out with Denise; whether you can ever really leave your daughters—something I could never ask you to do. We've never even discussed the subject. I'm also terribly worried about the case—my partnership is riding on it, Kevin. And that means a lot to me." The corners of Rachel's full mouth turned up in a forced smile as she tried to lighten her voice. "So let's help each other. Remember our commitment to take things one at a time? If all goes well, within a few months we will have tried and won the case for the first thirteen plaintiffs. Maybe you will have decided to separate from Denise and I will have bumbled my way into partnership. Then we can stop all this sneaking around and do it right. Until then, don't you see there's just too much at stake to rush it, no matter how much we want it?"

"I don't disagree with you, Rachel. But please," he said, moving toward her again, touching her shoulder, "let me come in for just one drink and then—"

Rachel suddenly felt exhaustion, impatience almost, invading every cell of her body, and involuntarily withdrew from the repugnant smell of alcohol and stale tobacco on Kevin's breath. She wanted very much to be alone, to turn off her mind and tune out the day. She impatiently cut him off in mid-sentence by opening the car door and saying, "Kevin, you haven't heard a word I've said. I really would like to talk with you, but later, please, when you're able to hear me." She was surprised to hear the tinge of annoyance in her voice.

Kevin only smiled and pulled her toward him again. This time his kiss was more demanding, his arms encircling her. She felt suffocated and spun away from him out of the car. She walked swiftly to her door and entered it, not looking back. Once inside, she closed the door behind her, leaned her head against it, then gave way to tears of yearning and confusion, for she knew that there would be no authoritative knock on the door this time as there had been that night in New York.

TWENTY-NINE

∎

At precisely ten o'clock the following morning Lieutenant Dan Conti, attired in his finest sport coat—a blue double-breasted raw silk number—presented himself to the receptionist at the Eagle's Nest. "Please be seated, sir," said the receptionist, "Mr. Barrington will be with you in a moment."

The inspector preferred to remain standing, however, as he surveyed the opulent surroundings. To the left of the reception desk, a perfectly printed black-and-white landscape by Ansel Adams hung austerely above a finely tufted Baker leather sofa flanked by matching wing chairs. Over to his right Conti's attention was drawn to an antique Chinese ceremonial robe, hand-sewn with an abundance of golden thread and so well-preserved in its hermetically sealed glass case that the expressions on each of the beautifully depicted weeping women were as clear as they had been when crafted hundreds of years before. *I'm definitely uptown,* he thought.

A tip-tapping sound on the dark-stained oak floors signaled the approach of Miss Tarkenton, who, seemingly all in one motion, caught the inspector's attention, turned around, and proceeded in the opposite direction, indicating without a word that the visitor was to follow her mincing steps down the hallway.

"I noticed you appreciating the ceremonial robe," she said finally. "You have never seen one like it, sir. It's a Chinese masterpiece, probably four hundred years old."

"You don't say?" said Conti, unimpressed by the pedantic

secretary. "They really made 'em to last in those days, didn't they?"

"Well," said the birdlike woman through puckered lips, "I suppose you could say that.

"Inspector Conti," said Ms. Tarkenton as she led Conti into Barrington's huge corner office. Her voice conveyed mild disdain as she completed the introductions: "This is Mr. Barrington, and this is Mr. Stone." Even as she spoke, Miss Tarkenton was economically executing another one-hundred-and-eighty-degree turn back to her busy desk.

"Nice to meet you," said Conti carefully. The senior partner was known by the inspector to be the most powerful member of San Francisco's Police Commission and a strong but rational ally of Conti's tough brand of law and order. Conti would need Barrington's office files on the victims and his full support in influencing Captain Mahan to open a formal investigation—which meant he had first to persuade Barrington that his murder theory was sound.

"My pleasure," said Barrington, proffering his hand.

"Hello," said Kevin Stone.

"Kevin Stone," said Conti, looking thoughtfully and directly into the taller man's unblinking eyes. "I've read a lot about you—a piece in the Sunday supplement just recently—'The Lawyer Who Refuses to Lose' or something like that."

Kevin smiled and said, "You can't blame me for the excesses of a free press, Lieutenant. But I will plead guilty to taking little pleasure in the thought of losing."

"A sentiment shared by us all, I'm sure, Mr. Stone," said Conti, turning back to the senior partner. "And you, sir. Your work on the Police Commission is well known and much admired."

"Thank you, Lieutenant, I do what I can. Would you like a cup of coffee? I'm sorry to have kept you waiting," added Barrington.

"Quite all right," said the inspector, as he took the cup of coffee. "Your reception area puts the Guggenheim to shame."

"Ah," said Barrington, "you enjoy art, then?"

"Well, I know what I like. For example, that 'Moon over Hernandez' you have in the lobby is a hell of a lot better print than mine, and I intend to find out why. May I ask you where you got yours?"

Barrington looked at the police inspector with new interest and tentative respect. "May I take the fifth on that, Lieutenant? I wouldn't want either to get in trouble with your purveyor for charging too much or to alert mine that he may have charged too little."

"I guess you're entitled to remain silent until you have a chance to talk with an attorney," said Conti, cocking his head to one side and tugging at an earlobe, "but I hope you'll be more open on the subject of your disappearing clients."

Barrington smiled and reached for his cigarette case as he said, "Doesn't that overstate it a bit, Lieutenant? You make it sound as if these deaths represent some kind of trend rather than just a tragic coincidence."

"That's because I believe it to be more than a tragic coincidence, Mr. Barrington, and see it as my duty to keep it from becoming a trend."

"Well," said Barrington, motioning to one of the large client chairs in front of his massive oak desk, "then let's get on with it. Tell us what you think."

Kevin took the chair next to Conti, whose incessantly curious eyes were already sweeping the room as he sought to position himself in relation to the universe of the moment, to become a part of the room's energy so as better to interpret the data it would soon produce. He noticed, for example, the conference table in the adjacent wing of the office and wondered why Barrington had chosen the security of his desk. And was it just his imagination or did the senior partner seem overfriendly and the younger one somewhat reserved? As usual, no movement escaped the homicide inspector's relentless need to process inferences and possibilities. Why did the younger partner now cross his legs at the knee and fold his arms? And what did it signify, if anything, that Barrington was already tapping an oversize fountain pen on his desk? Impatience? Hostility? If it were not a pen, what might it be?

"What do I think?" replied Conti finally. "I think they were murdered. And if I am right about that, your other clients might be in grave danger."

Barrington glanced at Kevin with widening eyes, then back at the inspector. "You can't be serious."

Conti said nothing, but alternated his gaze between the two lawyers, awaiting a more substantive response. Barrington looked at Kevin. "Is this as off-the-wall to you as it is to me?"

Kevin stared at Conti's profile as Conti gave Barrington a

below-the-eyes smile. "Could you tell us a bit more about your suspicions, Lieutenant?" said Kevin.

Barrington leaned forward and said, "Yes, Inspector Conti. On what facts do you base this astonishing hypothesis?"

Conti again cocked his head slightly to one side, and stared straight back at Barrington through narrowed eyes. Then, barely moving his lips, and in a tone spiked with confidence, he said, "Circumstance and intuition."

Barrington carefully placed the fountain pen flat on the oak desk and leaned back in his chair. "Could you be a little more specific?"

"The circumstances are that two men died within five weeks of each other; that both were scheduled to go to trial in the same case within the next six months; that both were seeking millions of dollars in damages; and that both had pretty good cases. Right so far?"

Barrington nodded once sharply in tentative affirmation, saying, "Go on."

"Charles Hallinan's car left highway seventeen," continued the inspector, "at one of only a handful of spots along the entire roadway between the summit and his destination where there was no protective barrier. A witness claims the victim was being harassed by a yellow pickup truck before taking the plunge. Skid marks ran for several hundred feet, and yet there was no indication of a blown-out tire. Hallinan simply couldn't have been going *that* fast on *that* road in *that* car, laying down skid marks *that* long, *unless he was being pushed*."

Inspector Conti glanced for the first time toward Kevin and flashed him an ironic smile, saying, "All circumstantial, of course."

Hearing no comments or questions, Conti continued. "As for Weisberg, the reason the sharks went after him was that he was bleeding. Whoever caused him to begin bleeding made a mistake. He or she automatically switched off the lights upon leaving, a common error, for even the most callous murderer seems to prefer to leave his deed covered by darkness. I conclude from this that unless Weisberg felt his way several hundred feet through three rooms, two of them in pitch darkness, somebody else was in there with him."

"But the newspaper account said there was a suicide note written in his own handwriting," protested Kevin.

"Now, there," said the inspector, shrugging his shoulders

slightly, "is a circumstance that does tend to point in the other direction."

"Well," said Barrington, "it seems to be a rather powerful circumstance. How do you counter it?"

Conti turned his head and stared for a moment out one of Barrington's north windows, stroking his nose with the index finger of his right hand. "That's where intuition comes in," he said quietly. "Intuition based on nearly fifteen years in homicide. I'm sure that in your work you sense when you've got a winning case or a loser? Well, there you have it; I know whether I've got an accident or a murder."

"But who would be interested in killing these two men?" asked Kevin, shaking his head. "It doesn't make sense. Neither would have lived through another year in any case."

"Is that because of the contamination they had consumed from their drinking water?"

"I see you've read the complaint," said Barrington. "Yes. They were both seriously ill. Terminally ill, in fact."

A momentary silence followed. Barrington allowed himself a cigarette. Kevin rose from his chair and walked to the east window-wall, hands in trouser pockets except for a purposeful glance at his wristwatch. Dan Conti watched Barrington light his cigarette as attentively as might an aborigine who had never seen fire, then shifted his intense gaze on the younger partner, saying, "Mr. Stone. You look a lot like Robert Redford. People tell you that?"

"Never."

Conti extended his arms, palms upward, then slapped them down on the arms of his chair. "Well, what do I know anyway? How would you rank the seriousness of their illness against your other one hundred or more plaintiffs?"

"They were probably the most seriously ill," said Barrington.

"Which means, I take it, that they were also likely to receive the largest monetary compensation," said Conti, slowly stroking his nose.

"That follows, yes," said Kevin, resuming his seat. "We had estimated verdicts of two to three million dollars."

"For both?" asked Conti.

"For each," answered Stone.

A low whistle issued from the inspector's full lips. "And now," he said, turning his head back toward Barrington and stroking his nose, "neither the North American Chemical Company, nor the city of Lileton, nor either of their insurers—if they have any—need be concerned about having to pay over five million dollars to you and these now conveniently departed plaintiffs.''

"You do have a point," said Barrington, thoughtfully tapping his pen against pursed lips. Conti noticed how the morning light streaming through the east window created a halo effect around the senior partner's large, erect head. *A regular Montgomery Street Buddha,* thought Conti admiringly. "And since the law does not permit heirs to recover for the pain and suffering of the victims before their deaths," continued Barrington, "it's standard practice to dismiss cases where an elderly plaintiff succumbs to disease or old age."

"Or is murdered," added the lieutenant.

Without comment on Conti's conclusion, Barrington confirmed the inspector's estimate that the defendants and/or their insurers stood to lose between 250 and 350 million dollars in all, plus that or more in punitive damages.

"Well, gentlemen," said Conti. "The cumulative effect of all this beats whatever I've seen in the realm of coincidence."

"That's your department, Lieutenant," said Barrington, throwing up his hands. "What do you want from us?"

"Your cooperation. Ever play baseball, Mr. Stone?"

"Not since the eighth grade," answered Kevin, a surprised look on his face.

"Hmm. Too bad about those Giants, huh? Baseball is in trouble everywhere, I guess: low attendance, players snorting everything but the baselines. What happened to all the heroes?" Without waiting for an answer, Conti cocked his head and shifted his attention back to Barrington. "First, I want to interview all personnel in your firm who worked with either Charles Hallinan or Bernard Weisberg. Second, I would like access to their files, together with the files of the remaining thirteen plaintiffs scheduled to go to trial in the first group."

Barrington replied without hesitation: "I can schedule meetings at your convenience with all team members who had any contact with Hallinan or Weisberg. Needless to say, whether we agree with your homicide hypothesis or not, it stands to reason that we wish to cooperate as fully as possible. If there is even a remote possibility that you are right, we would be the biggest benefactors of your diligence after the potential victims themselves. I am, however, concerned about the panic that could result among our plaintiffs if rumors about your murder theory got out. There might even be delays in our trial date. I must insist, therefore, that you exercise discretion, and speak to no one without clearing it with me. Moreover, all staff members have been instructed to observe the attorney/client privilege as to all facts other than those already a matter of public record.''

"Mr. Barrington," said Conti impatiently, "it will do me little good to talk to your staff members if they can tell me only what I've already learned from the public records. I must have more than that.''

"And I must ensure that my staff complies with the ethical restraints within which we must work. As you must know, I am a member of the Police Commission, and I have already assured you of our cooperation. But the question of privileged information is not negotiable," Barrington said with a hardening of his voice.

Conti returned Barrington's cold look with one of his own, then slowly rose and walked over to the west wall, where Levelor blinds fended off the morning sun. He absently created a small opening by delicately spreading two fingers and peered down toward the street. His disappointment was not surprising. If the firm continued to claim the privilege, a search warrant would yield nothing either. The files would have to be sealed by a special master and turned over to the Municipal Court for a hearing which, with a member of the Police Commission representing the opposing firm, he could only lose. Besides, Captain Mahan would not allow him to apply for the warrant in the first place in these circumstances.

Barrington remained at his desk, waiting; Kevin watched the detective's face and shifted in his chair. Conti seemed absorbed in the view. The Levelor blinds created a gridlike shadow that played across the detective's pale skin as he gazed absently through the openings. When at last he spoke, the tone of his voice had changed to a lower, grittier texture. "It's easy to talk about privileged information up here in the forty-second-floor penthouse, Mr. Barrington, but down there on the street—where I work and your clients live—it's a different world. Two of your clients have already been denied the most fundamental 'privilege' of all: the right to live out their lives. That's the only privilege I'm interested in; and unless you guys are more concerned about being lawyers than you are about the law, you'll hand over those records.''

Kevin, obviously irritated by the inspector's assertiveness, rose to his feet and said, "Listen, Lieutenant, Mr. Barrington has been damn patient with your theory. Murder is your job. But interpreting professional responsibility is ours, and if you don't like what we're offering you, then go out and get yourself a search warrant."

Inspector Conti turned from the window and gazed at Kevin with dark brown eyes that betrayed no emotion. "No formal investigation has been opened, Mr. Stone. And I think you know what would happen to my search warrant under Penal Code Section 1524 as well as I do."

"Then," said Kevin coldly, "I suggest that you also have no further business here."

Barrington cleared his throat and interceded in a placating tone: "I must reluctantly agree, Lieutenant, but if I am correctly following your line of thought, it would seem that your time might best be spent in investigating those who have the most to gain from these deaths: the North American and Lileton officials."

"Thanks for the advice, Mr. Barrington," Conti said, his face relaxing. "But as you know, our captain is a good politician and not likely to confront a neighboring police department, at this stage, at least."

"I understand," said Barrington, nodding his agreement, "but I hope you will also understand that our hands are absolutely tied by the attorney/client and work-product privileges. Now, do you wish to speak with Ms. Cannon or Mr. Johnstone, the two associates who worked with Hallinan and Weisberg?"

"For now, that will have to do," said the inspector with a shrug of his shoulders and an unexpected broad smile directed at Kevin Stone.

"Kevin," said Barrington, "please take Lieutenant Conti over to Rachel's office and ask her to introduce him to Johnstone when they are finished."

"Thank you, Mr. Barrington. I am sure we'll be seeing more of each other. Perhaps next time you'll be more open with me . . . at least concerning the source of your Ansel Adams." Conti said the last words with a wry smile, then turned, and with his head cocked and a flourishing gesture toward the door, added, "Mr. Stone?"

"Follow me," said Kevin, a coolness still apparent in his voice.

*   *   *

Both Adrian Fisher and Gardner White had asked Miss Tarkenton to signal them the moment Conti left, and within five minutes they were in Barrington's office. "Well?" asked White anxiously.

"Well *what*?" said Barrington, looking down at his rotund partner with overt contempt.

"You know what I mean," said White, shrugging his round shoulders and averting his eyes from Barrington's glare. "Your interview with the cop, of course. Look, Austin, I don't expect you to understand that there are two sides to this issue between us. But until we're out of the case, we're in it, and that includes me. Let's face it, if our little secret gets out, we're in something far worse."

"I believe it's called state prison," said Adrian Fisher with a sardonic grin. "But he's right, Austin. Like Yogi says, 'It's not over till it's over,' and whether the cop is right or wrong on his murder theory, it's nerve-racking to think of someone snooping around those records. Anyway, we need to forgive and stick together, no matter how deep the wounds."

"All right," said Barrington, taking his seat behind the desk and lighting a cigarette. "It went as well as could be expected. He's a tough little bastard. Highly unpredictable. Definitely not your average cop. Even knows a good Adams print when he sees one."

"Well, now you've lost me," said Fisher. "But what the hell does he want? Does he really think our chaps were murdered?"

"He's quite sure they were," said Barrington with a morose expression. "Of all the investigators in the universe, we had to get one straight out of Dashiell Hammett. Of course, he doesn't have a shred of hard evidence to support his conjecture. Kevin is taking him to see Rachel now."

"How did Kevin handle himself with Conti?" asked White.

"Not as well as I might have hoped; a little too spring-loaded. Quite frankly, our friend and partner Mr. Stone is exhibiting a few hairline cracks. Nothing I can't handle, but he did little to conceal his dislike for the good inspector."

"Austin," said Fisher, with the caution of a man walking through a mine field, "you *are* finished with the artificial supplement, are you not?"

"Of course I am," said Barrington testily. "We have all we need in that department."

"What about Rachel?" asked Adrian. "No pun intended, Austin, but she looks like a potential loose cannon to me."

Barrington reminded Fisher that he had continued to maintain tight control of the medical records—the sole traceable link to the artificial supplements and Project Salvation. But White paced back and forth with fists driven deep in suit coat pockets. "I'm concerned about Adrian's point. Is it possible that Conti's wild-goose murder chase could somehow reveal Project Salvation?" he asked.

"Oh, for Christ's sake, White, *sit down* and quit whining. That's an antique Khorassan prayer rug knotted in Birjand that you're threatening to wear out with your incessant pacing. I tell you there is absolutely nothing to worry about. No matter how deeply Rachel becomes involved in the case, there is no way she, Conti, or even the defense toxicologists could ever discover those few artificial supplements—even with the damn medical records! Sure, we could do without the spotlight, but without the support of his captain, Conti won't even get off the ground."

"But suppose he gets his search warrant?" asked White.

"How could that happen when an influential member of the Police Commission is about to let Captain Mahan know that his smart-ass detective is stepping on toes around here?"

Gardner White's face slowly relaxed into a smile.

"Furthermore," said Barrington, ringing Miss Tarkenton, "I suspect that this influential member of the Police Commission just might take the good captain to lunch during the next day or two."

THIRTY

∎

Inspector Dante Conti fared no better at his next meeting, as Rachel zealously complied with Barrington's orders and stone-walled the interview. Conti's normally inscrutable face was beginning to betray his growing frustration at his inability to break through the person he had assumed to be the weakest link in the chain of security surrounding the lawsuit.

"No problem, Ms. Cannon," said Conti, rising as if to leave Rachel's office, "I understand completely. As a nonpartner— and a lady at that—your activities in this case have probably been confined to library research anyway."

Rachel only smiled at the overt ploy. *This guy is too much*, she thought. *He makes the Neanderthal men around this place look fully evolved by comparison.* She pointedly looked at her watch and rose to encourage his departure. "Officer Conti," she said, deliberately demoting him in rank, "you can't bait me into saying any more than I've already told you. You're wasting your time as well as mine. If you wore a hat, I'd offer it to you at this point."

Conti shook his head slowly and smiled, but only with his mouth. "Tell me something," he said, "why would a pretty girl like you go to law school and let them turn you into such a tough cookie?"

Rachel flashed her own sardonic smile and said, "I did consider becoming a homicide detective, but I wasn't short enough."

Conti's head snapped back as the smile wilted on his face. Silenced and getting nowhere, he retreated to the doorway but then turned and threw both hands in the air, saying, "All right. I deserved that. I apologize."

"I accept," said Rachel, already regretting her unnecessarily personal remark.

"Can we start over?" asked Conti.

"Have a seat," said Rachel, "but I warn you, my lips are still sealed as to nonpublic medical information."

"I believe you, counselor," Conti said, arms extended and palms forward as if to ward off an attack. "Really I do. Now, Mr. Barrington indicates that you probably knew Hallinan and Weisberg better than anyone else in the office did."

"That's true, although I didn't know them very well. At the risk of being overly dramatic, the fact is, we cannot afford to get too personally involved with these people. They are very ill and may not be with us long."

"Could you give me an opinion as to whether Weisberg would have taken his own life?"

"That's a hard one. Bernard Weisberg was a tough little guy. Quite pushy, frankly. He was probably a decent enough person, but the toxins had taken a heavy toll on his central nervous system, and he seemed increasingly irritable and depressed each time we talked. Given his moodiness, and the fact that his system was loaded with lindane, I'd say he was a likely candidate for suicide.''

"Where would you rank Hallinan and Weisberg on the scale of potential monetary damages to be awarded by the jury?"

"I'd probably rank Hallinan first—he had only been given a few months to live—and Weisberg a close second."

"Does that suggest anything to you?"

"Not necessarily, but I've heard a rumor that it suggests something to you," said Rachel.

"Let me confirm that rumor," said Conti, unsmiling as he leaned forward, lowered his voice, and spoke in a rush of words. "North American Chemical is a privately held corporation, but we've recently learned that most of the stock is held by Carmine Romano, the head of a Mafia family who used to own two gambling casinos in Las Vegas. He lost his license when he was indicted with several other family members in New York City."

"What's that got to do with Weisberg?"

"Maybe nothing. Maybe everything. Romano's family has been moving his operations to the West, pursuing a new idea in creative management. They buy distressed 'straight' businesses, like this chemical plant, in depressed cities like Lileton, then slash costs by scaring off any unions they can't control, paying junk wages, and dismantling costly safety measures."

"I've heard something about under-the-table payoffs," agreed Rachel.

"In the first place," said Conti, "state inspectors visit a plant like North American as frequently as I visit my dentist. If someone does get pushy, it's handled by Joe Lucca in the traditional mob manner: He gives them a choice between a periodic C-note on the one hand or a bay swim in a cement jockstrap on the other. Follow?" Conti touched the tip of his nose and added, "Now, suppose that in order to maximize these profits they also skipped the little matter of insurance, a costly item in the chemicals industry. They could do that because they don't need it; they know they have the local enforcement authorities either scared or bribed or both. They've got themselves a regular cash cow. But then, all of a sudden, the hottest law firm in the Bay Area comes along and threatens to blow the whole banana. By the way, *does* North American carry insurance?"

"My, how neatly you slipped that in. You really should have been a trial lawyer, Inspector," said Rachel, smiling. "A very decent try, but no cigar this time. That information is not public yet. In any event, those are serious charges, and if you can make them stick, you might even get North American shut down and out of town before we can collect our jury verdict."

Dan Conti scowled. "You people are really something. I'm trying to put together a RICO claim that will smash the West Coast mob and you people want to talk about collecting money."

"Welcome to Planet Earth, Inspector Conti. Guess what? That's what lawyers do for their clients. And we, by the way, have been doing it pretty well. But then, all of a sudden, the hottest homicide detective—"

"Inspector—"

"—in town comes along and threatens to blow the whole banana. Sound familiar?"

"Vaguely, but what's your point, counselor?"

"My point is that if you now file a complaint under the racketeering act, our Mafia friends will be back in Vegas in an hour, with North American liquid assets stacked in a body bag, far beyond our reach. Thank you, Lieutenant. You've just given me yet another reason not to help you."

"Does that mean no insurance information?"

"I'll check with the man upstairs and if there's no problem in releasing this information, I'll call it in to you later today."

"Better yet," said Conti, "why don't we discuss it further at dinner, say, tomorrow night?"

Rachel laughed good-naturedly and said, "Sorry, the management does not permit us to date police lieutenants we meet during working hours, particularly those committed to deceit and treachery in their effort to ferret out confidential information."

Conti smiled broadly, his appreciation of Rachel now abundantly clear. "Well, anyway . . . thanks for the compliment. If you change your mind, just dial nine eleven. Now, where do I find this Jeffrey P. Johnstone?"

"One floor down. Check with the receptionist."

Conti had been gone but a few seconds before Rachel realized that she had rejected the offer to dinner for no rational reason; it had been an automatic response. *How long has it been,* she asked herself, *since I just allowed myself to go out and enjoy a relaxed evening with a man not in some way related to Stafford, Parrish, and MacAllister? Too damn long,* came the resounding reply, and on an impulse, she picked up her phone and dialed the receptionist. "Mimi, this is Rachel. There's a detective about to walk back into the elevator lobby—could you give him a message for me? 'Dinner meeting okay tomorrow night; Ciao at eight.' Got it? Thanks.''

Rachel slowly replaced the receiver on the hook, her smile cut short by the entrance of a haggard Kevin Stone. "Rachel," he said haltingly, "about last night. I guess I finally dropped one of those balls I've been trying to juggle, and it landed on you. Can you manage to forget the whole thing?"

"Consider it forgotten—for the time being," said Rachel with the hint of a smile. "And while you're here, would you enlighten me on how Austin is going to argue the motion to reconsider cancerphobia next week?"

"With his usual skill and daring, I suppose," said Kevin with an ironic smile. "What's your point?"

"I've been rethinking all this since last night," she said. "We haven't come up with anything new, so Judge Bainbridge will probably slaughter him, regardless of the old-boy connections. But what's even worse is the psychological lift the defense will get from viewing the carnage. Any settlement hopes will be destroyed. Shall I go on?"

"No. I get the idea, but hopes for a settlement at a decent price are shot now anyway. We've got to give it a try. How did your meeting with the cop go?" Kevin asked, quickly changing the subject.

Rachel was surprised to find herself feeling uneasy about the date she had just made with Conti—unease that had probably contributed to the ease with which she accepted Kevin's apology. It's ironic, she thought, that she probably would not have accepted Conti's dinner invitation in the first place but for Kevin's behavior the night before.

"It was fine," she said guardedly. "I gave him nothing but impressions. As for last night, all's forgotten, although there are terms to my unconditional forgiveness."

Kevin smiled, saying, "I thought I was sorry about last night, but I think you're about to make me even sorrier."

"Just kidding," said Rachel with a laugh, "but I've been thinking about something for several days and would appreciate your reaction and maybe a word to Austin."

"I'm listening."

"It has to do with my role at the trial. It's not that I don't appreciate getting to put on Saul Franks, but from the standpoint of the case, well, it could be counterproductive."

"What are you saying?" asked Kevin.

"This is going to be a long trial—six to eight weeks. Most of the men on the panel will be excused because of 'pressing business commitments,' and as you know, though it pains me to say it, we're going to end up with a whole lot of housewife jurors with a couple of retired male postal clerks thrown in. In other words, a substantial majority of our jury will be women. Doesn't this present an opportunity to exploit an advantage? Remember your lectures on the importance of the relationship of the jury and the trial lawyer. Isn't it obvious that if I do my part well, these women will identify with me? Will want me to 'make good'? Well, I'm suggesting we give them the opportunity to bring that all about—by returning massive verdicts in favor of our clients." Smiling sheepishly, she added, "And, of course, I have no personal axe to grind in the matter."

"Of course not," said Kevin, returning her smile and taking a seat. "What did you have in mind?"

"I was hoping that I might participate in some direct and cross-examination, perhaps even make the opening statement."

Kevin started to laugh, then caught himself, saying, "Are you sure you want Austin and me around at all?"

"Sure. I can't carry all those files myself," said Rachel, adding that if she were to put on but one witness, the female jurors would see it as tokenism. "So trust me on this," she concluded, "either involve me fully or keep me all the way in the background. I'll go along either way."

"Okay. It does make sense and I'll take it up with Austin. Now, can I buy you a nonalcoholic lunch today as penance for last night?"

"I'd love to, but I'm taking some lunch out to Emmett Dixon's house. We're having our final predeposition preparation today."

"Say hello to him for me. How's he doing?"

"Not so good, I'm afraid," said Rachel, her large gray-green eyes fogging with emotion. "I'm really worried about him."

"Hey, what's going on between you two?" said Kevin, standing up and taking Rachel tentatively by the shoulders. "You're not getting sweet on this old bird, are you?"

"He's such a dear man, Kevin. Those are from him," said Rachel, pointing to a bouquet of flowers on her credenza. "I think I'm the daughter he never had, and he's the spitting image of the grandfather I lost too soon."

"Well, give him my best, but keep that professional distance, okay?"

"Words of advice from the master on the subject?" said Rachel.

"Touché," said Kevin, smiling.

As Kevin left her office, Rachel felt another pang of uneasiness about her date with Conti and then swiftly caught herself. Why, she wondered, should she feel that in meeting Dan Conti for dinner she was betraying a man who was, after all, married to another woman? Nonetheless, her misgivings followed her as she left her office, her trial bag loaded with files and lunches.

Rachel was shocked to see how Emmett Dixon had deteriorated since their last meeting in February, just five months earlier. The mere act of answering the door seemed to exhaust him, and he quickly returned to his chair, where he remained throughout the brief meeting.

Rachel fought an engulfing sadness as she entered the tiny room. It had the smell of time, of shut windows.

"I don't look so good, do I?" said the old man with a wan smile. "It's not me, darlin'; it's these damn clothes that keep getting bigger somehow."

"Are you eating, Emmett?" Rachel asked, glancing into the kitchen, pleased to see that it seemed in reasonably good order.

"No appetite, but this food you brought looks mighty good."

"How have you been feeling?"

"Not too poorly up to recently. If last week was a fish, I'd throw it back. How are things in the outside world?"

"I have both good news and bad news. The good news is that the court granted our motion to advance the trial, which means that within six months this whole thing will be behind you, and you'll be able to take me out in the style to which I would like to become accustomed."

"Congratulations. But I'm not surprised. I can't imagine a judge saying no to you."

"Some have no trouble at all, but there's some bad news too: Remember our theory that money damages should be recoverable for the suffering involved in fearing cancer—without the necessity of tying a specific illness to the ingestion of a particular chemical? Well, it was thrown out last week."

"That sounds bad, but run it past me again, Rachel," said Dixon, picking at his chicken salad. "I don't know how to break this to you at this late date, but I'm the client, not the lawyer.''

"I keep forgetting," said Rachel, then reviewed the difficult problems involved in proving specific causation.

"I'm with you so far," said the old man, "but how do they explain the fact that every damn one of us who lived there very long has gotten sick in one way or another? I hear, for instance, that old Bernie Weisberg was crazy as a runover dog by the time he checked out."

"Good question, Emmett. The problem is that you all drank the same contaminated water, but you don't all have the same illness. The reason for this is that these chemicals break down the immune system, which then could result in a hundred illnesses which may all be different from one another. Like you said, Weisberg suffered depression, but you ended up with lung and kidney damage, while Charley Hallinan's main problem was deterioration of his liver."

"No, honey, Charley's main problem was his driving."

"I guess you're right, but you can see how this plays into the hands of the defendants. They will argue that we plaintiffs can't connect any particular chemical with any specific illness."

"Does this mean . . ." said the old man, his words interrupted by a coughing spell. Rachel quickly gave him some water and handed him his medicine. In a minute Dixon's distorted features slowly relaxed into a craggy smile. "Does this mean I better hold off booking passage for me and you to Ireland?''

"Well, I don't just go off with every man who invites me on a trip out of town. Play me a tune on your saw while I catch up on my lunch and think it over."

"Shoot, Rachel, I'm too tired to go and fetch the darn thing."

"Then let's get right to work. You'll be asked how you came to be living in North American housing and what did you do before that, so let's start today with your previous employment background."

"Let's see. My first and worst job ever was workin' up in the Minnesota north woods as a lumberjack for twenty-six dollars a month. They put us in bunkhouses infested with vermin. We'd boil our clothes on Sunday and burn sulphur in the bunkhouse to kill the bloodsuckers, but by Monday night the nits would hatch, and we'd be just as lousy as ever. We had no showers, not even cold water, and the company wouldn't hire anyone without his own blanket. All the signs in the employment offices looking for grafters, doggers, setters, or hokers said 'must have blankets.' For some reason, that was the last straw for me.''

"Why did you have to have a blanket to work as a lumberjack?"

"Well, it was cold, and the company was too cheap to provide them. It became a symbol of their power over us: You want to work? Then provide your own necessities—that was the message, which was the thing that led to me getting involved with the left. I'd been reading *Appeal to Reason* and decided to join the Wobblies.''

"So what did you do?" asked Rachel, putting down her pencil.

"We formed us a little committee of the biggest 'jacks in camp and started meeting all the boats and buses with incoming workers aboard. Then we took away their blankets and put 'em in a big pile and burned 'em. It got pretty rough sometimes, and I wasn't very big, though I was tougher than a boiled owl. Anyway, it worked; and the company had to start providing blankets and other essentials. That was the closest thing they'd ever seen to a successful 'strike' up there and I stayed on till we done logged out the whole area.''

The old man then recounted how he had moved to Everett, Washington, the lumber capital of the world in 1916, and joined another Wobbly movement. Pitted against company thugs, police, and ghastly working conditions, the party had chartered a tugboat to Seattle to confront management. Three hundred Wobblies came off the boat and were greeted by machine-gun fire; four killed on the spot and many wounded, including Dixon. "Instead of putting us in hospitals," he said, "they threw us in jail to die, but the Wobs got me out the next day just as I was about to bleed to death. After that, I became an active organizer for the IWW, which caught on big as a result of what came to be known as the Everett Massacre. Later on I took a job in Portland driving a forklift and got married. Lived there twenty-five years.''

Emmett Dixon paused for another convulsive coughing siege, then gave Rachel a weak smile and added, "So you can imagine, young lady, how good those workers' quarters at North American Chemical looked to me after some of the places I had seen.'' *They'd all felt that way, to some degree,* thought Rachel. *So innocent, these worldly-wise men. And to hear Professor Childhouse, Love Canal is no longer an isolated neighborhood experience. How many others around the country are drinking contaminated water, blissfully ignorant of the danger they are in? Dying in bits and pieces.*

Emmett Dixon tried to continue, but began to cough with such intensity that Rachel had to remove the plate of food from his lap. The racking cough continued for two or three minutes, during which Dixon took huge gulps of his medicine, clearly exceeding any prescribed dosage.

"I felt real lucky during those years at North American. There was a good bunch of guys to talk to with my darlin' Shirlee gone, and, well, I felt that the conditions me and the other guys had there proved that I hadn't wasted my life all those years with the Wobblies. There wasn't a night I went to sleep that I didn't pull that company blanket up around my shoulders and feel a little proud of what I'd done." Dixon went silent for a moment, his head lowered, and Rachel thought for a moment that he had gone to sleep. When he spoke again, there was a new sadness in his voice. "Shirlee never admired the Left much, but if she could have seen those workers' quarters at North American, she would have been proud of those four young men who were killed on the cold streets of Everett, Washington, in October of 1916, and maybe of her husband too."

Dixon finished his dessert and none too soon, for he began to cough again, but only for a minute. "But nothing's perfect," he said, shifting in his chair. "Like Willie Nelson says, 'If it ain't one thing, it's some other thing.' North American give us each a nice room, *two* free blankets, and a shower with hot water—hot with chemicals that ate our guts out." Dixon flashed an ironic smile. "Ain't it just like a bunch of poor working stiffs to be drinking themselves to death—on *water*. But we'll show 'em. The lucky thirteen of us who are left will open the door, and the rest can just walk in on our heels and pick up their checks."

"That's the plan, Emmett, just like you did it up in Everett, Washington, back in 1916. But now we had better talk a bit about your deposition. Then you can get some sleep."

After twenty minutes of reviewing the questions he might expect from the defense, the old man fell sound asleep in his chair. Rachel covered him up with a blanket, then held his hand for a few minutes before cleaning up the room and returning to the Imperial Building.

THIRTY-ONE

■

The morning blossomed near-perfect in Sausalito, and Rachel resolved upon awakening that today, nothing would dismay her. Yesterday had been a killer, but seven hours of sleep had performed its miracle and, at six sharp, she rose like Lazarus with renewed enthusiasm. A well-paced four-mile run along Sausalito Bay set her skin glowing and her heart singing. She even allowed herself extra time over coffee to catch up on a day-old *New York Times*, then dressed for work. She left Sausalito at seven-twenty, and drove south along Bridgeway Avenue toward the Golden Gate Bridge. Just offshore to her left, the herring fleet, with its convoy of freeloading sea gulls, bobbed like corks in the water, now electrified by the morning light from horizon to shoreline. The sun's aurora, reflected in the Bay's shimmering waters, looked like a vertical monolithic column, shooting like a Roman candle from shoreline to horizon. The foghorns had stopped their wailing, leaving the gulls to solo. She felt, as they were fond of saying in Marin County, centered.

But as she moved up onto the Golden Gate Bridge toward San Francisco, Rachel saw the funereal mattress of dense Bay fog that awaited her here every morning this time of year. Ahead, the Marin commuter parade of Jaguars, Mercedes, and Porsches slipped one after another into the oppressive stuff like letters into envelopes. Sometimes the fog was content just to drape itself across the Golden Gate Bridge. On such days it could be left behind at the south toll plaza, like a sullen hitchhiker whose fleeting dark look leaves one feeling somehow guilty and vaguely unsettled for a minute or two. But today the fog persisted past the Bay crossing into town, and she knew it would be noon before she saw the sun again.

This was just the beginning. As Rachel turned her car toward Lombard Street, more cars and city sounds began to assault her tranquil mood. She turned up her cassette player to drown out the staccato beat of the ubiquitous public works' jackhammers, eternally laboring on Van Ness Avenue to tear up last year's planting of the underground pipes and conduits that serve as the arteries and capillaries of every metropolitan city. Turning east down Bush Street and approaching the financial district, Rachel was next blasted by the din of compressors, concrete mixers, double-parked diesel trucks, and workmen's strained voices. She rolled up her windows and turned up the volume on Bob Seger's *You're Still the Same*, for nothing would get her down today. She would somehow hold on to "the feeling."

A downcast Jeffrey P. Johnstone greeted Rachel in the hall-way and she invited him into her office. Jeff nodded and shuffled toward her office. Rachel affectionately watched him from be-hind as he entered her room. Despite his best efforts to affect the manner of a lawyer, Jeff's walk looked like a break-dancer in slow motion, his clothes were early Missouri, and his head belonged on the shoulders of a punk rocker.

"I'll get right to the point, my friend," Rachel said. "You seem unhappy lately, particularly the last few months. I won-dered if there's anything you want to talk about."

"I'm not unhappy," came Jeffrey's quick response, delivered as he doodled on a yellow pad he was carrying.

"You're not unhappy," repeated Rachel, noticing Jeff's averted eyes.

Jeff finally looked up, his thin lips pursed into a sardonic grin. "I'm not unhappy," he said as he lay the pad on Rachel's desk. "I'm fucking miserable."

"Why?"

"Why shouldn't I be?" said the birdlike associate. "I'm nearly twenty-six years old and I'm not even on the Circuit Court of Appeals yet."

"Be serious."

"Serious is unhappy. I'm being funny, which is happy."

"Jeffrey," said Rachel in a friendly but no-nonsense tone, "do you want to talk about it or not?"

"Thanks, Rachel," said Jeff, smiling, "but no thanks. Not right now. But speaking of unhappy, does Kevin seem a bit edgy at times lately?"

"A bit," Rachel conceded. The sound of a pile driver drew her gaze out her window toward a construction project in prog-ress across the street. "He's under a lot of pressure, Jeff. More than we can probably realize."

"No doubt," said Jeff, then hesitantly added, "Rachel—I think I'd better tell you that I'm not sure you two are fooling anybody at team meetings."

The pile driver stopped and so did Rachel's heart. "What do you mean?" she asked as casually as she could manage.

Jeff gave her a look.

"So, what do you mean?" she repeated.

"Well," said Jeff, rising slowly, "for one thing, you light up like an arcade game when he walks in the room. He-too-you."

Rachel felt a flush spreading across her face. "It's that obvious?"

"Maybe only to me, but Stu Wallach said something the other day and, well, you know how fast something like this could spread once it got started."

"Thanks, Jeff," said Rachel quietly. "I'll try to watch it more carefully. I appreciate your candor."

"Is that all?" Jeff asked. "I guess it's ironic, Rachel, but here you are worrying about me while I've been worried sick about you."

"I'll be fine." Rachel smiled at her friend. "Please don't worry. Everything is under control."

"Everything?" Jeff said, and Rachel knew he was thinking of her loss of esteem among the partners should the word get out. Not surprisingly, Jeff would be a minority of one in blaming Kevin, she knew, but the thought provided no consolation at all.

"More or less. I guess there are times when your heart takes control and rationality takes a backseat."

"I know."

"You do?"

"Sure I do. Shit, Rachel, you weren't the only pretty girl who ever lived in the great Midwest, you know. But my love life—or lack thereof—isn't the issue before the court."

"And what, sage counselor, *is* the issue?"

"Simply put, the issue is: If he really cares about you, how could he let this happen when you're so close to making partnership? He's got his family, his partnership, his—"

"Jeff. *He* didn't just 'let it happen.' It just . . . well, things like this just happen. But don't worry. It's on hold now—until the trial is over. I'll either be a partner then or I'll be out of here. I know what I'm doing." She hoped that Jeff was more convinced than she was.

But Jeff was not satisfied. "He's married, Rachel, and I

haven't seen you date anyone for several months. That just ain't healthy."

"Well, doctor," said Rachel with a wink, "I'm taking your prescription this very night. Dating a cop no less."

"That detective from yesterday?" Jeff let out a whistle and ran his hand through his disheveled hair. "I didn't mean you should go *that* far. That guy eats baby ducks for breakfast."

"Well, I think," said Rachel, "that he'll be the perfect diversion. I want to relax, but not too much; the Big One is only three months off now. Which reminds me, I've got to get busy. I just heard there's a case very much like ours under way right now out at Superior Court. I might learn something." She planted a quick kiss on Jeff's cheek.

"Thanks for your concern, dear Jeffrey. Now, don't worry a minute longer. Okay?"

Jeff watched Rachel's shapely legs carry her back behind her desk, then reached up and touched his cheek. "Sure, Rachel . . . sure."

When Jeff had left, Rachel realized that his well-intentioned cross-examination had been more disquieting than she recognized at the time. She was feeling distinctly off-center, and beginning to see that she was not only in love but in trouble as well.

At noon the same day, Kevin met with Austin Barrington at the President's Club to deal with a matter that would influence the lives of everyone at S.P.&M. Barrington was visibly stressed, sipping an unprecedented second Glenlivet and already smoking his seventh cigarette of the day. Kevin appeared less anxious, but was staring into the bottom of his empty glass as if looking for answers among the melting cubes of ice.

"What I'm trying to say, Kevin, is that we're in a bind and we've got to quit squabbling among ourselves. For my part," said the senior partner, signaling Stefan to bring on the appetizer, "I want you to know I'm not blaming you for any of this."

"That's very nice of you," said Stone coolly, "because I never guaranteed the Court would rule for us on cancerphobia. I said only that it would be a relatively easy case if he did. He didn't. So it isn't." Kevin punctuated the last words with a wink and a mock toast as he held up his empty glass.

He's enjoying this, thought Barrington. *I'm about to lose everything I've worked for all my life, and he sits here in my club getting drunk and rubbing my nose in it.* "You might evidence a bit more concern, Kevin. You and Rachel gave me nothing new in your brief. In two days I have to stand in front of Matt Bainbridge with no new cases, no new facts, and no new theories."

"And you'll get no new rulings," said Kevin, "after which we'll just have to try the case on one leg."

"Dammit, Kevin, you heard the partners. They're not willing to let us do that. Besides, the bank's lawyers may be slow but they're not stupid. Within a week they'll figure out what's happened to our case and jerk our financing. And I won't be able to scare them out of it this time. It will be finished: the case, S.P.&M., all of it."

"I guess you're right," said Kevin, rattling the ice cubes in his glass. "I'm as sorry as you are about it," he added, but with no note of contrition in his voice.

Bullshit, thought Barrington. *After S.P.&M. closes its doors, you'll still be in demand. You may have to stay in the trenches for a few extra years, but at least you'll be working. And I? At my age, who will have me? I'll have nothing—except the ghoulish reputation as the lawyer who led his firm into bankruptcy. Never mind we would have been there anyway, but Tasker James, Gardner White, the press—they'll all be pointing at me as the fall guy. And W.W. II? Rolling in his grave with laughter.*

"I know you're sorry, Kevin, that's why you've got to come up with something. We can't just let it all . . . slip away. Don't you see, man? It's too *important*! It's, it's—"

Barrington quickly looked away from the younger partner, cursing his own garrulousness and catching himself on the verge of an unforgivable display of emotion. *I'm wasting my time,* he realized. *What is all this to him? To any of them, for that matter. I've given the ungrateful bastards everything and now . . . no one sees, no one understands, what I've done. If I hadn't told them about the supplement, they'd be behind me, sanctimonious bastards! Try to be forthright and . . .*

"I hate to suggest this," continued Kevin, seemingly oblivious to Barrington's inner turmoil and beginning to nibble at his crab cocktail, "but we could conserve our dwindling resources by halting all work on the case. We're spending about ten thousand a day . . ."

Barrington felt his last vestiges of hope deteriorating with each word Kevin uttered: ". . . keep the doors open a few more weeks, anyway . . ." *Christ almighty!* he thought as he slowly stabbed the ashtray with the stub of his eighth cigarette. *So this is how it all ends.* ". . . give people time to find new situations . . ." He began to feel nauseated, the bile of failure rising in his throat. Slowly, he rose to his feet, excused himself, and urged Kevin to stay and enjoy his lunch. Straightening, he tugged once on his vest, and with all the presence he could muster, said, "You're right, of course. Send out a memo, no explanation. Just 'Defer all North American projects until further notice.' "

Head erect, Barrington strode from the President's Club dining room, perhaps, he thought, for the last time.

THIRTY-TWO

■

Inspector Conti sat fidgeting at the bar at Ciao, resplendent in his most conservative suit, a gray sharkskin, a pearl-colored silk shirt, Hermès tie, and black Ferragamo shoes. It was still ten minutes before the appointed time. It had been eleven minutes the last time he checked. He had had no contact with Rachel Cannon since receiving the message from the receptionist, deciding not to confirm, fearful she might change her mind and decide not to come, although now he was almost more concerned that she would. He tried to analyze his anxiety and, getting nowhere, ordered another Campari and soda, then scanned the bar and the rest of the restaurant. He decided that if nothing else came of their date, Rachel had at least introduced him to a good spot close to his own neighborhood.

Dan checked his watch again: still ten minutes to eight. He was definitely on edge, but sipped his drink with deliberate care, for he knew he had to be at his best. He also noted that the place looked expensive, and that he'd better get enough info out of her to justify charging the check to the department. Either way, he rationalized, he was about to dine with the best-looking lawyer he had ever seen.

While Inspector Dan Conti continued to ruminate on his prospects for the evening, he kept an eye on the reflection of the front door in the bar mirror, occasionally turning slightly to examine himself. He scowled critically at the sawed-off little wop looking back at him through eyes as round as golf balls behind sloping lids that brought to mind Peter Lorre or Garfield the Cat. He started to brush his hair back with his hand, and then . . . Oh, shit, there was her reflection in the mirror, entering the restaurant as if it were her own dining room. The maître d' kissed her hand, and Conti could hear pieces of his greeting: ". . . much too long . . . *bellissima* Miss Cannon . . . yes, right over there."

The "there" was Conti, whose legs had suddenly turned to cement. By the time he slid off the barstool, Rachel had glided through the traffic and had extended her hand in warm greeting. "Hi" was all she said.

"Hi," he said back, his posture never better as he struggled for his one-inch height advantage.

"I saved your favorite table, Miss Cannon," said the maître d'. "Are you ready?"

"Thank you," said Rachel, and they both followed the maître d' to a corner table.

"May I start you with something?" asked a waiter immediately.

"May I?" asked Rachel, turning to Conti, who heard himself say "Sure," then listened as she ordered a very cold bottle of Mondavi fumé blanc and a platter of carpaccio.

"Excellent. Right away."

Rachel turned to the inspector and fixed her deep-set pastel eyes on him. "I hope you don't mind if this one's on me. It's one of my favorite places."

"We'll argue about that later," said Conti, cocking his head and massaging an earlobe. "Meanwhile, maybe we should introduce ourselves—*in*formally, I mean. I'm Dan."

"I'm Rachel," she said with a smile that turned him inside out. In a flash Dan knew why he'd been so anxious: It wasn't just that he felt that he was in over his head—although he was—but more the certainty that it wouldn't be enough just to sleep with this one. This was a woman to be loved, and he was a man who no longer had the heart for it.

As Rachel scanned the menu, Dan scanned her face, a face that seemed to shine with goodwill and innocent enthusiasm. Small town, he figured, probably Midwest. She could spend a little more time with her hair, he thought. He studied her mouth—if there was a flaw, it was the mouth—too wide, though her full lips, which tilted up at the corners like a cat's, tended to compensate. He felt himself relaxing.

"Do you like . . ."

Rachel had caught him in mid-stare, and now he noticed for the first time the incredible shade of gray-green in her eyes. He could also now see the symmetry and openness of her face, corroborating a look of genuineness seldom seen in a beautiful woman.

"Yes," said Conti, smiling. "Very much."

"But you don't know what I was about to ask you."

"The answer is the same."

"Well, all right," said Rachel, seemingly amused by his garish flattery. "Then it's liver and onions, collard greens, and blackeyed peas for you. I think I'll have the fettuccine carbonara as a first course, then fresh, broiled baby salmon with a light lemon-butter sauce."

"You didn't eat blackeyed peas where you grew up. I'd say Heartland—Iowa, maybe Illinois."

"Very good, Lieutenant. Kansas, then Missouri. How about yourself?"

"Right here."

"California?"

"No, right *here*."

"San Francisco?"

"Getting warmer," said Dan, smiling.

"You're from North Beach! The next time you say 'here,' I'll know you're talking '*here*.' "

"Well, it took you only three guesses. I think you'd make a pretty decent cop."

"And you'd make a good lawyer."

"I'm too short to be a lawyer," said Dan good-naturedly.

"Ouch," replied Rachel. "I'm sorry, Dan. I was in a very black mood yesterday."

"I wasn't exactly the Duke of York myself."

"You were just doing your job, and I was being nasty. The truth is, some of my best friends are . . ."

"Short?"

"No, Dan. *Cops!*"

"Are you serious? How do you know cops?"

"I started out in the Alameda County district attorney's office."

"Of course!" said Dan. "A fellow law enforcement officer. So *that's* why I like you."

Rachel smiled at him, her ingenuous eyes holding him willing hostage. "You're not overly keen on lawyers generally. Am I right?"

"I'll answer that with a riddle," Conti said. "What do you have when you've got a lawyer buried up to his neck in sand?"

"I give up," Rachel said.

"Not enough sand," Conti said.

Rachel laughed courteously. "We're not so bad, Dan, and I've met a few cops I'd like to plant at Stinson Beach at high tide."

"That may be so," he said, feeling comfortable at last. "Cops, however, can't always afford to be nice—the robbers outnumber us. But you take lawyers! Please! I mean, in another few years there will be more of you lawyers than available clients. What will you do then?"

"We'll represent each other, I guess," said Rachel, smiling. "I can see you've given a lot of thought to this."

"It's a serious situation. There are more lawyers right here in this country than there are in the whole rest of the world; and more of you right here in California than in all of England!"

"I'm not surprised," said Rachel nondefensively. "Our economy is far more productive and complex than England's and requires more laws to govern it."

"Maybe so, but I read a book not too long ago by a guy who claims there's an inverse relationship between the prosperity of lawyers and the development of America's productive capacity." Conti studied Rachel's face, pleased with his own observation and Rachel's attentiveness.

"That sounds like a tough case to prove," said Rachel, "and I don't think lawyer-bashing will solve anything." A flinty tone crept into Rachel's voice, signaling caution to Dan; *there is a limit to the girl's good nature,* he thought, irritated with himself that he would now have to further delay any attempt at obtaining information about Weisberg and Hallinan, and relieved to see the waiter approaching. "In any event," Rachel added, smiling an offer to truce, "I can assure you that my salary is not contributing to the problem."

Dan laughed overloudly and they turned to their menus as the waiter delivered the carpaccio and opened the wine. Meanwhile, Dan took advantage of the opportunity to study Rachel's small, well-formed nose, then stole a glance at her breasts which, while not large, rendered vain her best efforts at disguising them. He felt a sexual stirring just from being in her presence.

The wine poured and orders placed, they toasted the success of each other's cases, vowing at the same time not to discuss either of them during dinner. Dan rationalized that this understanding would expire with the dessert and coffee. Meanwhile, they talked about sports and watched the pasta maker, the local celebrities, and several singles on prowl for good food and bad company. Rachel probed Dan for information about his work as a police lieutenant, and he described his homicide investigations as highly overromanticized—"mostly just frustrated married people and lovers fed up with life and each other." Rachel commented that the overdramatization of both of their vocations on screen and TV was something they shared in common.

"That's true," said Dan solemnly, "but the similarity ends there. Lawyers live in courtrooms disciplined by order. We live on streets dominated by chaos."

"The difference," said Rachel, "is only on the surface. Any shrink will tell you why lawyers become lawyers. It's because they're trying to bring order to the chaos they feel inside."

"And I thought that was just your stomach rumbling. Let's dig into this carpaccio."

"Definitely. But don't change the subject. You must be working on something more interesting than boy-shoots-girl."

"Not really—other than our off-limits topic, of course—but next week we've got a full moon and business should pick up. Our motiveless killings soar when those intracranial fluids head out to sea with the tide. Last month a guy fired from his job drove his car right into a restaurant and killed two people. The same day we had a librarian in her sixties killed during her lunch hour chasing a vegetable truck she claimed was littering."

Rachel continued to bring Dan out during dinner and he responded readily, giving straight answers and revealing himself to be a person with a strict but compelling sense of morality and a vital love of life, matched only by an equally zealous hatred of those who would presume to deprive others of it. "I despise the thought of death," he said, "like others might hate bigotry or child molestation or paying taxes."

"So that's how you got into the homicide end," said Rachel.

"Probably, but the real motivation has more to do with a man who was murdered only about ten blocks from here."

"Really? Tell me about it," said Rachel.

Dan's mood instantly sobered. He realized he had been flattered by the woman's interest and was starting to talk too much. He debated for a moment whether he should confide so much so soon. How do you tell a stranger, even a perfect one, that you became a homicide detective because you were guilty of causing the death of your own father—well, maybe not guilty exactly, but responsible—a distinction he had been trying to make for years now. A distinction he realized made no difference to his father either way.

Dead is dead.

"The man was my father," he said finally, managing a matter-of-fact tone, "a grocer up on Columbus Street. He was killed during a robbery in the mid-fifties." *I'm going soft,* Dante thought. *I have not told this to three people in my lifetime.*

"I'm sorry, Dan," said Rachel. She paused for a moment. "Did they catch the killer?"

"Yeah, but he was just a kid only a few years older than I was at the time."

"Were you . . . there? I mean, when it happened?"

Dan Conti looked into his wineglass, thinking if only he *had* been there, and wondering how the facts—he knew most of them and could imagine the rest—remained so vivid in his mind, even now, as he pictured his wiry little father in his knee-length apron, moving among the jammed aisles of Mother's cookies, canned foods, Oxydol soap, shoe polish, Langendorf white bread, red and black licorice whips, Morton salt . . . When It Rains, It Pours, he thought, and, oh, brother, did the sky fall in on us that February in 1956! For the millionth time, his mind drifted back to that day that changed his life.

Dan knew Papa must have been expecting something like this since the day he opened his grocery store in 1937, but now it was finally happening, and it probably seemed no more real than a twice-seen movie happening to someone else. Dan could picture his father with razor clarity, standing there looking up at the tall, glistening, black youth, probably thinking 'Christ, I wish Dante was here. Where is that damn kid?'

"I was in school, Rachel," Dan said, so softly she had to lean forward to hear him. "Held after school for fighting."

And now the grocer would calmly try to reassure the kid, a scared punk for sure, brandishing a switchblade knife just inches from his face. And his father would carefully register the fea-

tures of the young man so there would be no problem identifying him later in a lineup—his dad was real good at details—tall kid; six feet two or three; deep scar running across the brow under an incongruous Greek sailor's cap; broad shoulders, made even broader by a girl's thin waistline.

"The kid waited until nobody was in the store but my Pop."

Francis Cesare Conti had always said he would be passive and cooperative when it happened, but as he looked into the dilated eyes of his assailant that day, the hate, the fear, and the vulnerability he must have seen there aroused his machismo, his pride, his anger.

"He always knew it would happen someday—promised Mama he'd go along with it when it did . . . ."

So the stage was set: in one corner, an overweight, fifty-eight-year-old gentle man, reaching into an ancient, yellow-bronze National cash register as calmly as if he were making telephone change for a nun. But there was a look in his eye now—Dan had seen it many times, but how was the punk to know—a look that said: I'm Francis Cesare Conti and nobody messes with me or my family. Pride. Anger.

And over in the other corner: the challenger, dancing from side to side like a drop of water on a hot griddle, his switchblade knife stabbing at the air in front of the older man's face, his left hand extended palm upward to receive the money.

". . . particularly since Papa never had a gun . . ."

Frank Conti must have appeared calm by comparison—he probably glanced once more out the front window to see if there was any help in sight—perhaps a last look for young Dante—before he lifted the tray, revealing the precious, hard-earned fifty and several twenties. Carefully, he scooped them up with both hands, checks and all, plus gleaming halfs and quarters, and turned, arms extended toward the youth. Then came the first surprise, for he suddenly threw the whole cache straight into the astonished face of the robber, and right behind the metal and paper shower came Conti's best Sunday punch smack into the face of the amazed kid, the fist hammering straight into yielding bone and tissue. Crunch! There goes the nose and some once-protruding upper teeth. No protective mouthpieces in this kind of fight. No referee, no rules.

". . . but my Pop was just . . . stubborn . . . and didn't know. . ."

The teeth were later found scattered over a ten-foot area, doubtlessly exiting the kid's bloody mouth with a gurgled protest that must have been music to the aging man's ears. And that's when the neighborhood bag lady said she looked in the window because the first thing she heard was Pop's maniacal scream, forming itself into words: 'Kill You . . . Kill You . . . Kill You Kill . . .' as his fist, now a deadly club, continued to rearrange the kid's features. Years of waiting, years of fear; now at last he had one of them! 'Shit, Dante, I didn't need you after all.'

". . . how much he needed me."

Old man Conti then seized the kid's right wrist with his left hand—time now to neutralize the knife—then followed his attack to the youth's bloody head with a knee to the groin as both of them crashed to the floor.

And that's when it all began to go wrong.

It must have happened so quickly Francis Conti didn't believe it at first—there probably wasn't even any pain . . . but there it was: the kid's hand suddenly lost deep in his gut and then . . . 'Oh my God,' the bag lady at the door heard him scream, 'I'm cut! GET IT OUT OF ME!'

"But I wasn't there to help him."

Now both the shopkeeper's hands seized the slippery wrist and the old woman, hypnotically drawn closer, stared at the blade as it grudgingly grew longer, each emerging inch smeared with the grocer's blood. From out on the street, the transient blare of a car radio, momentarily drowned out the shopkeeper's voice, much weaker now . . . 'Oh Christ, Dante, help me . . .'

"He said my name, but I wasn't there. I couldn't help him."

Then, unexpectedly, a bony black elbow slammed like a freight train into the older man's eye, ear, mouth, face . . . exploding light for an instant, then everything must have begun to turn dark and silent . . . 'Where's the knife, find the knife!' Papa was thinking now. 'There it is, but Jesus, Mary, and Joseph, look at the blade: It's getting smaller again; disappearing into my body again!'

Francis Cesare Conti was screaming now—so loud they finally heard him two doors down and came running just as the bag lady stumbled out the door and slipped in her own vomit. 'STOP HIM SOMEBODY,' shouted the grocer to no one, 'SOMEBODY PLEASE STOP THIS KID HE'S KILLING ME . . . KILLING ME . . . KILLING ME KILLING . . .'

"I wasn't there," Dan repeated, then, breaking out of his dazed reverie, added, "sorry. I'm afraid I drifted a bit there."

"No, I'm the one who's sorry. My prying was insensitive. The look on your face, Dan . . . as if you were having a bad dream."

Dan smiled grimly and said, "No dream, Rachel. I wish it were."

"So," said Rachel, trying to break the suddenly morose mood, "you were a fighter when you were a kid?"

Dan forced a smile. "Well, if you must know," he said, half filling their glasses with the chilled wine, and expertly curling spaghetti on his fork, "I was pretty small. My full given name is Dante, and when the class bully wanted to get my goat, he would make the other kids join him, chanting: 'Dante Conti, Dante Conti, Dante . . . ,' well, you see what I mean. One day I had all I could take, and I went after him. Unfortunately for me, the teacher walked in on the heels of my rare burst of courage. So I was kept after school writing 'Turn the other cheek' five hundred times and wasn't at work where I should have been when young Washington Jones, Jr., walked in and took one hundred and forty-three dollars and my father's life."

There was nothing left to say and Dan felt embarrassed by the ensuing silence, then found himself apologizing for the maudlin direction he had led them into. Rachel did the same, adding, "For what it's worth, Dan, I think I understand a part of what you went through."

"I don't think anyone could understand, but thanks anyway."

Rachel seemed to turn inward for an aching moment. Then she said, "I lost my father when I was practically the same age."

"You're kidding," said Dan.

"He just left. Took off. No one ever heard from him again."

"But why? Was it foul play? Or a . . . woman, maybe?" asked Dan, falling into his detective mode in spite of himself.

"Who knows? We were the all-American family pursuing the all-American dream. My dad was a partner in a law firm, civic leader, running for U.S. Congress. Seemed to everyone that he was on top of the world. Then, on the day after my twelfth birthday, he went off to work and never came back."

"Did he leave a note?"

"He left a note. Said he was tired of the rat race." Rachel's eyes narrowed slightly and her tone hardened as she added, "Left us the deed to the house—he had apparently been planning it for a while—and enough money to keep my mother in booze for the next year or so."

"Then what?"

"Then I went to live with an aunt. I attended high school during the day and bused tables. My aunt was as bad off as I was, but we made ends meet. By my senior year I had even saved enough to hire a private investigator to find my father."

"Did he find your dad?"

"No," said Rachel, her green eyes narrowing, and signaling the waiter in a way that told Dan the subject was closed, "I never actually hired one. By then I decided I didn't want to find him."

They sat in silence for a moment while the waiter cleared their plates, Dan staring at Rachel, thinking, *There's both toughness and vulnerability there. We're a pair of hard cases, this girl and I.*

"Anyway," said Dan, steering for calmer waters, "it's obvious why I became a homicide inspector. But what caused you to go into law?"

"I guess a panel of Zurich psychologists would take note of the fact that my father was a lawyer—maybe I was trying to take his place—but whatever it was, I've never regretted the decision for a moment."

"I bet it gave your mother a boost when you graduated from law school. Was she proud of you?"

"She was sure," said Rachel, unsmiling, "that it would ruin my prospects for marriage. She saw absolutely no point in it."

"But how about when you landed a job at the best firm on Montgomery Street?"

"She said she hoped I wouldn't start smoking cigars."

"Are you a good lawyer?" asked Dan, sensing that Rachel's mother was another taboo subject. He shifted course again, this time in a direction that might lead back to Weisberg and Hallinan. "Why did you leave the D.A.'s office? Did you lose your zeal for law and order?"

Rachel considered Dan's question thoughtfully before responding. "When I was little," she said finally, "I'd visit my father's office. He had a bronze plaque on the wall that said *The Law is the One Great Truth*. Those words made me feel good somehow, though I wasn't really clear on what they meant. I later claimed the plaque, like a treasure from the wreckage of my mother's life, and hung it on my own wall at the D.A.'s office. Then one day I realized I still had no idea what it meant. If there was one great truth, was there also one great lie? Or if there were many lies, must there not be more than just one truth?'' Rachel paused to sip her coffee. She seemed to be wrestling with something inside herself, or perhaps just looking for a tactful way to put it into words. ''Enforcing the law is your thing, Dan, and I respect you for it and thank God for you and others like you. But I'm not even sure what 'the law' means anymore. For example, I think I believe in the so-called 'Rule of Law,' but I see every day how the exceptions swallow up every rule made. First, we try to squeeze all human behavior into abstract categories; then, when we realize it can't be done, we start drafting exceptions to the abstractions. We end up with more words and less meaning.''

''What's the solution, counselor? Kill all the lawyers?''

Rachel smiled and threw up her hands. ''I haven't the slightest idea. We might start by ordering an extra-rich dessert.''

Dan laughed, but persisted in his earlier question, affecting a pontifical tone: ''Apart from your complex internal conflicts on the subject of absolute truth, Ms. Cannon, are you any good as a trial lawyer?''

''Yes, I'm pretty good,'' she said, ''and I hope to be a lot better. My goal has always been to be a partner in a firm that tries complex business litigation; you know, antitrust, securities, corporate disputes. I'm up for consideration at the end of this year at S.P.&M.''

''How does it look?''

''It looks good right now, so I don't want to jinx it by talking about it.''

''Partnership is really important to you, isn't it,'' Dan said.

''It's everything,'' Rachel replied with quiet intensity.

Dan looked at her and their eyes held for the first time. He gently covered her hand with his for a moment and said, ''Nothing is everything.'' They looked at each other in silence. ''Only death.''

Rachel regarded Dan with new interest, her head angled to one side so that a tangle of chestnut hair fell beneath her right shoulder. ''Are you sure you're a cop? You're sounding more like a philosopher.''

''To be a cop these days, you've got to be very philosophical. Also a fool.''

''But you like it. I can tell,'' Rachel said. ''You seem deeply committed.''

''I'm afraid the captain and even most of my friends think I'm overzealous at times. But I suspect that's something else you and I have in common: commitment.'' Rachel nodded as the waiter delivered the check. It seemed to Dan that they had just been seated, but his watch read ten-thirty and he knew he had to make his move. Stroking the tip of his nose, he said, ''Since we're on that happy subject—death, that is—did Bernie Weisberg ever talk to you about taking his own life?''

Rachel laughed, saying, ''Oh, you're a cop all right,'' then turned serious. ''This has been the best evening I've had in many weeks, Dan—strictly social and thoroughly relaxed. Let's keep it that way.''

Dan smiled back. *This will require patience,* he told himself, deftly spearing the check, *but with a woman like this, what's the hurry?*

''Hey, I thought we were going to discuss this check business,'' said Rachel.

''Uh-uh. I initiated this strictly social tryst.''

''Ah. Mr. Macho Man again?''

''No. Police policy. Never allow a suspect to buy you dinner.''

''I'm a suspect? I'm flattered.''

''Don't be. You qualify just by living in the Bay Area.''

''Isn't a good detective supposed to be able to narrow the list of suspects more than that? How would you question them all?''

''If they're pretty like you, with considerable pleasure. The rest I'll round up and interview in Candlestick Park.''

Rachel and Dan lingered over two cups of coffee. Laughter and light talk dominated their last few minutes. Dan astutely avoided any reference to the case. It was Rachel, in fact, who next compromised their agreement upon reaching the door of her automobile, to which Conti had insisted on accompanying her.

''Thanks for the protection, Detective Dan. Can I drop you at your car?''

''No, my clunker's right up the street,'' said Dan, instantly regretting his self-depreciating characterization. Her damn BMW had snapped him back to reality. But Rachel seemed to ignore his comment as she unlocked her door, then turned to face him.

''Thanks for keeping it almost entirely 'social,' Dan, but now my own curiosity is killing me. What do you *really* think is going on with these deaths?''

''I think it's murder,'' said Dan without hesitation, ''but to tell you the truth, I am functioning mainly on intuition, which is all I can do until I get some help from your law firm. Meanwhile," he added with a wry smile, "duty obliges me to keep an eye on you."

Rachel was surprised, surprised and pleased as Dan kissed her gently on the cheek, then walked quickly off into the fog. She sat in her car and watched until he was but a ghost, floating down a river of streetlights as mysterious and captivating as a string of natural pearls deep underwater.

At the scheduled team leaders' meeting at eleven the next morning, a pallid Austin Barrington stood with the passive despair of a man atop the gallows. He fingered copies of the Memorandum to Staff that Kevin had prepared at his direction, calling off all further work on the case. They had agreed that the team leaders were entitled to prior notice of its contents before general distribution.

"Does anyone know where Rachel is?" Barrington inquired without emotion, looking at Jeffrey and Kevin. "I want to get this meeting behind us."

"She should be here any minute, Mr. Barrington," said Jeff. "She said she had to go out to court and run down a rumor she had picked up."

"Well," said Barrington flatly, "we'll start without her. You all know I'm due in court tomorrow on what can best be described as a fool's errand." The senior partner glanced at Kevin, cleared his throat, then continued, "And, as the result of our motion to reinstate our cancerphobia theory is foreordained, we—"

The door burst open and all heads turned toward Rachel as she rushed in with apologies and a broad smile. "Kevin!" said Rachel, panting for breath and falling into an empty chair at the conference table. "It's happened . . . just as you predicted!"

"What's happened? What prediction?" said Barrington impatiently.

Rachel took a deep breath, continued to look at Kevin, and said, "I came from Judge Weston's department, where he has just ruled in *Arnett* versus *Dow Chemical* that cancerphobia is the law in California!"

"He extended emotional distress damages to toxic contamination victims?" Kevin asked through a tentative smile.

"With no difficulty whatsoever," said Rachel, "and tomorrow he will instruct the Dow Chemical jury accordingly."

While Barrington sat dazed in his chair, trying to assimilate this dramatic upswing in his destiny, Kevin pressed Rachel for the details. She readily complied.

"The plaintiffs in *Arnett* had been exposed to toxins over a long period of time—just like our clients—and were told by doctors that they had a good possibility of developing tumors. The objective guarantee of reliability in *Arnett* is that all of them have lowered sperm counts."

"It sounds like it's on all fours with our case," said Barrington, color beginning to return to his face.

"There's even a hidden dividend here, Austin," added Rachel, turning to the senior partner for the first time. "Once the plaintiffs' fear has become the main issue, we can roll in any and all evidence bearing on the dangers of toxic contamination that our plaintiffs may have seen or heard of—anything that has created an increase in their fear—*even though it would otherwise be excluded as hearsay*. Between our hundred-plus plaintiffs, I believe that we can—legitimately and in perfectly good faith—put before the jury just about everything that has been published, from newspaper articles to video replays of TV programs on the subject of potential harmful results of toxic exposure."

"Good point," said Barrington, sitting erect and in full command once more. Turning to Jeffrey, he added, "Start a collection of all articles and other scare media reporting on what these toxins can do to a body. Then we'll pick the best and make sure our clients *are* aware of them. How are we on emotional damage?"

"We already have a list of the five top forensic psychiatrists and psychologists in the area," said Rachel. "I will pick the best two for you to interview next week so that we can put them together with our clients next month."

"Excellent," said Barrington, rubbing his hands together. "Excellent. My congratulations to you all. No judge is more respected and admired by the other judges, including Matt Bainbridge, than Judge Weston. As I started to say a few minutes ago," the senior partner added with a wink at Kevin, "the court's ruling on our motion tomorrow is foreordained. So let's get back to work. We have," he continued as he slipped the copies of Kevin's stop-work memo under his notepad, "a record to set."

PART FOUR

·

THE CONFESSION

·

FALL, 1983

He got what he wanted,
But he lost what he had!
Shut up! Shut up! Shut up!
He got what he wanted
But lost what he had!
That's my boy, Little Richard, sure is.
Oo my soul.
                        —LITTLE RICHARD

THIRTY-THREE

∎

Austin Barrington privately congratulated himself as his quick review of status reports confirmed that all projects were on schedule. He glanced at his calendar—September 14, 1983—six weeks until trial, and only a handful of depositions remained before final pretrial motions began. There had been no further unforeseen glitches, not since Judge Bainbridge had reinstated cancerphobia in late July.

Stacked in front of him as he called a team leaders' meeting to order were the medical records on the remaining thirteen plaintiffs of Group A that he had carefully cleared for handing over to the defense. He had stalled as long as he could in order to give the defense as little time before trial as possible in which to spot any minor irregularities in the records, any hint he might have overlooked regarding the artificial supplements. Nobody but Newkirk had ever seen these records, not even Kevin, although Barrington would soon allow the younger partner to perform a cursory, fail-safe check on Barrington's own careful review. He had decided not to give even Kevin time for a more careful scrutiny, one that might detect the extent to which Barrington had expanded his administration of the supplement to five additional plaintiffs. Every one of the five men had been deficient, but now all would score high on blood and tissue tests soon to be administered by the defense; all would qualify for seven-figure verdicts. *A nasty business,* he thought to himself, but as W.W. II would say: "You've swallowed the whale; don't choke on the tail."

Yes, thought Barrington with satisfaction, his ordeal would soon be over, his place of honor in the firm's history and the national bar was assured. He could be president of the A.B.A. in three years, the American College of Trial Lawyers soon after that. And the firm—his firm—would rise to even greater heights. *Out of the ashes. . . .*

Barrington knew that others had made more money—his own father, for example—but few had exercised more real power, and none had single-handedly rescued a professional institution as important as Stafford, Parrish, and MacAllister from certain failure by acts of such unprecedented daring. *It's been neither easy nor pleasant,* he thought, *dealing with the stupidity of Newkirk and the treachery of his own partners, but there's no use agonizing over that now. The point is, I've done it, and victory is only months away.*

Which brought him to his one modest regret: that the world could never know and appreciate the enormity of the risks he had taken, not to mention the incredible genius of it all! He listened to the drone of voices around the table, planning the final stages of a certain triumph, voices of people who would be out on the streets now but for his *à couvert* fortitude; yet not even they would ever know. *Ah, well,* thought Barrington as he sipped his coffee, *that is a burden I can happily live with—like owning a stolen Rembrandt.*

"The defense filed another motion to compel the production of our clients' medical records today, Austin," Rachel was saying. "This time they've asked the court to dismiss the case."

Barrington, shaken out of his idyllic meditation, came out swinging: "Alan Hancock should be disbarred! Why the hell doesn't he just pick up the phone and be a gentleman about it?"

"He's been doing that," Rachel said cautiously, "for several weeks now. Three of our plaintiffs are scheduled for depositions and defense medical examinations next week, and he's of course demanding to see the records first. As you know, he's entitled."

"Of course I know that," said Barrington, shedding his frustration. "Anyway, it's now academic. Here they are—the medical records of all thirteen. Kevin, take a look through these and see if they appear to be in order."

"Austin," said Rachel, "it's worse than that. He has also filed a motion to delay the trial date indefinitely because of our delay in producing the medical records."

"How much delay can he justifiably claim we caused?" asked Barrington, his ill humor giving way to concern.

"No more than three to six weeks," Jeff said after a quick look at his notes.

"Can you hold him to a month, Rachel, so that we can still get our Christmas trial? That's crucial."

"I think so," said Rachel, "assuming we turn them over today."

"He will have them. Now, how about the progress of the economists in charting money damages?"

"They are charting actuarial data right now," said Rachel. "They're moving very slowly."

"Economists," muttered Barrington, "use statistics like a drunk uses a lamppost—more for support than illumination. What about that team of behavioral scientists you and Kevin convinced me we should retain? How are their interviews of the local citizens coming along?"

"Good," said Jeff. "We've collected almost all the responses and have a fairly good fix now on how the community from which the jury will be drawn feels about the issues in our case. We're now refocusing these issues in a way that meshes with these revealed attitudes. Then all we have to do is make sure we pick jurors representative of those attitudes."

"It still sounds like a lot of hocus-pocus to me," said Barrington, "but I'll go along. How will I communicate with the social psychologist once I'm selecting the jury?"

Kevin looked up from his perusal of the medical records. "It's simple, Austin. I've used it a couple of times lately with reasonably good results. The psychologist will sit two or three rows back so that the jury does not see her. She will already have quite a bit of data on each prospective juror from the jury service we subscribe to, but will signal me after she has had a chance to actually size up the juror with her own eyes. I will simply pass you a note that says yes or no."

"What if we disagree with her?"

"Then we ignore her, and we've lost nothing."

"Except a hell of a lot of money. I've seen her company's bills to date for the survey work and preliminary issue focusing: over one hundred fifty thousand dollars!"

"I expect we'll make that up on a hundredfold multiple if they help us make the right decision on only two or three jurors," said Kevin, returning to his review of the medical records.

"Nonetheless," said Barrington, "I still would like to meet the head of the team you've been working with."

"I'll get her in here right away," said Rachel.

"Good. Let's see now, what else is on our agenda?" asked Barrington, looking at his notes. "How is your coding going, Stu?"

Chief paralegal Stu Wallach reported on the routine coding and computerization of documents, and Jeffrey described in more detail some of the quick-retrieval features of S.P.&M.'s computerized support system.

"What's the head count on plaintiffs now, Jeffrey?" asked Barrington.

Jeff quickly scanned his notes. "With six weeks to go now before the scheduled trial date of the first thirteen plaintiffs, we have a total of one hundred and forty-seven plaintiffs signed to contingency agreements, plus twenty-five additional possibles awaiting test results from Newkirk's office."

"Excellent," said Barrington, his good mood fully restored. "It looks to me as if—"

"Austin!" interrupted Kevin. "Take a look at this."

Kevin handed Barrington Emmett Dixon's medical file folder, and indicated the printout concerning blood and tissue sample reports.

"So?" asked Barrington impatiently.

Kevin leaned forward and circled some tiny blurred letters that spelled out "chlordane" buried in a massive listing of other chemicals and metals found in Dixon's blood and tissue samples. He then scribbled a cryptic note on a piece of paper which he slipped inside the report and handed back to Barrington:

No chlordane at North American

"Ah, yes, Kevin. Thank you. Rachel?" said Barrington, clearing his throat as he casually handed the file back to Kevin.

"Yes, Austin?"

"I would like you to prepare and file an immediate motion to sever Emmett Dixon from the trial of the first thirteen plaintiffs."

"*Dixon?*" asked Rachel, nearly rising out of her chair. "Are you *serious*? Emmett Dixon is the most seriously injured plaintiff we have! If he doesn't go out on this first round, he may not *make* it to the second. And from the firm's standpoint . . ."

"From the *firm's* standpoint," said Barrington, fixing Rachel with a hard look, "I would like you to simply do what I ask on this without questioning my judgment. It happens that Dixon has some problems in his overall medical picture that will take some time to clear up. We cannot afford to have a single tenuous link—even the slightest flaw—in this first group of plaintiffs. As you yourself suggested from the start, Rachel, the results of this trial will establish the value of all the remaining cases for settlement purposes.''

"But Emmett Dixon is—''

"*Rachel*," said Kevin with quiet intensity. "Emmett Dixon is a liability. Austin's right. The old fellow is sick, very sick—we all know that. But our first group has to be *perfect*. We can't have a single weakness in connecting toxins to injuries. Remember, we still have to present a solid causation case—*Arnett* versus *Dow* could get reversed on appeal, so we can't be complacent and rely entirely on cancerphobia.''

"Well put, Kevin," said Barrington, softening his tone as he turned toward Rachel. "Besides, Rachel, you said yourself that Dixon may not be strong enough to sustain a trial. This might turn out to be the best possible outcome for him.''

"Austin," said Rachel urgently, "you don't understand—''

"After our verdict comes in," continued Barrington, slipping Dixon's file into a lower drawer in his desk, "he may well enjoy the benefit of a quick total settlement of all our cases without ever having to endure the rigors of a trial. Now, let's disperse and move on to our appointed tasks.''

Rachel, Jeff, and Stu Wallach left Barrington's office in a state of frustration and confusion. Once in the hallway, Jeff turned to Rachel. "Have you seen Dixon's records?''

"Of course I haven't seen Dixon's records. Nobody has, other than Newkirk and Barrington, and now Kevin.''

"Well," said Stu Wallach, "there must be some major problem with Dixon's tests or Kevin would not have seen it. When Kevin and Barrington agree on *anything* these days, the odds are overwhelming that they're right.''

"I know, Stu, but how do I explain this to Emmett? All that's holding the poor man together is the dream of re-creating his old Wobbly days of glory by getting up on the witness stand to strike a blow for the workingman. What do I say to him?''

No one answered her.

Meanwhile, Kevin had closed the door to Barrington's office and stormed Barrington's oak fortress. "Did you give Dixon A.S.?''

"Of course I did, Kevin; he was one of the first five. You knew that.''

"Yes, but you didn't tell me that Newkirk threw in the whole kitchen sink. What in the hell were you thinking of?''

"Well, Newkirk said—"

"*Newkirk!* Haven't you figured out yet that the guy can't scratch his ass with a handful of fishhooks? His brain cells are *gone*, Austin, and if I had not spotted the chlordane, you can bet the defense eventually would have—both in Dixon's records and in their own blood and tissue samples. It wouldn't only have fucked up Dixon's case, but all the other one hundred forty-six as well! Chlordane is carcinogenic, Austin, but it's neither produced *nor* dumped by the defendant. We just about handed North American a bullet-proof defense!"

"I know all that, Kevin, and to you goes all the credit for preventing a disaster." For the first time Kevin could remember, Barrington loosened his tie. "And it's my fault as much as Newkirk's. I told him I wanted quick results—to establish *your* theory, Kevin—so he gave it to me and, God help me, I gave it to poor Dixon."

"Any others?"

"No," said Barrington firmly. "Newkirk called to warn me that he had inadvertently included some bogus chemical and I destroyed the batch after only one administration of it. Unfortunately, I could not remember who got the contaminated batch, but I thought it was Weisberg. Well, now at least we know."

"Small comfort to Dixon," grunted Kevin, his face pale as he slumped against a wall for support. "No wonder the poor old bird is failing. That stupid, fucking Newkirk . . ."

"Calm yourself, Kevin. I intend to have very strong words with him as soon as we're finished. Now, let's not overreact. We are at war, and we must expect losses."

Kevin's eyes turned to ultramarine ice, his voice barely controlled as he spoke: "*Losses?* Jesus, Austin, you *created* the losses, the deaths. If this is war, you're the plaintiffs' enemy!" Kevin looked longingly at a chair, for fatigue was challenging his rage. "This thing has gone too far, Austin. You must see that. My God, you've *destroyed* this old man!"

"Come now, Kevin. It's not that bad. He's no worse off than the others."

"That's small consolation even if true, and it's not. Rachel says he's dying in bits and pieces. She's worried sick about him, and now so am I."

Barrington turned around and closed his Levelor blinds, as if,

Kevin reflected, to shield their deeds from the light. "There's no reason for you to be so upset, Kevin. He was merely supplemented in the most minuscule way, by a bad batch to be sure."

"There is no such thing as a 'minuscule' supplement when you're talking about something as potent as chlordane! He's not going to make it to trial, Austin. He's never going to see a nickel of his settlement. And you and I know why! *It's because you've killed him!*"

Barrington's face reddened as he leapt to his feet and charged toward the younger partner as if to physically assault him. "*Stop it, you whining bastard!*" he shouted, his stale, hot breath assailing Kevin's dulled senses. "I'm having trouble enough keeping our battle lines secure without you turning prima donna on me. So you think it's gone too far, do you? Then go report all this to Rachel so she can pass it on to her great and good friend Inspector Conti on their next date together. Oh? What's this?" he noted, drawing back with a smile at Kevin's unguarded expression. "You didn't know? No, I can see you didn't. Well, it's true, and it wouldn't take him long to come and cart us all away like a bunch of common criminals. And trust Alan Hancock to see to it that our one hundred and forty-seven clients— *your* clients, Kevin—don't see one penny! Let *that* be on your holier-than-thou conscience as you rot your moralistic life away in San Quentin."

Stunned by the senior partner's reaction, Kevin stepped back, shot Barrington a sideways glance, then reeled into the conference area, where he sank into a chair at the conference table and stared at his knees. His head was throbbing, a recurring malady in recent weeks. *Rachel with Conti. Chlordane in Dixon.* Nothing in his past had prepared him for this. Hope drained from him.

Barrington waited a few moments before he adopted a more conciliatory tone and slowly walked toward Kevin. "See here, kid. I've made my share of mistakes in this. And I'm sorry about Dixon. But Rachel's motion to sever him from Group A will prevent the defense from examining him and discovering the chlordane. We will then settle his case along with the rest of them—immediately after the trial of the twelve plaintiffs remaining in Group A. Everyone will be better off—even Dixon."

Barrington moved closer, tentatively resting his hand on Kevin's shoulder. "And while it is crass to observe it, your share of the verdicts and settlements, including your trial-team bonus, will be no less than three and probably closer to four million dollars. You will be able to take that long, long rest you've never had.''

Kevin massaged his temples and said nothing. Barrington reached over and picked up the conference room telephone. "Miss Tarkenton, I want Raymond Newkirk in my office immediately after lunch. If there is any reason on earth why he cannot be here, I want to speak with him personally."

Barrington pulled up a chair at the conference table next to Kevin and spoke gently into his ear. "I shall discipline Newkirk in my own way, but I am bringing him in here primarily so that you can be absolutely assured that Dixon was the only potential recipient of that bad batch."

Kevin's head snapped up like a punch-drunk boxer given smelling salts between rounds. "I don't want anything to do with Newkirk. He's your problem. You deal with him, and while you're at it, be thinking about how you're going to deal with Rachel. She is going to insist on some answers now."

Barrington's face relaxed into a smile. "Fair enough. I shall do just that, Kevin. Please be so good as to direct her to me if she has any more questions."

Barrington rose and gave Kevin two firm pats on the shoulder. "Now, listen to me, old boy. I know you're tired, perhaps even exhausted. But you've got to pull yourself together for one last hurrah. Let's get back to the business of uniting our efforts against the real villain in this piece: the North American Chemical Company. And when it's over, Kevin," he added, walking around the table and looking down at the downcast younger partner, "we'll bring you inside. Where it's warm."

After an explosive telephone conversation with Newkirk, Barrington assembled the Table of Three in his office. "There has been a minor hitch, gentlemen," said Barrington, affecting a relaxed mood. He spoke slowly, thoughtfully, his hands and fingers forming a bent steeple. "Kevin Stone spotted a contaminant called chlordane in the records of one of our plaintiffs today. I've just checked with Newkirk and he confirms that it is a carcinogen *and* that, like metals, it lingers in the system, shows up in tests for weeks, even months."

"But isn't that what you wanted? What's the problem?" asked Adrian Fisher.

"The problem," said Barrington, "is that this particular chemical was never produced by North American nor was it present in its dump site.''

"This sounds like more than a 'minor hitch,' '' said Gardner White, tugging at his second chin.

"It's nothing we can't deal with," said Barrington. "It had to be in one of the early batches, before Newkirk was able to survey the North American samples thoroughly. He's coming in after lunch to assure me that none of the other batches had chlordane or any other chemical not dumped at North American.''

"But what'll we do about Dixon?'' asked Fisher.

"I've already done it," said Barrington. "Rachel will file a motion to sever Dixon's case from the first group of remaining. That will eliminate the need to turn his medical records over to the defense and to subject Dixon for blood or tissue testing. Newkirk will then revise his records, and we will settle Dixon's case after the trial without the necessity for a pretrial medical examination. It will all blow over soon enough, but I wanted you to know in case Kevin wants to discuss it with either of you, which I suspect he might.''

"How is he taking this new development?'' asked White.

"He's a little shaken, but my main concern right now is that he doesn't unravel before the trial. He has a great deal on his mind—his home life for one thing. He just isn't focused lately.''

"The kid looks awful," said Fisher, nodding agreement. "I'm worried about him. Florence wants to have him to dinner with us, but she can't stand Denise.''

"Unfortunately," said Barrington, "I suspect that Kevin can't either. But don't worry. He'll be all right. I told you I can handle him and I will.''

"Well, I for one share many of Kevin's concerns and anxieties," said White. "You say Hancock will check the remaining plaintiffs' records. How about Hallinan and Weisberg? Will the defense want to see their paperwork? Do their medical records show chlordane?''

"Good point, Gard. Yes, the defense will, but no, the records won't," said Barrington, removing a small key from his vest pocket, "but why take chances?''

White and Fisher looked on as Barrington turned the key in a lock at the lower left side of his desk. He then produced another key from a silver chain attached to his belt loop and opened a metal document safe within the exterior wooden drawer. He lifted the lid and removed two thin files.

"These, gentlemen, are the original, and only medical records of Messrs. Hallinan and Weisberg. Since both are dead, dismissed, and no longer parties to the litigation, we are no longer precluded by law from destroying them. In fact, we owe a duty of privacy to our former clients to do just that. I want you to witness their destruction with your own eyes."

White and Fisher haltingly followed Barrington into his private bathroom, though White protested that he was busy and would take the senior partner's word for it.

"No, no, Gardner," said Barrington, lighting the first of the documents. "It's *your* frequent anxiety attacks I'm trying to put to rest here. Just bear with me." The two stunned partners looked on as Barrington burned the records, several sheets at a time, and dropped them into the urinal. "What about Newkirk's own records?" asked Fisher, ever the trial lawyer despite his uneasiness. "Doesn't he have the original test results?"

"He did," said Barrington, smiling, "until I helped him vacuum his office. These pages I am burning at this very moment *are* the only records made by Newkirk's office on Hallinan and Weisberg. Now you see them—now you don't," he added triumphantly as he lit the bottom corner of the final two sheets.

Macbethian witches in vested, pin-striped suits, the three lawyers huddled over the smoking urinal, watching the last possible threat to Project Salvation turn to ashes, then swirl out of sight.

THIRTY-FOUR

■

"So, where do you stand in the countdown to trial?" asked Beth Abelson of her two friends one week later, her eyes dancing back and forth between the two. She had just arrived to join Jeff and Rachel for lunch at Miyuki's, their favorite cafe and watering hole back when they were a threesome at S.P.&M.

"Do you want the short answer or the long one?" asked Rachel, handing Beth a menu. "Incidentally, I recommend the

Kaopai shrimp. They also have a great lobster ramen here, in case you've forgotten.''

"I'll skip the ramen, thank you—still on the goddamn diet,'' said Beth, ''and I'll take the short answer on your trial prep, by the way. I didn't come all the way over here to talk business.''

Rachel had forgotten how much she enjoyed her friend's directness.

"I see it's our same old no-nonsense Beth," said Jeff as the waiter appeared at their table. "Okay. I'll have the ramen. For you, Beth, here's my no-frills, condensed, quickie status report with six weeks to go before trial: Expert witness depositions have been completed on both sides except for one, which Rachel is taking on October third. Defense medical examinations are finished on all but three plaintiffs. We've filed a CCP 437(a) summary judgment motion. Notice of trial has been served in accordance with CCP 594(a). Defendants' motion *in limine* will be argued—''

"Excuse me," interrupted Beth, looking at Rachel and pointing at Jeff, ''is there any way to turn this thing off? I have to be back in court at one-thirty.''

"Not that I've ever been able to discover," said Rachel, laughing. She also realized how much she'd missed Beth's witty camaraderie, and resolved to revitalize their sisterhood even if it meant a weekly trip across the Bay.

"I can see," said Jeffrey, "that I'm losing my audience. So screw the exciting stuff—let's talk about your life instead, okay, Beth?''

The three friends talked and laughed their way through lunch, catching up with one another's lives and exchanging courtroom adventures. Rachel was also curious about the state of Beth's troubled marriage, but was content to see that she had apparently regained her balance and good humor. She also noted that, with their old friend around, Jeff's spirits were high for the first time in weeks.

"So, Jeffrey, I hear they're finally giving you a case to try on your own," said Beth.

"Yeah, I'm stoked, but also scared shitless. In fact, I'm afraid to open this fortune cookie. It's a plaintiff's personal injury case, representing a longtime S.P.&M. client. Respecting your obsession with brevity, Beth, I'll make it short. The case involves a dentist who rented an electric-powered Roto-Rooter to clean out a stopped-up drainage pipe.''

Rachel was unable to suppress a smile. "A dentist with a

Roto-Rooter?'' asked Beth. "Get outta here." Both Rachel and
Beth laughed while Jeffrey, undaunted, finished his recital of the
facts.

"He managed to get the snake deep into the pipe, with his
garden hose following along to flush out the dislodged crap,
when the garden hose got entangled in the rotating blades."

"Sounds more like a property damage case to me," said Beth.

"It would have been, but the middle of the garden hose was
wrapped around the dentist's ankle. Before he could reach the
on-off power switch, the marauding rubber snake had given his
left foot a full three-hundred-and-sixty-degree twist."

"At least his foot ended up pointing in the right direction,"
said Rachel, giving way to laughter again.

"Hardly a good defense," said Jeffrey, adopting her frivolous
mood in spite of himself, "as he's now two inches shorter on the
left side."

The arrival of the check—gallantly snapped up by Jeffrey—
signaled the end of their reunion. As Jeff went to the counter,
Beth leaned forward and asked for a report on Rachel's "social
life."

"Well," said Rachel, smiling and frowning at the same time
as she smoothed out the place mat in front of her, "I'm still in
love, but . . . well, it seemed time to break out of the rut I was
in and I've gone out on a real live date or two."

"Really?" said Beth. "Someone new? Who is he? What does
he do?"

"Fuzz," said Jeffrey, overhearing the question from his position at the counter and stepping back into the conversation.
"Heat. Pig. A *cop*, for Christ's sake!"

"You'd never know it, Beth, but Jeffrey doesn't approve,"
said Rachel. "The man happens to be a homicide inspector with
the San Francisco Police Department. I met him in July. He was
trying to establish something more than coincidence in the deaths
of our two plaintiffs—remember our chat back in February about
the suspected Mafia link with North American and Lileton?
Well, he's the guy you mentioned who was working with your
deputy D.A. trying to build a racketeering act case. He was
working on a murder angle to bolster the charges, but it never
got off the ground."

"Yet the intrepid lieutenant's romantic interest lives on," said
Jeffrey, affecting the clipped and dramatic flair of a radio
commentator.

"Jeffrey. Pay the bill," said Rachel. "And by the way, you're much nicer when you're depressed."

"Very interesting," said Beth, ignoring the exchange. "Now that I have to leave, you come on with the juicy stuff." She leaned even closer to Rachel and whispered, "Does Kevin know? What's happening with him?"

"The answer is 'I'm not sure' to both questions. My feelings are more or less the same, but he's still married and our sneaking around was beginning to get to me."

"Sneaking around doing *what* exactly?" asked Beth, smiling broadly.

"Just . . . sneaking around," said Rachel with an ironic laugh and extending her arms, palms up. "You know, stolen hugs and kisses in our offices, longing glances across a crowded elevator."

"Sounds frustrating."

"It has been," said Rachel, "and so I happened to meet Dan Conti at about the time I was deciding I had to get some distance from Kevin." Rachel paused reflectively, tapped one of her chopsticks against an empty water glass, then added, "I suppose I'm using my lieutenant to help with that."

"So?"

"So what?"

"So why do you look so worried?"

"I'm not," Rachel said, then looked up at Beth with glistening eyes, adding, "Yes, I am. Mainly I'm worried about Kevin."

"Why?"

"It's hard to explain. He's changed. I no sooner began to get to know him than he began to change into someone else."

"How so?" whispered Beth.

"Well, to begin with, everyone thinks of Kevin Stone as a killer because of his courtroom success, but he's really an incredibly sensitive and gentle person. At least he was. Lately, he's changed somehow. Part of it is the frustration I just mentioned, yet I can't help but feel that something else is working on him, something—"

Jeffrey returned with his change. "Okay, ladies, big bad Jeff approaching. No more secrets."

"Rachel was just agreeing with me that you get better-looking every day, Jeff."

"Sure she did. Sure I do. Knock off the bullshit and let's open our fortune cookies."

Rachel opened hers first. It read: YOU MUST SEEK MORE EXCITE-
MENT IN YOUR LIFE!

The three friends exploded in laughter.

"That was a good collar last night, Dan," said Captain Fred-
erick Mahan, his round red face beaming like a stoplight. "Two
rape-murders in two nights. Thank God you got him off the
streets. How did you find him?"

"Friends in low places," said Dan, ransacking his coat pockets for some crumpled notes. "The economics come to four
hundred and eighteen dollars in miscellaneous tips to informants.
Now all we've got to do is prove he's the one who did it."

"That should be no problem on this one." Captain Mahan
swiveled around so that he was directly facing Conti. "Dan,
close the door and sit down a minute. I think you know why I
wanted to talk with you."

"Why don't you just tell me?" said Dan. The direct gaze of
the inspector's sad eyes forced the captain to avert his own and
shuffle some papers in front of him.

"I got jumped again by the Lileton chief of police. Captain
Ciari says you've been poaching again—or at least trying to."

"Do I need a visa to enter the city limits of Lileton?"

"You know that's not the point," said Mahan, scowling. "I
thought we had an understanding two months ago that you were
to get the hell off that North American vendetta you like to call a
RICO case. It's not an investigation and it never will be. It's a
fantasy that you just can't seem to let go of. How many hours of
good time have you squandered on it? Ciari is mad as hell."

Dan rose to his feet. "If you're finished, Captain, I have a
question for you. Why does the captain of the San Francisco
Police Department give a shit what a tin-star bozo from a two-
bit, one-horse town like Lileton thinks about *anything*?"

"Why? I'll tell you why," growled Fred Mahan, nodding his
head and jamming a stubby finger in Conti's direction. "Because
one of his lieutenants is making a fool of himself and his captain
at the same time. Now, listen up, Dan, *okay*? These guys are
tough and we don't need any trouble with them. Just knock it
off."

"You want to keep peace in the 'family,' is that it?" said
Dan, cocking his head and smiling.

"What's that supposed to mean? Are you implying—"

"I'm saying it straight out, Fred," said Dan, rising and

leaning forward across the captain's desk. "The Mafia controls Lileton and North American Chemical, the city's major employer. You know it and I know it. That means they control Ciari and the police department too. I think we've got a slam-dunk RICO case against all of them if you'll just turn me loose. I can get them on extortion and I think they've killed two plaintiffs in that lawsuit—"

"*A racketeering case against a police force?* Holy God, you're even more brain-damaged than I thought! Are you trying to get me shit-canned? Or just murdered? Do you want my job, Dan? Is that it? Well, okay, you want straight, I'll give you *straight*. I wouldn't mess with those guys even if we had a case, which we don't. So this is final, *okay*? Once and for all, Lieutenant, *cool it*!" With his final words the captain rose to his feet and, hands in back pockets, waddled over to his window, where he stared out in silence, signaling the end of the meeting.

Conti walked to the door, then turned and said quietly, "When I was just an angry punk out on these city streets, heading for big trouble, a courageous cop became a second father to me. He channeled my rage in the right direction. That cop was afraid of nothing or nobody, and it showed. I wanted to grow up to be like him. He taught me that nobody had the right to violate the sanctity of another's life—even out of revenge. He explained how my life could give meaning to my Pop's death, a tall order at the time, but he pulled it off. I miss that cop, Captain, almost as much as I miss my father. What the hell happened to him?"

The captain remained turned away from Conti's hot eyes. When he spoke, his voice was flat and tired. "There's one thing I forgot to teach that young kid. In the real world, there sometimes have to be . . . accommodations made, okay?"

Dan stared at the back of the captain's head. "You mean compromises, don't you?"

Mahan spun back around. "Accommodations, compromises, call it whatever you want, Dan! God knows I've been making enough of them for you during the past two or three months since those two old birds died. Don't you hear the rest of the guys on the force talking behind your back? They're laughing at you!" The captain turned as he said these last words, then stiffly walked back to his chair and sat down, adding, "So I'm telling you for the last time, Dan, you leave this thing alone and face the fact that for once—maybe just once in your life—you're wrong! Your unauthorized inquiry on this matter is finished, *okay*? And so is this meeting.''

Captain Mahan again began shuffling papers in front of him, leaving Conti staring down at his balding head. Finally, the inspector shrugged his shoulders, turned, and walked out of Mahan's office. He returned to his own desk, picked up the phone, and dialed Rachel's number at the office.

"Hello?" said Rachel.

"It's me, Dan."

"Hi, Dan."

"I've got to see you tonight. Will you be home?"

"I was planning on it."

"How about eight o'clock? I could take you out for a quick hamburger. I've got to talk to you about how I can get some information on Hallinan and Weisberg—"

"Dan, I've told you—" A knock on Rachel's open door alerted her to Kevin's presence in the doorway. "I've got to go now. I'll see you later tonight."

Rachel replaced the receiver in its cradle and said, "Hi, Kevin. Come in. I need to talk to you about this motion to sever Dixon from the others. I'm arguing it tomorrow and it doesn't look good. I still don't even understand what's behind it or . . .'' Rachel's last words trailed off as she saw that Kevin was glaring at her through narrowed eyes.

"I have a suggestion, Rachel," he said coldly, "then a question of my own. My suggestion is that for once in your life you simply follow a senior partner's clear and specific instructions. My question is whether it's true that you've been dating Dan Conti."

"Why, yes, we've had dinner a few times and a movie or two." She was stunned by Kevin's manner even more than by his words. His jaw was clenched as his eyes continued to rake her face. He looked like a stranger.

"Was that him on the phone just now?"

"Kevin, this is not a courtroom, and you have no right to cross-examine me."

Kevin moved to within inches of Rachel's face. "That's where you're wrong. Do you have any idea what the hell you're doing? Don't you realize that Conti's using you to get at privileged information he couldn't pry out of Austin or me?"

Rachel stood her ground and matched Kevin's increasing intensity: "What I do and who I see on my time is my business.

As a matter of fact, Dan and I made a rule from the start never to discuss his case or mine.''

"Wonderful!" said Kevin. "The fox has agreed not to eat the chicken. Can you tell me that 'Dan' has never once asked you for information about our clients?''

The question stung Rachel into momentary silence as she tried to think of a single date when Dan had not at least mentioned the case, keeping his foot in a door she had been unable to close. It had even become a kind of ritual game between them. And now, with Dan's most recent demand still ringing in her ears, it was difficult to refute Kevin's argument, making her even more angry at both of them. "He's making a fool of you, Rachel,'' Kevin continued. "I shouldn't have to remind you of your responsibility to avoid even the appearance of jeopardizing the sanctity of the attorney/client privilege. And whether it's your personal time or not, the firm has the right to insist that you avoid even the appearance of, shall we say, a 'compromising position.' ''

Kevin's rudely transparent double entendre fueled Rachel's rising anger. "I'm well aware of my professional responsibility,'' she said in a cold but carefully controlled voice. "I also think you're masking your own personal feelings behind an inappropriate lecture on ethics and professional integrity. Whether you believe it or not, I am far too careful to hurt my clients—even unintentionally.'' Rachel paused and loudly tapped her pen twice on a book in front of her, then added quietly, "What I've done, Kevin, has hurt only you.''

Kevin stared at her for several seconds, then stalked out of her office. Rachel tried to work, but remained hurt and angry. After twenty minutes of frustrated failure she packed her briefcase and left for the day. She chose a circuitous route home, driving mindlessly through Pacific Heights and the Presidio before parking finally at the Palace of the Legion of Honor. She opened the windows but did not leave her car, for the fresh ocean air did nothing to clear the turmoil in her head and heart. Kevin was obviously jealous, but his statement about Conti's using her had cut deeply with the sharp edge of truth. She also knew that her own words to Kevin had also been painful to him. Then there was the whole matter of Emmett Dixon and how she would approach Judge Bainbridge tomorrow on the motion to sever his case from the others. What will I say to the Court? she wondered. What will I say to Barrington if I lose? And what will I say to Emmett if I win? She had not even told him about the motion, an unprofessional omission to say the least. If someone had put the question to her as to why, she would have to reply in all honesty, "Because I expect to lose and don't want to upset him needlessly." But if I *do* lose, she thought, and whatever it is about Emmett's medical picture causes damage to the entire case, I'll be blamed.

Getting nowhere in solving her dilemma, she started her car and pointed it toward Sausalito. The commuter traffic had cleared out, and she quickly crossed the Bay, hardly noticing the water-color sunset off to her left. She parked the BMW and entered her apartment, drained and dejected. She kicked off her shoes, made herself a white wine spritzer, and entered her bedroom. As she turned on the light, her heart froze at what she saw scrawled in lipstick across the large mirror above her vanity:

GET OUT OF NORTH AMERICAN

THIRTY-FIVE

■

Twenty-five minutes later Dan arrived at Rachel's door and found her badly frightened and disheartened. She had started to call Kevin at first, then remembered their angry exchange. Besides, maybe he was already home, and she certainly couldn't call him there. Moreover, this was, after all, police work.

Dan studied the scrawled message and maintained a professional manner that was reassuring to Rachel. In response to his questions, she described her movements since arriving and pointed out everything she had touched. He took careful notes and then called two of his best crime lab people at home and ordered them to the scene. Dan concealed any apprehension he might be harboring and, when questioned by Rachel, implied that the break-in was the work of a malicious prankster.

While waiting for the lab experts to arrive, he continued to play the incident down and prescribed "the official cop's cure for fear and trembling'': a stiff drink and a blood-rare hamburger at Sam's Grill in Tiburon. Rachel agreed, relieved to feel her initial fear beginning to subside, leaving depression in its wake. Her home had been her sanctuary, her secret hideaway from the noise of the city, rude encounters, assignments to suicide trials, or motions she knew she couldn't win. But here, nothing could get her. Until tonight.

Dan seemed to understand what she was feeling, and Rachel—despite Kevin's admonition and her own renewed suspicions about his motives—was relieved that he was with her. ''Are you okay?'' he asked. ''You seem pretty low, not that I blame you.''

''The worst part is that whoever did this could do it again. And just the thought of his handling my things, his *being* here. The way I feel now, I just don't want to live here anymore.''

Risking light humor, Dan said, ''Tell you what I'm going to do. I know of a lovely one-bedroom apartment in San Francisco . . .''

Rachel smiled as she said, ''I'll give it some thought,'' in a way that told Dan she was still not ready to sleep with him, certainly not tonight.

''Well, if you don't ask, you don't learn anything,'' said Dan. ''That sleazy trick having failed, let me tell you something from my own experience: Most people feel exactly the way you do at first, but it doesn't last. To make sure it doesn't, this house is going to be wired—even as we eat—with a state-of-the-art alarm system that would repel King Kong and which in the morning will be expanded and wired directly into the Sausalito Police Department's panel.

''In addition, by the time we get back from Sam's, we will know how he—or they—got in, just to make sure he—or they—don't do it again. That's going to make you feel better even faster. The trick in these things is to rid yourself of the unknown. Also, one of my own men will be staked out nearby when we return here tonight, and he will stay there until I have whoever did this behind bars.''

Relief, then gratitude, began to slice through Rachel's fear and dejection. ''Oh, God, I'm glad you're here,'' she said, bursting into tears and putting her head against his shoulder.

''And bring this lady lawyer a double kamikaze,'' Dan said to the bartender.

''If that drink is as lethal as it sounds,'' protested Rachel, ''I'd better pass. I have a very difficult motion before Judge Bainbridge tomorrow."

"So, you think you're the only one with a bad day ahead? I'm about ready to accelerate my running battle with Captain Mahan. The only good side of what's happened here tonight, incidentally, is that he may have to allow me to apply for a search warrant now, then take on your boss in a hearing to unseal the medical records."

"I'm glad I could be of this limited service at least," said Rachel with a dry laugh.

"Does that mean you still won't help me? The process I've just described may take weeks!"

"If helping you means disclosing nonpublic information about my clients without a subpoena, the answer was, is, and forever shall be no, I won't help you."

Dan clenched his strong, lean hands together, pursed his lips, and seemed to go within himself. Rachel wondered whether he was angry at her again and whether she was being too stubborn. *What if he's right about all this?* she thought; *that certainly wasn't Mother Teresa who just paid my apartment a visit.* But when she looked back at Dan, he was smiling at her warmly, his eyes radiating goodwill.

"Okay, counselor," he said gently. "You've made your point. I give up—for now at least."

The drinks arrived. "Drink one half of it now," said Dan, "the other half in five minutes, and you won't even notice how bad the hamburger is."

Rachel turned to Dan with her glass raised and her eyes suddenly misty. "My hero," she said.

Dan continued smiling and touched her glass with his, leaving them connected. "My heroine," he said, and they gratefully drank.

The alcohol went straight to Rachel's brain, filling her with a pleasant, numbing sense of well-being. She looked at Dan's reflection in the mirror running behind the bar. This guy's got his own agenda, she thought, but don't we all? And he does make me feel good. "What's the matter with your captain?" she asked after another moment of thoughtful silence. "Is he as cynical as I am—or was—about this murder theory of yours?"

"He makes you look totally supportive," said Dan. "But then, I'm thoroughly pissed and disillusioned with Captain Mahan right now. That he could have been elevated to the rank of captain in the first place only proves that hot air rises.''

"You say that, yet you don't sound like you mean it.''

"I really don't know what's going on with him. He's under a lot of heat right now from Cleo Barnes. That may explain some of his concern about me taking on what could be a controversial and high profile investigation of a neighboring city. You've read about Cleo, I'm sure.''

"The black developer who was recently appointed to the Police Commission?''

"Right. Barnes is a pretty good man actually; a token minority member whom Mahan recently charged with lack of concern for law and order. Cleo called his own press conference the next day and characterized Captain Mahan as a village idiot. Mahan demanded a written public apology and retraction. You know the rest: Barnes took out a half-page ad in the *San Francisco Examiner* in which he indeed apologized 'to all the village idiots in Christendom' and retracted his earlier characterization on the grounds that Mahan was 'not the village idiot, but an idiot of state, possibly even national, stature.' ''

Rachel laughed and finished her drink. She was beginning to feel the exhaustion of a day she would never forget. "How long will it take those guys to sanitize my condo? I feel like I could sleep forever.''

"Let's get our table. They should be well along by now.''

Upon their return to Rachel's, Conti met privately with his lab people and then returned to pronounce the place safe and fully protected. After seeing the lab technicians off, he offered to stay on the couch.

"No, Dan, although I'm sure your intentions are honorable.''

"My intentions are the very worst,'' he replied, and took her into his arms, kissing her deeply for the first time. She returned his kiss, feeling a rush of emotions that momentarily cut through the fatigue. She knew she was beginning to care for Dan, whom she now knew to be far more sensitive and intelligent than she would ever have guessed that first day in her office just over two months ago. He was strong and attractively intense—like Kevin— but refreshingly less complicated. Now, as he kissed her on the cheek, the neck, she heard his voice hypnotically repeating her name in her ear. He began to gently push his hips against her, whispering, "Rachel, Rachel,'' in rhythm with his movement.

Pleasantly alarmed at her own surging passion, she reluctantly pulled away.

"Dan. Not tonight, please. It's been a long day, an awful day, and I've got another big one tomorrow," she said, looking deep into his longing eyes. *Such gentle eyes,* she thought, *even now.* "Am I going to have to call a cop?"

Dan held her face gently in his hands. "Rachel," he said quietly, but with laser intensity, "I'm a patient man, as long as there's reason to think that my case isn't hopeless." He paused, catching his breath. "You're both the lawyer and the judge in this one. I trust you to tell me if you decide I haven't a chance at winning."

Rachel smiled, her clear skin reflecting the moonlight off Sausalito Bay: "Dan. Dearest Dan. I'm in a . . . very difficult situation right now. I—"

"Don't say another word," Dan interrupted. "I haven't read you your Miranda rights. Meanwhile, good luck on your motion tomorrow, and wish me luck with Mahan."

Dan walked toward the door without enthusiasm, then turned and said, "This new gadget here is a dead bolt that can't be beaten. Your earlier visitor came right through your front door. The lab guys tell me you forgot to set both locks. Now you've got three to think about. The keys are on the counter there. Can you handle all that?"

"I'll write notes to myself," said Rachel, giving him a final kiss on the cheek.

Dan brushed his lips across her cheek and buried them in her silken hair, then gently pulled it against his own face. "Take care of yourself," he said, and walked swiftly toward his car, nodding at the plainclothes officer positioned across the street.

As Rachel arrived at the courthouse the next day to argue her motion to sever Emmett Dixon's case from the other Group A plaintiffs, she was surprised to see Kevin already seated in the back of the courtroom. *Just what I need,* she thought, *a classroom monitor.*

Appearing for the defense was Chuck Parnell, Alan Hancock's junior partner. This was also discomforting, for Parnell was nearly as experienced as Hancock but more sensitive and therefore more dangerous. An uncomfortable heat consumed her body. Her intuition began flashing red lights.

"Before you commence oral argument," said Judge Bainbridge,

"the Court feels compelled to say that I am not overly impressed with the grounds cited in plaintiff's motion to sever Mr. Dixon's case from the other Group A plaintiffs."

Chuck Parnell saw an opening and seized it, appropriating Rachel's right as the moving party to argue first: "I agree, your honor—if I may be heard for just ten seconds—I'm sure the Court will remember that Ms. Cannon was out here just a few short months ago arguing that Mr. Dixon, along with others, should have their cases advanced for trial. At that time, your honor, it was imperative to plaintiffs' counsel that Dixon be *advanced*. Now it's equally imperative that he be *delayed*. I think we're being played with here, your honor."

"Well, Ms. Cannon?" said Judge Bainbridge. "Do you have anything to add to your moving papers?"

Rachel felt trapped. She could hardly admit in the presence of opposing counsel that the real reason Barrington wanted the severance was to eliminate a questionable medical case from the first group going to trial, yet her voice sounded confident as she said, "Your honor, this is primarily an internal administration matter for the plaintiffs to deal with. No one is prejudiced by the severance, and if we, as counsel for over one hundred forty plaintiffs, are for any reason unable to prepare one victim's case as fast or as fully as the others, we should be permitted to drop that plaintiff back into the next group for trial. For this, and the other reasons cited in our moving papers, we urge that Mr. Dixon be severed for a later trial."

"I can't see it, Ms. Cannon," said Judge Bainbridge. "I think the answer here is simply for you and your firm to devote some additional energy to the Dixon case. You have plenty of time to get it up to speed with the rest and Lord knows you've got enough people—at least three times the number of lawyers in Mr. Parnell's firm. Otherwise—and I must agree with Mr. Parnell on this—my efforts to administer this complex matter will be made all the more difficult." Judge Bainbridge was already searching for the next motion on his calendar and Rachel felt the scalding dampness of defeat flooding her body.

"Thank you, your honor," said Parnell. "Next up for consideration, I believe, is our motion for monetary sanctions for counsel's delay in turning over plaintiffs' medical records and our motion to continue the trial for three months on the grounds of this delay."

Rachel cleared her head. *Put Dixon behind you*, she admonished herself. How important could it be anyway? But this was more serious: The defense had finally figured out how they had been mousetrapped into a Christmas verdict and were now trying to exploit Barrington's delays into a delay of their own—into January or even February! Before she could protest, however, the judge spoke. "Again, Ms. Cannon, I find no reason in the record to excuse plaintiffs' delay in providing the defense full access to plaintiffs' medical records. You understand that they are entitled to see these records before they conduct their own defense medical examinations of the plaintiffs."

It was not a question but a statement with which Rachel could only agree, but she rose quickly to her feet, saying, "You will note, however, that all records have now been turned over—except Dixon's, of course, pending the Court's ruling today—and defendants can present no reasonable argument for delaying the trial one day longer than we delayed their own medical preparation."

"But, your honor," said Parnell, "that fails to take into account the extra time it will now take us to reschedule our own medical examinations of plaintiffs and—"

"Our clients are available," said Rachel, interrupting him, "seven days a week, twenty-four hours a day. As long," she added somewhat melodramatically, "as they are still alive."

"All right, counsel. I've heard enough. My rulings are as follows: First, on the motion to continue the trial date—motion granted, but only to the extent of the delayed production. Assuming production of Dixon's records and answering all interrogatories no later than October eighth, for example, the date certain for trial will be continued only to December thirteenth." Rachel breathed a sigh of relief. The spirit of Christmas would still prevail in our case, she thought. "As for the request for sanctions, defendants' request is denied. Mr. Clerk, call the next case."

Kevin was waiting at the courtroom door.

"Hello, Kevin," Rachel said with a tentative smile. "I guess it could have been worse."

"It could *hardly* have been worse," Kevin shot back in far too loud a voice, it seemed to Rachel. "*You lost the goddamned motion!*"

"Correction, I lost *one* of the motions. We won on the sanctions, and we held the line on the motion to continue the trial. Yes, we failed to sever Emmett Dixon, undoubtedly against our client's own will. Can that be so damn important?''

"More important than you'll ever know," said Kevin, still visibly enraged and blocking her path. "I suppose that the date I heard you making for last night left you little time for preparation."

Rachel stopped abruptly in the courtroom corridor and stared at Kevin, feeling powerless to do justice to her anger. She cursed the tears she felt coming, fearing that Kevin would misunderstand them, take them for hurt feelings rather than indignation. "Please get out of my way," she said finally in a voice that crackled like a forest fire. Kevin took three steps back, an insufficient distance to avoid the force of her fury as she added, "If you insist on leveraging your position as a partner in the firm to manipulate my personal life, I can't stop you. But to suggest that I have given this matter less than my very best effort suggests to me that you never knew me at all." She started to walk off, then added, "You and Barrington make a great team: He sends me out on a suicide motion, and you come out to harass me when I predictably fail!''

Before Kevin could speak, Rachel accelerated and with long, swift strides whipped out of the courthouse. He caught up with her and walked beside her as they crossed Polk Street to the taxi stand and then jumped into the backseat of her cab.

"Imperial Building," said Rachel, ignoring him.

"The time has come, Rachel," said Kevin, shifting to a more controlled but still unyielding manner, "for you to choose between our case and your little lieutenant's case. Barrington is the one who told me about you and Conti. It must be all over the office. We've agreed that if you're going to be involved in our trial team, you must have no further social contact with him. After the trial, of course, your life is your own, and presumably no longer includes me. But meanwhile, you've got to accept our view. The man is exploiting you in order to enhance his own reputation in a very high-publicity situation, no matter what he's saying to you. These so-called dates are just one small part of his total picture, and so are you. He's shooting for the whole damn mob, Rachel.''

"It's good somebody is. They seem to be shooting for me."

"What's that supposed to mean?"

Rachel was too angry to answer, and they rode in tense silence nearly all the way to the financial district. Kevin slowly regained his composure and, as they approached the Imperial Building, apologized and admitted that he had been unfair to her, that he and Barrington had counted on Judge Bainbridge to be liberal to the plaintiffs, as was usual in these matters, and that when Kevin saw the motion fail, he had taken his frustration out on Rachel. A few blocks later he also admitted his jealousy of Dan Conti and pleaded for Rachel's understanding.

"It's no secret to you that I've been struggling for control lately," he said. "I know I have no right to influence what you do outside the office when I'm still . . . married to Denise. It's just that I feel so damned trapped and helpless right now."

Kevin's candor and exposed vulnerability had a cooling effect on Rachel's anger. She looked at him for the first time and saw that his face was drawn—pinched actually—and that his eyes were pleading and forthright, almost fearful. She experienced a resurgence of feeling for him and conceded to him that she was also feeling the pressure, particularly after the warning scrawled on her mirror the previous night.

"My God, why didn't you tell me sooner?"

"You haven't given me much of a chance."

Kevin took her hand and kissed it gently. "I'm sorry, darling, really sorry. Jesus, I don't know what I'm doing or saying lately."

Kevin promised to bury his personal feelings about Conti and to press Barrington to insist on police protection for Rachel and all other members of the trial team. "It sounds like maybe the cop is not so crazy after all," said Kevin. "If he is right, this thing might get dangerous. If you prefer, Austin and I could handle this trial alone if necessary."

"I won't dignify that with a response," said Rachel, smiling for the first time.

As Kevin reiterated his love for her, Rachel was both pleased and saddened to see how much he still needed her. She wished she could do more, but forgiveness was all she could manage right now. They seemed to be riding the same emotional roller coaster, but each would have to take responsibility for his and her own survival; at least until the verdict was in and this growing nightmare behind them.

As they left the cab and entered the Imperial Building in silence, Rachel realized that with both Kevin and Dan, she was gradually allowing herself to be diverted from her ultimate objective. She had once blamed her first husband, Justin Parks, for "doing this to her," but now she knew that the blame lay entirely within her own irresolute heart. She had wanted so to please Justin and had desperately feared his disapproval even though she thoroughly disapproved of him. She left him, but only after a frivolous two years during which she learned that she could not afford the price she was paying for being totally pampered and cared for. It struck her now that until she was stronger, she could neither risk dependency on a man, nor support a man's dependency on her. *I must,* she told herself, *get off this slippery slope that can only lead me again into that same warm, comforting quicksand. I've got to center my fading energies and refocus my attention more fully on the case. The case is where I'll find my strength.*

Myself.

Without telling Kevin, Rachel decided on the spot that it was time to put all further dating on hold—including Dan—until the trial was completed. It was time to commit every waking moment to the success of the case and thus to the attainment of her life's dream—now nearly within her grasp: to become one of the partners at Stafford, Parrish, and MacAllister.

THIRTY-SIX

■

One week later Rachel entered the austere offices of Dr. Emery Heller, principal expert witness for the defense. His barren, shoe-box waiting room on the eighth floor of the 50 Sutter Medical Building suggested either a very small or a very select clientele, with chairs that were covered in traditional leather and a magazine rack that contained just two A.M.A. journals, a *Scientific American,* and a current *National Geographic.*

Rachel smiled at the certified shorthand reporter already seated, selected a chair across from her, and continued to look around. The beige walls were bare but for two tasteful Kollwitz conti crayon drawings and a calendar reporting that it was October 3, 1983, just two months from trial.

Rachel had spent hours trying to find skeletons in the closet of the defense toxicologist, but Childhouse had affirmed that Heller was not only highly respected but "at the top of his field." Bad news for them. This, then, would be not only the most important deposition she had ever taken, but her most difficult, and she was appropriately tense.

"Is everyone here now for Doctor's deposition?" asked the pert receptionist.

"There will be someone from the Hancock firm," replied Rachel, hoping it would be someone young and inexperienced. From all she had heard about Dr. Heller, Rachel knew she would need a relatively unfettered hand if she were to get anywhere with him.

"Oh, you mean Mr. Hancock? He has been here all morning. He instructed me to send you in when you and the shorthand reporter had both arrived."

Rachel's heart sank. She could see that Hancock had taken charge of Dr. Heller's office, and as she picked up her briefcase and followed the receptionist down the hall, she wondered if he had by now also taken possession of the doctor's mind.

"Ah, there you are," said Alan Hancock, looking even more smug than usual. Hancock, a heavyset but solid man, had one of those eternally youthful faces—a selfish, pugnacious face that was topped by thick white hair clipped trim as a toothbrush. "Let's get started."

Rachel recognized that Hancock's rudeness in failing to introduce her to the witness was calculated, and countered by holding out her hand to the expert. "Dr. Heller, I presume?"

"Yes, indeed. And you are . . . ?"

"Rachel Cannon, counsel for the plaintiffs, and this is Joyce Enrick, who will be our shorthand reporter today."

"I am very pleased to meet both of you," Heller said, as he responded with a surprisingly warm handshake.

Dr. Heller was sworn as a witness by Joyce Enrick and Rachel turned to the task at hand, to both "pin down" and "set up" the witness. Pin down, so that they would know exactly what he was going to say at trial. Set up, because it was important to try to develop flaws and inconsistencies that Austin or Kevin could exploit during cross-examination.

As Rachel finished her first hour of examination, fighting Hancock all the way, she knew the partners would not be disappointed by the transcript. Dr. Heller was turning out to be one of those rarities in the forensic field—a totally honest and straightforward expert witness. She suspected that Hancock would work hard during the ten-minute recess to inhibit some of his expert's candor, and she decided to come right off the floor with a haymaker on the first question after they resumed.

"Dr. Heller, wouldn't you agree that the symptoms and illnesses sustained by the thirteen plaintiffs in Group A are consistent to a reasonable medical certainty with those you would expect from people who had consumed the toxins listed on exhibit thirteen, which we discussed earlier today?"

"Well, I think there is a definite—"

"*Objection!*" screamed Hancock.

"On what grounds, counsel?" said Rachel.

"I object to the form of the question. You are asking what is essentially a hypothetical question without the necessary foundation."

"In the interests of expediting Dr. Heller's testimony," Rachel shot back, "I will withdraw that question temporarily and ask this one first: We established this morning, I believe, Doctor, that your own samples from the dump site revealed substantial quantities of 2,3,7,8– tetrachlorodibenzoparadioxin?"

"That's correct."

"Are you familiar with Evans's *Handbook of Toxins*?"

"Yes. It is a well-respected and useful resource."

"Then I take it you agree with Dr. Evans that just three ounces of tetradioxin, evenly distributed and ingested by a million people, could kill all of them?"

"Objection! Objection!"

"State your objection for the record, Mr. Hancock," said Rachel in a bored tone, "so I can get my answer."

"The grounds for my objection," said Hancock with despotic conviction, "are obvious."

"The only thing that is obvious, Mr. Hancock, is that there is no conceivable objection to the question I have just asked. The defense has already admitted that this particular chemical was dumped at North American." Rachel then turned back to Dr. Heller: "You may now answer the question, Doctor."

"I object to the question and I instruct the witness not to answer," Hancock said angrily. He scribbled a note and passed it to Dr. Heller. "The question is vague, compound, argumentative, and cannot possibly lead to admissible evidence."

"I want the record to show that Mr. Hancock has just written a note and handed it to Dr. Heller. I respectfully request, Doctor, that you hand me the note so that I may also make it a part of the record.''

Heller, confused, stared incredulously at Hancock, who, to Rachel's surprise, had deftly snatched the note from the doctor's hands and crumpled it into a ball.

''I further note for the record,'' said Rachel calmly but with growing irritation, ''that Mr. Hancock has retrieved the note from Dr. Heller, wadded it into a ball, and presumably refuses to allow me to make it a part of this record. What are you going to do now, Mr. Hancock? Chew it up and swallow it?''

''I can talk to my witness anytime I please, either in writing or orally!'' shouted Hancock. ''Put that in your record!''

''Dr. Heller,'' said Rachel, ''you must be very confused by now. Let me assure you, however, that Mr. Hancock has no authority to instruct you not to answer. This authority exists only where a lawyer is representing a client at deposition, not where he is trying to protect his retained expert witness. Now, Doctor, please answer my question.''

''No, counsel, he will *not* answer your question,'' said Hancock smugly. ''You see, Dr. Heller has retained me to represent him for the purposes of this deposition; thus, I am authorized to instruct him to answer, even under your interpretation of the rules.''

''Is that right, Dr. Heller?'' asked Rachel, her voice rising.

''Well . . . I . . . whatever Mr. Hancock says, I guess—''

''The record will show,'' said Hancock, ''that my law firm does represent Dr. Heller and that I have instructed him not to answer. Now, move on to your next line of questioning and stop wasting our time.''

Rachel looked at the befuddled Dr. Heller, then at Alan Hancock, then back at the witness as she rose to her feet. ''Good day, gentlemen,'' she said quietly.

Before Hancock could protest, Rachel had her coat on and was packing her briefcase.

''Where do you think you're going—''

''*Please,*'' interrupted the court reporter. ''Is this still on the record?''

''Absolutely,'' said Rachel, snapping her briefcase shut. ''I want the record to show that Mr. Hancock has engaged in the following activities: *One*—he has made frivolous objections to valid questions; *two*—he has, in the middle of cross-examination, offered to represent the witness for the sole purpose of evading fair and proper questions by claiming the right to instruct him not to answer; and *three*—he has improperly attempted to control the order of my cross-examination of his witness by precluding an answer to an appropriate foundational question—objectionable conduct even if he did legitimately represent Dr. Heller.''

Hancock shrugged his shoulders and began packing up his own briefcase. ''Well, counsel, if that's the way you want it, we will deem this deposition completed.''

Rachel paused at the doorway and glanced at the court reporter to make sure she was still taking everything down. ''You are also wrong about *that,* Mr. Hancock. This deposition is far from completed. I'll be back quicker than you can say 'obstruction of discovery,' and I'll have a court order with me calling for monetary sanctions for your interference.''

''Tell it to the judge,'' said Hancock derisively, rising to his feet.

Rachel gave Hancock a sardonic smile as she walked back and firmly set her case on the table in front of him. ''You know, Mr. Hancock, I think I will do just that.'' She then walked to the telephone and began dialing a number written on the inside of her file.

''What the hell are you doing? Who are you calling?'' asked Hancock, betraying more than idle curiosity.

''I'm taking your advice to 'tell it to the judge.' I'm calling Judge Bainbridge to tell him that you have instructed an expert toxicologist not to answer a question concerning the lethal effect of a chemical you have already stipulated was contained in North American's dump site. Let's see what he thinks of the Hancock view of relevancy. Excuse me. Hello, may I speak with Judge Bainbridge, please? I want to see if he could see counsel for a few minutes concerning a dispute which has arisen . . .''

Hancock leapt to his feet, traveled the eight feet to the phone in two strides, and pushed the disconnect button on the telephone. Rachel gave him a dry smile as she handed him the receiver, removed her jacket, and resumed her seat.

''Now, Dr. Heller, I believe we can get on with our business here. You remember the question, don't you?''

The remainder of the deposition went smoothly, so smoothly in fact that she called Jeffrey from the downstairs pay telephone and invited him to meet her for lunch to celebrate the neutralization of the defendants' key toxicologist.

"Perfect!" he said. "I've also got some good news to celebrate for a change. I just settled my dentist mechanical snake
case for forty-five thousand dollars! The client is ecstatic and has
written a letter saying as much to you-know-who."

"Barrington?"

"The very same. Where do you want to meet?"

"See you at Mulhern's in fifteen minutes, okay?"

Rachel and Jeffrey returned to the Imperial Building in high
spirits owing in no small part to a pair of Irish coffees downed
by each of them after an excellent lunch. As they entered the
building, however, Jeffrey's mood leveled off, then sank lower
the higher they went. "Well," he said glumly as they reached
Rachel's floor, "I'll pick up a couple of files, then return to my
monkey cage."

"Jeff, it's an office, not a cage, and you're not considered to
be a monkey by anyone around here," Rachel began, worried
about his obvious discontent. But her attempt at consolation was
broken off.

"Inspector Conti has been waiting for you." The receptionist
tilted her head, indicating a small conference room area. "He's
using the phone in the conference room right now. He says it's
important."

"I'm sure you will excuse me, Rachel," said Jeffrey, frowning and executing a one-hundred-eighty-degree turn back into the
elevator.

"Jeff, wait. What's eating you lately? I can't keep up with
your moods. Is it Dan? You needn't worry; we're not even
dating anymore."

Jeff pushed the elevator hold button and shrugged his shoulders. "It's not just that; it's hard to explain," he said, removing
his glasses and blowing on them. "You're right, Rachel. I'm
moody and zero fun to be with."

"I didn't say that, but I would like to know what's going on
with you."

Jeff gave his head a quick shake. "I just don't feel that I'm
doing what I was trained to do. You're dismantling the key
defense expert in the country's biggest case while I'm screwing
around making some rich dentist even richer, then trying to
persuade myself it's important."

Jeffrey let the doors start to close, but Rachel parted them.
"Jeff, you're less than two years out of school and—"

"Don't get the idea I'm comparing the two of us, Rachel. I'm just trying to say that I was doing more for that fucked-up world out there before I became a lawyer than I'm doing now." A warning buzzer sounded harshly and Rachel watched helplessly as the doors slowly closed on her friend.

Rachel turned and walked into the conference room, feeling both worried about Jeff and annoyed at Dan's interruption. One look at Dan's face, however, convinced her that he was on business, serious business. He walked past her and closed the door to the conference room. "Sit down, kid. I have some bad news."

Rachel obeyed automatically, such was the gravity of Dan's suggestion. He perched on the edge of the table and looked down at her. His features seemed sharpened by tension, his large nose casting a shadow against his unusually pale skin.

"Rachel," he said finally. "Emmett Dixon is dead."

A few seconds of silence passed before the words took hold, then Rachel began to slowly shake her head from side to side. Her eyes remained fixed on Dan's, looking for a reprieve, a denial. "I know how you felt about him," Dan continued. "I'm sorry. Really sorry."

"Thanks for being the one to tell me," said Rachel, fighting back tears. "When did he die?"

"Last night, early this morning," said Dan, "but I just found out about it. It came across the arson wire."

Rachel's head snapped up. "Arson? What are you talking about?"

"He didn't die from his illness. His cottage caught fire. It went up like a tinderbox. No hope of getting him out. For whatever consolation it might be to you, I'm sure the smoke got him before he even woke up."

"Oh, my God," said Rachel, face buried in her hands. She turned away from Dan and began to weep quietly.

Dan saw she did not want to hear more and put both hands gently on her shoulders from behind. "I have to go report this to your bosses. I'll call you later. Okay?" Dan closed the door softly as he left the room.

Barrington scowled as Margaret Tarkenton's metallic voice announced an unwanted message: "Inspector Conti is in the reception area. He says it's extremely important."

"Tell that pest that if he wants to see me, he can make an

appointment and . . . oh, well, you might as well go get him, but tell him I am interrupting a meeting and that he has only a few minutes.''

Barrington clicked off and stared over steepled fingers at the door through which Conti would soon emerge. He must have found something, thought Barrington; better find out what it is.

Miss Tarkenton's efficient twin rap on the door signaled the detective's brisk entry. ''Good afternoon, Mr. Barrington. I bring bad news so I'll get right to the point. Early this morning—around four o'clock—Emmett Dixon was killed. He was trapped in his burning cottage.''

''Oh, my God,'' said Barrington, sinking into his chair. ''The poor devil. How did it happen?''

''That question has preoccupied me since I heard about it mid-morning. You see, the fire department thought it originated in the kitchen: spontaneous combustion in a closet where he kept his cleaning supplies. When I heard it was another one of your clients, I sent the arson squad in. They found some residue that could be kerosene in the victim's bedroom. The fire department paid it no attention because he had a kerosene space heater in his bedroom, and two one-gallon cans stored in his kitchen closet.''

''So why was the arson squad suspicious?''

''They weren't,'' said Conti, smiling his humorless smile and touching the tip of his nose with his index finger, ''but I am. I've talked so far to three neighbors and one of his close friends. It's far from a sure thing, but so far I can't find anyone who ever saw a kerosene space heater in Dixon's house.

''Now, let me guess what you're thinking, Mr. Barrington. You're thinking, *Here goes that crazy inspector again*. And I'm the first to admit there is nothing but circumstantial evidence here. But whether or not Dixon had a space heater is not the only issue. Nearly as important is whether Dixon was or was not the most seriously ill of the thirteen remaining plaintiffs in Group A.''

Barrington's face arranged itself into a more tolerant look as he lit a cigarette and inhaled deeply. ''You're quite right, Lieutenant. If not the most seriously ill, he was certainly one of them and—anticipating your next question—yes, he would have been the largest monetary threat to the defendants.''

''And isn't it true that he was a widower without heirs?''

''To my shame,'' Barrington said thoughtfully, ''the thought was just entering my own mind. You see, these men were all bachelors or widowers when they lived in the company-supplied housing, so it's not too surprising. And since they are poor, they leave no one who can claim lost support. The suit just dies with the victim. I'll have to check, but I'm reasonably certain Dixon was no exception." The senior partner rose for the first time and walked over to his north window-wall, leaving Conti in a haze of cigarette smoke. He spoke in a resigned, tired voice. "This probably means another dismissal, another two or three million dollars eliminated from the verdict and, obviously, another million-dollar-fee loss to my firm."

"I don't think you should be ashamed at all, Mr. Barrington," said Conti deliberately. "In addition to being lawyers, you have a business to run here. That's why I know you will be cooperative and turn over the complete records of Hallinan and Weisberg to me now, as well as Dixon's."

Barrington turned abruptly and headed straight for the door, signaling the end of the meeting. "Lieutenant Conti, I believe we have been through this already. And I don't have time for another of your lectures on legal ethics today. I interrupted a meeting to see you and must return to it. If you wish to come back tomorrow morning, we'll discuss it further."

Conti checked his watch, then looked up into Barrington's determined face. "All right, Mr. Barrington, nine o'clock then. Meanwhile, I can't leave without stating the obvious: This confirms to me that all three of these men have been murdered. Rachel Cannon has received a threat, as was reported to you. Your continued withholding of cooperation could be costing lives, perhaps even endangering your own staff."

Barrington exhaled an audible grunt of exasperation. "And I must say again to you, Lieutenant Conti, that next to the victims themselves, no one is losing more as a result of these untimely deaths than my law firm. But you must understand that it's my job to protect the attorney/client privilege just as it is your job to follow the search warrant procedures under Penal Code Section 1524. We are at a standoff by virtue of the laws and canons of ethics that bind us both. If it's any consolation," he added as Conti turned to leave, "I'll talk to Captain Mahan again. God knows some protection for our staff couldn't hurt."

With a slight upward tilt of his head and an arid smile, Conti replied, "Thank you. That would be nice," and left Barrington's office.

The senior partner stared for a moment at the doorway, then

buzzed Miss Tarkenton. "Yes, sir," came the secretary's crisp voice.

"I'm leaving for the day. I want you to prepare a dismissal in the case of Emmett Dixon—with prejudice—to be filed this afternoon. It can follow exactly the same form as Hallinan's and Weisberg's. Then tell Kevin Stone that I must meet with him tomorrow morning here in my office at eight o'clock sharp. Tell him we have been hit by another dark cloud, but that this one at least has a silver lining. Got that?"

The inevitable affirmative response issued from the speaker box. Barrington double-checked the locked safe in the lower left-hand part of his desk, grabbed his cashmere topcoat, and headed for the elevator.

THIRTY-SEVEN

■

Kevin arrived at Barrington's office five minutes late, his eye red and swollen. "My God, Kevin," said Barrington in a tone more critical than compassionate. "You look as though you've been hit by a two-ton truck."

"No," grunted Kevin, "but I had a close call with a one-hundred-ten-pound wife."

The senior partner frowned. "That's not very funny, Kevin," he said. "Are you two having problems?"

"You and Catherine had a ringside seat just a few months ago," Kevin answered.

Barrington paused, then assumed an avuncular, if annoyed tone. "You're a very fortunate man," he said. "You have two lovely daughters, and Denise is a gorgeous woman. Anyone would be happy to trade places with you."

Kevin immediately experienced the pang of guilt he often felt when people reminded him how lucky he was. Why didn't he *feel* lucky? It seemed lately that he was playing a role of a guy with complete control in a play directed by everyone but himself, to an audience who should know better than to watch. Yet, it was the lead role and he'd be crazy to complain about it; anybody would want the part. But dammit, the play never stopped—it only became more demanding and now he was hardly ever offstage. He had recently found himself sleeping longer hours and cherishing his occasional dreams, for only in sleep did the theater go dark.

"You've got it all, Kevin. Make the most of it, man!" continued Barrington. "You're one of the firm's few candidates for membership to the President's Club and you know that admission there wouldn't hurt your chances to eventually succeed me here as . . . in other things as well. You also know that the club's membership committee values strong family ties. I know I was held back three years simply because I—Catherine and I—never had children, for God's sake! A separation or divorce, even those wagging tongues we hear in the office could kill you, Kevin. Then there's old man Mason himself. Your father-in-law is now one of our biggest clients, Kevin—"

"Jesus, Austin, ease up. All I said was we're having problems. Tell me a couple who doesn't? How's Catherine, by the way?"

"All right, Kevin, point made—but just what *is* the matter with you today? Are you ill?"

"Just a touch of the one-day pneumonia, complicated by an eight o'clock meeting with a senior partner. What's all this about dark clouds and silver linings?"

"Lieutenant Conti will be back in here at nine. An incident occurred early yesterday morning that has refueled his interest in the case. Emmett Dixon is dead."

"Dixon? *Dead?*" said Kevin, suddenly straightening in his chair.

"I know; it's unbelievable. Our three biggest verdicts out the window, not to mention our three biggest fees."

Kevin's pallid face became drawn even tighter as he stared in disbelief at the senior partner. "You never cease to amaze me, Austin. A man dies and you count the loss in dollars. I'm surprised you don't mention how this solves the severance problem."

"We wanted him severed," said Barrington, his dark eyes turning to flint, "not dead. But since you mention it, that's the silver lining."

"Was it his heart? A stroke?"

"Neither. Either spontaneous combustion in a closet or his space heater blew up. His cottage went up like a matchbox."

Rachel, thought Kevin, *how will I tell her? She loved the old fellow.* "What a way to go," he said quietly. "Leave any family?"

"It turns out there's a sister who had not spoken to him in years. Your own view concerning my compassion to the contrary notwithstanding, I felt that I would be obliged to break the news to whoever survived him. She says she's the only one."

"Perhaps she'll substitute into the suit as executrix."

"No," said Barrington, clearing his throat. "I asked her that, as a matter of fact."

"Got right down to business, I see. 'Your brother's dead, ma'am, want to make a buck?' "

"That's enough of that, Kevin," Barrington said sharply. "She heard about the other deaths and seemed a little nervous about getting involved. She instructed me to dismiss the case, and I've done so."

"Does Rachel know?"

"Conti told her late yesterday afternoon."

"*Conti.* That's nice," said Kevin, running his hand through his hair. Of course it would be Conti to tell her, offer his shoulder to cry on, exploit the situation. Kevin, who had so far held the line against drinking before noon, suddenly felt the need to bend the rules.

Barrington interrupted Kevin's unhealthy musings. "I'd like you to sit in on my meeting with Conti. It will come as no surprise to you that our little crimebuster has had his pet theory resuscitated by this most recent tragedy. He was prowling around here late yesterday insisting on seeing the records of Hallinan, Weisberg, and Dixon."

"That could present a problem," said Kevin. "If Conti finds out about Dixon's chlordane, the defendants will soon know about it also."

"Exactly my point," said Barrington, holding up a thin folder in front of Kevin. "That's why we've got to get rid of his records."

Kevin looked at the manila folder with the name "Emmett Dixon" neatly typed on the side. It seemed impossible that this was all that was left of a man he had spoken with just a week earlier. "Jesus, Austin, it seems a bit too coldly efficient. The man's not even buried yet."

"That may be true," countered Barrington, "but the good lieutenant will be walking through that door in about forty-five minutes and for all I know, he may have a search warrant this time. You're supposed to be one of the smartest lawyers around; you tell me what's wrong with destroying the records of an ex-client who's been dismissed from the case."

"You know as well as I do," said Kevin mechanically, "that we're entitled. The case is closed and dismissed."

"Exactly. Come with me for a moment. I want you to witness this in the event Gardner White suffers another one of his ever-increasing anxiety attacks."

Puzzled, Kevin followed Barrington into his private bathroom and was surprised to see the senior partner remove his gold lighter and begin applying it to the documents, two or three at a time, over the urinal.

"Isn't this a bit on the cloak-and-dagger side, Austin? It seems so . . . tacky."

"We're protecting the client's privacy," said Barrington, lighting the last of the papers.

"What we're really doing," said Kevin flatly, staring at the building flames with a strange, detached look, "is protecting *our* privacy; destroying evidence, to put it more directly."

"If you must put it directly," said Barrington.

But Kevin no longer heard him; he had retreated within his own guilt. Staring at the hypnotic flame, he recalled a night at Elaine's in New York when he was told to make a wish, then to light the bottom of a tubular cookie wrapper. He was assured that if it rose from its own convective heat toward the ceiling, his wish would be granted. *If I had but one wish now,* thought Kevin, *it would be that I had stopped this insanity when I first heard about it.* Perspiration dotted his forehead as he watched the flame grow brighter, felt himself lost in the flashing yellow tongues of fire. He vaguely heard Barrington's distant voice: ". . . And with this gone, we're absolutely clear . . ." Kevin continued to stare at the flame and was vaguely conscious that a black butterfly of ash was rising from one of the charred sheets toward the ceiling.

He began laughing, quietly at first, then louder. "What's so damn funny?" grunted Barrington.

"Your wish will be granted," said Kevin, staring at a black smudge the ash had deposited on the ceiling. "Your wish, my wish, Dixon's wish . . ."

"Kevin! Go out and wait for me in the conference area. Get hold of yourself!"

"Gladly," said Kevin, leaving the bathroom.

Kevin heard Barrington flush the toilet for the last time and reenter the office, vigorously drying his hands. His voice as he addressed Kevin was now warm, even sympathetic. "It's Dixon, isn't it? I didn't know you two were that close."

"We weren't," said Kevin, seeming himself again. "It's a lot of things, Austin."

"Are you sure you're okay?" asked Barrington, standing over Kevin, a huge ham of a hand resting firmly on his shoulder.

"I'm fine," he lied, absurdly hoping Austin would offer him a drink. Instead, Barrington walked to the telephone and buzzed Miss Tarkenton. "Has Lieutenant Conti arrived yet?"

"Please hold, Mr. Barrington," came the raspy voice, audible even to Kevin. "I'll check with reception."

Barrington drummed on his desktop, then reentered his bathroom. Kevin heard water running. *Final checking,* thought Kevin. *The man is nothing if not meticulous.*

"Yes, Mr. Barrington," came Miss Tarkenton's voice over the intercom speaker. "He is meeting with Ms. Cannon."

Kevin's head snapped up. "*What?* How long has he been there? He might as well take an office here," he added. "At least we'd get some rent out of the little shit."

"Kevin," Barrington instructed him, "get down to Rachel's office right away and break that up. But do it *casually*, Kevin. Tell them that I'm waiting for him and have another meeting to attend. And be civil for God's sake."

Kevin approached Rachel's open door slowly, catching snatches of their conversation. "I have all the pressure I need right now, Dan—"

"I know that, Rachel, that's why I want you to get off this case. You don't have to consult the stars or study the entrails of a hawk to see that—"

Kevin fought for control as he loudly cleared his throat and said, "I see we have a new assigning partner now. How nice, Inspector Conti, that you could take the time off from your busy schedule to instruct our associates on whether they're on or off a case."

"Relax, Mr. Stone. I'm sure we're both concerned about the same thing. There's a murderer out there who has warned her to do the same thing. I am simply urging her to take his advice, at least until I can get some cooperation out of you people and stop him."

Kevin slowly shook his head and exhaled, remembering Barrington's admonition. "Look, Conti, we can't stop you from trying to turn these accidents into murder, but unless you have a warrant or specific authority, you're to stop harassing our staff. Austin Barrington is waiting. Follow me."

"Kevin," interceded Rachel, "he wasn't harassing me. He was only concerned—"

"Oh, I'm aware of his concern, Rachel," said Kevin, keeping his hard gaze fixed on Conti. "And as long as you keep welcoming it, he'll keep right on providing it. Let's go, Lieutenant. Now!"

"Kevin," said Rachel, "listen to him. He may have a point here."

"Please, Mr. Stone," said Conti, smiling and seeming unperturbed. "All I want or need from you is a look at the decedents' medical records. Clearly your plaintiffs are being chopped down in the descending order of their monetary threat to North American. You can no longer deny it, Mr. Stone. I think the medical records of the three decedents will confirm it and force my reluctant captain into a full, formal investigation. And by the way, the medical records might even permit prediction of the next victim so that we could provide focused protection."

"What you're telling me," said Kevin, "is that you still have no search warrant. And what I am telling you is to stay away from here."

"Mr. Stone, I am trying to explain to you the reasons why I can't do that. You see, unless I stop him—or them—somebody is going to keep on killing your clients. The funny thing is," he added, slowly shaking his head, "nobody seems to care but me."

"The only funny thing," Kevin said sharply, "is a publicity-happy policeman who's trying to turn a series of tragic mishaps into serial murders so that he can round up the whole Mafia."

Conti's half smile vanished. "You refuse to turn over the records of the Group A plaintiffs? I must ask you that for the record, Mr. Stone."

"Yes, I refuse. On the same grounds as before: the attorney/client privilege and the attorney work-product privilege."

"Then give me the records of Hallinan, Weisberg, and Dixon. You don't represent them anymore."

"You're right for once—and for that very reason their records no longer exist."

"You've destroyed their records?"

"All right, you two," Rachel cut in, "I think you've both forgotten that you are in my office and that I've got work to do."

"I'll leave," said Dan with a penetrating glance at Kevin, "but I won't stop." Then, shifting his gaze to Rachel he added meaningfully, "I'm a very patient man."

Kevin returned Conti's hard look. "And Austin Barrington is not. I'll tell him that we have already had our talk and that you've left. Come back when you have a search warrant . . . and not before."

Kevin stalked out of Rachel's office, pointedly leaving the door open.

"I'm sorry about this, Rachel," said Dan. "But don't you see what's going on here?"

"Dan. I don't *care* what's going on here! And I cannot and will not take any more pressure from you! I'm still an associate here trying desperately to become a partner, and I simply can't go behind the senior partner's back to help you. And even if I wanted to, Barrington alone sees those medical records. I have no access to them."

Dan seized Rachel roughly by the shoulders and spoke in a tone totally alien from anything she had seen in him. "Then *get* access."

"That's really what you want from me, isn't it, Dan?" said Rachel, her eyes blazing back at his. "That's what you've always wanted."

"Rachel, it's not that way—"

Rachel shook free of his grasp. "Listen, Dan. Like the man said, the next communication I have with you will be pursuant to a court order. Now, please leave."

"Come on, Rachel, I really didn't mean—"

"Now!" she repeated.

Dan's extended arms fell noisily against his hips, then he turned and walked slowly out.

Kevin strode back to Barrington's office like a middleweight boxer, fighting the grim reality that his anger at Conti was rooted

in jealousy and fear, his two most despised emotions. Jealousy—
because Conti was clearly an announced rival for Rachel, and
Kevin knew she couldn't be expected to wait forever. Fear—
because he saw in Conti that same powerful intuition that he
himself possessed. *Am I being paranoid?* Kevin asked himself.
No, he thought. Conti was the enemy all right, now threatening
the two things in life he held most dear: his future with Rachel
and his very freedom. He realized that he had never hated
anyone the way he now hated that meddling little cop. Too bad
that Conti, not Dixon, wasn't in that house when it went up in
flames!

Kevin stopped dead in his tracks. *What am I thinking?* he
asked himself. *What in the hell is happening to me?* He squeezed
his eyes shut tight, then opened them and started walking again,
more deliberately now, as if to calm the maelstrom inside his
throbbing head. There was, after all, no way Conti could be
suspicious. What could his so-called "murders" have to do with
the artificial supplement? Not even intuition can make connections where none exist. We'd be better off just to give him the
damn records now that the last chlordane exposure is safely out
of the picture, he thought; otherwise, the little bastard is going to
keep thinking we're hiding something, which is crazy because
what we've been hiding has no connection whatsoever to his
fantasy serial murders.

Or does it?

A blade of ice stabbed at his backbone, nearly freezing his
movement again as he reached the outer door to Barrington's
office.

What if . . . Oh Christ, no, he thought. *It's too absurd.* Yet
Dixon's demise undeniably provided a convenient solution to an
otherwise insoluble problem. How did Austin put it? A "silver
lining." As Kevin passed through Barrington's doorway, the
coldness spread out from his spine, and by the time he had
walked through Miss Tarkenton's entry office, he knew he had
to put some difficult questions to his partner.

"Ah, Kevin. Where's the good inspector?"

"I'm afraid I didn't manage the assignment very well," said
Kevin grimly. "I caught him pressuring Rachel to provide medical records."

"And?"

"And," said Kevin, forcing a smile, "I more or less threw
him out of the office."

"Well," said Barrington, "I suppose there's no use catering to him any longer. Even if he comes back with his search warrant, he can't hurt us now." The senior partner returned to the file he had been reading.

"Austin?"

"Yes?"

"Why did you destroy Hallinan's and Weisberg's medical records?"

"Why? Why not? With the great Kevin Stone as my authority, there was neither need nor legal reason to keep them."

"But we had a good reason to destroy Dixon's records. A very specific reason. They showed that you had administered chlordane. I think you destroyed Hallinan's and Weisberg's records for the same reason."

"Very good," said Barrington without looking up. "To the head of the class with you."

The sensation of coldness that Kevin had felt across his back now spread to his face, to his chest. The immobilizing chill ran down his arms into his hands. He sat down in one of Barrington's client chairs because the sensation had spread down his legs, rendering them weak. He felt ill as he sat staring at the floor, seeing nothing. Just the truth. The harsh, ugly truth.

"Kevin, you'll have to excuse me. As I told you, I have an important meeting at ten. Kevin?"

Kevin slowly raised his eyes to meet Barrington's, and when the words finally forced their way into the room, he was surprised at how calm his voice sounded: "But you didn't just destroy their records, did you, Austin? That wasn't enough. You had to destroy the old men as well. You had all three of those people killed so that the defense medical examinations would not reveal the presence of chlordane in their blood or tissue samples, chlordane inadvertently supplied by your brilliant friend Newkirk."

Barrington did not reply, but merely lit a cigarette, then leaned back and exhaled smoke, looking at Kevin in a way that instantly confirmed his worst fears. Slowly, he lifted himself from his chair and walked to the north window-wall, where he stood motionless, arms folded, looking out over the Golden Gate Bridge toward the Pacific Ocean. Finally, he began to speak in a tone that was resigned, but without apology. "All right, Kevin, you're entitled to the complete story. Actually, you've already had most of it. All I failed to tell you—to protect you, of course—is that Newkirk initially discovered that same damnable chlordane in the blood and tissue samples of both Hallinan and Weisberg. I blew my stack, of course, but there was no way to undo the damage. To complicate matters, both of them were scheduled for defense medical examinations and biological testing within the next few weeks. This was back in late May. You will recall, Hancock was accusing us of stalling. I was desperate, Kevin. I didn't know what to do.''

Even in his anguished state Kevin realized that this was the first time he'd noticed a contriteness in Barrington's tone, not from guilt over what he had done, but that for once in his life he simply hadn't known what to do. Kevin wondered whether Barrington's own difficult role in life—the man who is always right and keeps everyone under control—was made harder or easier by his apparent lack of awareness that he was in fact playing a role. But maybe he wasn't playing a role at all. Was everyone Kevin knew simply playing himself and only Kevin acting a role? Another wave of damp heat coursed through his body and he wondered if he was going crazy. Could his recent preoccupation with roles portend a total break with reality? Well, maybe that wouldn't be such a bad thing right now.

Meanwhile, Barrington dragged deeply on his cigarette, and Kevin was conscious of wanting one badly. ''You will never know, Kevin, how I agonized over the decision. On one side I had these two old men, one who had insisted on artificial supplement and one who was scheduled to die within the next several months from natural causes anyway. Neither would leave relatives or loved ones.

''On the other side, I had well over one hundred people whose lives had been genuinely shattered by the North American Chemical Company, and whose only hope for a decent few years of life rested on our shoulders, Kevin—yours and mine. Christ, I don't have to tell you what Alan Hancock would have done with all the other plaintiffs once he had found chlordane in just two of them. We've already been through all that. The defense would simply have established that one of the most deadly chemicals in the case had entered our clients' drinking water *from some other source*. All one hundred forty-seven cases would have been thrown into doubt. *What was I to do?''*

Kevin felt very tired. *As soon as I call the police, I'll go to bed and sleep until they come for me. It's over. I can sleep now.* All he had to do was get up, go to his office, and call Dan Conti. He raised his head and managed to look Barrington squarely in the eye. "What you did is monstrous, Austin," he said finally. "You can talk all day, but nothing can justify it. Nothing." *Now the harder part,* he thought, *the part about getting to his feet and calling Conti.*

Barrington, meanwhile, ignored Kevin's comment and continued his peroration, a hypnotic drone that Kevin felt powerless to turn off. "It was necessary, of course, not only to eliminate Hallinan and Weisberg from the case, but to insure that they be disposed of in a way that would eliminate the possibility of autopsy or post-mortem testing. Finding someone to do this took two and a half weeks. You'd be surprised, incidentally, how many people there are out there who are willing to kill someone for a few dollars. But to find a truly professional assassin—competent as well as discreet—was no easy matter." Kevin noticed that Barrington could not keep a note of pride out of his voice and manner. He walked back over to his desk and crushed his cigarette into a bronze ashtray with a single stabbing motion. Austin Barrington, thought Kevin absently, never wastes himself on the slightest unnecessary movement.

"I worked backward through a good friend in a New York law firm who used to be with the U.S. attorney's office. He had no idea what kind of information he was giving me, but it wasn't hard to make the contacts one step at a time. Our man fulfilled his end of the bargain by insuring that each death appeared to be accidental or suicidal *and* that the bodies were sufficiently destroyed to avoid autopsy or testing."

Kevin noticed that Barrington, for all his apparent composure, looked ten years older now in October 1983 than he had just a year and a half earlier, when all this had begun. He experienced a brief stab of sympathy, a feeling he quickly dispelled to avoid a concomitant sense of his own corruption. While studying Barrington's face, Kevin misconstrued the brief pause in the senior partner's discourse as completion and began to summon the strength to rise and do what he must do. But Barrington was far from finished.

"I know all this sounds insane coming to you for the first time, but put yourself in my position. I could not let these two old men—well, three now—who had already lived long, full lives and who were dying anyway, destroy the hopes and dreams of nearly a hundred and fifty clients, who were depending on us for medical treatment, nursing care, and a decent last few years. Can't you understand that?"

Kevin shivered, then whispered, "No, I can't. You played God. You had no right."

"I had no *choice*!" Barrington slammed his hand down noisily on the desk and strode to where Kevin now sat, hunched over, hands pressed together between his thighs. "*Surely* you can see that," he said. "How could I have sacrificed this law firm, and a hundred and fifty clients to whom we owed the highest professional duty, for three terminally ill old men, one of whom had created this whole damn problem in the first place!"

Kevin was vaguely aware of warm breath on his neck and the faint smell of stale tobacco. He felt Barrington's hand on his shoulder as the senior partner continued: "And then there is Adrian Fisher—I know you don't give a crap about Gardner White, and neither do I—but *Adrian*! To allow Adrian to go to prison would have been to pronounce his death sentence." Barrington moved around in front of Kevin and leaned back against the front of his desk, their legs almost touching. "Yes, I may have played God, but now it's your turn, Kevin. You must make the same decision: whether to save Adrian, your clients, and the rest of us, on the one hand, or to make Dan Conti a hero, on the other. Your call, old boy." Kevin's eyes involuntarily flashed and Barrington, ever the perceptive trial lawyer, must have noticed the spark ignited by the mere mention of Conti's name. "But other than making Conti a hero," he continued, "tell me one thing you would accomplish. You can't bring them back, Kevin. So, you see? You have the same decision I had, but your path is so much easier. Your burden so much lighter. All you have to do, Kevin, is do *nothing*. Nothing at all. Simple acceptance of what is now beyond your power to alter. That's all. Simple acceptance. You can't change anything that's happened. Neither of us can do a damn thing for those three dead men now. It's time to leave the dead to bury the dead. Your duty, like mine, is now to the living, including yourself."

Kevin was assailed by a touch of vertigo and had to dig fingernails into his palms to steady himself. He tried to think of his hands as the base of a triangle, at the top of which must be his head. But if this were so, why couldn't his head then simply command his legs to rise and move the rest of him out of this room, away from this voice? But Barrington's words now came in a rush, though his tone had modulated to a more sympathetic key.

"Listen to me, Kevin. You're no kid anymore. We've talked

about this, but isn't it time you gave yourself a break? Haven't you been thinking about what I said before? Isn't it getting a little tougher every year out there? Everybody out to beat you, cases getting tougher, clients expecting more? How many more stressful years do you want to spend getting sucked dry by clients who gross five times what you make every year?" Barrington now moved to Kevin's side, bent down beside him on one knee. Kevin felt the huge arm again encircle his shoulder. He could smell Barrington's expensive aftershave as the embrace tightened. Kevin was suddenly conscious that he could no longer warm his hands.

"I'm doing all right," he offered lamely, his voice as thin as a gum wrapper.

"You haven't fooled me, Kevin. Remember, I've been in your place myself. I saw the first signs of it in your eyes long before you started hitting the cocktail circuit. By the way—where was it last night? Mulhern's? Washington Square Bar & Grill? *Perry's*, for God's sake? You're getting a bit ragged around the edges, old boy, and you know it. But your four-million-dollar share in the North American fees will secure your future. And there's something else, Kevin. The Table last week decided to expand to a foursome, at least until Adrian decides to take his overdue retirement. And you'll be at that table, Kevin. You'll be by far the youngest of the three of us, so I don't have to spell out the rest, do I? I'm not getting any younger either, Kevin, believe me."

Barrington, weary from his effort, exhaled audibly as he lifted himself up with great apparent effort and stood behind the still-seated Kevin. Placing both hands on Kevin's shoulders, he added in the quiet tone of a foregone conclusion: "Cumulative events—none of which could have been foreseen—bind you and me together, Kevin. Neither of us can accomplish anything constructive by surrendering Conti his victims. The past cannot be altered, but the future is in our hands, the future of our clients and our firm."

Barrington paused, seeing that Kevin was about to break his silence again.

"That business with Rachel. Why in God's name did you have her condo broken into?"

"Isn't it obvious?" asked Barrington. "Can you think of a better way to divert suspicion from us than to have threats made against us?"

"But why Rachel?" asked Kevin.

"Because the most efficient way of getting misinformation to Conti was through his girlfriend."

Kevin's shoulder muscles tightened under the weight of Barrington's last words. Silence engulfed the room but for the ticking of the grandfather clock in Barrington's entryway. The portrait of Whit Stafford looked down upon the scene, while diffused light from the muted sun fell across Barrington's back. For a moment, staring at the portrait of the founding partner, Kevin could see the scene—and himself—as it might have appeared to the great Stafford: a young man, a boy even, dwarfed by the spacious office, the seventeenth-century Mediterranean credenza bearing a bronze scales of justice, the fortress of a desk, the presence of Austin Barrington, whose own massive stature dominated the younger man, on whose shoulders those giant hands remained resting so firmly.

Waiting.

When Kevin finally spoke, he asked a question that gave Barrington his answer.

"Who else knows?"

Barrington applied a firm pat to Kevin's shoulder, then walked back around behind his desk. "Nobody, not even Adrian or Gardner know about the . . . more recent developments. Adrian is no fool, of course, and may have figured it out when he heard about Dixon, but he doesn't need or want confirmation."

Barrington stared at Kevin, waiting for his next words. When they came, they were anticlimactic—like a referee's gun sounding the end of a lopsided game.

"I'd better get ready for my eleven o'clock deposition," he said, glancing at his watch and walking from the room.

THIRTY-EIGHT

∎

Barrington sat at his usual table at Jack's Restaurant, rehearsing in his mind what he would say to Captain Mahan. It would be important to push hard enough to gain token police protection for the S.P.&M. staff, yet avoid creating the impression that he felt Conti was right in wanting to launch a full-scale investigation. It would be a delicate operation despite Mahan's obtuse nature.

He sipped his Glenlivet and permitted himself a moment of relaxed satisfaction as he awaited the arrival of the police captain. Jack's Restaurant always soothed him; it was the one restaurant outside the Club worth walking to. It looked and felt the way a restaurant should. He liked the way the waiters—some even older than he—greeted him in a way that caused curious strangers' eyes to glance surreptitiously in his direction. *Hello, Mr. Barrington. Your drink is coming right up, Mr. Barrington. We have your favorite today, Mr. Barrington.* He liked the overlighted and spacious room, its soaring ceiling with bas-reliefs high on the walls, and brass coat hooks always within easy reach. This was a straight-from-the-shoulder place to eat fine French country cooking, right down to the simple white tablecloths, the carefully beveled mirrors, and, most important of all, a tradition that even preceded Stafford, Parrish, and MacAllister in time. Barrington's beloved Montgomery Street was a quagmire of oozing mud, connected by random planks and boardwalks, when Jack's had been born in 1864. While the Comstock Lode poured silver, Jack's had poured drinks downstairs and provided ladies upstairs. Destroyed in the 1906 earthquake, Jack's Restaurant had emerged from the ashes and was restored to the same spot: 615 Sacramento Street, where it had served the San Francisco elite ever since. Jack London had dined here, Louie Lurie reigned over his real estate empire here, Whit Stafford controlled San Francisco politics here, and now Austin Barrington was proud to be one of the few men to command his own table, an honor accorded only rarely in the restaurant's century-long history. Louis Lurie had held his for fifty-five years. Whitcomb Stafford had enjoyed this privilege for ten years before his death in 1958, and Barrington had been granted permanent rights to the very same table in 1971. As he glanced at the empty bentwood chair that Mahan would soon occupy, he wondered how many congressmen, mayors, and police chiefs had fallen prey to Stafford's cunning at this very spot.

Barrington's reverie was interrupted by the arrival of Captain Mahan. The heavyset red-faced captain was a sight to behold in a baggy blue-green herringbone suit that seemed to change colors as he moved. *Where does one get a suit like that?* pondered Barrington while conveying just the opposite impression—respect and sincerity—by his warm handshake and greeting. "Fred, my friend, you're looking wonderful! How have you been?"

"I've been worse," said Fred Mahan. He smiled broadly, revealing a one-eighth-inch gap between his two front teeth which gave his entire face a rough, disheveled look. All in all, Fred Mahan was a man totally lacking in style, an impediment particularly obvious when he was not in uniform. He took his seat opposite Barrington, looking like a stevedore wearing a stolen suit.

Mahan glanced around the room with a furtive but respectful attitude and said, "I wish the other police commissioners had your good taste in restaurants, Austin. Do they still have the best fish in town here?"

"Actually," said Barrington agreeably but in a manner that subtly began to assert control, "the fish *is* quite good—the Rex sole meunière and sole marguéry are the best in town—but one must avoid the tourist's misconception that this is another San Francisco fish restaurant. The thing to order here, in my opinion, is the mutton chop; beautifully aged—cut it with your fork."

"You don't say?" said Mahan. "I just might try that myself."

"Good," said Barrington, "let's start with some Olympia oysters and a celery root salad."

At that moment, the waiter placed Mahan's double bourbon with a splash of water—ordered beforehand by Barrington—in front of him. It was a flattering gesture that brought another broad smile to the captain's pumpkin face. The men toasted—"Happy Pearl Harbor Day," said the captain wryly—and engaged in the small talk that inevitably preceded major agenda items; indeed, not until lunch was winding down and the captain had asked, "So how's business at your shop?" did Barrington seize the moment he had been waiting for.

"Couldn't be better," Barrington replied. "You may have heard that our trial date went over to December thirteenth."

"Only a week away," said Mahan. "Are you ready to sock it to 'em?"

"We should do quite well indeed." Barrington signaled the waiter for coffee. "Care for dessert? They offer a nicely glazed rum omelet I think you'd enjoy." The portly captain shook his head, patting his bloated stomach. "Understood," said Barrington, nodding sympathetically. "In any event, as you recall, we were plagued with two accidents and a suicide between June and early October, taking three out of our first fifteen plaintiffs."

"Do I *recall*!" Mahan exclaimed. "My young homicide inspector has been driving me—and probably you, too—nuts since that fire your client died in last month. Conti. Sorry about him."

"A conscientious young man, no doubt about it. I suppose it's important to have people around who see a disaster lurking around every corner. Occasionally they're going to be right, you know." *That smokescreen of tolerance should elicit exactly what he thinks about Conti*, thought Barrington, studying the captain's open face.

"He's a good enough cop, all right. I probably put up with too much from him. You might say he's a protégé of mine." Mahan paused. "He's a fanatic all right, but a damn good cop. 'Course he's as full of shit as a Christmas goose this time, although there *is* something that worries me about this one."

Barrington's voice betrayed nothing but idle curiosity: "Oh? What's that?"

"That message scrawled on your young associate's bathroom mirror: 'Get off the case' or something like that. What do your people make of that?"

"Well, for what it's worth," said Barrington, "I think some antifeminist crank saw an opportunity to terrorize a young female lawyer who—let me tell you in strictest confidence—is about to become a partner in my law firm."

"You don't say? Going liberal on us, huh, Austin?"

"You know better than that, Fred—you've known me too long. But this girl is going to be important to me in this case. It would certainly make her more effective if she had the security a little police protection could provide. Nothing elaborate and only for the next few weeks. Can you spare a good man? Or maybe I should say 'can you spare a good woman?' ''

Both laughed, knowing Mahan's sensitivity to recent demands for more female members on the police force and his well-publicized but grudging acceptance of the inevitable.

"Sure. No problem. Dan Conti had a man on her for a while until I found out about it. I'll put somebody back on it. I assume Conti has her address?"

"I'm sure he does," said Barrington, containing a smile. "Speaking of Conti, there is one other little thing you could do for me. Your young lieutenant's fertile imagination has involved a great deal of my staff's time over the past several months. It's been several weeks now since the Dixon mishap; may I assume that we will not be bothered during this difficult trial period by your young fanatic?"

"No sweat," grunted Mahan. "If he takes just one step inside your offices, you'll be doing me a favor by letting me know, and I'll have him walking a beat south of Market Street in ten minutes."

"Well, don't misunderstand me, Fred. I hardly know the man, and I'm sure he's a fine police officer. We all lose our heads once in a while—I've done it myself on a case or two—but this situation . . . well, I appreciate your cooperation. Another whiskey?"

Later that afternoon the trial staff gathered for its final weekly team meeting and an interview with Dr. Judith Barkheim, the psychologist who would be working with Kevin and Barrington during the jury-selection process. Barrington, Kevin, Rachel, Jeffrey, and Stu Wallach were seated around the senior partner's conference table as Dr. Barkheim finished reviewing the status of her firm's preparation.

"So, having analyzed the results of our survey of San Francisco residents typical of those who will make up your jury," the psychologist said in a forceful, efficient voice, "and having found them to possess a surprisingly low level of sensitivity to the matter of contaminated water in general, we provided Ms. Cannon with what we thought had to be done to fill this vacuum in the opening statement and to minimize cognitive dissonance when the jury begins hearing the testimony."

"Cognitive dissonance?" interrupted Barrington, his skepticism obvious. "The words you people use these days are sometimes more confusing than enlightening. This is beginning to remind me of my first meeting with Desmond Childhouse—the same damn déjà vu all over again.''

Jeffrey leaned over and whispered into Rachel's ear: ''Holy shit—a triple redundancy!'' Rachel stifled a grin while Dr. Barkheim explained that jurors do not leave their prejudices and personal experiences behind; they try to focus the trial issues in a way that is compatible with these prejudices and any other generalized community values.

''It turns out,'' she continued, ''that your jurors will probably not realize that most drinking water is contaminated to a greater or lesser extent. We have, therefore, included a great deal of information in the opening statement which we'll videotape tomorrow. Our objective will be to stir them up a bit, bring the issue home to them, break through their complacency, get them angry at the defendants. We'll test our success by showing our videotaped opening statement to randomly selected surrogate jurors, then interviewing them in depth to get their reactions. We will then rework the opening statement to meet any remaining objections of the people interviewed.''

''Sounds good,'' said Kevin in a hoarse voice Rachel attributed to his smoking. ''Tailor our opening statement and proof to the jury's own values and beliefs.''

''Exactly,'' said Dr. Barkheim, who then explained her own role in trying to select jurors at trial who will typify the community attitudes. ''I will observe them from the time their names are drawn by the court clerk through to their selection or rejection. I will be looking at much the same things you do: how they are dressed, the condition of their shoes, what if any jewelry they wear—I can tell you worlds about a man just by looking at his watch—accent, voice tone, and, of course, what they say in answer to questions which I will assist you in framing. When it comes time for you to accept or reject a juror, I will simply touch my right ear if I believe the juror is acceptable, or the left one if I don't. I recognize that my role is only advisory, but I think you will find it helpful.''

Barrington was impressed, and reluctantly said so. Jeffrey, however, was not. ''This sounds like jury-stacking to me,'' he said.

Kevin swiftly interceded. ''Johnstone—please. Let's thrash that issue out at our next Tuesday staff meeting or, better yet, over a victory drink after the trial.''

Everyone smiled, but Dr. Barkheim had the last word: "You lawyers have been trying to stack your juries for years, sir; we're just helping you do it more effectively."

"She's got us there, Jeff," said Kevin.

"There is something else I would like to say," said Dr. Barkheim with an apologetic smile, "although I find it a bit awkward because of my gender."

"Go ahead," said Kevin. "Speak freely."

"All right, I will. Estimates for this trial run from a minimum of six weeks to as high now as ten or eleven weeks. Most executives will excuse themselves because of the press of business and, because most executives are still male, you are going to end up with a heavy majority of female jurors, as you always do in long cases. Our past surveys on long trials clearly tell us that women jurors tend to identify with the side that has a woman lawyer—fully involved, of course, not just put on display at counsel table and occasionally dusted off."

Barrington smiled, saying, "I think I know where you're going, Doctor, so let me save you some time. I've given this very matter considerable thought and have reached a decision: Rachel Cannon will make our opening statement."

Rachel was so stunned she did not notice the look of surprise on Kevin's face as well. By the time she turned to him, he had regained his composure sufficiently to give her a half smile as he ground his cigarette butt into an ashtray. Before Rachel could speak, Dr. Barkheim, who was already clicking her briefcase shut, said, "An excellent decision, Mr. Barrington. Having Rachel merely sit at the counsel table might have suggested tokenism to the female jurors and perhaps even have offended some of them. Jurors aren't easily fooled."

Barrington smiled. "Thanks for coming in, Dr. Barkheim," he said. "We look forward to working with you on this case. Okay, people," he added, "that does it for today. Kevin, Rachel, I'll see you back here at four o'clock. We'll go over to Hancock's office together for the settlement conference.

"Incidentally," he added, "although I am convinced that the deaths of our three clients were purely tragic coincidence, there remains the matter of the break-in at Rachel's condominium in late September. I just had lunch with Captain Mahan of the Police Department and was able to pressure him into providing us with limited police protection. His personal belief, as well as mine, is that this was the sick joke of a crank, but one we cannot take lightly. So watch yourselves.''

The associates and Stu Wallach filed out of the office in a disciplined manner, but broke ranks immediately once they were in the hallway. ''Can you believe it?'' cried Jeffrey, trying to control the volume of his voice. ''Rachel Cannon—*making the opening statement*!''

They all knew that the literature was now persuasive: Over eighty percent of interviewed jurors admitted they had made up their minds during or just after opening statements. The subsequent evidence and closing arguments thus merely support a decision the jury has already made. To Rachel, then, would go much of the glory for victory . . . and all of the responsibility for defeat. *Be careful what you ask for,* thought Rachel, the old cliché never more appropriate, *you just might get it.* She had hoped for some additional direct examination, a little cross-examination maybe—but the opening! Kevin must have sold his soul to Austin for this. How, she thought, can I ever repay him?

''Congratulations,'' Stu Wallach was saying. ''You'll be terrific. Most lawyers wait a lifetime for an opportunity like this.''

''And the newspapers, Rachel, the goddamn press!'' added Jeffrey. ''*Newsweek, Time, The Wall Street Journal,* they'll all be there to cover the biggest monetary verdict of all time! And there, from Hutchinson, Kansas, in the white wings and halo, the golden scales of justice held high above her glowing head, stands Rachel Cannon, girl lawyer!''

''Okay, okay, Jeff. Now all I've got to do is deliver! If we lose the first trial, guess who will be a convenient scapegoat just when it's time for a decision on that particular lawyer's partnership? Blaming my opening could give the moral majority the excuse they need to dump me—the way they dumped Beth.''

''But if we *win,* Rache. If we *win,* you're home free! And what could possibly stop us now?''

Kevin, meanwhile, had remained standing in the conference area, glaring at Barrington, trying to read the motivation behind his cold, dispassionate eyes.

''I take it,'' said Barrington finally, breaking the tense silence between them, ''that you disagree with my uncharacteristic display of fair play and tolerance for the weaker sex?''

''I think you've gone barking mad, Austin. You know the significance of the opening statement as well as I. Rachel's good but she's too young to be saddled with this kind of responsibility. Besides, I expected . . . I assumed that I would—''

"Oh, come now, Kevin! This is no time for nursing our egos."

Ego, thought Kevin, knowing what Denise would say about this humiliating maneuver. She would be utterly convinced that Barrington, apprehensive about delivering the opening himself, had given it to Rachel to avoid being upstaged by a younger partner who was already far too popular with the press. "But bear in mind," Barrington continued, "that I—you and I—shall approve Rachel's outline in advance; I'll fly-speck every word! So cheer up, Kevin. She's an unusually bright and talented girl." The senior partner paused and arched a thoughtful eyebrow as he added, "I'm rather surprised, in fact, that you've never suggested she be given a more active role."

Rachel's phone was ringing as she entered her office. "Inspector Conti," came the voice of her secretary. "He says it's important."

Rachel's first impulse was to have her secretary report that she was out and to call back early next year. She hadn't seen Dan for two months (though he continued to pester her by telephone), and she felt oddly guilty and resentful about this at the same time. She was becoming disappointed in Dan and, ironically, angry that his insensitive persistence was destroying her affection for him. It had happened before with other men. She ultimately came to see their affection as fawning, their compliments as flattery, their courtesy as weakness. She would become hypercritical of even the most normal male weakness until, suddenly, all feeling would be gone. This introspection put into question her capacity to love *any* man—an extremely depressing thought.

Tolerance, she thought as she picked up the phone. *Give the guy a break*. "Hello, Dan."

After a few seconds of silence a subdued voice said, "It's been a while, Rachel. How are things going?"

"Fine. How have you been?"

"Same old game," said Dan, followed by another few seconds of silence and then a sharp exhale. "I've missed you, counselor. I called to wish you luck. I read in the paper that the trial starts next week, but, to tell you the truth, I also called to try one last time to get your help."

Rachel felt her good mood evaporate, her joy at the new assignment temporarily swept away.

"I know what you're thinking, Rachel," he added in a pleading tone. "Just hear me out. It took forever but I finally found the very last purchaser of Equator Space Heater number 641-B. I have now accounted for every space heater like the one found in Dixon's bedroom sold in northern California in the past two years. None of them was purchased by Dixon, and not one of Dixon's friends, including a Veterans Administration doctor who visited him several times when he was ill, ever saw a space heater like that in his bedroom. Rachel, he never had one. His cottage was small, but it had a central heating system that worked, according to the arson squad."

Rachel said nothing, listening to the silence.

"Rachel . . . your friend was murdered. Somebody went in there with that rigged heater and blew him up."

Rachel's shoulders fell, and she leaned against her desk as fatigue reasserted itself. "Dan, I—"

"Listen to me, Rachel. I'm not asking for much. Just a shot at stopping the next innocent victim from being murdered. All I want is a look at the medical records. I know you've turned over the twelve remaining Group A plaintiffs' medical records to the defense, but they're under seal and I can't get access to them. Newkirk and the internists won't talk to me without signed consents to release medical records. I also need to see—"

"Dan, stop it!"

"No, Rachel, I won't stop it. If you'll show them to defense counsel so that they can defend North American against your clients, why the hell won't you show them to me so that I can defend your clients against North American! Rachel? Are you there?"

"Yes, I'm here," said Rachel, unable to deny the logic of Dan's argument. "I need time to think, Dan. I'll call you. I've got to go now."

Rachel hung up the phone, grabbed her coat, told her secretary she'd be back in thirty minutes, then left the building. Once on the street, she paused for a moment, trying to decide which of her two places of meditative refuge she would seek. When chaos and confusion threatened to overwhelm her—more and more frequently of late—she often drove out along the Bay to the old South Embarcadero area and drank a beer or an Irish coffee on the outside deck of the old Mission Rock Resort, a rustic oasis in the middle of urban confusion, that catered to fishermen and the occasional outlander seeking a friendly atmosphere. When chaos accelerated to apparent catastrophe, however, she chose the more tranquil and private setting of the Coit Tower lookout, where one could sit in privacy and scan the length of San Francisco Bay, three bridges, and her beloved Sausalito. After a few seconds of consideration she walked up Montgomery toward Coit Tower.

Rachel returned to the Imperial Building at three forty-five. She paused for a moment in front of the building, noticing that the old brownstone facia on the left portal was beginning to crack; probably the four-point-eight earthquake last month, she thought.

When she appeared in Barrington's office at three fifty-five, she noted that her Coit Tower retreat had produced both relaxation and conviction.

"I came a few minutes early to thank you again for your confidence, Austin," she said. "I just want you to know that I realize how important the opening statement will be and that you'll have my best effort. I guess I had assumed you or Kevin would be doing it and, well, I appreciate the opportunity."

Barrington eyed her appreciatively. "You deserve it, and I know you'll do a good job. I do, however, expect to review and approve the outline. In fact, I would like to see the video cassette after you have taped it tomorrow."

"Of course," said Rachel, "and I'll welcome any suggestions you might have." She thrust her hands deep into her skirt pockets and peered at the toes of her shoes. "Austin . . . there's another matter I wanted to discuss. I just heard from Lieutenant Conti, and he tells me that he has developed some support for his theory that Dixon was murdered."

"Oh?" said Barrington. "What's our little sleuth up to now?"

"He thinks he can prove that the space heater that exploded and caused the fire was brought into Dixon's cottage by the murderer."

"Nonsense!"

"I don't necessarily buy his theory, Austin, but he is quite insistent. He wants to prevent any more 'tragic coincidences.' Would it cause any great harm for us to show him the plaintiffs' medical records, now that we've given them to the defense?"

"Oh, I suppose not," said Barrington, his voice more casual. "I'll put together a package for him."

What a day of surprises, thought Rachel, and beamed her appreciation. "Oh, Austin, thank you! You can't know what a relief it will be to get him off my back. Incidentally, for some reason, he seems particularly interested in the records of Hallinan, Weisberg, and Dixon."

"Well, now, that will be quite impossible," said Barrington. "Their cases have all been dismissed and, accordingly, their records have all been destroyed."

"Destroyed?"

"Yes, it's office policy to retain documents of living clients for three years after a case is closed. When clients die, however, we destroy them immediately to avoid a repetition of the problem we had once when a distant relative crawled out of the woodwork and sued us for releasing a decedent's personal records—even though our records had been properly subpoenaed! We've religiously adhered to this policy ever since. Those records are gone forever, Rachel, but I'll be happy to put together something on the other twelve for you to give Conti."

"Well, thank you. Thank you very much."

"Ah," said Barrington. "There's Kevin. I don't want Hancock to think we're too eager, but I did tell him four o'clock. Let's be on our way."

Minutes later the three lawyers entered the offices of Hancock and Wolfe. Although the Hancock firm was on the same street as S.P.&M., there the comparisons stopped. Hancock and Wolfe was a high-volume insurance defense firm whose cost-conscious clients were content to see their favorite lawyers in modest quarters, driving Detroit vehicles. Thus, while S.P.&M. partners took quiet pride in their opulent surroundings, viewing them through clients' eyes as a testament to their success and competence, Hancock and Wolfe delighted in their demonstrated austerity and its tacit promise that low overhead would translate to low rates.

The meeting started in the manner typical of most settlement conferences: bluster in place of reason; substance surrendering to posturing. After twenty minutes of this, Hancock finally got to the point. "Look, Austin, we both know the rules. We have to be able to tell the judge that we've at least talked. So now we've talked. Do you want to cut through the crap and tell me how much you want for those twelve old birds?"

Austin's bushy eyebrows crept upward in an attitude of apathy, emphasized by a shrug of his shoulders. "Alan, I haven't the slightest idea. You've seen our reports, and we've seen yours. I don't have to tell you that they are practically identical and that we could send our experts packing and win the race on the testimony of the horses in your own stable. To put it bluntly, these cases are of such incredible value, I don't know how to quantify them.''

"Well done, Austin.'' Hancock clapped his hands slowly in mock admiration. ''Thank God I don't have to play poker against you, but you know as well as I do that you've got to start somewhere.''

"Not necessarily,'' said Barrington, rubbing his eyes wearily, ''and I'm not bluffing. This may be one of those cases where we just have to let the jury decide. What has happened to these men is bigger than anything our small minds can visualize.''

Hancock slammed his pencil down on the table and said, ''Do you want to knock off the bullshit, Austin? There's no jury here to impress.''

Austin Barrington flashed his laser eyes on Hancock, his disdain palpable. Hancock stirred uncomfortably under the glare, then in a conciliatory tone said, ''Oh, come on, Austin. Let's hear your demand. You know that nothing either of us says or does in a meeting like this can be made public. Let's be candid with each other. Then if we can settle it, fine. If we can't, that's fine too.''

Not once taking his eyes from Hancock, nor by his tone suggesting forgiveness for his earlier remark, Barrington said softly, ''You want a demand? All right, I'll give you one. Our demand, which will expire when I leave this room, is three million dollars per client.''

Chuck Parnell let loose a contrived outburst of laughter and began shaking his head in mock amusement.

"Let me help you with the arithmetic, Mr. Parnell,'' Barrington said, launching a rocket glare at Hancock's younger partner. ''That's thirty-six million dollars for the first twelve. The other hundred plaintiffs we'll talk about later.''

Hancock joined in his partner's feigned and incredulous laughter, but Barrington was undaunted. ''Funny? You think that's *funny*? You asked for a demand, and you have one. I repeat, once rejected, our demand will expire and never be reopened. Now then, may I have your response?''

"My response is that you're bluffing,'' said Hancock, turning serious. ''No case in the history of mankind has been worth that kind of money, certainly for men this age with no significant earning power. I should think that with all the mishaps you've had, you would be happy to settle this case and be done with it.''

Barrington fixed Hancock with a dark look and said, ''I'm sure that's exactly what you think.''

''Austin,'' Kevin said, ''it looks like we're wasting our time. We've fulfilled our obligation under the local court rules. Let's get back to work.''

''I agree,'' said Rachel. ''We'll report to Judge Bainbridge that we've made our demand and the defense chooses to make no offer.''

''Hold on—not so fast,'' said Hancock. ''Let's all cool down a bit here.'' After a moment of tense silence and a quick *sotto voce* consultation with Chuck Parnell, Hancock said, ''I would be willing to recommend to my people that they consider an offer at ten percent of your demand: three hundred thousand dollars per plaintiff for a total of three million six hundred thousand.''

For the first time Barrington granted Hancock a small smile, but one bereft of amusement, as he said, ''There seems to be a communication problem here.'' Abruptly, he rose to his feet, gathered up his file, and headed for the door, pausing only to say, ''When you're ready to move the decimal point back into its proper place, call me. Otherwise, we'll see you in court.''

''Well now, Austin . . . *Austin!* Hold on a minute there!'' But Kevin and Rachel had shot from their seats and followed Barrington out of the conference room, down the hall, and into the elevator, where it was their turn to explode into laughter. ''Beautifully done, Austin!'' said Kevin.

Rachel vigorously nodded agreement and said, ''Did you see Hancock's face when we went out the door? Austin, how much authority do you think he really has?''

''My guess is that if we had allowed them to coax us back into the room, we would have gotten another three hundred thousand each, a total of seven point two million,'' Kevin said. ''Frankly, I'm amazed they started as high as they did.''

''I tend to agree,'' added Barrington, ''and I think they'll come up with three times that after opening statements.''

''Well, put a little pressure on me, why don't you,'' said Rachel, smiling.

As the trio returned to the Imperial Building, Rachel was pleased to see that Kevin seemed charged with his old enthusiasm again. He appeared to be back in control and ready to take charge. He had stopped smoking nearly as suddenly as he had started, the puffiness was gone from his face, and she noticed that his eyes had regained much of their ultramarine clarity. This pleased and relieved her. *Maybe we can find each other somewhere at the end of all this after all,* she thought. He'd been respecting their moratorium on romance. His only deviation, one that charmed and delighted her, was a single red rose that waited for her at the end of each day in her doorway at home.

The three lawyers paused in front of the Imperial Building to review the activity assignments for the next two days; then Kevin said good-bye to Barrington and reminded Rachel to take time to keep up her running. "We'll all need to be in good physical condition for this one," he said. "I started last week—my first trip to the club in so long I had forgotten my locker number. See you all later."

Barrington and Rachel watched as he hailed a cab. "He sure looks fit to me," said Rachel, forgetting herself.

"That's Kevin," Barrington said, smiling. "He trains for a trial as if it were a triathlon or a fifteen-round boxing match. He won't even touch a drink now until this thing is ended. He knows that when it's behind us, he'll have his reward."

And, thought Rachel, smiling a good-bye to the senior partner, *I will have mine.*

THIRTY-NINE

∎

The Bay was growing restless as Rachel and Jeffrey parked in front of the breakwater adjacent to the St. Francis Yacht Club. "There's going to be a storm before this party's over," Jeffrey said. Rachel nodded agreement as she looked out beyond the surging Bay, where dark clouds now blotched the horizon and the sun's last rays stabbed at the approaching night. "And now that I think of it, Ms. Cannon, it was damned insensitive of your social committee to schedule the annual firm Christmas party four days before the trial starts. I bet you're not going to be leading an after-hours dance party to Club Montmartre tonight."

"Right you are, Jeffrey. This is strictly a cameo spot for me. You'll have to find your own ride home."

"No problem, Rachel. I just might give Pam Spalding her big chance tonight."

"And just who gave you permission to stay out late, young man? You're on this trial team, too, you know." Jeffrey stood silent. His sad face shone in the dying sunlight, reflecting the troubled Bay waters. "Jeff," said Rachel, "something's still bothering you." Jeffrey merely shrugged his shoulders. "Talk to me, Jeff. What is it?"

"What's the use?" he said finally. "It's my same old harangue. I just think too much lately about how I'm doing too little. Maybe I should have been around in the sixties when things were really happening. Now all I can do is be appropriately cynical, and join the Sierra Club. I see our poor old plaintiffs shuffling in and out of our office and listen to Childhouse and Saul Franks talk about what we're doing to our drinking water, and I do *nothing*." He bent over, picked up a rock, and hurled it far into the night.

"What do you mean nothing? In four days we'll start what could be the biggest damages trial in history. We—all four of us—are going to go public with the pollution problem in a way that will be heard around the world. You call that *nothing*?"

Jeff threw another rock. "For you, Rachel, it's everything. But for me, I'm just a highly educated gofer, making sure Barrington has fresh water and sharp pencils. And don't think, by the way, that Mr. Establishment is going to let you send out that message to the world. Has he seen your outline yet? Your videotape?"

"Well . . . no, but . . . ."

"Rachel, I'm not trying to rain on your parade," Jeff said as he flung another rock at the darkness, "but you asked me, and I'm telling you. Our job here at S.P.&M. is to make money, not send messages to a waiting world about industry's rampant greed."

"That's Barrington's view all right. But Kevin agrees we should reveal the danger outside Lileton as well as inside and I intend to do just that in my opening."

"Sure, but that's just because Kevin knows we can get the jury excited and make more money that way, not because of any social altruism.'' Rachel made no reply and started walking toward the club.

"Hey, Rache—I'm sorry. I didn't mean to put down your . . . friend. I'm just down on everybody right now, including myself.''

Rachel turned back and put her arm around Jeff's shoulders. "It's okay, Jeff. We'll get our message across and make a dollar or two in the process. And I couldn't do my part without you. So cheer up, it's Christmas, and there's a party in there. Pam Spalding awaits you!''

Jeff managed a half smile of appreciation, if not conviction, and the friends stood together for another quiet moment, watching the rapidly changing seascape. A straggling sailboat under motor power putted into the protective harbor beyond the clubhouse, from which the din of the revelers could already be heard in the intervals between the crash of waves pounding against the breakwater. Kevin would be inside, Rachel knew, and Denise too. It was, after all, the annual S.P.&M. family Christmas party.

Family.

What would it be like? Sixteen days before Christmas usually signaled the start of a bad case of seasonal blues for Rachel, but she had no time for it this year. She would dutifully post her semiannual card to her mother—expecting and getting no reply. There it was. Her "family.''

But never mind, for if all went well in the next few weeks, she would soon be asked to join the most prestigious professional family in town. That would be enough.

Well, almost enough. She found herself missing Kevin, wanting him lately as never before. Why now? Was it the holiday season? Or because she had put her one romantic diversion—Dan Conti—on the shelf? Perhaps it was simply because Kevin had backed off, giving her room to breathe. Whatever the reason, she felt herself again drawn closer and closer, answering need with need. She no longer discouraged—indeed, now looked forward to—those rare late-night telephone calls, whispered promises of a "new life together.'' Yet Rachel also knew that it was only because her restless mind and energy were now consumed by "the case'' that this kind of relationship could sustain her. January would have to bring more than just the start of a new year.

"It's starting to rain,'' she said. "Pop your umbrella, Jeffrey.''

The two friends turned together and walked toward the main

building. "You were telling me earlier that Dan Conti called you
again the day before yesterday. What did he want this time?"

"The usual."

"Wanted you to enlist in his crime-stoppers army, right?"

"Exactly."

"Well, did you tell him to fuck off or what?"

"No, actually, I decided to help him—partly to get him off
my back, and partly because he just might be right."

"You turned over the medical files on the twelve plaintiffs?"
Jeff asked, stopping in his tracks.

"As a matter of fact, I did," Rachel said, kicking aside a
fallen pine bough, "but after getting Mr. B's consent."

"He agreed to it? You're kidding!" Jeffrey said, catching up
and staring both incredulously and admiringly at Rachel's profile. The wind had blown her long hair off one shoulder, revealing the straight line of her neck. "That's some turnabout. What
got into him?"

"I'm not sure. Maybe the fact that any claim of attorney/client
privilege dissolved as soon as we turned the records over to the
defense. I even asked him for the records of Hallinan, Weisberg,
and Dixon, too, but they had all been destroyed."

"Destroyed? How come?"

"Well, the guys are dead, and dismissals have been filed. It's
an office policy."

"Hmm. I wonder if they've purged the computer files as
well."

"What computer files?" Now it was Rachel who came to a
stop.

"The litigation support system, dodo. Don't you remember?
Everything is automatically logged in as soon as it comes in the
office."

"You're right, of course," said Rachel, slowly resuming her
walk toward the club. "I had forgotten. But Barrington has had
those files locked up in his desk all this time. He wouldn't have
allowed them to be put on computer."

"You're right too, Rache," said Jeffrey, "unless, like you, he
forgot that it's all automatic." A thunderclap of lightning flashed
through the sky, and the friends ran the remaining thirty feet to
the entryway of the club. "All I'm saying," Jeff went on,
panting from the exertion, "is that if they came into the office,
they went on the computer. It's automatic. From mailroom to
records to computer, *then* to addressee. Barrington, like most of

the old-timers, resists all this high-tech stuff and probably wouldn't even think of it. Of course, if he *has* thought of it, he undoubtedly purged the computer disks when he had the records shredded. Do you want me to check it out?''

"Oh, forget it, Jeff. He'll just be upset by being reminded of it,'' said Rachel. "Let sleeping dogs lie.''

"You're the doctor, lawyer,'' he said, checking his umbrella and topcoat in the lobby while Rachel brushed the rain out of her hair.

As they entered the firm's reserved room, they encountered a reception line headed by Catherine and Austin Barrington, Florence and Adrian Fisher, and two other senior partners and their wives. "*Ra-chel*,'' gushed Catherine Barrington, "you look *lovely* as usual. How can you *possibly* be such a fine lawyer and still look good on a night like this?''

Rachel returned Catherine Barrington's flowery compliment with an extra squeeze of her hand. "Thank you, Mrs. Barrington. You look very pretty yourself.''

She next shook hands with Austin Barrington, who said quietly, as he maintained the firm hand contact, "Catherine is right, Rachel. You are an incredibly attractive woman. If I have to be locked up with someone over the next two months, I'm glad it's you.'' Rachel avoided his eyes and smiled politely as she assessed the words, striving for an innocuous intent.

Jeffrey caught up with her later at the bar and was about to speak, when Tag Wickman approached, obviously drunk. "Well, well, it's the exciting and glamorous Rachel Cannon. We've been waiting for you.''

"Is that the sovereign 'we,' Tag, or is there a mouse in your pocket?'' said Rachel, unsmiling. Rachel had already had her fill of sexual innuendo and was beginning to realize she was just not in a party mood.

Wickman ignored the barb. "Thank you, Rachel, but I was referring to 'we' as in every red-blooded male lawyer in the office. Which one of us will you be favoring tonight? Which humble frog will you turn into a prince at midnight?''

"I don't do frogs,'' Rachel said, grabbing her drink and turning to walk away. "Nor do I suffer fools gladly.''

Wickman lurched after her, still oblivious to her insults, and encircled her waist with his free hand. "Hey, Rachel, you're right here on my dance card. Come on, it's a slow one.''

"Tag. Please, I just arrived. I want to drink my drink and walk around a bit."

"Great! I'll walk with you."

"Tag, please go away. Perhaps we can talk later."

Undaunted, Wickman stayed close to her side, talking directly into her ear. "You'd do well to remember, your royal highness, that any two men in the partnership can vote you out of here."

Rachel stopped and faced the junior partner. "Men?" she said. "Did you say *men*? Then I certainly don't have to worry about your vote counting against me, do I, Tag?"

While Wickman unraveled this latest insult, Rachel escaped into a crowd of litigation support coders and emerged within several feet of the place where Florence Fisher, Catherine Barrington, and Gardner White's wife were now engaged in animated conversation. All but Florence seemed to be complaining about something or other, and Rachel slanted off in another direction, where she spied Stu Wallach standing alone. She was just beginning to engage him in conversation when she felt a firm tap on her shoulder, turned, and found herself standing face-to-face with Denise Stone.

"Well, hello, Rachel," she said. "You're looking quite lovely, particularly for someone who has been so very, very busy."

Denise's breath was strong with alcohol and an ominous aura belied her half smile. "Hello, Mrs. Stone," said Rachel, backing up and ignoring the double entendre. "Yes, we're about ready to go at last."

"Not on another trip, I hope." Still the ironic smile, but the tone now hardening. "Although I realize it's been over a year now since duty called you and my husband to New York."

"I meant . . . ready to start the trial," Rachel said, turning to walk away just as Kevin quickly approached from behind Denise.

"Hi, Rachel. Nice party," he said perfunctorily, then taking his wife by the arm, he added, "Would you excuse me if I steal Denise away for a second? There are some people . . ."

"Of course," Rachel said gratefully, but Denise shook out of Kevin's grasp, all pretense instantly gone as she jammed her face close to Rachel's. "And will you excuse *me*, Miss Cannon, if I do *not* permit you to steal my husband away?"

Shocked anxiety engulfed Rachel as she stared first into Denise's accusing eyes, then glanced at Kevin's blood-drained face. Denise's words were hot needles; harsh, unanswerable words she knew were burning their way into that part of her brain that would never forget. Rachel stood there, feeling never more alone as the crowd seemed to retreat around her.

"Let's go, Denise," Kevin said with quiet intensity. "The party's over." His features frozen, he led her firmly toward the door, not once looking back.

Kevin maneuvered Denise across the yacht club's parking lot and into his Jaguar.

"Christ, it's pouring, Kevin. My poor fur is ruined!"

"What do you think you were doing in there?" Kevin said quietly as he stared at the ignition key in his hand.

"Just calling a slut a slut, dear boy."

The lightning blow from Kevin's open hand to Denise's face echoed in the darkness like a gunshot, but her head snapped back quickly and defiantly. "It's true then, isn't it?"

Kevin was not sure whether she meant is it true that he and Rachel had gone to New York or that her coat was ruined or that he was in love with Rachel, but he met her eyes and said without hesitation, "Yes, Denise. It's true."

Later that night he said good-bye to his daughters and drove in a torrential downpour to the Ascot Hotel, where he took a room, paying three months in advance.

FORTY

Two days later—one day before the start of trial—Kevin looked up to see Rachel standing in his doorway. He was both preoccupied and late for a meeting, but a quick glance at the way her jaw was set and the way her fingers clutched her sweater convinced him that she would have to be dealt with here and now.

"I'm sorry about the night before last, Rachel. I had no idea—"

"I understand that, Kevin. And I see no point in prolonging the incident by rehashing it. It wasn't your fault. What I don't understand is what Desmond Childhouse is doing here."

"Desmond? Oh. You saw him?"

She had seen him all right; seen him, greeted him as if she had known he was coming, a cheap, face-saving artifice.

"Would you like to tell me why I've been excluded from this meeting?" she asked.

Kevin rose, seeking the advantage of height. "It's his style, Rachel. Barrington's. He believes in every person focusing on his or her own particular segment of the overall performance, after which he, as stage director, will pull it all together. He's doing the same thing to me. Really. I should think you'd be satisfied—if not overjoyed—to be making the opening statement and putting the groundwater expert on the stand at trial. A pair of damn good roles, I'd say."

Rachel stared at Kevin in silence, frustrated by his rationality and the appalling possibility that she might be overreacting. Kevin shrugged, turned away from her, and continued. "Austin has insisted from the beginning that he intends to handle the medical part himself, and the sole agenda for today's meeting is microbiology and pathology, fields in which Childhouse is also an expert."

"Bullshit," said Rachel.

"I don't know whether the professor is also an expert in bullshit, but I'll ask him," Kevin said, turning back toward her, "if you'll move out of my doorway, that is."

"By all means. I certainly wouldn't want to stand in the way of men at work, despite the fact that I'm the one who selected Childhouse, prepared him, took him through his three-day deposition, and knows his strengths and weaknesses better than anyone."

Rachel turned to leave, knowing she was saying too much but unable to stop herself. She was already beginning to regret her emotionalism, when Kevin suddenly grinned, threw his hands up in surrender, and said, "Hold on, officer, I'll talk."

Rachel softened her tone as she said, "I'm listening."

"It's really quite simple. He knows you've been dating Conti, and he also knows that Conti has been hounding us for more privileged information on who are the most seriously ill clients. Austin believes that if there is any truth to Conti's theory that the Mafia owners of North American are killing off our biggest potential verdict-winners, the leak of information might be right in Conti's backyard: the police department."

Rachel, abandoning her effort at restraint, charged Kevin's

desk, and said, "And the leak to Conti? That has to be me. Right? Well, take this back to your partner: In the first place, I am—in case you two have forgotten—a lawyer, and understand the importance of respecting privileged information. In the second place, I have nothing Conti needs, although he doesn't believe it. So if in fact our plaintiffs are being murdered in the order of the severity of their symptoms and the dollar value of their cases, it's not because of a leak in the police department, because Conti knows nothing about the medical profiles of our people. In the third place, I've gone out with Dan Conti a grand total of half a dozen times and—"

"Were they really grand?"

"My last date with him was in September! Not even Barrington can be so paranoid."

"And you can't be so naive as to think that you don't have something Conti needs."

Rachel said nothing, but gave Kevin a look that communicated both resignation and disgust. Kevin received the message and said, "Yes, I know. I'm doing it again. Macho innuendo in response to your legitimate questions. Right? Okay, I'm sorry; the guy just pushes my button. As for Austin, I'm not saying I agree with him. I'm just telling you what he thinks, and he *is* senior on this case, even to me, remember? But don't worry about coordination at trial. I'm sure he'll open up as the trial gets under way. Consider yourself lucky; this kind of meeting is the most boring part of the case as far as I'm concerned. Personally, I'd be delighted to miss it."

"You couldn't be more delighted than I am," said Rachel coldly, walking toward the door.

"Bullshit," said Kevin, smiling after her.

Rachel halted in the doorway, then turned slowly back toward Kevin and studied his face for a moment. The warmth she saw there slowly melted her set features into a half smile. "I'm being a creep, aren't I?"

"It's called," said Kevin gently, "pre-game jitters."

"And injured pride. I guess I just feel left out. Say hello to Desmond for me."

"Sure. Now will you listen to me for ten seconds?" Kevin rose from behind his desk, but remained there. "I've left Denise. I'm going to seek a divorce as soon as the trial is behind us."

Rachel's eyes turned to meet his. "You're serious, aren't you?" she asked. "When did you leave?"

"The night of the party. I'm staying at the Ascot—it's close to the courthouse."

"Kevin, I . . . don't know what to say."

"You don't have to say anything. I didn't even plan on telling you until after the trial. Our romance moratorium, remember? Besides, I don't want anything to interfere with your performance tomorrow."

"Don't worry," she said, recovering from her surprise and smiling broadly. "I won't disappoint you."

"There's only one way you could ever disappoint me, Rachel," said Kevin, walking over to her and gently taking hold of her shoulders, "and that would be to refuse to give me another chance. I know I've been erratic, even weird at times. At a place in your career when you've had your own concerns I've tried to saddle you with mine. I'm sorry for all of it, but as soon as the trial is behind us, I intend to invite you to join me on an extended visit to Nantucket."

Rachel smiled and nodded her head, her feelings a potpourri of relief, joy—and a grain of doubt. She reached up and spread her hands across his chest. "I know it's been difficult for you," she said. "You seem much better lately, but for months you've been, well . . . different. Is there anything else troubling you? Something you're not telling me?"

Kevin met her gaze and replied without hesitation. "There's nothing else, Rachel. Nothing at all."

Still, Rachel sensed that Kevin was concealing something—*to spare me more anxiety*, she thought, touched by the nobility inherent in his denial.

"All we need," he continued, as if he'd run it through his head a thousand times, "is to get the trial behind us. I'll have more money than I ever thought possible and can buy my peace with Denise. You will be a partner at Stafford, Parrish, and MacAllister, and then we can finally be ourselves. Find ourselves. Be together." His hands closed tighter on her shoulders, pulling her closer.

"But what will they say at the firm—"

"They'll all come to the wedding," Kevin said, kissing her deeply. "Married, my darling Rachel, my wife—"

"Kevin . . . the door—" but Rachel's token protest was muffled by Kevin's lips covering hers as he gently guided her against the wall, out of the view of anyone passing by. His hands were everywhere, touching, tracing erotic memory paths, filling her with electric desire. She now returned his kiss and welcomed his hardness pushing against her, all resistance short-circuited as sensation replaced thought. She could not believe the suddenness of the exquisite feeling, the building pressure. *Oh, God,* she whispered, *it's been so long.*

Rachel clung to Kevin for another few moments, spent from the exertion and amazed at what had happened. Finally, she smoothed her skirt and closed the door. "After the horse is stolen?" said Kevin, smiling. "By the way," he continued, "I think I was in the middle of a proposal, but perhaps I've bent the rules enough for one day."

"Bent? How about smashed and shattered?" Rachel said, her skin glowing like a sunrise.

"Guilty as charged, your honor, but before I join Barrington, I have one last thing to say: There's nothing wrong with me that our being together won't take care of. You see that now. There's only one thing in the way—winning the case—and I know now that we can do it."

Rachel was pleased to see the infectious confidence back in Kevin's eyes. "We *will* win, Kevin. I know we will."

The owl-like professor had barely perched in his chair after Kevin's late arrival, when Barrington went to work. "You must be particularly patient with us today, Professor. In my case, I hated high school chemistry and biology and avoided both in college. But before I put you on the stand in a few days, I will need to know every detail I can learn about the manner in which these chemical toxins have attacked the bodies of our plaintiffs. This must be our focus today.

"But first, Desmond," Barrington continued, affecting a casual tone, "I need to cover a minor housekeeping matter. I believe I showed you some medical records early on relating to three of our clients who are now deceased. Do you recall that?"

"Yes, I believe I did see those records—Dixon, Halloran or Hallinan, something like that; I can't remember the third."

"Weisberg?" said Barrington, shooting Kevin a worried look.

"That's the one, Weisberg. Terribly ill, all of them, shot through with toxins."

"Yes, well, Desmond," said Barrington as he strolled over to his desk and picked up a cigarette. "I was wondering if, by any chance, you made any notes off those records."

Kevin studied the expert's face, trying to anticipate his an-

swer. Here's the whole ball game, he thought. The last potential
flaw in Project Salvation. Barrington merely lit his cigarette and
stared out the window. Professor Childhouse cleaned his glasses
as if to clear his memory.

"I don't recall, Austin," he said finally. "Would you like me
to check my files?"

Barrington snapped his lighter shut, but his voice tone was
matter-of-fact as he said, "Yes, Desmond, why not take a look
right now?"

The professor began to leaf through his papers one by one,
sometimes pausing—causing Kevin's heart to jump—before moving on to the next one. Barrington remained standing by his
desk, apparently incurious, his eyes diverted from both Kevin
and the expert witness, but Kevin's mind raced wildly at the
possible existence of damning, written evidence of chlordane in
each of Barrington's three murder victims. How would Barrington handle it? Would Childhouse have given copies to others?
Consultants? Assistants? Secretaries? If so, it would be like
trying to get smoke back into a bottle.

"Ah, here it is. Yes, I do have notes on their records. What
would you like to know, Austin?" asked Childhouse, his pink
skin glowing with satisfaction.

Kevin had to resist the impulse to snatch the papers from the
expert's hand, but Barrington's outward calm remained intact as
he asked, "What do you show for their test results?" Both
lawyers' eyes were now fixed upon Childhouse as he studied the
sheets of paper.

"This just confirms what I said earlier—all were heavily
contaminated, as revealed in both blood and tissue samples from
Newkirk's lab."

"Do your notes describe the, ah . . . specific chemicals revealed in the tests?"

"Oh, no, Austin. That really wasn't my job, was it? I just
note here that dioxin seemed the principal culprit. My note here
says, 'See Newkirk file for breakdown by chemical.' I'm sorry,
but I'm sure we can check Newkirk's records for—"

"No, no, Desmond, it's quite irrelevant now anyway," said
Barrington. Kevin replicated the senior partner's casual smile,
but realized he had stopped breathing. "I was just curious,"
continued Barrington, "about what we would be turning over to
the defense pursuant to their subpoena. We're very protective of
the privacy of deceased ex-clients." *Jesus, that was close,* thought

Kevin. *No wonder Austin wanted me to keep Rachel out of this meeting.* "Anything else in there?" Barrington asked.

"About the decedents?"

"Right."

"No, that's it." Childhouse handed his file to Kevin. "Check my papers, please, Kevin, but I think these are the only notes I made on Newkirk's work. I now have his complete set of records, of course, on the twelve who are going to trial."

"That's fine," said Barrington, now hiding his relief as adroitly as he had previously concealed his concern. Kevin's heartbeat returned to normal as he confirmed that there was no reference to chlordane in Childhouse's file.

"And this is your entire file?" Kevin asked.

"That's it," said the professor.

"Very good, then," Barrington said as he joined the others at the conference table, "let's get down to work."

The next few hours were spent discussing the insidious way the "synthetic intruders" could alter the functioning of a cell's DNA and affect the chromosomes' ability to engage in proper cell division, rendering the body helpless to prevent the growth of a pathological mass that would slowly starve the defenseless surrounding tissue.

"How," asked Barrington, "do we deal with the defense claim that the well water was within safe limits as to some of the toxins?"

Childhouse vigorously shook his head. "Gentlemen, there *are* no safe limits. Remember, four thousand human cells placed side by side constitutes a row only an inch long. The mitochondria, which contains packets of enzymes, are even smaller. Think of it: *Cancer may be initiated if even a single one of these cells is transformed.* Thus, it's a myth that there are so-called 'safe threshold levels,' for a mere one part per billion of any carcinogen may easily implicate one of these cells and initiate a full-blown cancer."

"And once the first domino falls," said Kevin, "I take it different people will be affected in different ways, even though they may have absorbed the same toxin."

"That's right," said Professor Childhouse, thrusting his pipe into his mouth. "And that's also a good way to put it. The jury must be educated that there is no chemical out there we can label 'cancer-producer' or 'liver-destroyer' or 'lobotomizer.' A chemical enters the body and invokes the immune response, thus initiating a drama that will be played out differently in each person's body. I noticed, however, that the plaintiffs do have a few things in common. Newkirk's tests show that all had evidence of synthetic compounds stored in the body tissue. Some show signs of bone marrow and thymus cellular disruption, and most display various forms of organ pathology. In other words, all of them have altered immune systems, but the pathological manifestations of this phenomenon are never exactly the same in any two victims.''

"Then tell us, Professor," said Barrington, "how will we deal with all this at trial.''

"Simple. These men were exposed to chemicals and, as the toxicity built up in their systems, so did their symptoms; thus we find a correlation both in dosage and time. At Love Canal, for instance, when we began to find numerous miscarriages and babies born with three ears, club feet, and six toes, you could not ignore the evidence that something they shared in common was the cause. Similarly, you've got plaintiffs who shared contaminated drinking water who are now suffering far more disability than test groups of people outside their area who did not drink it.''

"But some of these men haven't been on the property for years," said Barrington.

"That's physiologically irrelevant," Childhouse said. "Let me give you an example. In the summer of 1973, around two thousand pounds of PBBs—polybrominated biphenyls—were accidentally substituted for a feed additive for farm animals in Michigan. Cattle grew ill and hens stopped laying eggs, but nobody realized what the problem was. It took nearly a year before they figured it out, during which time some of the animals had been recycled into feed for other livestock, and the poison had been spread to consumers through milk, meat, butter, eggs, and cheese. They had to destroy thirty thousand cattle, a million and a half chickens, and seven thousand other farm animals. But here's my point: In 1978—five years later—the Environmental Sciences Laboratory of the Mount Sinai School of Medicine examined more than seventeen hundred people representing a cross-section of Michigan citizens. After completing blood serum and fatty tissue studies, they found that ninety-seven percent of the fatty tissues of the people tested showed clear signs of PBBs—*just from ingesting milk and eggs from animals who had eaten a bad batch of food five years earlier!*''

At this, the lawyers exchanged a knowing look.

"I take it," said Barrington, "that all of these chemicals and metals you have traced into the plaintiffs' blood and tissue are by-products of something produced regularly at North American," said Barrington.

"Yes. That's Saul Franks's job, and he has done it well. His team, for example, has confirmed the existence of TCE, a very common industrial waste by-product used as a cleaning solvent. It has been proven to cause cancer in rats. Benzene and toluene are other solvents, petroleum based, that were both manufactured at North American. Benzene has been proven to cause cancer in humans; it attacks bone marrow, causes deafness, and will literally take the paint off of walls. In addition, lindane, another restricted pesticide, was made for years at North American. It attacks the central nervous system and causes great hyperirritability. I've already mentioned that Mr. Weisberg was depressed largely because of the high amounts of lindane he had absorbed. Depression and suicide are common symptoms of lindane."

The lawyers exchanged another quick look and Kevin quietly rose to his feet and began to pace as Barrington took the expert through a detailed question-and-answer session. An hour later Barrington was ready to sum up: "Finally, Professor, what is your opinion with respect to whether or not the twelve plaintiffs' injuries and illnesses are related to and caused by the contaminated well water you have described?"

"I conclude," said Desmond Childhouse, stroking a thin fringe of hair over his right ear, "on the basis of the symptomatology and dose response of the plaintiffs, Dr. Newkirk's initial tissue and blood samples, together with my own epidemiological studies, that the plaintiffs' injuries and illnesses were caused by their consumption of water from the North American well."

As he finished the last sentence, Professor Childhouse jammed his pipe into his mouth and, for the first time since Kevin had known him, lit it. It was not an act of arrogance, merely an acknowledgment of finality. Closure.

Kevin stared at the expert witness for a full minute, trying to find a gap, a flaw in the scenario. Finally, he smiled and turned toward Barrington.

"Bingo," he said, and leaned back into his chair.

Meanwhile, behind her closed office door, Rachel began work on the opening statement, struggling to discipline her concentra-

tion away from Kevin, Kevin, Kevin. The afterglow was still
there, yet something still nagged at her. Was it Kevin's erratic
behavior the past few months? Was it really him at all, or her
own imaginings; the same old quest for flaws to justify her
reluctance to make a full commitment, her inability to place her
total trust in another? *It's me,* she thought. *Kevin is everything
I've ever dreamed of, so it must be me. I'm the erratic one—
caught between wanting the security of the white picket fence
and the fear that I'll be trapped behind it. But I won't think
about that now. I can't think about that now.*

Rachel turned to the matter at hand. On her desk before her sat
a fresh yellow pad. Surrounding her were lab reports, engineering diagrams, twelve bulging medical files, state and federal
regulations, at least fifty depositions, epidemiologic surveys, and
jury data. Paper, paper, everywhere. Documents demanding to
be read. Thick reports, like insistent children, screaming for
attention. Rachel thought of the Hydra.

She spun away from her desk and stared at the clearing sky
outside. She knew that her opening was not only a chance to
score an early knockout for her clients, but also an opportunity to
awaken people to the dangerous contamination levels of much of
the nation's diminishing freshwater reserves. She had worked for
nearly a year now with clients in the prime of their lives who had
been reduced to incontinent and retarded invalids, their skin
melting with running lesions, their livers turned to leather. She
had wept while watching Desmond Childhouse's videotapes of
babies born blind, bladders outside their bodies, without hands
or feet or with extra fingers or toes. Love Canal—first thought to
be an isolated disaster—had crept unchecked toward neighbor-
hoods all over America and tomorrow, with the national press as
captive audience, she could prove it.

There was, however, an obstacle blocking her concentration.
Several actually, if you counted an anonymous crackpot threatening God knows what; Kevin and his news; Dan Conti and his
endless pestering; Jeffrey's growing demoralization, which had
begun to show itself in his work; and Tag Wickman's declared
negative vote on her imminent proposal for partnership. Her
most immediate problem, however, was Austin Barrington, whose
opposition to her "save the world" rhetoric still echoed in her
ears. He had been openly angry upon viewing the video recording of her opening statement and had slashed from her outline
even the most innocuous reference to anything vaguely related to

what he sarcastically referred to as "the national peril." Difficult choices had to be made now, for she knew that Barrington was at least partly right when he warned her that "preaching the apocalypse" could be a turnoff to some of the jurors and that her well-intentioned efforts might jeopardize her clients' cases, not to mention her own chances for partnership. Yet, to confine a rampant national epidemic to the tiny city of Lileton would not only be a missed opportunity, but a lie as well. As she reviewed her notes, the telephone seized her attention. "Jack, I thought I'd asked you to hold—"

"Sorry, Rachel, but it's Inspector Conti. He says it's an emergency."

"Just give me thirty seconds . . ." he said before she could express her irritation.

"No, Dan, for once I will *not* give you thirty seconds. I have given you the medical records of the living plaintiffs and have learned that Barrington destroyed the rest in accordance with office policy. So there's nothing else I can do."

"But there is, dammit—"

"No, there isn't, *dammit*! Now just leave me alone!" Rachel slammed down the receiver, missed the cradle completely, and watched it fly out of her hand to the floor. She picked it up and studied a crack in the mouthpiece, fighting back tears. The click of her door opening drew her eyes to Jeffrey Johnstone, looking as if he had walked in and caught his parents in *flagrante delicto*.

"It's okay, Jeff, come on in," said Rachel, pulling some Kleenex from her drawer.

"Shit, Rachel, I'm sorry, but since I'm here, what's the matter?"

"I'm not sure I know," said Rachel, smiling through glistening eyes. "I just hung up on Dan Conti without even letting him tell me what he wanted. I'm taking out all my frustrations on him."

"That's because you *know* what he wanted. Number one, he wants more information, and number two, he wants you. I take it that neither is available right now, so what the hell are you supposed to do?"

"Exactly what I told him," said Rachel, "but the truth is I'm curious now as to whether there are any new developments. After all, that guy who ruined my best lipstick writing threats on my bedroom mirror just might be for real . . . there's also a part of me that has difficulty saying no to Dan Conti."

"On number one or number two?" said Jeffrey, giving her a sideways look.

"Did you come in here to pry or just to finish off my already-dwindling powers of concentration?"

"Neither. I came to wish you good luck. But I'll throw this in as an extra: I went ahead and checked the computer file, and guess what. The files are there. Hallinan, Weisberg, and Dixon. Test results and all. Do you want me to get you hard-copy printouts?"

Rachel got up and closed her door again. She returned to where Jeffrey stood, then sat on the front edge of the desk so that their eyes were at the same level. "Listen to me carefully, Jeffrey. I told you not to check this out, and you checked it out anyway, and that's okay. I'm not your mother. But I tell you now, stop while you're ahead. You are a sometimes intelligent, often impulsive junior associate with decent prospects for partnership someday. If Barrington catches you reproducing records that were supposed to have been destroyed as a matter of office policy, you are one dead rookie."

"Jeez, Rachel, lighten up. I was just trying to help. I just feel so frigging *useless*. I've got this need to *do* something, that's all."

"Then finish those two new jury instructions, but stay out of this medical records matter. Have I made myself clear?"

"Yes, your eminence—I will obey your divine will. Please see fit to forgive my unholy transgressions." As Jeffrey smiled and quick-stepped out of view, Rachel started back around her desk. But seeing that darkness had fallen on the city, she decided she had better get out of the building before any more well-wishers dropped by.

The drive across the Bay Bridge cleared Rachel's head, and the germ of a perfect compromise on her opening statement began to form in her mind as she whipped the black BMW into her stall at the condominium. She had just started up the steps toward her front door when she heard a rustling from the shrubbery behind her, followed by the unmistakable sound of footsteps. Startled, she turned to see a huge figure separating itself from the shadows and moving swiftly toward her. Cold with terror, she raced to the door and frantically turned the key in the first lock.

But there were now too many locks, and as she glanced over

her shoulder she saw that the approaching figure was a large dark man and that there was the glint of metal at the end of his extended arm. Trapped in the entryway, nowhere to run, Rachel prepared for the worst.

"Sorry to startle you, Ms. Cannon," came the stranger's voice as he stepped into the light holding out his police badge. "Dan Conti has put me on extra for the duration of the trial, and I just wanted you to know I'm here." Rachel fell against the door, gasping with fatigue and relief. "He told me to keep an eye on you," the plainclothesman continued. "Sorry."

Rachel, not yet trusting her voice, returned his smile and let herself in the door, triple-bolting it behind her.

Neither Rachel nor the officer was aware that across the street a dark silent figure was keeping an eye on both of them.

FORTY-ONE

■

There is nothing like the first day of a jury trial, thought Rachel as she entered the courtroom. The tension was physically palpable, almost overwhelming. It occurred to her that anxiety ran highest at the very beginning of a trial and spared no one connected with it: the parties, who feared their testimony would be rejected by the jury; the judge, who knew that jury trials always evolve into a struggle for control of the courtroom by aggressive, competent lawyers who would eventually challenge even his own dominance; the panel of jurors, whose names might be called at any minute, thrusting them onto center stage, hoping they would be able to state their names audibly and to deal gracefully with the often embarrassing *voir dire* questions; and, finally, the trial lawyers themselves, who paced back and forth inside the rail like restless matadors, and on whose shoulders rested not only the fate of their clients, but their own reputations—for only one side could win and only lawyers who won today would be called upon by new clients tomorrow.

The local and national press added yet another dimension of

excitement, for their very presence suggested that something important was about to happen. Ordinarily, only capital offenses or sex cases attracted the interest of the press, but today, two full rows had been reserved—the second and third—for reporters and the courtroom artists who were already busy trying to capture the suppressed excitement in the faces of the main combatants.

Rachel nodded the traditional greeting to Hancock and Parnell, then joined Barrington and Kevin at the plaintiffs' counsel table, traditionally the one closest to the jury box, as the court reporter entered from a door behind the bench and took her seat, signaling the imminent appearance of the judge.

Showtime.

Rachel looked back as Jeffrey assumed his position in the row immediately behind the counsel table with Stu Wallach and other support staff. Jeff's job during the trial would be to provide case citations and quick answers to any knotty legal questions that might arise during the trial, while Wallach's task as head of the computer litigation support team would be to quickly retrieve hard-copy printouts of any piece of evidence that might unexpectedly become important. In the first row outside the rail, immediately behind Johnstone, sat the twelve plaintiffs, who would soon be introduced to the jury, then be excused from time to time for medical and other necessities. There was, of course, another blatantly tactical reason why they were there—this pitiful lot of victims, some of them coughing, many of them wearily clawing at their scarred flesh, all of them with chalky complexions and vacant eyes.

At the defense counsel table, to Rachel's left, Alan Hancock and Chuck Parnell whispered instructions to their own contingent of backup associates and paralegals, behind whom sat several clean-cut executives: Joseph Lucca, the president of North American Chemical, and Delbert Norville, production vice-president. Just to their left sat Aldo Petri, Lileton's city manager.

Jeffrey leaned forward to get his first look at Petri, whose deposition, taken by Kevin Stone, Jeff had recently outlined and computerized. Kevin had described him as "cool under fire," but Jeff wondered how well he would hold up when confronted with the information he had recently discovered that Petri's brother-in-law was related to Carmine Romano and had been a longtime soldier for the notorious Romano family.

A hush fell over the courtroom as the door to the judge's

chambers opened and Judge Mathew Bainbridge moved purposefully up the six carpeted steps to the bench.

"All rise!" shouted the bailiff into the high-ceilinged, paneled courtroom, his echo muffled by the sound of the people jammed into every available seat scrambling to their feet. Twenty minutes later, seven women and five men had been seated in the jury box, and questioning of the prospective jurors by counsel was under way. Barrington handled the *voir dire* for the plaintiffs, with Kevin relaying Dr. Barkheim's surreptitious signals on whether to accept or reject a juror.

By holding the entire panel until well into the lunch hour, unexpected progress in jury selection insured that Rachel would start her opening statement by mid-afternoon, and just before the afternoon recess at three o'clock, a jury of nine women and three men was sworn. They had selected their jury in record time for a case of such magnitude. Rachel slipped out of the courtroom and went downstairs for a solitary last walk around the third-floor corridor to gather her thoughts, no longer rehearsing now, just centering her energy and holding anxiety at bay. Her moment had arrived.

As counsel filed back inside the rail after the recess, Rachel noticed a note tucked under her pad. She had been looking for Dan in the courtroom all day, and suspected that it was a note from him wishing her well. What she saw, however, blasted both her expectations and composure. The note, printed in a child's scrawl, read:

> Hope you got plenty fire insuranse.
> You going to nead to.

Rachel turned, the searing pain of fear slicing up from her stomach and into her throat. She both hoped and feared that she would somehow be able to recognize and confront her tormentor. Unable to speak, she handed Kevin the note just as Judge Bainbridge resumed the bench.

"Oh, Christ," said Kevin, seemingly more angry than surprised. "Don't worry about it, darling. I promise you, it's just the same vicious crank. Just do your thing."

As Rachel wondered how she would get to her feet, let alone force coherent words out of her sawdust throat, she saw Kevin turn to his right, thrust the note under Barrington's eyes, and watched as the senior partner's face winced with pain. What she could not see was that Kevin had taken Barrington's arm in a vise hold. "What in the fuck are you doing, Austin!" he whispered. "You told me this charade was over! And why *now*, for God's sake? Are you trying to scuttle our entire case?"

Barrington stared open-mouthed at the note, saying, "Kevin, I swear to you—"

"Are the plaintiffs ready with their opening statement?" said Judge Bainbridge, looking down at Barrington.

The senior partner rose to his feet, cleared his throat, and said, "Ms. Cannon . . . will deliver . . . the opening statement for the plaintiffs, if the Court pleases."

As Rachel tried to gather herself, Barrington whispered back at Kevin with equal intensity, "Christ, Kevin, I wouldn't cut my own throat. I swear I know nothing about this. It must be some nut who picked up on the newspaper story. Believe me—"

"All right, Ms. Cannon," said Judge Bainbridge. "We are ready if you are. Ms. Cannon?"

Still stunned, Rachel rose to her feet and stiffly walked around the end of the plaintiffs' counsel table, dragging the fingertips of her right hand along the top of the table as she walked toward the jury like a blind person approaching an intersection. Finally, her mouth opened, but nothing came out. One of the jurors coughed, and the effect was awkward and uncomfortable. Rachel's mind seemed full of flying moths, and she cursed her decision not to use notes. *Think*, she admonished herself, *and say something, for God's sake. Stop fighting it and go with your . . .*

"Fear," she heard herself say finally. "This case . . . members of the jury . . . is, above all, a case about . . . fear." Another gap of silence had the jurors stirring uncomfortably in their seats, some of them exchanging glances. Rachel was conscious of this, and of the turmoil her hesitation must be creating in the minds of Barrington and Kevin. *Control the turmoil in your own mind*, she ordered herself. *Forget theirs*. It wasn't the beginning she had planned, but she began to see its possibilities.

"Fear," she repeated in a voice that sounded to her like a bad telephone connection, thin and metallic, "of the unknown. Living in dread of another day of suffering. Living in terror of dying . . . from the deadliest disease . . . known to mankind. Fear . . . of cancer." Rachel took a deep breath and a step closer to the jury.

"Cancer. A disease so terrifying that, as a child, I mostly heard it called simply 'C' or, later, as the 'big C.' A disease so frightening we try to avoid even uttering the word, yet that ugly word will be on the lips and in the minds of these twelve men every minute of every day for the rest of their abbreviated lives.

"Fear . . . and suffering and . . . hopelessness. That's what this case is about."

The courtroom had gone silent as a tomb.

"Now, members of the jury," she continued in a more matter-of-fact tone, "these twelve men have faced their fear and suffering in the past, but it is you to whom they must now look for hope in the future. They come before you to seek the only relief the law can now afford them from these two defendants: North American Chemical, which knowingly and systematically poisoned them, and the city of Lileton, which idly stood by and did nothing to stop it. You see, ladies and gentlemen, this is also a case about greed. Cold, malevolent . . . greed."

Rachel stopped for a moment, her mind crazily darting to Dan Conti's harangues about her doing "nothing to stop them," to dear Emmett Dixon, and then to a faceless man—probably watching her from the back of the courtroom at this very moment—a man who wanted to kill her. Her legs felt suddenly limp. *Adrenaline is playing games with my body,* she thought. She hoped the jurors might interpret the pause as dramatic effect. Kevin must have known otherwise, because he poured a glass of water for her and pushed it across the table toward where she stood.

Rachel took another deep breath, then turned and looked to her right, past Kevin, focusing her eyes on the twelve plaintiffs just outside the rail. The jury also turned and could not have missed the look that passed among them. Then Rachel finally began speaking again, not in the strident tone that jurors have come to expect from trial lawyers, but softly and, it seemed, to each one of them personally.

"These men really don't want to be here," she said in a voice cracking with compassion. "They would rather be working, or playing with grandchildren. But they can't work because they are so physically devastated they can barely sit up. And most of them can't play with grandchildren because they were rendered sterile before they even knew they were sick. Sick from a deadly poison which North American knowingly and callously allowed them to ingest day after day for years upon years." Rachel paused, then walked closer to the jury rail and pointed to her clients, one at a time. "Poison that destroyed Jack Lamphere's lungs, Tim Martin's liver, and Gerald Grey's kidneys. Poison that has turned each day into a nightmare of torture for every one of these victims. *Look* at them, ladies and gentlemen of the jury. Look if you can into the faces of fear. Of suffering. Of hopelessness. Look at the victims of the defendants' greed and corruption. The greed, as the evidence will show,'' said Rachel in a more vigorous voice as she took several steps toward the defendants and then jammed her finger straight at Joseph Lucca, ''of North American Chemical. The corruption,'' she added, redirecting the accusing finger toward city manager Aldo Petri, ''of the city of Lileton.''

As Rachel continued for the next thirty minutes, the jury—the entire courtroom—seemed caught in Rachel's web of rhetoric, so convincing and sincere, so emotional yet softly stated, that three of the jurors began involuntarily nodding in agreement by the time she concluded that ''when you compare the chemicals found in these men's bodies with the chemicals found in the dump site, the water from the test drillings into the aquifer, and the samples from the water well, there will not be a shred of doubt in your minds but that they all came from the very same place and for the very same reason.

''The place? North American Chemical Company.

''The reason? To save money and to maximize profits.''

Rachel paused for a few seconds to satisfy herself she had each juror's full attention. ''Now, you have heard there are two sides to every story, and this case is no exception. You see, members of the jury, we have already taken testimony in this case and we know what the defense will be. Their defense? 'Progress' in science and agriculture. Yes, you heard me right. The defense you are going to hear is that North American Chemical acted reasonably, was innocent of any wrongdoing and, indeed, that their work was and is essential to . . . '*progress.*' ''

Rachel had not only commanded the jurors' rapt attention but had mesmerized the cadre of reporters as well. A number of them seemed torn between accurately writing down her every word and the pleasure of watching her say them. For a final ten minutes Rachel excoriated the defendants, explaining with excruciating clarity the relationship between their callous behavior in the name of progress and the pain and suffering it had caused. Then she was ready to close.

''In summary, members of the jury, it will be for you, as representatives of the community, to send a message to polluters—

here and *everywhere*—that it's time they come down off their high horse; the high, white horse they hypocritically call 'progress.' That it's time to compensate the people who rendered up their most precious possession—their health—in the service of this very profitable enterprise they call 'progress.' Compensatory damages? Yes, of course, but punitive damages as well, for when you hear the evidence, you will know that *this* white horse was tainted with greed and splattered red with the blood of its victims; that *this* white horse was not progress at all, but rather Satan's own stallion, belching noxious flame from its nostrils and trampling its innocent victims with phosphorescent hooves of case-hardened steel.

"I am confident, therefore, that when you have heard the evidence, you will ask yourselves—as I have asked myself—how can we stop this marauding beast? The answer? There is only one way: by the award of punitive damages in an amount that will send a message not only to polluters, but to those legislators and other government representatives throughout this land who are too busy to care, who sit in ivory towers drinking bottled water, breathing filtered air, and making laws they know will never be enforced. They don't care—because *they* don't have to live day after day in pain, looking in their mirrors each morning for new scars of their misplaced trust, at the running sores and lesions that will be their constant companions during their last lonely days of agony on this once-natural planet. They just don't care.

"Yes, members of the jury, there is but one way to communicate this message loudly and clearly, and that's to award each of these plaintiffs no less than two million dollars in compensatory and general damages, then an additional three million each in punitive damages. For when you see the massive profit figures on North American's financial records, you will recognize that a verdict of this magnitude is the only way to get their attention."

Jurors number two, five, eight, and eleven almost imperceptibly, and entirely unknowingly, nodded their agreement.

"Ladies and gentlemen of the jury," said Rachel, her voice now strong and clear as she concluded, "this willful and wanton conduct has gone on for years now, unchecked and unpunished. When you have heard the evidence in this case, you will know that the time to stop it is here and now, not only for these innocent victims before you, but for you . . . and your children . . . and for all humankind. We cannot allow—and I know that you *will* not allow—either industry's avarice, or government's apathy, to further despoil our remaining resources, to deprive us of our precious health, and to rob our heirs of their legacy on this planet.

"If *you* won't act, who will?

"If not now," she ended in a whisper that carried the intensity of a storm, "*when*?"

As Rachel finished, she became aware that it had become so quiet in the courtroom she could hear herself breathe. The jurors were still riveted on her as she took her seat, and there was not a sound for ten full seconds. Even the judge maintained an awed silence. Then suddenly the courtroom exploded as reporters raced for telephones and spectators shouted their approval. Judge Bainbridge quickly restored order and admonished the jury to disregard the outburst, then excused them and called a recess. As soon as the jury had left the courtroom, Barrington nodded his approval. Kevin smiled, an ironically sad smile it seemed to her, and shook her hand, saying, "Rachel, you were truly great. No one could have done it better."

Rachel thanked them both and Barrington assured her that he would personally deliver the threatening note to Captain Mahan and insist upon more security. Rachel looked past Kevin's shoulder and saw Dan Conti standing by the door of the courtroom. Their eyes met briefly before he turned and left the courtroom, his departure somehow diminishing the glow of her triumph.

Later, back at the office, Kevin angrily pursued his probing of Barrington concerning the threat to Rachel: "How can you be sure your hired assassin didn't just throw this in on the house?"

"The person whose services I engaged," Barrington said stiffly, "does not perform those services 'on the house,' and he never misunderstands instructions. He's probably smarter than either one of us, Kevin; he just happens to kill people for a living. I don't even know how to find the son of a bitch. He reaches me from time to time at his own convenience and pleasure."

"Well, we were damn lucky," said Kevin. "Anyone without Rachel's spunk would have fallen apart and blown the opening. As it stands now, she's still goddamn upset, and I can't blame her."

"Can't you calm her down?" asked Barrington.

"Sure. I'll just assure her that the professional assassin you hired to kill our clients and break into her apartment isn't involved this time."

Barrington placed his glass down on the bar and walked over to his desk, a signal that the meeting was over. "I'll overlook your sarcasm, Kevin. I know how upset you are. But we've both got other things to think about now. Leave the cop work to the cops. Tomorrow, you're cross-examining the production manager, and I'm putting Childhouse on the stand."

Kevin remained standing at the bar in Barrington's conference area, absorbed and inscrutable. He rotated the glass of Perrier in his hand, seemingly oblivious to Barrington's words. "Kevin. Come *on*! I tell you there's nothing to worry about. The parts are all in place; now all we have to do is assemble them and drive the damn thing home. With the start Rachel gave us today, nothing can stop us now. Things could not be better!"

Kevin put his glass down with studied care, then gave Barrington a cold look and headed for the door without a word.

FORTY-TWO

Rachel was home at last, yet feeling strangely sad and ill at ease. A letdown from her afternoon triumph was beginning to set in. She worried about whether her new celebrity status would create tension among other lawyers in the firm. She felt sad that Dan had left the courtroom before she could talk with him. He was probably angry at her for hanging up on him. She now regretted it, but could not bring herself to apologize. Worst of all, the trial lawyer in her was beginning to dredge up things she might have done differently in her opening statement and to remember points she had forgotten to make—the inevitable, retrospective masochism of a perfectionist.

She moved to another chair and stared meditatively at the Bay. Part of her melancholy mood was just loneliness, she told herself; the biggest night of her life and no one to share it with. She thought of Kevin, and wondered what he was doing. She turned from the window, rose, and walked into the kitchen, poured herself a glass of chardonnay, then suddenly realized that neither loneliness in general nor Kevin in particular was the main reason for her darkening mood.

She was still afraid.

It was that damn note—the instrument of fear that she had somehow been able to cordon off to a separate chamber of her mind earlier this afternoon—now clamoring for recognition. She had always wondered what it would be like to be the target of hate, and now she knew. Somewhere in the crowded courtroom tomorrow, and every day until it was over, a psychopath capable of murder might be sitting, watching her every move. For the first time, she fully appreciated the plainclothes security guard who had waved to her earlier as she entered her apartment.

She decided to read for a while, but soon found herself puttering around the house until finally it was bedtime. She was about to disconnect the telephone and head for the bedroom, when she was startled by the shrill ring of her doorbell. She tiptoed to the door and looked through the peephole. Relieved, she saw the profile of Dan Conti. One chain and two sliding bolts later, she opened the door partway, saying, "Hello, Captain Midnight. Working the late shift this week?"

Dan did not laugh. "I was passing by and saw your lights on. Got a minute?"

"I was just going to bed, Dan."

"Sorry, I haven't got time for that right now." His stern features eased into a smile. "A cup of coffee will have to do."

Rachel could not contain her own smile. After all, there were worse things for a case of the jitters than a visit from a policeman. These past months, she had missed him, missed his cool decisiveness, a trait he wore as comfortably as Melvyn Douglas wore a smoking jacket. She remembered that other terrible night and the way he had handled the lab technicians. They would have climbed into her refrigerator and shut the door if he had told them to. When he wasn't badgering her for help, she had always felt so comfortable with him. *Why?*

"Take off your coat," she said. "Instant coffee okay?"

"Sure," Dan said, throwing his topcoat over a chair. "Did you see the news on TV? Pictures of star plaintiffs' lawyer Rachel Cannon triumphantly leaving the courtroom?"

"The answer is no." The truth was she had looked, but not seen anything.

"You want to tell me what was going on up there at the counsel table before you started your opening statement?"

"Didn't Barrington give you the note?"

"No, but I heard about it. Exactly what did it say?"

"It asked me whether I had fire insurance. Told me I would definitely need it—spelled n-e-a-d, if that narrows your list of suspects any. Was it that obvious that something was going on inside the rail?"

"Not really. The popular conception was that the brain-trust triumvirate was trying to make a decision on its next diabolically brilliant stratagem. It appeared for a moment, however, that your friend Kevin was about to throttle your senior partner."

"I missed that completely," said Rachel, "but I often feel the same way myself."

Dan stared down into his freshly poured coffee. Rachel knew what was coming. She absurdly flashed into Barrington's recent triple redundancy: *It's the same old déjà vu all over again. This guy never stops,* she thought. *Why do I humor him? Partnership is within reach, the man I love will soon have his freedom, and I'm about to receive more than my fair share of credit for one of the biggest verdicts of all time. Enter Dan Conti with another pitch for me to rock the boat that's carrying me to Paradise Island.*

"The answer is no, Dan," said Rachel firmly but without malice.

Dan just shook his head. "You've been reading my mind again. Rachel, that note you got today was a message from Emmett Dixon's murderer! Some maniac is telling you that you are going to die the same way your friend Dixon did—by fire—and you stand there—"

"Dan, it's been a long day. I simply can't—"

"Yes, I know. You're a very busy woman, so I guess my time is about up. But dammit, Rachel, while you're out there sounding the clarion call for water reform tomorrow, there's a murderer on the loose, bent on killing your clients—and you. You can't keep sitting on the sidelines, Rachel. You've got to help me find this guy and stop him, and if you don't, you're as responsible as he is because you aren't crazy and he is!"

Stung by the tirade, Rachel snatched the cup from Dan's hand and emptied it into the sink. "I don't *have* to do *anything*, Lieutenant. You're just going to have to put the next notch in your gun without my help. I don't have time for it."

"That's just fine," Dan said, grabbing his coat, "because I don't have time to debate motivation with a rich lady lawyer too busy earning big fees to be concerned whether her clients will still be alive to collect their share."

The bitterness of his denunciation rendered her speechless. Rachel had never felt so misjudged, so angry, so tired.

"Good *night,* Lieutenant!" she said finally, but Dan stood staring at her, rooted in place, as the shrill ring of the kitchen telephone split the bitter silence. Rachel snatched the receiver. "*Yes?*" But there was no response from the other end, and yet another warning light flashed red in Rachel's overloaded central nervous system. "*Hello? Who is this!*" she demanded. Dan swiftly moved in closer to listen in and Rachel tilted the receiver so he could hear, their argument temporarily forgotten.

"Jeez, Rachel—some welcome," came the voice of Jeffrey Johnstone. "Have you considered a career as a wild animal trainer?"

"Jeffrey," said Rachel, more perturbed than relieved, "why are you calling at this hour, and where did you go after court today?"

"Well . . . uh—I think the answer to either question answers both. To sum it up, I'm in jail. Busted for trespass and vandalism."

"You're *where*? For *what*? In jail?" Dan, who had begun to leave, stopped at the door, turned, and walked back into the kitchen.

"That's right," said Jeff. "I'm using my one call to talk to my lawyer, though you're probably out of my price range after that opening statement today."

"Jeff, stop clowning. What happened?"

Rachel heard the raucous, echoing, unmistakable sounds of a jail as Jeff's volume and bravado began to fade. "It's a bit hard to talk here, but the bottom line is that I joined some friends over in Richmond at Systron Chemical, the company that makes pesticides and plastics. They've been pumping heavy metals and organic chemicals into the Bay for fifty years."

"Talk louder, Jeff. I can't hear you with that racket in the background."

"I'll try. We set up a portable pump at an outflow pipe and started pumping the waste material right back onto their own property, made a hell of a mess of their executive putting green. They had to turn their own pumps off, of course, then some of us chained ourselves to the main outflow opening."

"*Jeffrey!* Were you hurt?"

"Not a bit, and Rachel—I've never felt better. I was kidding about the lawyer call, but you will need a replacement gofer tomorrow."

"Jeff!" Rachel exclaimed. "Why didn't you tell me you were planning to do this?"

"Well, it was more or less impulsive. Besides, you would have tried to talk me out of it. Oh, shit, Rachel, I don't know. I just decided it was time to do something. After all, didn't you say today that it was time to *act*—and that 'if you won't, who will?' Whoops . . . I gotta get off. The good news is that there's no room at the inn, and they're releasing people who have a responsible party to claim them. Knowing none, I called you."

"City jail? Give me thirty minutes. And listen, you little shithead, you *will* be in court tomorrow . . ."

"Come on, Rachel, no way. No more. After tonight, you don't even know me."

"Don't be a creep, Jeff," said Rachel. "I'm just *starting* to know you. 'Bye."

Rachel slowly replaced the receiver in the cradle and told Dan what had happened. He persuaded her to let him handle Jeff's release. "The paperwork will keep you there until at least four in the morning if you do it. I can walk him out in five minutes and drop him home in another twenty-five. You get some sleep now."

"You'll be . . ."

"Yes, I'll be nice. A real big brother. I don't approve, but I'll be nice, mainly because I know you need him on your case."

Rachel looked at Dan's tired face as he reached for the door. *What if he's right?* she asked herself. What if their collective lawyer-like stubbornness should result in another death? *My own, for instance.* Dan was the only one who didn't shrug off this threat, and she felt herself weakening from compassion and gratitude.

"Here's your cup back. Have some before you go, Dan. I'm sorry about the temper tantrum, and I guess I'm also sorry it took another threatening note from the nut factory and my little sidekick's bravado to wake me up. Maybe I can help you and your crazy theory after all. I'll put together a package of my own notes and other papers from interviews with Hallinan, Weisberg, and Dixon."

"You're kidding! How soon can I get all this?" he asked.

"My secretary will put together a package tomorrow morning. And Dan, there's something else. We've found that the original medical records of Dixon, Hallinan, and Weisberg were recorded on computer when they first came into the office and that they are still there."

Conti was obviously excited and why not? She was giving away the store and this time he hadn't even asked.

"Can you get me hard-copy printouts?"

"I'll give it a try as soon as I can."

"Tomorrow?"

"I have to do it when Barrington isn't around, but maybe late tomorrow night."

Rachel saw Dan smile broadly for the first time in months. "Rachel Cannon, I love you." He then moved close to Rachel and took her hand. "It's crazy," he added, "but I think I really do. Maybe after this thing is behind us we'll get a chance to know each other." Dan turned away, picked up his coat, and walked toward the door. "By the way," he added, "I know about Kevin."

"You know what about Kevin?" asked Rachel, feeling her face flush.

"That he loves you," said Dan, stopping at the door. "It's nothing you've said or done, though I suspect you're aware of the fact yourself. It's the way he is with me. He senses how I feel about you. Some of us macho pigs have intuition, too, you know."

Just as he pulled the door closed behind him, Dan grinned and said, "Oh, yeah—good job today."

The case resumed the following morning with Kevin Stone cross-examining Delbert Norville, the North American production manager called for cross-examination by the plaintiffs. After nearly thirty minutes of sparring, during which he appeared to grow more and more evasive, Norville was finally forced to admit that chemicals identical to those found in the plaintiffs' drinking water were often dumped into an open pit. When asked about the toxic properties of the chemicals, however, he rigorously denied any danger.

Kevin seemed unperturbed as he picked up plaintiffs' exhibit six, a five-pound sack containing a sample core taken directly from the dump site, and held it up in front of the production manager. "Let's see if we really have a disagreement, Mr.

Norville. Are you saying that the scientists, both yours and ours, are wrong when they say that this bag of chemical waste taken from your dump site is full of contaminants dangerous to humans?"

"Damn right I am!" Norville said. "I've run this operation for five years and don't need some college boys telling me what's safe and what isn't."

Kevin stared at the bag in his hand as if he expected it to speak out in disagreement, then slowly extended it toward the witness. Turning his head toward the jury, he said quietly, "Then, of course, sir, you will have no objection to putting your hand down into the waste and leaving it there for a period of, say, two minutes?"

Norville's eyes flickered to where Hancock was already jumping to his feet. "Your honor," cried the defense lawyer. "This is a trial, not a circus."

"So far I'd like to think you're right," said Judge Bainbridge amicably, "but what's your objection?"

"Well, it's . . . prejudicial and a patent attempt to embarrass an officer of the defendant corporation by requiring him to soil his hands in a plaintiff's exhibit. I don't see Mr. Stone doing it."

"And you're not likely to," said Kevin, smiling. "The scientists are unanimous that contact with these chemicals will result in severe chloracne—running sores and lesions—and that merely inhaling from the open bag could cause nausea and damage to the central nervous system."

"You see what I mean," protested Hancock, still standing. "Now he's threatening my client's health!"

"Only," said Judge Bainbridge, "if the scientists are right and your client is wrong. Objection overruled."

"Well, Mr. Norville?" said Kevin, more firmly now.

Delbert Norville's face turned crimson with anger. "Give it to me!" he demanded.

Kevin handed him the bag, saying, "You need only unzip the top. But first," he added, producing from his pocket a small plastic mask and tendering it to Norville, "you should wear this mask and keep your eyes closed after you unzip the bag."

The witness eyed the mask suspiciously for an instant, then took it and put it on. Rachel winked back at Jeffrey, looking tired but otherwise none the worse for wear as a result of his jailhouse experience, then nudged Austin Barrington, whispering, "Strike two on Mr. Norville—he's just put on a protective mask he denies he needs."

"Very good," said Kevin, stepping backward from the bag in exaggerated haste. "Now, sir, all you need do is unzip the top of the bag and immerse your hand. I will tell you when two minutes are up."

With a murderous look at Kevin, the production manager unzipped the bag and gingerly worked his hand partway through the opening. After a few seconds he squinted back at Kevin, but with eyes more pleading than angry. Kevin's tone remained casual, even pleasant, as he said, "I believe, Mr. Norville, we agreed that it would be your entire hand. And I do urge you to keep your eyes closed."

As the hand disappeared farther into the bag, Kevin noted the time on his watch, then, after a seemingly endless period of silence, announced the passage of fifteen seconds. The witness' face was now heavily beaded with perspiration, and he, along with the jurors, watched the slow passage of the courtroom clock's sweep second hand. Finally, as Kevin announced the passage of thirty seconds, the witness jerked his hand out of the bag as if it had been bitten.

"This is ridiculous!" he said, addressing the judge in a whining tone.

Showing no surprise, Kevin took the bag back and, in a matter-of-fact manner, said, "Let's not forget to zip it up tight, Mr. Norville." Later, he would explain to Jeff and Stu that Dr. Judith Barkheim had assured him that if the witness believed sufficiently in the danger, his hand would be burning in thirty seconds even if the bag had contained baking flour. Mainly, however, Kevin would have been willing to settle for what he knew he could get: North American's key witness, hopping mad, with a mask on his face and his hand in a bag of filth. Stifling a grin, Kevin continued. "Your honor, may I suggest a recess so that the witness might be excused for a few moments."

"This court is in recess for ten minutes," announced Judge Bainbridge. Over the din of the crowd, Rachel smiled at Barrington again, and said, "Strike three."

FORTY-THREE

■

At eight-thirty the next morning Rachel cradled the phone against her shoulder as she finished packing her briefcase for court. "Hello, Dan," she said, "I'm at my office and about to leave. I wasn't able to get the thing we talked about last night. There was no privacy here, if you understand what I mean."

"I understand," Conti said.

Rachel heard the disappointment in his voice. "Today's a big day for Austin," she said. "He's putting Childhouse on the stand and worked with him last night here in his office until well after midnight. I'll try again tonight; we're off all day tomorrow. So I doubt Austin will be working tonight. I'll do my best."

"That's all I can ask," he said. "Are you doing anything in court today? It's my day off, and I might come down if the star will be onstage."

"Thanks," she said, "but I'm coasting today—at least I think so. It's Austin's day, and it should be a good one for the home team, but hopefully not a very exciting one for observers. Did the package I sent to you yesterday help any?"

"So far, not much," he said. "I plan to go through it again today. Stu Wallach's client interview notes discussing the victims' medical history tend to support my theory, and the packet of miscellaneous papers that Weisberg's sister sent you make interesting reading." Conti was referring to copies of notes Weisberg had written Barrington, describing his medical symptoms and emotional distress, notes that were then recycled into answers to the defendants' written interrogatories. Dan also had to admit that Weisberg was in constant pain and apparently suicidal. "But I'll keep at it," he added. "Meanwhile, watch yourself; I'll be right here if you need me."

The direct examination of Dr. Childhouse was everything they had hoped it would be. When asked by Barrington to identify the

contents of plaintiffs' exhibit six, he did so with professional
ease, providing the specific description and history of each chemical found at North American, including its potential for causing
injury and illness. Where animal studies provided the only data,
he was scrupulously candid, yet quick to point out the high
correlation between animal studies and epidemiological surveys
and other tests on humans. He was also quick to commend the
wisdom of the previous witness in removing his hand from the
contents of exhibit six, as laboratory analysis had shown the
sample to be heavily laced with solvents such as trichloroethylene, a common dry cleaning agent, which would indeed have
eventually inflicted his hand with "Hooker's bumps." "Just five
gallons of this solvent flushed down a toilet," he added, looking
at the jury as he polished his Ben Franklin glasses, "can poison
the well water necessary to serve fifty thousand households for a
full year."

Most of all, the professor was plainspoken and clear. He had
his class's full attention. The team's months of work had molded
the honored intellectual into a perfect forensic expert.

Later, Hancock's effort to cross-examine Childhouse similarly
backfired as he walked into one carefully set trap after another.
But just as it looked as if the plaintiffs were about to have yet
another perfect day, Hancock jolted them by seeking leave to
call a witness out of order.

"I apologize to counsel and regret the inconvenience to the
Court and to the jury," said Hancock, directing his most winning smile at the nine women and three men. "As you know,
your honor, we originally thought this trial was going to start last
month which, through no fault of ours, it failed to do. My expert
psychiatrist has since been taken seriously ill, and I have found a
replacement—Dr. Emily Fairchild—who I learned last night must
leave the country immediately for a teaching appointment in
Zurich. Unless I am permitted to briefly interrupt the plaintiffs'
case, her testimony will be lost to the defense. It is difficult to
see how plaintiffs will be in any way prejudiced by this minor
but essential rescheduling."

Judge Bainbridge excused the jury in order to hear further
argument on the issue in chambers, and Barrington did his best
to oppose the interruption, pointing out that there would indeed
be serious prejudice since the order of their presentation would
be disrupted and, as they had not had the opportunity to take the
deposition of the new expert, they had no idea what she was

going to say. Following a lively exchange in which Hancock admitted he had retained the expert only a week earlier and had decided only early that very morning to put her on the stand, the trial judge followed the general rule of liberality and ruled she could testify out of order. "But before we go back out there," added the judge with a hard look at Hancock, "you'll now tell counsel here what she's going to say and I'll be listening to make sure she doesn't deviate from your representation. I also intend to inform the jury that through no fault of plaintiffs, they have not been permitted an opportunity to examine her in deposition."

"Very well, your honor," said Hancock, obviously pleased with the compromise. "These plaintiffs are trying to prove they have suffered, and will continue to suffer, severe and long-term emotional distress as a result of traumatic neurosis sustained by virtue of their ingesting water allegedly contaminated by my clients. Dr. Fairchild will simply state that her studies and experience have established that psychiatry is unable to predict with any reliability whatsoever the evolution of traumatic neuroses such as claimed by plaintiffs here. She has read the specific prognoses contained in the reports of plaintiffs' psychiatric expert and will testify that the state of the art in psychiatry has not advanced to a point where such prognoses can legitimately be made."

Kevin leapt to his feet. "Your honor! This is extremely prejudicial. The defense is offering a witness to rebut testimony from a plaintiffs' witness not yet even presented to the jury."

"I'll explain all that to the jury, Mr. Stone," said Judge Bainbridge. "Besides, her testimony may fall on deaf ears for that very reason. Have you considered that, Mr. Hancock?"

"I have, your honor, and I heartily agree," said Hancock, affecting a tone of despair, "but Dr. Fairchild's schedule leaves me no choice in the matter."

"Well, one thing's for sure," said Judge Bainbridge, sniffing as he rose to his feet, "testimony like you've described won't make her popular with her colleagues. All right, let's get on with it."

As the witness was called and made her way through the rail toward the witness box, Stu Wallach leaned close to Jeffrey asking, "Isn't this unusual?"

"It's in the category of marginally acceptable dirty tricks," said Jeff. "The judge probably chewed out Hancock for not listing her as an expert witness and giving us a chance to depose her. He knows that it's practically impossible to cross-examine an expert witness when you don't know in advance what she's going to say."

Dr. Emily Fairchild took the oath and sat poised in the witness box. Rachel figured her for fifty-five to sixty years of age. Her gray-streaked hair was closely curled, and she wore a conservative blue suit that cloaked her slender, erect body with an impression of sincerity. "If she testifies as smart as she looks, she could be trouble," Rachel whispered to Kevin while Hancock led the psychiatrist through a long list of frighteningly impressive qualifications.

"And how long have you been a full professor there?" continued Hancock.

"For eighteen years," replied Dr. Fairchild in a strong throaty voice. "And as you indicated," she added, "I am leaving for Zurich, Switzerland, tomorrow night to engage in a six-month teaching sabbatical there."

"And what will you be teaching in Zurich?"

"I will be teaching a course on newly discovered limitations on predictability of emotional and neurological pathology."

Rachel saw worried looks exchanged between Barrington and Kevin and could understand why. Hancock was scoring the perfect interdiction: putting on a witness to discredit the plaintiffs' planned expert testimony on the high cost of treating traumatic neuroses before the jury had even heard it! "And how did you become interested in this subject, Doctor?" said Hancock, skillfully leading the witness through the preliminaries.

"As I've indicated, I have been in private practice now for nearly twenty-five years in addition to my teaching, and have closely observed my results and those of my colleagues. I began to realize that while we could achieve moderate levels of success in correcting certain forms of emotional pathology, we were committing a dangerous disservice both to the profession and to our patients by claiming to be able to predict anything whatsoever about the future course of traumatic neuroses cases. I began compiling test data on the subject and, as you know, wrote a treatise on the subject last year."

"And was the book based on those studies?"

"Yes, and on a paper I delivered to the American Psychiatric Association's national convention."

Rachel saw Barrington's hands tighten into fists.

"How did your colleagues take to the idea of being told they were ineffectual in a major part of what they were doing?'' asked Hancock, displaying his perfect teeth and swaggering back and forth in front of the trio of plaintiffs' lawyers.

''The good ones already know better than to try to predict, so they applauded my efforts. The rest I don't care about.''

She's good, thought Rachel. She's wiping out the monetary recovery on our cancerphobia theory, taking away our best hope for a big verdict.

''Turning to this case,'' Hancock said, barely able to conceal his pleasure as he picked up the speed and intensity of his questions, ''based upon your study of the medical records of the plaintiffs and the testing methods employed by the plaintiffs' expert psychiatrist, do you have an opinion as to whether *anything* can be predicted to a reasonable degree of medical certainty concerning their prognosis and the need for future medical treatment?''

''My opinion, Mr. Hancock, is that a real professional would not attempt to so testify. If he or she did, it would have no value.''

Hancock glanced over at Rachel, caught her eye, and actually winked. ''And why is it, Doctor,'' he continued, ''that psychiatrists and psychologists cannot make accurate predictions in this area of pathology?''

''Because we have no reliable methods for testing victims of traumatic neurosis. Our tools—Rorschach, Thematic Aperception, and so on—are antiquated and useless. And without the ability to test the degree of pathology, we surely cannot make predictions concerning duration of the supposed illness.''

''Or the need for costly monitoring and maintenance?''

''Or the need for monitoring or maintenance.''

''Would you say that estimates of monetary allowance for these functions would be difficult?''

''I'm saying it would require rank speculation and conjecture.''

''In this case?''

''In all cases.''

''Thank you, Doctor. Your witness, counsel.''

Kevin caught the judge's eye, then pointedly redirected his gaze toward the courtroom clock. Judge Bainbridge picked up the tacit plea and announced the afternoon recess. ''Ten minutes,'' he said, striding from the bench.

While reporters headed for the telephones and Hancock floated back to his chair, Barrington turned to Kevin: ''What in the hell

do we do with this one?'' Kevin was silent, staring at his notes.
"You'll handle the cross, Kevin?'' Barrington asked in a low,
pleading whisper.

Kevin looked up from his notes and slowly shook his head. "I
think we had better leave her alone, get her out of here before
she sinks us even deeper."

"But we've got to do *something*."

"Austin, did you see her up there? Butter wouldn't melt in her
mouth. She's smart as a whip, makes a great impression, and
she's written a book on the subject. If I try to strong-arm her, it
could be construed by the jury as bullying, because she'll be
smart enough to play the woman when it suits her purpose. On
top of that, I can't think of a hell of a lot to ask her. I think this
is one where we do our best to act like she hasn't hurt us and get
her on her way to Zurich as quickly as we can."

"I guess you're right," said Barrington glumly. "But the
jury's expectations . . . Christ, I hate to . . .''

"Kevin?" said Rachel.

"Yeah?"

"Well, I was just thinking. Nobody could accuse us of bullying a woman if a woman were asking the questions."

"That's true, Rachel, but what in the hell would you ask
her?"

"Umm, well, I've got the same problem there that you do.
But I can at least point out her obvious lack of hands-on knowledge of the plaintiffs and her late entry in the case. Anyway,
maybe something will develop as I go along. I don't see any
downside to giving it a try."

"I'm inclined to let her have a go at it, Kevin," Barrington
said, after considering the proposition for a moment. "The jury
knows that we were taken by surprise here and won't expect
much, but they certainly expect *something*. And with Rachel
being twenty years younger than the good doctor, the 'bullying'
might cut the other way. What is there to lose?"

"The downside," Kevin said, scowling, "is that the witness
may get to drive her points home two or three more times."

"I know she'll try," Rachel said, "that's her job. But mine is
to prevent it. The minute she scores on me, you can give me the
hook."

Kevin emphatically shook his head. "If anyone is going on a
suicide mission," he said, "it's going to be—"

"I think she should give it a try," said Barrington, interrupting Kevin, "but be conservative, Rachel. No risks."

"I'll be careful," Rachel said. She poured herself a glass of water and exchanged a look with Jeffrey, who had been listening in. He gave her a smile and a thumbs-up, though what he really wanted to do was persuade her to change her mind.

"If all else fails," he whispered as Rachel walked out toward the hallway to gather her thoughts for a minute, "challenge her to a duel."

Meanwhile, Kevin leaned close to Barrington and spoke with muted vehemence. "That does it, Austin. First the opening statement, now this. It seems obvious that you and our new star litigator can handle this job without me."

Barrington feigned a smile for the benefit of onlookers, then replied with equal intensity. "Easy, Kevin," he said. "I'm merely doing what's best for our clients—as I see it, of course."

"I have a different theory, Austin." Barrington looked around anxiously, but Kevin continued in an intense whisper. "Though I really must credit Denise for it. She had you pegged right all along. You've lost it, Austin, and you hate me because I'm now doing what you used to do, plus I've been doing it better. You would rather risk the outcome of this whole damn case than let me do what you're now afraid to do yourself."

"That's absurd and unworthy of further comment," retorted Barrington, now also coloring with anger. "You're the one whose ego is running amuck here, my boy. The truth is that you liked Rachel better when she was carrying your briefcase, and now you're afraid after her opening statement that you might soon be carrying *hers*. You're afraid you won't be able to handle her on an equal footing. Isn't that what's really eating you?"

Kevin shot the senior partner a murderous look and began to respond, but Rachel returned and the trial resumed with the cross-examination of Dr. Fairchild.

Rachel's initial questions were delivered on eggshells, harmless banter about the major strides in psychiatry since Freud. Then, gradually, Rachel turned more bold. "I'm curious about why we haven't had a chance to talk before," said Rachel casually. "Just when did you get involved in this case?" At least, thought Rachel, I'll remind the jury I haven't had the normal advantage of a deposition.

"One week ago," said the witness without hesitation.

"No, Doctor, excuse me, I apparently didn't make myself

clear," said Rachel, feigning surprise. "When is the very *first* time you were approached by the defense to render testimony in this case?"

"One week ago," said Dr. Fairchild icily. "You heard me *quite* correctly the first time."

Ah, thought Rachel. *Did my sleazy lawyer's trick reveal a tiny crack in the impervious calm?*

"Were you given any reason why Mr. Hancock was ringing you in at the last minute or—"

"*Objection,* your honor!" screamed Hancock. "It's argumentative to suggest that I was 'ringing in' an expert witness at the last minute."

Rachel interrupted before the Court could rule: "Forgive me, Mr. Hancock, you're quite right. I meant to say '*bringing* her in' at the last moment. In any event," said Rachel, spinning back on the witness, "*isn't it a fact that you did not know a single thing about any one of these twelve men until one week ago?*" It wasn't really a question.

"That's right," said Dr. Fairchild, crossing her legs, then uncrossing them.

Rachel dwelled on the point that the witness had never spoken to or examined the plaintiffs, then spent the next ten minutes cautiously probing for a major weakness, a flaw, something to develop. During this process, she momentarily lost her concentration and gave the witness a chance to expand on her supporting studies, at the end of which Dr. Fairchild added with an upraised chin and a flashing of her eyes, "In fact, my studies established that patients in test groups deprived of treatment sometimes did even *better* than those who received prolonged and expensive treatment."

Hancock shot Kevin a twisted smile, though Rachel looked surprisingly unperturbed.

"That's a very interesting point, Doctor," said Rachel, also glancing at Kevin, "and I'm glad you raised it, because it makes me wonder just how you were able to come to your conclusions. How many groups did your study involve?"

"I used three groups with six traumatic neurosis patients in each one. Quite standard blind testing procedure."

"And how did you select your groups of people in a way that would allow you later to determine whether some had made progress and others had not?"

"I ranked the people according to the seriousness of their

symptomatology. One group was composed of an equal blend of seriously and mildly traumatized patients. A second group was comprised of seriously traumatized patients. And the third group was comprised of mildly neurotic people.''

As Rachel slowly paced back and forth in front of the witness, she began to move closer and closer, glancing sideways long enough to cast a quick, confident smile at Kevin. Despite his anger, Kevin's head involuntarily nodded almost imperceptibly, though Barrington and Jeff maintained looks of concerned confusion. "And then, as I understand your testimony," continued Rachel, "you treated all of the mixed group, and half of each of the other two groups. You left the rest of them completely alone and then at the end of a period of one year, you found—"

"That those without treatment," said the witness with obvious impatience, "had improved as much as—sometimes even more than—those who had received treatment."

Rachel stopped her pacing and gave the expert another look of mock surprise, then asked in an offhand manner, "I assume you used the same testing procedures at the end of the study that you used at the beginning so that your results would be correlatable."

"Of course," said Dr. Fairchild. "I used—"

Dr. Fairchild stopped in mid-sentence, coughed twice, and reached for a glass of water. She crossed her legs again and clasped her hands firmly in her lap. She sat even more erect than before and abandoned all traces of the tolerant, bored look. *She knows that I know*, thought Rachel, her heart pounding. *Now it's time to let the jury know.*

Killing time.

Rachel now moved in oppressively close, forcing the psychiatrist deeper into her chair. "Did you finish your last answer, Doctor?" she asked with ostensible courtesy. "I believe you were about to tell us that you used certain tests in order to insure the accuracy of your study. Isn't that correct?"

Kevin elbowed Barrington and smiled in spite of himself.

"Yes," said the witness respectfully now, her imperial manner missing.

"I'd like you to tell the jury which testing methods you used," said Rachel. It was not a question; it was an order.

"I used . . . several methods: TAT—that's the Thematic Aperception Test—Rorschach, clinical judgment, and the like."

"Standard and accepted methods?" asked Rachel.

"Well," said the witness, struggling to find high enough

ground to fight a rearguard action, "they are considered to be by many in the profession."

"And that," said Rachel, "would include yourself, would it not, Doctor? I trust you would not base your conclusions on tests you did not consider to be standard and accepted?"

Dr. Fairchild colored. "That's true," she said.

Rachel spun and shot her next words at the witness. "Then aren't you saying that the conclusions reached in your study, your paper, your book, and your testimony here today were all based on the very same tests used by the plaintiffs' psychiatrist?" The question seemed to slap at the face of the witness, and she visibly winced from its intensity.

"Yes," she answered finally in a barely audible voice.

"And did you not employ these very testing methods to justify your prognosis that the most seriously ill test group had not improved and would not improve as a result of the treatment they had received?"

"Yes," said the witness. "The testing revealed . . . certain trends which allowed me—"

Rachel finished the sentence. "*Which allowed you to predict the future course of their illness!* Am I not right?"

Dr. Fairchild stared at Rachel with hatred as Barrington clutched Kevin's arm and several of the jurors began to make notes on the small writing pads the judge had allowed them to use.

"Yes," came the delayed reply.

Rachel now slowly turned away from the witness and rested both hands on the jury rail, looking from one juror to another as she spoke. "So, Doctor, can we say in summary that the study upon which you based your testimony on direct examination here today relied upon the very same traditional therapeutic techniques, methods, and predictability that your testimony purported to discredit?"

There was no reply. None was required.

Finally, as the witness looked up at her interrogator with defeated eyes, Rachel added in a more gentle voice, "I think that will be all, Doctor. I would not want to further delay your departure to Switzerland."

Seeing that she was free to go, the witness left the witness stand without delay or even a glance at Hancock, who sat staring at his own clenched hands. His brilliantly designed bomb had blown up in his face. The case was only three days old and he, along with everybody else in the courtroom, already knew that the verdict would not be a question of whether, but how much.

Rachel's relief was so great, she barely noticed the perfunctory quality of Kevin's handshake before he snapped his briefcase shut and strode from the courtroom.

PART FIVE

·

THE CHIMERA

·

WINTER, 1983

All that we see or seem
Is but a dream within a dream.

—EDGAR ALLAN POE

FORTY-FOUR

■

"Give it up, Rachel!" said Barrington with an unusually broad smile, his huge presence filling up her doorway. "Haven't you had enough for one day? Besides, we're off tomorrow."

The Grace Cathedral chimes had just rung seven times and, with a day off coming up, Rachel had been counting on Barrington's early departure from the office.

"I'll be out of here pretty soon, Austin. Just cleaning up a few things. By the way, thanks again for your kind words after court today. Your confidence has really given me a boost."

"I meant every word," said Barrington. "As a matter of fact, I'd like to say more, but will exercise restraint until the trial is behind us." The remark exploited Barrington's genius for ambivalence—*is this another of his oblique romantic allusions?* wondered Rachel. *Or is he suggesting that with the now-inevitable trial victory would come my partnership as well?* Today she had demonstrated skill and courage in managing the enemy; sufficiently, perhaps, to counterbalance her "one flaw," her inability to manage her own peers. *But really,* she asked herself, *does one have to make straight A's in every subject in order to make partnership?* "Yes," came the answer—if one is a woman.

"Well, the wait will do me good," she replied, steering a neutral course, "because I've had enough ego-stroking since four-thirty this afternoon to carry me through a lifetime."

Barrington laughed. "Well then, no more of that. But can I offer you a lift anywhere?"

"No thanks, Austin. I've got my car. Have a good evening," she added in a tone that was cordial yet intended to encourage him out the door.

"It's probably best," said Barrington, concealing any disappointment or rebuff he might be feeling. "This is opening night of *The Nutcracker* for me. Annual penance for my sins of the past year—curtain at eight. I trust you will have a nice evening though—God knows you deserve it. See you in the morning.''

Rachel closed her door and spent the next hour reviewing retrieval procedures for calling up data on the IBM terminal located in the litigation support center on the thirty-eighth floor. The eight o'clock curtain provided a sense of security. She would wait until nine, then make her move.

Although her desk was loaded with backed-up work, the time crept by. When, finally, she heard the church's nine chimes, she checked Kevin's office to insure his departure, then caught the elevator to the deserted thirty-eighth floor. Committed now, and not looking back, she made straight for the computer terminal, turned it on, and typed the North American retrieval code three times before she got it right. *Slow down,* she told herself, punching the Enter button after again punching in the code for the medical records category. The records had been indexed and sorted in various ways: age, group, primary disease, alphabetically, and so on. She entered group code "A," added an alphabetical indexing instruction, then pushed Enter again.

"*Voilà,*" she said aloud as fifteen Group A names flashed on the screen in alphabetical order. Excited, she pushed "DIX" for Dixon and, a second later, a dozen pages were indicated. She called them up and scanned them one by one before finally concluding that Jeffrey had been right: There was nothing unusual in Emmett Dixon's records. She repeated the procedure with Hallinan, then Weisberg. Nothing. Dan would be disappointed. So much for men's intuition.

Because the records of Hallinan, Weisberg, and Dixon were so similar to the other twelve sets already in Dan's possession, Rachel wondered whether she really ought to take the time and risk printing them out for Dan. She reached up to turn off the computer. Better take one more quick run-through, she decided.

One by one she scanned the pages again, first Dixon's, then Hallinan's, and then finally Weisberg's. It was not even clear from the records—though undoubtedly true—that the three decedents were in fact the most seriously ill. All were heavily contaminated, but then, so were the others. Then she remembered the day when Barrington became so concerned about Dixon's records and focused her attention on his file, trying to discover what had been missing from his test results that had bothered Kevin and Barrington, initiating her failed effort to have his case severed from the others. Getting nowhere, she called up the medical records of Efrem Weschler, one of the twelve remaining plaintiffs. Alternating between Weschler and Dixon, she tried to find something in Weschler's record that was missing in Dixon's but could find nothing. She was about to give up when, with spine-tingling clarity, there it was: not something missing, *something extra.* She quickly scanned Hallinan and Weisberg again, her heart pounding in her temples.

Her tentative conclusion now confirmed as to all three victims, she slumped back in her chair and tried to slow her racing mind. The blood and tissue samples of each of the three dead men— and *only* the three—showed a high concentration of a chemical called chlordane. Trembling with excitement, she checked the master index, then called up the chemical log file to find out that chlordane was a potentially lethal carcinogen known to cause liver and kidney damage, convulsions, and central nervous system disorders.

Rachel's face glowed with excitement in the eerie light of the cathode ray tube as she scanned forward in order to execute the final step: corroborate the finding by checking out the complete list of chemicals dumped at the North American site. She searched the list in vain for any reference to chlordane. Turning back to the other Group A plaintiffs' test results, she found that not one of them showed a trace of the chemical. As the ramifications of this discrepancy hit home, Rachel felt the strength drain from her as the excitement of a moment ago congealed into a mass of dense confusion. *What was going on?*

Rachel again sunk back into her chair and tried to sort through the possibilities. One thing was obvious: These records in the hands of the defense could destroy everything they had worked for. Everything *she* had worked for. It was also clear now that Barrington had honestly forgotten that these computer files even existed. But exist they did, and with a heavy heart Rachel picked up the phone and dialed Kevin's number at the Ascot Hotel. There was no choice; he had to know what she had found.

Why *me*? she asked of the ceiling as the phone rang. Kevin was not in his room, so she left word for him to call her at home, ran off hard copies of the three decedents' records, and sealed them in a manila envelope.

She considered calling Dan, but felt the need to talk to Kevin first. Maybe . . . somehow, there was an explanation. There *had* to be an answer. It couldn't be as bad as it seemed.

As the elevator took her to the lobby floor, her mind was

generating questions faster than she could process them. Where did the chlordane come from? Should we have added some other chemical company as a defendant? How come three of the plaintiffs showed it and none of the others? The data base had emphasized that once in the system, chlordane was a chemical that stubbornly refused to metabolize. It literally raced to its resting place in adipose tissue—fat. So why didn't the other twelve clients show it in their fatty tissue samples as well? *What am I missing here?* she wondered, staring into the uneasy silence of the darkened underground garage.

Her need to talk to Kevin dominated her thoughts as she moved toward her car, then a rush of growing anxiety as cold as the concrete floor enveloped her as she started to open her car door. *Ridiculous*, she thought. *I do this practically every night.* But now there it was—the unmistakable sound of footsteps.

As she started to turn in the direction of the sound, a voice came at her from out of the semidarkness.

"*You're going to die a young woman,*" said a harsh, deep voice Rachel vaguely recognized, "*unless you stop working these long hours.*"

"*Edgar!*" said Rachel, gasping, her hand clutching her sternum and staring wide-eyed at the security man. "If I die young, it's going to be your fault for giving me a heart attack!"

"Sorry I startled you, Ms. Cannon, just making my rounds. Take care now."

"Thanks, Edgar. I'm a bit jumpy tonight. See you tomorrow."

Rachel drove quickly across the Golden Gate Bridge with her windows wide open to the mid-December air in a vain attempt to clear her clogged mind. She slowed to a crawl as she reached Sausalito and gazed sadly at the full moon illuminating the wildly tossing Bay as she drove along the harbor's edge. The water was boiling so furiously that the neon-white spears of water glancing off the breakwater nearly reached her car before dying on the asphalt.

With similar force a nagging thought kept pushing up through the surface of her intuition, resisted less and less by the gravity force of rationality. An insane thought struck her. Perhaps Dan had been right all along about the murders, but wrong about the murderer and the motive. But that's insane, she thought, turning into her carport; these crazy ideas are the moon's doing.

*   *   *

Within the next hour, Rachel left a trail of urgent messages for Kevin but heard nothing back. Feeling helpless and frustrated, she reluctantly dialed Dan's apartment. *He deserves to know,* she thought, but hung up after the first ring. She looked up Jeffrey's number but then closed her book. She knew she had to wait. She had to talk to Kevin before anyone else. Fifteen minutes later he called.

"Kevin," she said, carefully controlling her voice. "I need to talk to you right away. Could you possibly come over?"

"Of course I can," he said, unable to contain the anticipation in his voice. "Just give me thirty minutes."

FORTY-FIVE

■

While Kevin unknowingly prepared for his moment of bitter disappointment, Alan Hancock railed on the subject of his own unanticipated misfortune.

"Come to sleep, dear," urged Rhoda Hancock. "It couldn't be as bad as you think. Tomorrow's another day."

Hancock slowly shook his head. "You're not hearing me, dear. My key expert witness on cancerphobia self-destructed today in open court."

"But there will be other experts, won't there?"

"Yes, there will be other experts, and they will do better, but they'll be too late to save me. Emily Fairchild was my flagship and she sank today in deep water. I went down with the ship, Rhoda. You should have seen the way the jury looked at me— like *I* was the one who poisoned those guys' water. The bitch Cannon didn't just destroy my witness, she destroyed *me*!"

"Is there any chance the case will settle?"

"Hell, yes, it's got to now. It'll settle tomorrow, in fact. The insurance carrier just authorized me to put up the city's policy limits of thirty million dollars. North American's got to come up with another thirty to forty million."

"Can they? Will they?"

"They can, and they will. They can't take this heat any more than I can. The word came in from the stockholders an hour after we broke for the day: 'Settle by Monday morning at the latest.' We're off tomorrow and I'll have enough money together by early afternoon to satisfy even that bloodsucking Barrington."

Rhoda, ever the optimist, stroked her husband's rigid shoulders and said, "Then it will be behind you, dear."

"The sooner the better," said the lawyer, staring almost unseeing at a mound of records and deposition summaries through ravaged eyes. "You know what really pisses me off? I've been sitting there taking it in the chops for three days now at one hundred sixty bucks an hour, and the fucking insurance company bitches to me about legal expenses. Stafford, Parrish, and MacAllister's fee for doing the same goddamn work we're doing will be a minimum of fifteen to twenty million dollars!"

Silence. "Can you believe that, Rhoda?" he asked. "Is it fair?"

Rhoda shook her head in commiseration and said, "No, darling, it's outrageous. That firm is getting away with murder."

Meanwhile, the Table of Three, peace restored, sat at a table for six at L'Etoile, relaxing with their wives to Peter Mintun's piano following a long evening at the ballet.

"Wasn't it absolutely *beautiful?*" asked Catherine Barrington, evoking fervent agreement from Cecilia White and Florence Fisher.

The men, clustered on the other side of the table, were less enthusiastic. Adrian Fisher wistfully eyed Barrington's Glenlivet and said, "Florence will have to apply a nutcracker to *me* if she expects me to sit through that thing again next year."

"Speaking of nutcrackers," Gardner White said, "it appears that our Ms. Cannon did quite a job on the bad guys today."

"My view on female lawyers is well known, Gardner," Barrington said, "but I must say I have never seen a better piece of surgery in my life."

"Present company excluded, of course," Fisher said, chuckling and slapping Barrington on the knee.

"Present company *included*," Barrington said, "and you can throw in Kevin Stone, who, incidentally, is less than ecstatic about Rachel's rise to fame."

"He'll adapt just as we all will," White said, "to a whole lot of money and a different kind of partnership."

"Correct on both counts," Barrington agreed. "I'd appreciate it, Gardner, if you would start arranging a surprise partnership-announcement party for Rachel. Let's make it something special. We've swallowed the whale; let's not choke on the tail. We might as well let the world think we like it."

"Well, I'll tell you something that may surprise you, Austin," said Adrian Fisher, "I *do* like it. She's made a believer out of me."

"Very well, then," said Barrington. "Here's to our new partner."

If Rachel had decided to call Dan before reaching Kevin, she would not have reached him unless she had dialed the Tosca, Dan's favorite North Beach bar. Weary of staring at the same files and finding no answers, he had wandered up the street for a quick White Nun before bedtime, which had led to three or four. While starting into the second one, he had been joined at the bar by a pair of unusually attractive women in their mid-twenties, then had engaged in some light flirtation via the back bar mirror, leading ultimately to the usual small talk. The one who introduced herself as Dorothy had a boyfriend, but he was out of town and she was showing her companion—an old high school pal now living in Ohio—around San Francisco.

"Lea likes funky places like this. You too?"

"Sure, I like funky places," Dan said agreeably, then recommended some other popular San Francisco bars. The talkative one named Dorothy, however, seemed to think the Tosca would do just fine as long as Dan happened to be drinking there. The one called Lea was a knockout despite a minor cosmetic impediment, the product of several sticks of gum in her mouth at once combined with a fierce resolve to chew them out of existence. There also began to build in Dan's mind considerable doubt concerning Lea's ability to string words together in a complete sentence.

"So what do you do, Dan?" Lea said, breaking her silence, as she continued to savage the lifeless wad.

"Law enforcement," he said.

"Are you FBI? My ex-brother-in-law was FBI in Cleveland."

"I'm not FBI."

"Actually, it was Cincinnati. So what does an FBI agent do in a nice town like this?"

Dan downed his third drink and returned his attention to

Dorothy, saying, "Since I'm the law here, how about I ask the questions now. What's your boyfriend doing letting a pretty lady like you loose on the streets?"

"He travels a lot. In fact, he won't be back in town until the day after tomorrow. How about you? Do you have someone special?"

For the first time, Dan realized he was feeling the drinks. I should be out of here, he thought; drunk on only three White Nuns, or was it four? He turned back to Dorothy and studied her face—a nice face, even pretty in profile. He pictured her breasts under the silk blouse and knew exactly how they'd feel and yet felt a rising desire to find out for sure.

"Well?" asked Dorothy. Dan liked the way her lips pouted just before she rolled out the word. For a crazy instant he considered putting his mouth on those lips, just to see what she would do. Instead, he picked up his change and swung off the stool.

"Yeah, I have a girl—it's just that she doesn't know it yet. You ladies have a good time."

Rachel looked out at the Bay from her kitchen counter, but found neither answers nor consolation there. She became unnerved by the groaning of her coffee maker and decided to rinse her face before Kevin arrived. In the bathroom she looked in the mirror and was disappointed, but not surprised, to see a pale and uneven face looking back at her, and though she knew she should not expect to look anything less than exhausted, the sight of her pallor, the worried line that had formed across her forehead, depressed her. She angled her head and spotted several gray hairs in the mirror. Maybe she should have her hair cut; not stylishly short, rather just above her shoulder—she'd seen a style she'd liked last month in *Cosmo*.

Then, she caught herself up short: Her anxiety had nothing to do with the newly discovered signs of age and everything to do with the fact that Kevin Stone was on his way to Sausalito at this moment, no doubt thinking her summons meant the end of the moratorium between them, a romantic victory celebration. And instead, he was about to learn that something—something possibly devastating—was very, very wrong.

FORTY-SIX

■

Kevin Stone had raced across the bridge, negotiating the twenty-minute drive from his hotel in fifteen, certain that Rachel's call meant the resumption of their relationship. A new beginning.

As he entered Sausalito, however, he slowed down, suddenly nervous, plagued by Barrington's words and a growing concern that Rachel was indeed no longer the worshipful associate he'd dazzled in New York just over a year ago. Nor was it even clear after today that he was still the champion of S.P.&M.'s trial staff. Yet with his financial future soon to be secured, his dark secret almost buried, and his reservation at the Table of Three now confirmed, he could live with that. He would, of course, make his peace with Barrington. After all, accommodations had to be made in life—the trade-offs one must endure to survive. Yet, the thought had continued to nag him as he'd neared Rachel's condo: Even if he could live without top billing, could he live with the one who had succeeded to it? Well, time would tell, he'd thought, a smile crossing his face. God knows, Rachel was worth taking a shot at it. It seemed he had lived his life either in the illusion of a successful relationship or the reality of its failure. Perhaps Rachel was the alchemist who would turn years of illusion into reality.

It had not taken long for him to discover that another illusion was about to shatter. One look at Rachel's face as she opened the door had done it.

Now, as he sank heavily into a chair in her living room, he tried to deal with the catastrophic import of her words. It had been obvious from the moment she started to speak that his romantic optimism had been foolish and unjustified. But then the bombshell had landed.

She knew.

What Rachel still didn't know was that she was telling Kevin things *he* already knew.

"What do we do, Kevin?"

Kevin composed himself. "Why do anything?" he said tentatively.

"Why do anything," she repeated in a flat, emotionless tone. Then, her voice rising: "Need I remind the teacher that we are officers of the court, and that I'm holding here in my hand evidence requested by the defense and which you and I—probably even Barrington—legitimately but erroneously thought had been destroyed. I'm beginning to have my suspicions about all this convenient innocence, by the way," she added, one eyebrow arched as she regarded Kevin.

"Suspicions?"

"From the start, Austin has been unusually circumspect concerning these medical records. You convinced me that this was his style, that we all do our separate parts, but I'm now beginning to think that maybe he hastened to destroy them intentionally— I mean, he intended to destroy them intentionally even though he didn't. Oh, God, I'm tired, but you know what I mean."

Kevin knew what she meant.

"Don't you see? Our three clients who died just also happened to be the only ones who had chlordane in their tests. Just to play detective for a minute—don't laugh—suppose Barrington found out about the chlordane, realized our whole case was blown because North American doesn't produce it, then, well, you told me about the firm's utter dependence on the success of this case . . ."

"Yes?" said Kevin, his voice casual, belying his growing despair as Rachel approached the predictable and final step in her deductive process.

"Well, what if Barrington concluded that the only way he could cover it up was to . . . to, well, get rid of the three men?"

"Don't you think you've been spending too much time with Detective Conti?" asked Kevin, trying to derail her line of thought, but Rachel was too engrossed to respond to his jibe.

"I realize it's probably crazy. Paranoia about homicide is indeed Dan's department. We'll just have to see what he thinks about all this."

"Rachel, wait a minute," Kevin continued calmly. "You want to give those records to Dan Conti?"

"What else can we do, Kevin? I think we've also got to give them to Hancock. The spirit, if not the letter, of our pretrial discovery rules requires their disclosure."

"And the canon of ethics requires us to vigorously represent our clients," responded Kevin. "We have to decide where our loyalties lie. Remember that although you and I know that not one of our present, living clients has any chlordane in his blood or tissue samples, Hancock is a good enough lawyer to blow all one hundred and forty-seven cases out of the water if we give him this to work with."

"But Kevin," said Rachel, regarding him through narrowed eyes, "you could justify nearly anything using that kind of rationalization."

Tell me about it, thought Kevin grimly. "No 'buts,' Rachel. I want those records," he said, extending his hand, an expression of determination on his lined face. "This is a partnership decision," he added, "and Austin and I will make it."

Rachel, puzzled, gave him an injured, curious look. His manner had shifted to a cold insistence she had never seen in him, even when angry. She remained silent, but Kevin saw her hands tighten on the envelope, and finally averted his eyes from hers. After a tortuous moment of silence he rose and walked over to the window-wall, his back to her.

"There's even more to this than I have guessed, isn't there, Kevin," she said.

He said nothing.

"Conti was right, wasn't he," she said. Again, it was an assertion, not a question; a statement that pleaded for a denial, for an incredulity and outrage to match her own.

Silence. Kevin stared out toward Alcatraz.

Rachel looked down at the envelope in her hands, then back up at Kevin. "And whatever it is," she said, her voice breaking, "you're in it too, aren't you?" Kevin remained silent, his back still turned against her pleading eyes, in which tears had begun to form.

"Kevin. You've got to *talk* to me. Tell me what's going on."

Kevin's mind whirled around the possibilities, none of them promising. *Perhaps,* he thought, *it's time to resort to the truth. Austin was able to persuade me, after all, and if Rachel really loves me, my job should be easier.* He turned and met her pleading pale, gray-green eyes. *She loves me, all right,* he concluded, walking back to her and taking her hand.

"Okay, Rachel, here it is. All I ask is that you hear me out from start to finish and that you never forget for a second how much you mean to me. Remember that I'm the guy who left his family out of love for you and that's just the beginning of what I'll do once we're together and this is all behind us. Do you understand that?''

"I . . . well, yes, Kevin, but . . ."

"Then sit down and listen. Please." Rachel complied while Kevin gathered himself to argue the toughest case of his career.

"It all started with Newkirk, when he blew the exploratory test results on the first five prospective plaintiffs. Remember how excited everybody was? Remember the press release? The detailed complaint we filed? Well, it all began to unravel when Newkirk admitted to Barrington that his lab technician had inadvertently exaggerated the toxicity in Hallinan's, Weisberg's, and Dixon's bodies. It turned out Austin had picked, by the worst possible chance, some of the weaker cases from a testing standpoint. The first guy he broke the news to was Weisberg, who—"

"Kevin . . ." said Rachel, starting to interrupt.

"Please, Rachel, let me finish," said Kevin as he came back and sat down across from her. "Believe me, I didn't know anything I'm telling you until it was already over and done with." He paused, and shook his head. "If I had, I swear to you we wouldn't be having this conversation."

Rachel sat back with an obvious effort of will and Kevin continued, explaining Weisberg's insistence and Barrington's acquiescence and how it had worked so well, Austin decided to administer the supplement to the other two as well. The only problem was the chlordane in one lot of the supplement, a chemical that North American had never produced. "Barrington originally thought that only Weisberg had received doses from the bogus batch, but then it showed up in Hallinan's next blood test and Barrington realized that his problem could no longer be solved by altering records or running new tests. Chlordane stores itself in fat; hardly any is metabolized, so he . . ." Kevin's voice broke, revealing the strain beneath his outward calm. "So he would have to dispose of the people themselves—"

Rachel's body stiffened as if struck by a deadening cold wind. She looked ill. *This isn't working,* Kevin thought, fighting a rising panic. His words were coming faster now, as if he were fighting a deadline. "Believe me, darling, I knew nothing of this. It was presented to me as a *fait accompli.* As for Dixon, neither Newkirk nor Barrington realized that he had also been given doses from the bad batch until I spotted it that day in Barrington's office. The full import didn't hit me at the time, since I still thought that Hallinan was an accident and Weisberg a suicide. If I had known what Barrington was planning, I would have stopped it, of course.'' Tears, beginning to fill Rachel's eyes, told Kevin that she had just realized the consequences of her failed attempt to get Dixon severed from the first trial. ''Maybe I should have known what Barrington would do, but in my wildest imagination I didn't think it possible.''

Kevin saw that Rachel had curled her legs up underneath her, her arms folded and shivering. He wanted to go to her, hold her, but he feared her reaction and he knew he must continue until he had finished. ''I was wrong, of course. He had Dixon killed too. We were just a week away from having to turn over his medical records and to present him for blood, tissue, and general physical testing by the defense that would have shown the presence of chlordane. The game would have been up. You know the rest. Austin brought me in when it was over, when it was too late to change anything. And he'd rationalized everything so perfectly that it was hardly like he was talking about people at all, about . . . murder—''

Rachel looked at Kevin's tortured face and finally spoke. Now she appeared calm, almost removed from what she was hearing. ''Dan Conti told me once that death by murder was the ultimate weapon of greed; the ultimate obscenity. He was so right, wasn't he, Kevin? He was right on just about everything, I guess.''

Her words sliced into Kevin's heart. He had lost her. Involuntarily, his throat constricted with anger and despair. He wanted to scream the pain out of his suffocating lungs, to shake Rachel, slap her if necessary, until she understood the reasons for his silence, his collaboration. *It wasn't me! I could do nothing!*

But he said nothing, stood mute. *Nolo contendere.*

Rachel unwound her long legs, rose to her feet, and slowly walked across the room to her window-wall. Outside, flashing white wings of gulls bolted in and out of ribbons of light shooting from the deck of a neighboring restaurant. A curtain of glowing mist gave the birds a preternatural appearance that made her shiver again. ''Just when,'' she said quietly, ''did you learn all this, Kevin, and how?''

Rachel's voice sounded flat, drained of emotion and utterly lacking in charity, while Kevin had reached that state of fatigue where even his own words sounded alien to him—seemingly logical when spoken but of doubtful merit by the time they were heard. Yet those brave and self-serving utterances continued to march relentlessly from his mouth, like doomed soldiers. "In bits and pieces," he replied at last. "I know it seems incredible, but every time I learned something, it had already happened, and there was nothing I could do about it. I learned about the artificial supplement after it had been completed. I learned about the murders after Dixon's death. Each time Barrington had all the answers. *Nothing can be accomplished by blowing the whistle now,* he would say. *You will only be depriving one hundred and forty-seven living plaintiffs—your clients—of their rights under the law against the truly guilty parties. All three of them were old men, soon to die anyway, leaving nobody dependent on them.* On and on. He was right, of course, and on top of all that, there was the fate of Adrian Fisher. Imagine, Adrian in jail!" But Kevin could see that his words were having no impact on Rachel. The "logic" that had won him, had silenced him all these months, held no suasion for her, invoking only incredulity and disdain.

"The Table was in on it? All along?"

"Almost from the beginning, which gave Austin another leverage point. He kept challenging me to name one thing I would accomplish by coming forward, other than to send Adrian Fisher to prison and a wretched death. I agonized over it, Rachel, then went along. That's it. That's the story."

"And the break-in here at my apartment?"

"It was Barrington, still planting Mafia seeds. He figured that you were the quickest route to Conti, and Conti went for it." Kevin marveled at his own pettiness in taking a modicum of satisfaction in his last uttered words. "When you told me about what had happened, I went crazy, and forced Barrington to give me his word—"

"His *word*!" cried Rachel, awakened from her lethargy.

". . . never to play that game again and on that—dammit, Rachel, *listen to me*—on that, at least, I still believe him. Whoever left the note in the courtroom was a copycat nut, just trying to get into the act." His words were hollow. *He'd lost her.*

Rachel stood immobile, turning the sealed envelope over in her hand. She turned her head southward and stared across the charcoal Bay. The lights of San Francisco blinked through a film of fog.

"Well?" said Kevin anxiously.

"Well what?" said Rachel without emotion.

"What are we going to do?"

"*We?*" she said, then brusquely walked to the chair over which Kevin had flung his coat. She picked it up and held it out to him, saying, "*I'm* going to bed. Good night, Kevin."

For a brief moment their wounded eyes met in a confused embrace of crossed messages: disillusionment, mingled with the shreds of longing, and tangled by fear. Then Kevin turned away and walked to the door. But as his hand touched the door handle he stopped, and with his back to Rachel he spoke in a voice so flat and quiet as to be barely audible. "When I was just a kid, they took my class to the zoo in Golden Gate Park. Fleishhacker Zoo. Just as we got to the reptile area, a small dog had wandered in and had become caught in the coils of a boa constrictor. We were all pretty upset but we just stood there and watched. I had always thought boas crushed their victims, but it turns out they don't have the strength to do that. They just hold on, and then each time their victim exhales, they tighten up a little bit, holding them in that new position—like living Velcro—so that their victim dies in pieces, not all at once."

Kevin paused for what seemed a full minute, but Rachel said nothing, and he slowly turned to face her, his face now gray with despair. "Do me one last favor," he said, finally. "When you decide, let me know first." Rachel thought for a moment, then nodded her agreement.

As he opened the door, he turned again and added without smiling, "I won't jump bail. I'll be in my office early."

Rachel turned her head to the side and quickly closed the door, determined that he not see her tears again.

FORTY-SEVEN

Distant thunder, sounding the approach of another storm, awakened Rachel at four o'clock, just as she had begun to doze for the first time. A spark of lightning just off the horizon caught her eye, then was quickly absorbed by the mud-gray sky. She counted

the seconds it took for the sound of the thunderclap to reach her.
Was the storm coming closer or moving away from her? Her
father had taught her how to tell the difference.

Her father. What would he tell her to do if he were here? God
knows it was time to resort to solid values of generations past.
She had to smile, realizing that her father was hardly the person
to turn to for solid values. She tried to picture him in a character-
istic pose or in something other than the suit depicted in the
photograph displayed on her mantel. But the picture on the
mantel *was* her father, all she would ever know of him. Moral
training? Ethics? All she recalled now were vague images of
occasional visits to his law office on weekends, drawing count-
less pictures while he studied briefs.

Pictures in crayon. A photograph on the mantel.

Father.

Sleep crept up from behind her thoughts, but she awoke again
after two hours, just ahead of the alarm's intrusion. A glance out
the window confirmed that winter was still in control, though
daylight had now delineated water from sky. The phone rang.
She did not answer. But arose, made tea and sat, sipping it, long
legs folded beneath her, watching the standoff between the sun
and the fog until her decision was made. By the time she had
showered, dressed, and driven to the Golden Gate Bridge, Tiburon
had broken partially free from the grasp of morning fog, though
Alcatraz remained its prisoner.

Rachel had never seen Kevin look so haggard. A sleepless
night had set deep lines on either side of his mouth, and his brow
was so pinched that he looked like a gravely perplexed, much
older man, as he crouched behind his desk, staring at a picture of
his daughters. His sad, red-blotched eyes stabbed at her heart.

Kevin knew, had always known, what her decision would be.

Unable, unwilling to deny her instinctive reaction, she walked
around his desk and held his head tenderly against her breast.
How she had loved him. She held him that way for what seemed
like minutes, then walked back around to the other side of his
desk. Tears were again beginning to streak her face.

"It's funny," said Kevin with a twisted smile and running a
hand through his disheveled hair. "The first case I ever lost—
argued to a friendly judge."

Rachel smiled. "You're still the best, Kevin. You always will
be."

Kevin maintained his ironic smile, but now his eyes too were filled with tears as he acknowledged her words with a quick nod of his head. They said nothing more, and she slowly turned and left his office.

Dan Conti's headache was nonspecific but unyielding. As he splashed cold water on his face, it occurred to him that he had not eaten for twenty-four hours. He shuffled into his kitchen and was just opening the refrigerator when the phone rang.

"Good morning, Lieutenant," came the cheery voice of the desk sergeant: "We've had some call-ins; the damn flu is taking us one by one. Can we get you to come in at six and work swing?"

"My pleasure." Conti groaned and plopped into a chair at his document-laden kitchen table. "Assuming I'm still alive by then."

"Are you sick, too, Lieutenant?" came the gruff but concerned voice. "Fever?"

"No, Sergeant, nothing so respectable. I've just got a few White Nuns pounding repentance into my head this morning. If they don't stop soon, I don't think I want to live till six."

"Wash down two aspirin with an Alka-Seltzer and you'll drown the good ladies," said the sergeant, chuckling. Conti blinked, shook his head, blinked again, then fell into a dinette chair so hard the plastic cracked. "If they don't stop soon, I don't think I want to live," he repeated.

"Yeah, Lieutenant, I heard you the first time. Lieutenant? Are you still there? You all right?"

"Yeah . . . I'm fine . . . in fact, I've just taken a major turn for the better." *If they don't stop soon, I don't want to live,* he repeated to himself as he hung up and began to rummage wildly through the notes, documents, and answers to interrogatories. Then, at last. He grabbed at a page in front of him. He read it as if it were a long-awaited letter from a cherished lover, shaking his head and smiling ruefully, stroking his nose all the while. There, sitting in front of him all the time, had been his answer: copies of Bernard J. Weisberg's message from the grave, compliments of his sister:

Dear Mr. Barrington:

As you requested, I enclose my rough ideas about how to answer the written interrogatories from the defendant. I have tried to be very complete but you will please consider these to be my first attempt. I have put my thoughts for answers to some of the questions on separate 3x5 cards so you can pick the best one for my case and throw away any you don't like.

Sorry about no answers to some questions because I had already given information to Rachel, i.e., medical bills, time off work, etc.

Please hurry my case to trial because I need money for surgery, debts, etc. As you know, I've taken a turn for the worse. No one but myself to blame, I guess, but please hurry the case to trial.

Sincerely yours,
Bernard J. Weisberg

Conti hurriedly shuffled through the cards until he found Weisberg's scribbled reply to interrogatory number eighty-three; the interrogatory read as follows:

Question: If you claim damages for pain and suffering, state in detail the nature and duration of said pain and suffering.

Bernard's notes were draft answers, ideas to be put on three-by-five cards, largely illegible and difficult to read, but Conti found the sheet entitled "notes to #83" and reread the following excerpts:

"Constant humiliation . . . pills okay on pain but feel like Dr. Jekyll and Mr. Hyde . . . how do you win? *I'd as soon be dead*."

Conti clapped his hands together loudly and began scavenging through his own files before removing an envelope marked "7/19/83: Bernard J. Weisberg suicide note."
He placed the note beside the scribbling and reread the note:

Everybody knows that cancer means pain. I have learned that it also means the day by day humiliation of your spirit and the destruction of your soul.

Pills help the pain but they turn me into someone else I don't know and don't like. The more pills I take, the more I change. Every day now I need more of them.

I would prefer the pain, except that it grows too strong for me to bear so that I weaken and take the drugs and become someone else again. I have tried them all. It's always the same.

I am rambling a bit. The point is, what kind of life is this? I hurt physically without the pills. I suffer even more emotionally when I take the pills. And the Grim Reaper is always there in the wings waiting for me.

The answer is: it's no kind of life at all and I'm sorry, but you can have it.

Laughing like a maniac, Conti fell back into his chair, the scribbled handwriting of the victim in his left hand, the "suicide note" in the other.

"*Barrington!*" he shouted out loud. "*It was that pontifical asshole Barrington all along!*"

Conti glanced at his watch: eight-twenty A.M. He grabbed a shirt, stuck one arm through while grabbing the telephone. A quick call to headquarters; pants, shoes, an apple out of the icebox. The telephone rang again. Conti took three steps toward the door but swung around and grabbed it. "Yeah?" he shouted impatiently.

"Dan, it's Rachel. I'm so glad you're off the phone . . . Dan . . . it's about Austin Barrington—"

"I know. He's our murderer," said Dan, interrupting. "But I haven't yet figured out why."

"You know?" She was incredulous for an instant. "How did you find out?"

"It just this minute hit me. The so-called 'suicide note' was really a proposed answer to an interrogatory Weisberg sent to Barrington." He continued as if resuming a conversation they'd recently left off. "Fortunately, Weisberg kept some drafts and they were in the package of documents his sister sent you. Maybe Barrington worked it out that way or maybe it just happened, but either way it turned out looking like a perfect suicide note—perfect because it was in his own handwriting. And since Barrington concealed from me the fact that it was really just an answer to an interrogatory, it has to be him. And you? How did you find out?''

''As you said all along, it was in the medical records,'' said Rachel softly; the topic itself demanded a hushed tone; they were now co-conspirators in the truth. ''Barrington killed Weisberg and the others—had them killed—because their bodies contained a chemical that North American neither produced nor disposed of. It would have blown our case.''

''Christ!''

''There's more, Dan. Barrington was poisoning our own clients to qualify them for a new, almost foolproof legal theory for recovery. Weisberg even volunteered for it, but then the toxicologist screwed up and three of them took in heavy doses of the wrong stuff.''

''Anybody else in on it?''

Dan listened as Rachel's attempt at controlled breathing echoed in the telephone receiver. ''The Table of Three, Newkirk and—''

''Stone?'' said Dan quietly, intuiting the struggle at the other end of the line.

''Dan, listen to me. He did none of it, he only found out about it afterward.'' She knew it sounded weak; she would do better later. ''He was afraid to say anything because of what would happen to the rest of the clients . . . and to Adrian Fisher. Barrington convinced him that nothing could be changed anyway. So he went along.''

''Where are you, Rachel?''

''In the office.''

''Stone?''

''He's here.''

''Barrington?''

''I saw him a few minutes ago.''

''Does he know what's happening?''

''I don't know,'' she said. ''Kevin knows, but he won't leave.''

''How do you know he won't?'' he asked.

''I know,'' she answered.

''Rachel, do exactly as I say. Walk directly to the elevator and take it down to the street. Turn to your right as you hit the street, and don't stop until you find a cop or an empty taxicab. *Get out of the Imperial Building!*''

Conti hung up and redialed the desk sergeant.

*   *   *

Kevin looked up to see his doorway filled by Austin Barrington. "Kevin, I need to discuss my unforgivable insensitivity yesterday and review a few things with you before the nine o'clock team meeting. Which one of us, for example, is going to take on . . . Jesus, Kevin, you're a mess! What in God's name is the matter with you?"

"Sit down a minute, Austin. Close the door."

Without taking his eyes off Kevin's distraught face, Barrington complied, and lowered himself into a client chair. "Are you ill? Are you still upset about yesterday?"

"The answer to both those questions is yes, but that's not what I want to talk to you about."

"Well? You've certainly got my attention. What is it?"

"Austin," said Kevin, slowly raising his bloodshot eyes to face Barrington, "it's all over. We're finished. All of us."

"What's over? Who's finished?"

Kevin only half met the irritated senior partner's eyes. "Rachel knows everything," he said in a tired voice, "and by now she's told Conti."

Barrington leapt to his feet and leaned across Kevin's desk, snarling his words: "Everything? She's told Conti . . . *everything*?"

Kevin instinctively rolled his chair back a foot or two to distance himself from the reddening face of the senior partner and said, "Your victims, Austin; their records were not all destroyed after all. You forgot about the computer disks. Everything is automatically programmed as it comes into the office now and—"

Barrington exploded with a cry of anger and advanced around the desk. He seized Kevin by the lapels, pulled him out of his chair, and slammed him against the wall. "Stop babbling, you idiot! Are you saying she found out about the chlordane?"

"Yes."

"But she can't know about the *murders*!" It was the first time Kevin had heard the Great Equivocator say it like it was.

"She knows," said Kevin quietly, offering no resistance to Barrington's physical explosion. "I told her."

"You . . . did . . . *what*?"

"I told her everything."

Barrington's head snapped up, then angled skeptically to one side. "You didn't. You're joking, Kevin, and it's not at all funny."

"I told her everything, Austin." The defiance of truth was in Kevin's eyes. Barrington no longer had any power over him. That was finished, done with.

"I don't believe you. You can't have done that. I thought . . ."

"You thought I'd become just like you, Austin. Well, maybe I almost did. Maybe the only difference between us is that I know when I'm stuck with the check and it's time to pay up."

Kevin saw first astonishment, then fury register in Barrington's eyes, yet he found himself strangely relaxed and passive. Barrington tightened his hold on Kevin's coat, threatening to lift him off his feet. The senior partner's huge neck and head were nearly purple with bulging veins, his eyes almost popping out. With incredible strength, Barrington lifted him off the floor and jammed him even harder against the wall. Then, panting for breath, he released the younger man, who had to struggle for a moment to maintain balance atop weakened legs. "*Why?*" he said, hissing through a clenched jaw. "Why in God's name did you tell her?"

"What does it matter now, Austin?" Kevin shook his head impatiently. "She discovered the chlordane herself and was suspicious about the rest. Complete candor was our best hope. It just didn't work." Kevin shrugged his shoulders in a matter-of-fact way. "What's really odd is that I'm telling *you* that I told *her*. I guess in some strange way—habit I suppose—I feel obligated to . . . keep you informed." The last words were followed by an ironic laugh. "But you must have a backup plan, Austin," he added conspiratorially. "An escape route; someone else to blame, some way out. You've always thought of *everything*. Surely this can't be the end of the line."

"Your treachery and stupidity is one thing I never counted on," said Barrington, backing up a step. "How long ago did she tell Conti?"

"Ten, maybe fifteen minutes ago."

"She discovered the chlordane this morning? How?"

"No, she told me last night what she had learned."

Barrington flared again. "Then why the hell didn't *you* call *me* last night? I could have talked her out of it! *I could have kept her quiet!*"

Kevin faced Barrington squarely as he said: "Oh, yes, I know you could have silenced her, Austin; and that's precisely why I didn't tell you last night."

Barrington again exploded with fury, this time lashing out

with his giant right hand and smashing Kevin with a violent blow to his chin. Kevin had seen the punch coming, and might have deflected its full impact had his head not been so muddled to begin with. It should have been obvious that Barrington's mallet fist was in motion toward his face, but it registered in Kevin's brain as a mass frozen in space, like the illusory inertia, at first glance, of the second hand of a watch. Thus unprepared, he absorbed the full force of the blow and felt himself sinking into unconsciousness. He fell backward, dizzily struggling to maintain his footing, then felt another sensation—like being struck by something behind him—and this time his brain seemed to detonate: flashing lights turning into warm reverberations, slowly absorbing him . . . into the warmth.

Barrington, his left hand clutching shattered right knuckles, walked swiftly out of the room without noticing the flecks of blood on the corner of the oak bookcase behind Kevin's bleeding head.

FORTY-EIGHT

■

Conti did not wait to be announced this time as he and two police officers strode from the elevator toward Barrington's corner office. Dan paused only long enough to confer briefly with a uniformed officer who had reached the floor a few minutes ahead of him. The receptionist warned Barrington of Conti's imminent intrusion just as the inspector and two uniformed police officers were already entering his office.

"Yes, my dear, it's quite all right. Thank you," said Barrington, gently replacing the receiver. "Come in, Lieutenant, come in," he added with a welcoming smile, gesturing to a chair in front of his desk. "Your friends may join you if they wish."

"Wait outside the door," said Conti to the others.

"So, copper," said Barrington, a crooked smile on his pallid face, "I guess the jig's up, eh?" He dropped the pseudo accent, but could not resist one more cliché: "I've been expecting you."

"I take it you've seen Mr. Stone?" said Conti, not amused.

"Indeed I have. He had the belated courtesy to tell me that you'd be coming here to read me my rights or whatever it is you fellows like to do." Barrington casually sipped his coffee, then lit a cigarette, adding, "Have you already placed Mr. Stone in chains?"

"We'll be placing him in an ambulance as soon as one arrives," said Conti.

"An ambulance, you say! Perhaps I've been in the wrong line of work all this time. My uncharacteristic tantrum culminated in but one punch, surely not enough to send that hard-headed Irishman to the hospital. He'll recover."

"There's a very deep indentation in the back of his skull," said Conti with restraint. "His head apparently struck the book-case after you hit him."

Barrington drew deeply on his cigarette, sipped his coffee again, then resumed his relaxed half smile. "Although I regret Kevin's inconvenience, I think you would agree that my modest assault constitutes a relatively venial offense when viewed against the backdrop of my more ambitious undertakings."

"Before you say another word," said Conti through clenched teeth, "it is my duty to warn you that anything you say may be held—"

"*Oh, stuff your Miranda Rule!*" said Barrington, slamming his cup on the desk. "I won't be patronized like a common criminal."

"You're entitled to remain silent and to have the benefit of counsel," continued Conti, adding, "I want you to know your rights for my benefit, Barrington, not yours, because if you do say anything, I want to be able to use it to lock you up in state prison, where you belong."

"Jail, you say? You'd settle for jail after all the mischief I've caused? After all the trouble you've gone to? Does this suggest the possibility that you possess a modicum of sympathy, or at least understanding, concerning the pressures that have governed my difficult choices?"

"None whatsoever, Barrington. As I told you once before, I'm opposed to killing, irrespective of who's doing it. But nothing will stop me from seeing you rot behind bars for what you've done."

Barrington maintained his dry smile. "A cliché worthy of Robert Stack," he said, then looked around his office as if viewing it for the first—or last—time. Conti watched Barrington's eyes travel in and out of his conference area, across the wall of his main office, fixing for a moment on a hanging behind where Conti was seated. "Do you like it?" asked Barrington. "It's my favorite. It's a Persian Armanibaf Bakhtiari, similar to the one hanging in the reception room. Fourteenth century. Picked them both up in an auction in Hong Kong for a mere fifty thousand. I wish I could take it with me."

"Not where you're going," said Conti, meeting Barrington's smile with his own.

"But you don't know where I'm going. In fact, Inspector, you don't know very much about anything. You couldn't even figure out what was going on until a young lady had to explain it all to you." The senior partner winced suddenly with pain, then added, "Isn't that right?"

"If you say so," said Conti. "Now, if you've had your fun, I think it's time to go."

"Fun?" said Barrington, flashing anger. "You think this has been *fun*? You think it was *fun* working all my life to become the head of the greatest law firm on the West Coast, only to see it all threatened by an economy beyond my control? Recession, deregulation, inflation, interest rates, austerity programs, client bankruptcies, bad debts, you name it! Then I try to somehow salvage everything, to put it all back together, only to have a meddling female, a love-struck partner, and a cop ruin everything I had accomplished! *Fun* you say?"

Barrington had lost his earlier composure. His outburst left him breathless and even more pale, yet he continued speaking, but now in a quiet, conversational tone. "Have you ever lost something very precious to you as a result of your own mistake—something or someone more important than your own life? Yes, I can see you know what I mean. You made a mistake once, too, didn't you, Detective? Oh, yes, Captain Mahan told me all about your little secret. You see, Inspector Conti, you and I have something in common after all. The difference is that your mistake only cost a man's life. My mistake—putting my trust in incompetent fools—will result in the death of an institution, a tradition more important than you or I or anyone else."

Conti said nothing. He felt himself drawn into Barrington's strange peroration and strangely reluctant to end it. He noticed, however, that Barrington was beginning to perspire heavily and that his voice was becoming more strained as he struggled to continue.

"Yes, Detective, I learned from Captain Mahan all about your preoccupation concerning death. I've become very interested in the subject myself . . ." Barrington's face now became even more distorted and gray, and he suddenly doubled over, knocking a marble fountain pen set off his desk as he folded his arms together tightly over his stomach.

"Are you all right, Barrington?" he asked. Conti started to rise, but the senior partner quickly straightened and dismissed Dan's concern with a quick wave of his hand. He then resumed his attitude of apparent calm, and continued speaking.

"And you know, Inspector, we are also alike in our dedication to our chosen professions. I believe I have been every bit as zealous in protecting the life of my firm as you seem to be about protecting life in general."

"And if you had to murder a few people here and there—"

"Oh, come now, Lieutenant, let's not get righteous. Isn't it obvious to a man like yourself that this country was not built on the principle that a few should determine the lives and fortunes of the many?"

Conti stared coldly at Barrington. "You killed them to perpetuate the ideals of democracy, Mr. Barrington; is that what you're saying?"

"I'll ignore your sarcasm," Barrington said, "for in a manner of speaking it's true. Those three doomed and lonely men died so that others might live out their lives in relative comfort, financial independence, and dignity." Barrington took a long drink from his coffee cup, scowled, then lit another cigarette. "But it was not meant to be. You and I, Inspector Conti . . . you and I with our own private obsessions . . . both doomed to become failed zealots."

"Yes, I should have figured it all out long ago," said Conti, breaking his silence. "To that extent I have failed."

"That's not what I mean," said Barrington with a forced laugh. "There was nothing you could do, nothing *anyone* could do to save those three men's lives. I was referring to your failure to save my own . . . to your failure to see me subjected to the whim of a jury of my . . . peers . . . to see me 'rot behind bars' as you so inelegantly put it."

"What are you talking about?" said Conti with a puzzled look at the senior partner.

"I'm talking about failure, Lieutenant. How, for example, do you think I administered the toxins to those old fools? Hasn't that even interested you? You really disappoint me, Inspector Conti."

As Barrington raised his coffee cup to his lips, Dan suddenly leapt from his chair and threw himself across the desk at Barrington, slamming the cup out of his hand and across the room, where it shattered against the wall.

"You *bastard*!" said Conti, pushing himself away from Barrington, then falling back into his own chair. "*You rotten bastard!*" Hearing Conti's voice, the two officers crashed into the room.

"Has anyone ever talked to you about your style, Lieutenant?" said Barrington, straightening his suit coat with suddenly shaking hands. He attempted a mocking smile, but his face was now too contorted, his eyes nearly closed. "Why should I not be allowed to pick my own time and place? Like you, Conti, the law has been my religion and, well . . . this firm has been my church. How many are so fortunate as to be able to die in church?"

Barrington reached out a palsied hand and took a cigarette from a package on his desk, then hesitated and dropped the cigarette back down near the open pack.

Conti picked it up and offered to light it for him.

"Thank you, no," Barrington said with a quickly abandoned attempt at regaining his characteristically erect posture. "Spare me your sympathy. Besides, I've already had my tenth today." Barrington smiled, then added, "And you're already burdened with enough problems as it is . . . like dealing with the reality that . . . despite your righteous pretensions . . . you're just another cop."

Barrington slumped forward onto the desk. Conti felt his pulse weaken, and within a minute he was dead.

Dan turned to the nearest officer and ordered him to secure the room's contents for analysis, especially the residue of Austin Barrington's last pot of coffee.

Dan Conti reached the street in front of the Imperial Building just as Kevin was being put into the ambulance. Rachel was already inside, and Dan joined her there as the attendants closed the door behind them.

"What in the hell are you doing here?" he demanded of Rachel. "I told you to—"

"I work here, Dan, remember?"

Dan remembered and dropped it. He nodded his head toward Kevin. "How is he?"

"Not good," replied a young paramedic. "Looks like rampant internal hemorrhaging to me. He was conscious and lucid for a few minutes upstairs, but he doesn't appear to be fighting it."

"Did you arrest Barrington?" asked Rachel.

"He's dead," said Dan through tight lips. "Killed himself with some kind of poison in his coffee."

"*What?*"

"He administered it to himself—apparently the same way he did to the others he killed—in the coffee. He casually drank the stuff while I sat there like a dope listening to him talk about his bloody law firm and my preoccupation with preventing death."

"Oh, Dan," said Rachel, shaking her head slowly back and forth and instinctively putting her hand over his.

"How about you? You okay?" asked Dan, his eyes searching Rachel's face. He found only deep sadness.

"It's hard to say," she said quietly, turning to look at Kevin's inert face as new tears filled her eyes. She shook her head again in disbelief. *Gone. All of it gone.*

The sound of their ambulance's siren seemed strangely distant to Rachel. *Kevin, dear Kevin, please. Not you, too.*

Conti interrupted her thoughts, saying, "Barrington admitted he hit him. Stone then apparently fell backward and struck his head on a bookcase."

Rachel said nothing, for Kevin was beginning to stir, then suddenly both eyes fluttered open. "Rachel," he said with surprising clarity, eyes darting around him. "Am I in an ambulance?"

"Yes, Kevin," Rachel said, touching his face. "But you're going to be fine."

"I feel funny," said Kevin, then closed his eyes as quickly as he had opened them. After an anxious silence, he opened them and began to speak again. "This is not good," he said simply, then lapsed into another moment of silence.

A minute later, though his eyes remained closed, his voice was clear and coherent as he said, "And the police are here to insure my safety. How decent of you, Conti."